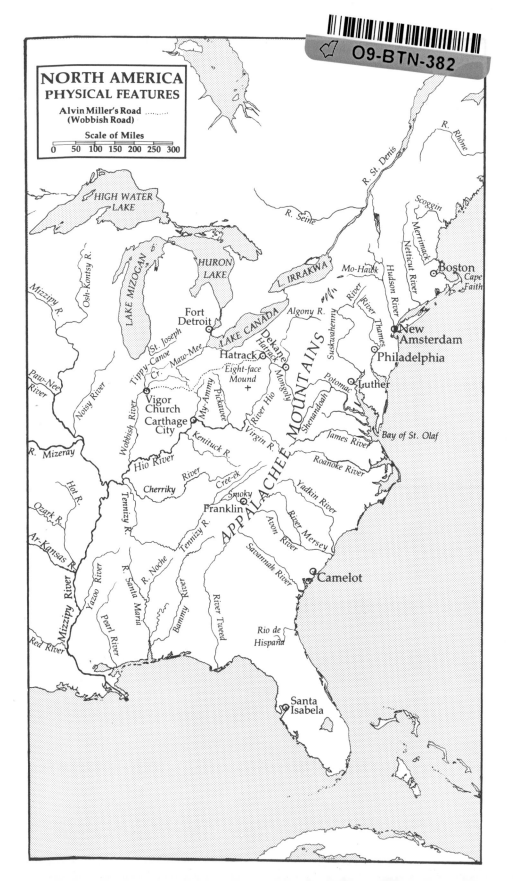

NORTH AMERICA
PHYSICAL FEATURES

Alvin Miller's Road ....
(Wobbish Road)

Scale of Miles
0 50 100 150 200 250 300

O9-BTN-382

HIGH WATER LAKE

HURON LAKE

LAKE MIZOGAN

Osh-Kontsy R.

Mizzipy R.

Paw-Nee River

St. Joseph

Tippy-Canoe

Cr. Maw-Mee

Noisy River

Fort Detroit

LAKE CANADA

L. IRRAKWA

R. Seine

R. St. Denis

R. Rhône

Scoggin

Merrimack

Netticut River

Boston

Cape Faith

Mo-Hawk

River

River

Hudson River

River Thames

New Amsterdam

Philadelphia

Algony R.

Dekane

Hatrack

Hatrack River

Mongoly

Suskwahenny

Eight-face Mound

Vigor Church

Carthage City

Wobbish River

My-Ammy

Pickawee

River Hio

Virgin R.

Luther

Potomac

Shenandoah

APPALACHEE MOUNTAINS

James River

Bay of St. Olaf

R. Mizeray

Hot R.

Ozark R.

Hio River

Kenituck R.

River

Cree-ek

Roanoke River

Cherriky

Smoky

Franklin

Yadkin River

River Mersey

Ar-Kansas R.

Tennizy R.

Tennizy R.

Avon River

Savannah River

Camelot

Mizzipy River

Yazoo River

R. Santa Maria

R. Noche

Bammy River

River Tweed

Rio de Hispana

Red River

Pearl River

Santa Isabela

Tor Books by Orson Scott Card

The Folk of the Fringe
Future on Fire (editor)
Future on Ice (editor)*
Lovelock (with Kathryn Kidd)
Pastwatch: The Redemption of Christopher Columbus
Saints
Songmaster
The Worthing Saga
Wyrms

THE TALES OF ALVIN MAKER
Seventh Son
Red Prophet
Prentice Alvin
Alvin Journeyman
Heartfire

ENDER
Ender's Game
Speaker for the Dead
Xenocide
Children of the Mind

HOMECOMING
The Memory of Earth
The Call of Earth
The Ships of Earth
Earthfall
Earthborn

SHORT FICTION
Maps in a Mirror: The Short Fiction of Orson Scott Card (hardcover)
Maps in a Mirror, Volume 1: The Changed Man (paperback)
Maps in a Mirror, Volume 2: Flux (paperback)
Maps in a Mirror, Volume 3: Cruel Miracles (paperback)
Maps in a Mirror, Volume 4: Monkey Sonatas (paperback)

*forthcoming

ORSON SCOTT CARD

HEARTFIRE

**THE
TALES OF
ALVIN MAKER
V**

TOR®

A TOM DOHERTY ASSOCIATES BOOK
NEW YORK

HEARTFIRE

A TOR BOOK
Published by Tom Doherty Associates, Inc.
175 Fifth Avenue
New York, NY 10010

Tor Books on the World Wide Web:
http://www.tor.com

Tor® is a registered trademark of Tom Doherty Associates, Inc.

Library of Congress Cataloging-in-Publication Data

Card, Orson Scott.
 Heartfire / Orson Scott Card.—1st ed.
  p.   cm. —(The tales of Alvin Maker; 5)
 ''A Tom Doherty Associates book.''
 ISBN 0–312–85054–9 (acid-free paper). —ISBN 0–312–86728–X (ltd.
 ed.: acid free paper)
 I. Title. II. Series: Card, Orson Scott. Tales of Alvin Maker; 5.
PS3553.A655H43   1998
813'54—dc21   98–3041

First edition: August 1998

Printed in the United States of America

0 9 8 7 6 5 4 3 2 1

To Mark and Margaret,
for whom all heartfires
burn bright

Acknowledgments

SEVERAL BOOKS WERE of incalculable value in developing the story of Alvin's search through America for patterns he might use to build a community that is both strong and free. Most important was David Hackett Fischer's *Albion's Seed: Four British Folkways in America* (Oxford University Press, 1989, 946 pp.), a brilliant, well-defended exposition of a non-reductionist theory of the origins of American culture; in its pages I found both detail and rich causal reasoning, greatly helping me take this book from plan to page. William W. Freehling's *Road to Disunion: Secessionists at Bay, 1776–1854* (Oxford University Press, 1990, 640 pp.) gave me details of life, obscure historical characters, and the economic and political realities of Charleston in the 1820s, which I could then distort into my American "Camelot." Carl J. Richard's *Founders and the Classics: Greece, Rome, and the American Enlightenment* (Harvard University Press, 1994, 295 pp.) provided me with the attitudes of educated American leaders toward the Greek and Roman classics that were a part of traditional education at the time.

As so often before, I thank Clark and Kathy Kidd for providing me with a retreat where I could jump-start this book.

Thanks also to Kathleen Bellamy and Scott J. Allen for help above and beyond the call of duty; to Jane Brady and Geoffrey Card for their collection of data from the earlier books.

As Alvin wanders through the world, it is his wife who provides his harbor; this my wife, Kristine, also provides for me. All my stories are told first to her.

Contents

1

Gooses

ARTHUR STUART STOOD at the window of the taxidermy shop, rapt. Alvin Smith was halfway down the block before he realized that Arthur was no longer with him. By the time he got back, a tall White man was questioning the boy.

"Where's your master, then?"

Arthur did not look at him, his gaze riveted on a stuffed bird, posed as if it were about to land on a branch.

"Boy, answer me, or I'll have the constable . . ."

"He's with me," said Alvin.

The man at once became friendly. "Glad to know it, friend. A boy this age, you'd think if he was free his parents would have taught him proper respect when a White man—"

"I think he only cares about the birds in the window." Alvin laid a gentle hand on Arthur's shoulder. "What is it, Arthur Stuart?"

Only the sound of Alvin's voice could draw Arthur out of his reverie. "How did he see?"

"Who?" asked the man.

"See what?" asked Alvin.

"The way the bird pushes down with his wings just before roosting, and then poses like a statue. Nobody sees that."

"What's the boy talking about?" asked the man.

"He's a great observer of birds," said Alvin. "I think he's admiring the taxidermy work in the window."

The man beamed with pride. "I'm the taxidermist here. Almost all of those are mine."

Arthur finally responded to the taxidermist. "Most of these are just dead birds. They looked more alive when they lay bloody in the field where the shotgun brought them down. But this one. And that one. . . ." He pointed to a hawk, stooping. "Those were done by someone who knew the living bird."

The taxidermist glowered for a moment, then put on a tradesman's smile. "Do you like those? The work of a French fellow goes by the name 'John-James.' " He said the double name as if it were a joke. "Journeyman work, is all. Those delicate poses—I doubt the wires will hold up over time."

Alvin smiled at the man. "I'm a journeyman myself, but I do work that lasts."

"No offense meant," the taxidermist said at once. But he also seemed to have lost interest, for if Alvin was merely a journeyman in some trade, he wouldn't have enough money to buy anything; nor would an itinerant workman have much use for stuffed animals.

"So you sell this Frenchman's work for less?" asked Alvin.

The taxidermist hesitated. "More, actually."

"The price falls when it's done by the master?" asked Alvin innocently.

The taxidermist glared at him. "I sell his work on consignment, and he sets the price. I doubt anyone will buy it. But the fellow fancies himself an artist. He only stuffs and mounts the birds so he can paint pictures of them, and when he's done painting, he sells the bird itself."

"He'd be better to talk to the bird instead of killing it," said Arthur Stuart. "They'd hold still for him to paint, a man who sees birds so true."

The taxidermist looked at Arthur Stuart oddly. "You let this boy talk a bit forward, don't you?"

"In Philadelphia I thought all folks could talk plain," said Alvin, smiling.

The taxidermist finally understood just how deeply Alvin was mocking him. "I'm not a Quaker, my man, and neither are you." With that he turned his back on Alvin and Arthur and returned to his store. Through the window Alvin could see him sulking, casting sidelong glances at them now and then.

"Come on, Arthur Stuart, let's go meet Verily and Mike for dinner."

Arthur took one step, but still couldn't tear his gaze from the roosting bird.

"Arthur, before the fellow comes out and orders us to move along."

Even with that, Alvin finally had to take Arthur by the hand and near drag him away. And as they walked, Arthur had an inward look to him. "What are you brooding about?" asked Alvin.

"I want to talk to that Frenchman. I have a question to ask him."

Alvin knew better than to ask Arthur Stuart what the question was. It would spare him hearing Arthur's inevitable reply: "Why should I ask *you? You* don't know."

Verily Cooper and Mike Fink were already eating when Alvin and Arthur got to the rooming house. The proprietor was a Quaker woman of astonishing girth and very limited talents as a cook—but she made up for the blandness of her food with the quantities she served, and more important was the fact that, being a Quaker in more than name, Mistress Louder made no distinction between half-Black Arthur Stuart and the three White men traveling with him. Arthur Stuart sat at the same table as the others, and even though one roomer moved out the day Arthur Stuart first sat at table, she never acted as if she even noticed the fellow was gone. Which was why Alvin tried to make up for it by taking Arthur Stuart with him on daily forays out into the woods and meadows along the river to gather wild ginger, wintergreen, spearmint, and thyme to spice up her cooking. She took the herbs, with their implied criticism of her kitchen, in good humor, and tonight the potatoes had been boiled with the wintergreen they brought her yesterday.

"Edible?" she asked Alvin as he took his first bite.

Verily was the one who answered, while Alvin savored the mouthful with a beatific expression on his face. "Madame, your generosity guarantees you will go to heaven, but it's the flavor of tonight's potatoes that assures you will be asked to cook there."

She laughed and made as if to hit him with a spoon. "Verily Cooper, thou smooth-tongued lawyer, knowest thou not that Quakers have no truck with flattery?" But they all knew that while she didn't believe the flattery, she did believe the warmheartedness behind it.

While the other roomers were still at table, Mike Fink regaled them all with the tale of his visit to the Simple House, where Andrew Jackson was scandalizing the elite of Philadelphia by bringing his cronies from Tennizy and Kenituck, letting them chew and spit in rooms that once offered homesick European ambassadors a touch of the elegance of the old country. Fink repeated a tale that Jackson himself told that very day, about a fine Philadelphia lady who criticized the behavior of his companions. "This is the Simple House," Jackson declared, "and these are simple people." When the lady tried to refute the point, Jackson told her, "This is *my* house for the next four years, and these are my friends."

"But they have no manners," said the lady.

"They have excellent manners," said Jackson. "Western manners. But they're tolerant folks. They'll overlook the fact that you ain't took a bite of food yet, nor drunk any good corn liquor, nor spat once even though you always look like you got a mouth full of *somethin'*." Mike Fink laughed long and hard at this, and so did the roomers, though some were laughing at the lady and some were laughing at Jackson.

Arthur Stuart asked a question that was bothering Alvin. "How does Andy Jackson get anything done, if the Simple House is full of river rats and bumpkins all day?"

"He needs something done, why, one of us river rats went and done it for him," said Mike.

"But most rivermen can't read or write," Arthur said.

"Well, Old Hickory can do all the readin' and writin' for hisself," said Mike. "He sends the river rats to deliver messages and persuade people."

"Persuade people?" asked Alvin. "I hope they don't use the methods of persuasion you once tried on *me*."

Mike whooped at that. "Iffen Old Hickory let the boys do *those* old tricks, I don't think there'd be six noses left in Congress, nor twenty ears!''

Finally, though, the tales of the frolicking at the Simple House—or degradation, depending on your point of view—wound down and the other roomers left. Only Alvin and Arthur, as latecomers, were still eating as they made their serious reports on the day's work.

Mike shook his head sadly when Alvin asked him if he'd had a chance to talk to Andy Jackson. ''Oh, he included me in the room, if that's what you mean. But talking alone, no, not likely. See, Andy Jackson may be a lawyer but he knows river rats, and my name rang a bell with him. Haven't lived down my old reputation yet, Alvin. Sorry.''

Alvin smiled and waved off the apology. ''There'll come a day when the president will meet with us.''

''It was premature, anyway,'' said Verily. ''Why try for a land grant when we don't even know what we're going to use it for?''

''Do so,'' said Alvin, playing at a children's quarrel.

''Do not,'' said Verily, grinning.

''We got a city to build.''

''No sir,'' said Verily. ''We have the *name* of a city, but we don't have the *plan* of a city, or even the idea of the city—''

''It's a city of Makers!''

''Well, it would have been nice if the Red Prophet had told you what that means,'' said Verily.

''He showed it to me inside the waterspout,'' said Alvin. ''He doesn't know what it means any more than I do. But we both saw it, a city made of glass, filled with people, and the city itself taught them everything.''

''Amid all that seeing,'' said Verily, ''did you perhaps hear a hint of what we're supposed to tell people to persuade them to come and help us build it?''

''I take it that means you didn't accomplish what you set out to do, either,'' said Alvin.

''Oh, I perused the Congressional Library,'' said Verily. ''Found many references to the Crystal City, but most of them were tied up with Spanish explorers who thought it had something to do with the fountain of youth or the Seven Cities of the Onion.''

''Onion?'' asked Arthur Stuart.

"One of the sources misheard the Indian name 'Cibola' as a Spanish word for 'onion,' and I thought it was funny," said Verily. "All dead ends. But there *is* an interesting datum that I can't readily construe."

"Wouldn't want to have anything constroodled redly," said Alvin.

"Don't play frontiersman with me," said Verily. "Your wife was a better schoolteacher than to leave you that ignorant."

"You two leave off teasing," demanded Arthur Stuart. "What did you find out?"

"There's a post office in a place that calls itself Crystal City in the state of Tennizy."

"There's probably a place called Fountain of Youth, too," said Alvin.

"Well, I thought it was interesting," said Verily.

"Know anything else about it?"

"Postmaster's a Mr. Crawford, who also has the titles Mayor and— I think you'll like this, Alvin—White Prophet."

Mike Fink laughed, but Alvin didn't like it. "White Prophet. As if to set himself against Tenskwa-Tawa?"

"I just told you all I know," said Verily. "Now, what did *you* accomplish?"

"I've been in Philadelphia for two weeks and I haven't accomplished a thing," said Alvin. "I thought the city of Benjamin Franklin would have something to teach me. But Franklin's dead, and there's no special music in the street, no wisdom lingering around his grave. Here's where America was born, boys, but I don't think it lives here anymore. America lives out there where I grew up—what we got in Philadelphia now is just the *government* of America. Like finding fresh dung on the road. It ain't a horse, but it tells you a horse is somewhere nearby."

"It took you two weeks in Philadelphia to find *that* out?" said Mike Fink.

Verily joined in. "My father always said that government is like watching another man piss in your boot. Someone feels better but it certainly isn't you."

"If we can take a break from all of this philosophy," said Alvin, "I got a letter from Margaret." He was the only one who called his wife by that name—everyone else called her Peggy. "From Camelot."

"She's not in Appalachee anymore?" asked Mike Fink.

"All the agitation for keeping slavery in Appalachee is coming from the Crown Colonies," said Alvin, "so there she went."

"King ain't about to let Appalachee close off slavery, I reckon," said Mike Fink.

"I thought they already settled Appalachee independence with a war back in the last century," said Verily.

"I reckon some folks think they need another war to settle whether Black people can be free," said Alvin. "So Margaret's in Camelot, hoping to get an audience with the King and plead the cause of peace and freedom."

"The only time a nation ever has both at the same time," said Verily, "is during that brief period of exhilarated exhaustion after winning a war."

"You're sure grim for a man what's never even killed anybody," said Mike Fink.

"Iffen Miz Larner wants to talk to Arthur Stuart, I'm right here," said Arthur with a grin. Mike Fink made a show of slapping him upside the head. Arthur laughed—it was his favorite joke these days, that he'd been given the same name as the King of England, who ruled in exile in the slave shires of the South.

"And she also has reason to believe that my younger brother is there," said Alvin.

At that news Verily angrily looked down and played with the last scraps of food on his plate, while Mike Fink stared off into space. They both had their opinions of Alvin's little brother.

"Well, I don't know," said Alvin.

"Don't know what?" asked Verily.

"Whether to go there and join her. She told me not to, of course, because she has some idea that when Calvin and I get together, then I'll die."

Mike grinned nastily. "I don't care what that boy's knack is, I'd like to see him try."

"Margaret never said he'd kill me," said Alvin. "In fact she never said I'd die, exactly. But that's what I gather. She doesn't want me there until she can assure me that Calvin is out of town. But I'd like to meet the King my own self."

"Not to mention seeing your wife," said Verily.

"I could use a few days with her."

"And nights," murmured Mike.

Alvin raised an eyebrow at him and Mike grinned stupidly.

"Biggest question is," Alvin went on, "could I safely take Arthur Stuart down there? In the Crown Colonies it's illegal to bring a free person of even one-sixteenth Black blood into the country."

"You could pretend he's your slave," said Mike.

"But what if I died down there? Or got arrested? I don't want any chance of Arthur getting confiscated and sold away. It's too dangerous."

"So don't go there," said Verily. "The King doesn't know a thing about building the Crystal City, anyway."

"I know," said Alvin. "But neither do I, and neither does anyone else."

Verily smiled. "Maybe that's not true."

Alvin was impatient. "Don't play with me, Verily. What do you know?"

"Nothing but what you already know yourself, Alvin. There's two parts to building the Crystal City. The first part is about Makering and all that. And I'm no help to you there, nor is any mortal soul, as far as I can see. But the second part is the word *city*. No matter what else you do, it'll be a place where people have to live together. That means there's got to be government and laws."

"Does there *have* to be?" asked Mike wistfully.

"Or something to do the same jobs," said Verily. "And land, divided up so people can live. Food planted and harvested, or brought in to feed the population. Dry goods to make or buy, houses to build, clothes to make. There'll be marrying and giving in marriage, unless I'm mistaken, and people will have children so we'll need schools. No matter how visionary this city makes the people, they still need roofs and roads, unless you expect them all to fly."

Alvin leaned back in his chair with his eyes closed.

"Have I put you to sleep, or are you thinking?" asked Verily.

Alvin didn't open his eyes when he answered. "I'm just thinking that I really don't know a blame thing about what I'm doing. White Murderer Harrison may have been the lowest man I ever knowed, but at least he could build a city in the wilderness."

"It's easy to build a city when you arrange the rules so that bad men can get rich without getting caught," said Verily. "You build such a place and greed will bring you your citizens, if you can stand to live with them."

"It ought to be possible to do the same for decent folks," said Alvin.

"It ought to be and is," said Verily. "It's been done, and you can learn from the way they did it."

"Who?" asked Mike Fink. "I never heard of such a town."

"A hundred towns at least," said Verily. "I'm speaking of New England, of course. Massachusetts most particularly. Founded by Puritans to be their Zion, a land of pure religion across the western ocean. All my life, growing up in England, I heard about how perfect New England was, how pure and godly, where there were neither rich nor poor, but all partakers of the heavenly gift, and where they were free of distraction from the world. They live in peace and equity, in the land most just of all that have ever existed on God's Earth."

Alvin shook his head. "Verily, if Arthur can't go to Camelot, it's a sure bet you and I can't go to New England."

"There's no slavery there," said Verily.

"You know what I mean," said Alvin. "They hang witches."

"I'm no witch," said Verily. "Nor are you."

"By their lights we are."

"Only if we do any hexery or use hidden powers," said Verily. "Surely we can restrain ourselves long enough to learn how they created such a large country free of strife and oppression, and filled with the love of God."

"Dangerous," said Alvin.

"I agree," said Mike. "We'd be insane to go there. Isn't that where that lawyer fellow Daniel Webster came from? He'll know about you, Alvin."

"He's in Carthage City making money from corrupt men," said Alvin.

"Last you heard of him, maybe," said Mike. "But he can write letters. He can come home. Things can go wrong."

Arthur Stuart looked up at Mike Fink. "Things can go wrong lying in your own bed on Sunday."

Alvin at last opened his eyes. "I have to learn. Verily's right. It's not enough to learn Makering. I have to learn governing, too, and city build-ing, and everything else. I have to learn everything about everything, and I'm just getting farther behind the longer I sit here.''

Arthur Stuart looked glum. "So I'm never going to meet the King."

"Far as I'm concerned," said Mike Fink, "you *are* the real Arthur Stuart, and you've got as much right as he has to be king in this land."

"I want him to make me a knight."

Alvin sighed. Mike rolled his eyes. Verily put a hand on Arthur's shoulder. "The day the King knights a half-Black boy . . ."

"Can't he knight the White half?" asked Arthur Stuart. "If I do something real brave? That's how a fellow gets hisself knighted, I hear."

"Definitely time to go to New England," said Alvin.

"I tell you I got misgivings," said Mike Fink.

"Me too," said Alvin. "But Verily's right. They built a good place and got good people to come to it."

"Why not go to that Tennizy place as calls itself Crystal City?" asked Mike.

"Maybe that's where we'll go after we get run out of New England," said Alvin.

Verily laughed. "You're an optimist, aren't you."

They mostly packed before they went to bed that night. Not that there was that much to put in their satchels. When a man is traveling with only a horse to carry himself and his goods, he gets a different idea of what he needs to carry from place to place than does a man riding a coach, or followed by servants and pack animals. It's not much more than a walking man would be willing to tote, lest he wear down the horse.

Alvin woke early in the morning, before dawn, but it took him no more than two breaths to notice that Arthur Stuart was gone. The win-dow stood open, and though they were on the top floor of the house, Alvin knew that wouldn't stop Arthur Stuart, who seemed to think that gravity owed him a favor.

Alvin woke Verily and Mike, who were stirring anyway, and asked them to get the horses saddled and loaded up while he went in search of the boy.

Mike only laughed, though. "Probably found him some girl he wants to kiss good-bye."

Alvin looked at him in shock. "What are you talking about?"

Mike looked back at him, just as surprised. "Are you blind? Are you deaf? Arthur's voice is changing. He's one whisker from being a man."

"Speaking of whiskers," said Verily, "I think the shadow on his upper lip is due to become a brush pretty soon. In fact, I daresay his face grows more hair on it already than yours does, Alvin."

"I don't see your face flowing with moustachery, either," said Alvin.

"I shave," said Verily.

"But it's a long time between Christmases," said Alvin. "I'll see you before breakfast is done, I wager."

As Alvin went downstairs, he stopped into the kitchen, where Mistress Louder was rolling out the dough for morning biscuits. "You didn't happen to see Arthur Stuart this morning?" asked Alvin.

"And when wast thou planning to tell me ye were leaving?"

"When we settled up after breakfast," said Alvin. "We wasn't trying to slip out, it was no secret we were packing up."

Only then did he notice the tears running down her cheeks. "I hardly slept last night."

Alvin put his hands on her shoulders. "Mistress Louder, I never thought you'd take on so. It's a rooming house, ain't it? And roomers come and go."

She sighed loudly. "Just like children," she said.

"And don't children come back to the nest from time to time?"

"If that's a promise, I won't have to turn these into salt biscuits with my silly tears," she said.

"I can promise that I'll never pass a night in Philadelphia anywhere other than your house, lessen my wife and I settle down here someday, and then we'll send our children to your house for breakfast while we sleep lazy."

She laughed outright. "The Lord took twice the time making thee, Alvin Smith, cause it took that long to put the mischief in."

"Mischief sneaks in by itself," said Alvin. "That's its nature."

Only then did Mistress Louder remember Alvin's original question. "As for Arthur Stuart, I caught him climbing down the tree outside when I went out to bring in firewood."

"And you didn't wake me? Or stop him?"

She ignored the implied accusation. "I forced some cold johnnycake into his hands before he was out the door again. Said he had an errand to run before ye boys left this morning."

"Well, at least that sounds like he means to come back," said Alvin.

"It does," said Mistress Louder. "Though if he didn't, thou'rt not his master, I think."

"Just because he's not my property don't mean I'm not responsible for him," said Alvin.

"I wasn't speaking of the law," said Mistress Louder, "I was speaking the simple truth. He doesn't obey thee like a boy, but like a man, because he wants to please thee. He'll do nowt because thou commandest, but does it only when he agrees he ought to."

"But that's true of all men and all masters, even slaves," said Alvin.

"What I'm saying is he doesn't act in fear of thee," said Mistress Louder. "And so it won't do for thee to be hot with him when thou find him. Thou hast no right."

Only then did Alvin realize that he was a bit angry with Arthur Stuart for running off. "He's still young," said Alvin.

"And thou'rt what, a greybeard with a stoop in his back?" she laughed. "Get on and find him. Arthur Stuart never seems to know the danger a lad of his tribe faces, noon and night."

"Nor the danger that sneaks up behind," said Alvin. He kissed her cheek. "Don't let all those biscuits disappear before I get back."

"It's thy business, not mine, what time thou'lt choose to come back," she said. "Who can say how hungry the others will be this morning?"

For that remark, Alvin dipped his finger into the flour and striped her nose with it, then headed for the door. She stuck her tongue out at him but didn't wipe the flour away. "I'll be a clown if thou want me to," she called after him.

It was far too early in the morning for the shop to be open, but Alvin went straight for the taxidermist's anyway. What other business could Arthur Stuart have? Mike's guess that Arthur had found a girl was not likely to be right—the boy almost never left Alvin's side, so there'd been no chance for such a thing, even if Arthur was old enough to want to try.

The streets were crowded with farmers from the surrounding countryside, bringing their goods to market, but the shops in buildings along the streets were still closed. Paperboys and postmen made their rounds, and dairymen clattered up the alleys, stopping to leave milk in the kitchens along the way. It was noisy on the streets, but it was the fresh noise of morning. No one was shouting yet. No neighbors quarreling, no barkers selling, no driver shouting out a warning to clear the way.

No Arthur at the front door of the taxidermy shop.

But where else would he have gone? He had a question, and he wouldn't rest until he had the answer. Only it wasn't the taxidermist who had the answer, was it? It was the French painter of birds, John-James. And somewhere inside the shop, there was bound to be a note of the man's address. Would Arthur really be so foolhardy as to . . .

There was indeed an open window, with two crates on a barrel stacked beneath it. Arthur Stuart, it's no better to be taken for a burglar than to be taken for a slave.

Alvin went to the back door. He twisted the knob. It turned a little, but not enough to draw back the latch. Locked, then.

Alvin leaned against the door and closed his eyes, searching with his doodlebug till he found the heartfire inside the shop. There he was, Arthur Stuart, bright with life, hot with adventure. Like so many times before, Alvin wished he had some part of Margaret's gift, to see into the heartfire and learn something of the future and past, or even just the thoughts of the present moment—that would be convenient.

He dared not call out for Arthur—his voice would only raise an alarm and almost guarantee that Arthur would be caught inside the shop. For all Alvin knew the taxidermist lived upstairs or in an upper floor of one of the nearby buildings.

So now he put his doodlebug inside the lock, to feel out how the thing was made. An old lock, not very smooth. Alvin evened out the rough parts, peeling away corrosion and dirt. To change the shape of it was easier than moving it, so where two metal surfaces pressed flat against each other, keeping the latch from opening, Alvin changed them both to a bevel, making the metal flow into the new shapes, until the two surfaces slid easily across each other. With that he could turn the knob, and silently the latch slid free.

Still he did not open the door, for now he had to turn his attention to the hinges. They were rougher and dirtier than the lock. Did the man even use this door? Alvin smoothed and cleaned them also, and now, when he turned the knob and pushed open the door, the only sound was the whisper of the breeze passing into the shop.

Arthur Stuart sat at the taxidermist's worktable, holding a bluejay between his hands, stroking the feathers. He looked up at Alvin and said, softly, "It isn't even dead."

Alvin touched the bird. Yes, there was some warmth, and a heartbeat. The shot that stunned it was still lodged in its skull. The brain was bruised and the bird would soon die of it, even though none of the other birdshot that had hit it would be fatal.

"Did you find what you were looking for?" asked Alvin. "The address of the painter?"

"No," said Arthur bleakly.

Alvin went to work on the bird, quickly as he could. It was more delicate than metal work, moving his doodlebug through the pathways of a living creature, making tiny alterations here and there. It helped him to hold the animal, to touch it while he worked on it. The blood in the brain was soon draining into the veins, and the damaged arteries were closed. The flesh healed rapidly under the tiny balls of lead, forcing them back out of the body. Even the ball lodged in the skull shrank, loosened, dropped out.

The jay rustled its feathers, struggled in Alvin's grasp. He let it loose.

"They'll just kill it anyway," said Alvin.

"So we'll let it out," said Arthur.

Alvin sighed. "Then we'd be thieves, wouldn't we?"

"The window's open," said Arthur. "The blue jay can leave after the man comes in this morning. So he'll think it escaped on its own."

"And how will we get the bird to do that?"

Arthur looked at him like he was an idiot, then leaned close to the bluejay, which stood still on the worktable. Arthur whispered so softly that Alvin couldn't hear the words. Then he whistled, several sharp birdlike sounds.

The jay leapt into the air and flapped noisily around the room. Alvin ducked to avoid it.

"He's not going to hit you," said Arthur, amused.

"Let's go," said Alvin.

He took Arthur through the back door. When he drew it closed, he stayed for just a moment longer, his fingers lingering on the knob, as he returned the pieces of the lock to their proper shape.

"What are you doing here!" The taxidermist stood at the turn of the alley.

"Hoping to find you in, sir," said Alvin calmly, not taking his hand off the knob.

"With your hand on the knob?" said the taxidermist, his voice icy with suspicion.

"You didn't answer to our knock," said Alvin. "I thought you might be so hard at work you didn't hear. All we want is to know where we might find the journeyman painter. The Frenchman. John-James."

"I know what you wanted," said the taxidermist. "Stand away from the door before I call the constable."

Alvin and Arthur stepped back.

"That's not good enough," said the taxidermist. "Skulking at back doors—how do I know you don't plan to knock me over the head and steal from me as soon as I have the door unlocked?"

"If that was our plan, sir," said Alvin, "you'd already be lying on the ground and I'd have the key in my hand, wouldn't I?"

"So you *did* have it all thought out!"

"Seems to me *you're* the one who has plans for robbing," said Alvin. "And then you accuse others of wanting to do what only you had thought of."

Angrily the man pulled out his key and slid it into the lock. He braced himself to twist hard, expecting the corroded metal to resist. So he visibly staggered when the key turned easily and the door slipped open silently.

He might have stopped to examine the lock and the hinges, but at that moment the bluejay that had spent the night slowly dying on his worktable fluttered angrily in his face and flew out the door. "No!" the man shouted. "That's Mr. Ridley's trophy!"

Arthur Stuart laughed. "Not much of a trophy," he said. "Not if it won't hold still."

The taxidermist stood in the doorway, looking for the bird. It was long gone. He then looked back and forth from Alvin to Arthur. "I know you had something to do with this," he said. "I don't know what or how, but you witched up that bird."

"No such thing," said Alvin. "When I arrived here I had no idea you kept living birds inside. I thought you only dealt with dead ones."

"I do! That bird was dead!"

"John-James," said Alvin. "We want to see him before we leave town."

"Why should I help you?" said the taxidermist.

"Because we asked," said Alvin, "and it would cost you nothing."

"Cost me nothing? How am I going to explain to Mr. Ridley?"

"Tell him to make sure his birds are dead before he brings them to you," said Arthur Stuart.

"I won't have such talk from a Black boy," said the taxidermist. "If you can't control your boy, then you shouldn't bring him out among gentlemen!"

"Have I?" asked Alvin.

"Have you what?"

"Brought him out among gentlemen?" said Alvin. "I'm waiting to see the courtesy that would mark you as such a one."

The taxidermist glowered at him. "John-James Audubon is staying in a room at the Liberty Inn. But you won't find him there at this time of day—he'll be out looking at birds till midmorning."

"Then good day to you," said Alvin. "You might oil your locks and hinges from time to time. They'll stay in better condition if you do."

The taxidermist got a quizzical look on his face. He was still opening and closing his silent, smooth-hinged door as they walked back down the alley to the street.

"Well, that's that," said Alvin. "We'll never find your John-James Audubon before we have to leave."

Arthur Stuart looked at him in consternation. "And why won't we?" He whistled a couple of times and the bluejay fluttered down to alight on his shoulder. Arthur whispered and whistled for a few moments, and the bird hopped up onto Arthur's head, then (to Alvin's surprise) Alvin's shoulder, then Alvin's head, and only then launched itself into the air and flew off up the street.

"He's bound to be near the river this morning," said Arthur Stuart. "Geese are feeding there, on their way south."

Alvin looked around. "It's still summer. It's hot."

"Not up north," said Arthur Stuart. "I heard two flocks yesterday."

"I haven't heard a thing."

Arthur Stuart grinned at him.

"I thought you stopped hearing birds," said Alvin. "When I changed you, in the river. I thought you lost all that."

Arthur Stuart shrugged. "I did. But I remembered how it felt. I kept listening."

"It's coming back?" asked Alvin.

Arthur shook his head. "I have to figure it out. It doesn't just come to me, the way it used to. It's not a knack anymore. It's . . ."

Alvin supplied the word. "A skill."

"I was trying to decide between 'a wish' and 'a memory.' "

"You heard geese calling, and I didn't. My ears are pretty good, Arthur."

Arthur grinned at him again. "There's hearing and there's listening."

There were several men with shotguns stalking the geese. It was easy enough to guess which was John-James Audubon, however. Even if they hadn't spotted the sketchpad inside the open hunter's sack, and even if he hadn't been oddly dressed in a Frenchman's exaggerated version of an American frontiersman's outfit—tailored deerskin—they would have known which hunter he was, by one simple test: He was the only one who had actually found the geese.

He was aiming at a goose floating along the river. Without thinking, Alvin called out, "Have you no shame, Mr. Audubon?"

Audubon, startled, half-turned to look at Alvin and Arthur. Whether it was the sudden movement or Alvin's voice, the lead goose honked and rose dripping from the water, staggering at first from the effort, then rising smoothly with great beats of his wings, water trailing behind him in a silvery cascade. In a moment, all the other geese also rose and flew down the river. Audubon raised his shotgun, but then cursed and rounded on Alvin, the gun still leveled. "Pour quoi, imbecile!"

"You planning to shoot me?" asked Alvin.

Reluctantly, Audubon lowered the gun and remembered his English, which at the moment wasn't very good. "I have the beautiful creature in my eye, but you, man of the mouth open!"

"Sorry, but I couldn't believe you'd shoot a goose on the water like that."

"Why not?"

"Because it's—not sporting."

"Of course it's not sporting!" His English was getting better as he warmed to the argument. "I'm not here for sport! Look everywhere, Monsieur, and tell me the very important thing you do *not* see."

"You got no dog," said Arthur Stuart.

"Yes! Le garçon noir comprend! I cannot shoot the bird in the air because how do I collect the bird? It falls, the wing breaks, what good is it to me now? I shoot on the water, then splash splash, I have the goose."

"Very practical," said Alvin. "*If* you were starving, and needed the goose for food."

"Food!" cried Audubon. "Do I look like a hungry man?"

"A little lean, maybe," said Alvin. "But you could probably fast for a day or two without keeling over."

"I do not understand you, Monsieur Americain. Et je ne veux pas te comprendre. Go away." Audubon started downstream along the riverbank, the direction the geese had gone.

"Mister Audubon," Arthur Stuart called out.

"I must shoot you before you go away?" he called out, exasperated.

"I can bring them back," said Arthur.

Audubon turned and looked at him. "You call geese?" He pulled a wooden goose call from his the pocket of his jacket. "I call geese, too. But when they hear this, they think, Sacre Dieu! That goose is dying! Fly away! Fly away!"

Arthur Stuart kept walking toward him, and instead of answering, he began to make odd sounds with his throat and through his nose. Not goose calls, really, or not that anyone would notice. Not even an imitation of a goose. And yet there was something gooselike about the babble that came from his mouth. And it wasn't all that loud, either. But moments later, the geese came back, skimming over the surface of the water.

Audubon brought the shotgun to his shoulder. At once Arthur changed his call, and the geese flew away from the shore and settled far out on the water.

In an agony of frustration, Audubon whirled on Arthur and Alvin. "When did I insult you or the cauliflower face of your ugly mother? Which clumsy stinking Philadelphia prostitute was your sister? Or was it le bon Dieu that I offended? Notre Pere Celeste, why must I do this penance?"

"I'm not going to bring the geese back if you're just going to shoot them," said Arthur.

"What good are they if I don't shoot one!"

"You're not going to eat it, you're just going to paint it," said Arthur Stuart. "So it doesn't have to be dead."

"How can I paint a bird that will not stand in one place!" cried Audubon. Then he realized something. "You know my name. You know I paint. But I do not know *you*."

"I'm Alvin Smith, and this is my ward, Arthur Stuart."

"Wart? What kind of slave is that?"

"Ward. He's no slave. But he's under my protection."

"But who will protect *me* from the two of you? Why could you not be ordinary robbers, taking my money and run away?"

"Arthur has a question for you," said Alvin.

"Here is my answer: Leave! Departez!"

"What if I can get a goose to hold still for you without killing it?" asked Arthur Stuart.

Audubon was on the verge of a sharp answer when it finally dawned on him what he had just seen Arthur do, summoning the geese. "You are, how do you say, a knack person, a caller of gooses."

"Geese," Alvin offered helpfully.

Arthur shook his head. "I just like birds."

"*I* like birds too," said Audubon, "but they don't feel the same about me."

"Cause you kill 'em and you ain't even hungry," said Arthur Stuart.

Audubon looked at him in utter consternation. At last he made his decision. "You can make a goose hold still for me?"

"I can ask him to. But you got to put the gun away."

Audubon immediately leaned it against a tree.

"Unload it," said Arthur Stuart.

"You think I break my promise?"

"You didn't make no promise," said Arthur Stuart.

"All right!" cried Audubon. "I promise upon the grave of my grandmother." He started unloading the gun.

"You promise *what*?" demanded Arthur.

Alvin almost laughed aloud, except that Arthur Stuart was so grim about it, making sure there were no loopholes through which Audubon could slip once Arthur brought the geese back.

"I promise, I shoot no gooses! Pas de shooting of gooses!"

"Not even powder shooting, whatever that is. No shooting *any* birds *all day*," Arthur said.

"Not 'powder,' you ignorant boy. J'ai dit 'pas de.' *Rien! No* shooting of gooses, that's what I say!" In a mutter, he added, "Tous les sauvages du monde sont ici aujourd'hui."

Alvin chuckled. "No shooting savages, either, if you don't mind."

Audubon looked at him, furious and embarrassed. "Parlez-vous français?" "Je ne parle pas français," said Alvin, remembering a phrase from the few halting French lessons Margaret tried before she finally gave up on getting Alvin to speak any language other than English. Latin and Greek had already been abandoned by then. But he did understand the word *sauvage*, having heard it so often in the French fort of Detroit when he went there as a boy with Ta-Kumsaw.

"C'est vrai," muttered Audubon. Then, louder: "I make the promise you say. Bring me a goose that stand in one place for my painting."

"You going to answer my questions?" asked Arthur Stuart.

"Yes of course," said Audubon.

"A real answer, and not just some stupid nothing like adults usually say to children?"

"Hey," said Alvin.

"Not you," said Arthur Stuart quickly. But Alvin retained his suspicions.

"Yes," said Audubon in a world-weary voice. "I tell you all the secret of the universe!"

Arthur Stuart nodded, and walked to the point where the bank was highest. But before calling the geese, he turned to face Audubon one last time. "Where do you want the bird to stand?"

Audubon laughed. "You are the very strange boy! This is what you Americans call 'the brag'?"

"He ain't bragging," said Alvin. "He really has to know where you want the goose to stand."

Audubon shook his head, then looked around, checked the angle of the sun, and where there was a shady spot where he could sit while painting. Only then could he point to where the bird would have to pose.

"All right," said Arthur Stuart. He faced the river and babbled again, loudly, the sound carrying across the water. The geese rose from the surface and flew rapidly to shore, landing in the water or on the meadow. The lead goose, however, landed near Arthur Stuart, who led it toward the spot Audubon had picked.

Arthur looked at the Frenchman impatiently. He was just standing there, mouth agape, watching the goose come into position and then stop there, standing still as a statue. "You gonna draw in the mud with a stick?" asked Arthur.

Only then did Audubon realize that his paper and colors were still in his sack. He jogged briskly to the bag, stopping now and then to look back over his shoulder and make sure the goose was still there. While he was out of earshot, Alvin asked Arthur, "You forget we were leaving Philadelphia this morning?"

Arthur looked at him with the expression of withering scorn that only the face of an adolescent can produce. "You can go anytime you like."

At first Alvin thought he was telling him to go on and leave Arthur behind. But then he realized that Arthur was merely stating the truth: Alvin could leave Philadelphia whenever he wanted, so it didn't matter if it was this morning or later. "Verily and Mike are going to get worried if we don't get back soon."

"I don't want no birds to die," said Arthur.

"It's God's job to see every sparrow fall," said Alvin. "I didn't hear about him advertising that the position was open."

Arthur just clammed up and said no more. Soon Audubon was back, sitting in the grass under the tree, mixing his colors to match the exact color of the goosefeathers.

"I want to watch you paint," said Arthur.

"I don't like having people look over my shoulder."

Arthur murmured something and the goose started to wander away.

"All right!" said Audubon frantically. "Watch me paint, watch the bird, watch the sun in the sky until you will be blind, whatever you want!"

At once Arthur Stuart muttered to the goose, and it waddled back into place.

Alvin shook his head. Naked extortion. How could this be the sweet-tempered child Alvin had known for so long?

2

A Lady of the Court

PEGGY SPENT THE morning trying not to dread her meeting with Lady Guinevere Ashworth. As one of the senior ladies-in-waiting to Queen Mary she had some influence in her own right; more importantly, she was married to the Lord Chancellor, William Ashworth, who might have been born the third son of a schoolteacher, but by wit, dazzle, and enormous energy had clawed his way to a fine education, a good marriage, and a high office. Lord William had no illusions about his own parentage: He took his wife's family's name upon marrying her.

A woman is a woman, regardless of her parents' rank or her husband's office, Peggy reminded herself. When Lady Ashworth's bladder was full, angels didn't miraculously turn it into wine and bottle it, though from the way her name was spoken throughout Camelot, one might have thought so. It was a level of society Peggy had never aspired to or even been interested in. She hardly knew the proper manner of address to a daughter of a marquis—and whenever Peggy thought that she ought to make inquiries, she forced herself to remember that as a good Republican, she *should* get it wrong, and ostentatiously so. After all, both Jefferson and Franklin invariably referred to the King as "Mr.

Stuart,'' and even addressed him as such on official correspondence between heads of state—though the story was that clerks in the ministry of state "translated" all such letters so that proper forms of address appeared on them, thus avoiding an international incident.

And if there was any hope of averting the war that loomed among the American nations, it might well rest on her interview with Lady Ashworth. For along with her lofty social position—some said the Queen herself consulted Lady Ashworth for advice on how to dress—Lady Ashworth was also leader of the most prominent anti-slavery organization in the Crown Colonies: Ladies Against Property Rights in Persons. (According to the fashion in the Crown Colonies, the organization was commonly called Lap-Rip, from the initials of its name—a most unfortunate acronym, Peggy thought, especially for a ladies' club.)

So much might be riding on this morning's meeting. Everything else had been a dead end. After all her months in Appalachee, Peggy had finally realized that all the pressure for maintaining slavery in the New Counties was coming from the Crown Colonies. The King's government was rattling sabers, both figuratively and literally, to make sure the Appalachian Congress understood exactly what abolition of slavery would cost them in blood. In the meantime, union between Appalachee and the United States of America was impossible as long as slavery was legal anywhere within Appalachee. And the simplest compromise, to allow the pro-slavery New Counties of Tennizy, Cherriky, and Kenituck to secede from Appalachee, was politically impossible in Appalachee itself.

The outcome Peggy most feared was that the United States would give in and admit the New Counties as slaveholding States. Such a pollution of American freedom would destroy the United States, Peggy was sure of it. And secession of the New Counties was only slightly more acceptable to her, since it would leave most of the Blacks of Appalachee under the overseer's lash. No, the only way to avoid war while retaining a spark of decency among the American people was to persuade the Crown Colonies to allow the whole of Appalachee, New Counties and all, to form a union with the United States of America—with slavery illegal throughout the nation that would result.

Her abolitionist friends laughed when Peggy broached this possibility.

Even her husband, Alvin, sounded doubtful in his letters, though of course he encouraged her to do as she thought right. After hundreds of interviews with men and women throughout Appalachee and for the last few weeks in Camelot, Peggy had plenty of doubts of her own. And yet as long as there was a thread of hope, she would try to tat it into some sort of bearable future. For the future she saw in the heartfires of the people around her could not be borne, unless she knew she had done her utmost to prevent the war that threatened to soak the soil of America in blood, and whose outcome was by no means certain.

So, dread it as she might, Peggy had no choice but to visit with Lady Ashworth. For even if she could not enlist Lady Ashworth and her Lap-Rip club in the cause of emancipation, she might at least win an introduction to the King, so she could plead her cause with the monarch directly.

The idea of meeting with the King frightened her less than the prospect of meeting Lady Ashworth. To an educated man Peggy could speak directly, in the language they understood. But Southern ladies, Peggy already knew, were much more complicated. Everything you said meant something else to them, and everything they said meant anything but the plain meaning of the words. It was a good thing they didn't let Southern ladies go to college. They were far too busy learning arcane languages much more subtle and difficult to master than mere Greek and Latin.

Peggy slept little the night before, ate little that morning, and kept down even less. The most acute nausea from her pregnancy had passed, but when she was nervous, as she was this morning, it returned with a vengeance. The spark of life in the baby in her womb was just beginning to be visible to her. Soon she would be able to see something of the baby's future. Mere glimpses, for a baby's heartfire was chaotic and confusing, but it would become real to her then, a life. Let it be born into a better world than this one. Let my labors change the futures of all the babies.

Her fingers were weak and trembly as she tried to fasten her buttons; she was forced to ask the help of the slavegirl who was assigned to her floor in the boardinghouse. Like all slaves in the Crown Colonies, the girl would not meet Peggy's gaze or even face her directly, and while she answered softly but clearly every question Peggy asked, what passed between them could hardly be called a conversation. "I'm sorry to trouble you, but will you help me fasten my buttons?"

"Yes ma'am."

"My name is Peggy. What's yours?"

"I's Fishy, ma'am."

"Please call me Peggy."

"Yes ma'am."

Don't belabor the point. "Fishy? Really? Or is that a nickname?"

"Yes ma'am."

"Which?"

"Fishy, ma'am."

She must be refusing to understand; let it go. "Why would your mother give you such a name?"

"I don't know, ma'am."

"Or was it your mother who named you?"

"I don't know, ma'am."

"If I give you a tip for your service, do you get to keep it?"

"No tips please, ma'am."

"But if you were to find a penny in the street, would you be permitted to keep it as your own?"

"Never found no penny, ma'am. All done now, ma'am." And Fishy was out the door in a heartbeat, pausing in the doorway only long enough to say, "Anything else, ma'am?"

Peggy knew the answers to her questions, of course, for she saw into the woman's heartfire. Saw how Fishy's mother had shunted her off on other slavewomen, because she could hardly attract the master's lust with a baby clinging to her thighs. And when the woman grew too slack-bellied from her repeated pregnancies, how the master began to share her with his White visitors, and finally with the White overseers, until the day the master gave her to Cur, the Black foreman of the plantation craftsmen. The shame of being reduced to whoring with Blacks was too much for Fishy's mother and she hanged herself. It was Fishy who found her. Peggy saw all of that flash through Fishy's mind when Peggy asked about her mother. But it was a story Fishy had never told and would never tell.

Likewise, Peggy saw that Fishy got her name from the son of the first owner she was sold to after her mother's suicide. She was assigned to be his personal maid, and the senior maid in the plantation house told her that meant that she must do *whatever* the master's son told her to do. What that might have meant Fishy never knew. The boy took one look at her, declared that she smelled fishy, and wouldn't let her in his room. She was reassigned to other duties for the months that she remained in the house, but the name Fishy stuck, and when she was sold into a household in the city of Camelot, she took the name Fishy with her. It was better than the one her mother had given her: Ugly Baby.

As for tipping, if any slave in this house were found with money, it was assumed that it had been stolen and the slave would be stripped and branded and chained in the yard for a week. Slaves might walk with their heads downcast, but in this house, at least, they saw no pennies on the ground.

The worst frustration for Peggy, though, was that she couldn't say to the slave, "Fishy, do not despair. You feel powerless, you *are* powerless except for your sullen contempt, your deliberate slothfulness, the tiny rebellions that you can carry out and still survive. But there are some of us, many of us working to try to set you free." For even if Peggy said it, why should Fishy believe a White woman? And if she did believe, what should she do then? If her behavior changed one iota from this obsequiousness, she would suffer for it, and emancipation, when and if it came, was still many years away.

So Peggy bore Fishy's unspoken scorn and hatred, though she knew she did not deserve it. Her black skin makes her a slave in this country; and therefore my white skin makes me her enemy, for if she took the slightest liberty with me and addressed me with anything like friendship or equality, she would risk terrible suffering.

It was at moments like these that Peggy thought that her fire-eating abolitionist friends in Philadelphia might be right: Only blood and fire could purge America of this sin.

She shrugged off the thought, as she always did. Most of the people who collaborated in the degradation of Blacks did so because they knew no better, or because they were weak and fearful. Ignorance, weakness, and fear led to great wrongs, but they were not in themselves sins, and could often be more profitably corrected than punished. Only those whose hearts delighted in the degradation of the helpless and sought out opportunities to torment their Black captives deserved the blood and horror of war. And war was never so careful as to inflict suffering only where it was merited.

Buttoned now, Peggy would go to meet Lady Ashworth and see if the light of Christianity burned in the heartfire of a lady-in-waiting.

There were carriages for hire in the streets of Camelot, but Peggy had no money to spare for such luxury. The walk wasn't bad, as long as she stayed away from King's Street, which had so much horse traffic that you couldn't tell there were cobbles under the dung, and flecks of it were always getting flipped up onto your clothes. And of course she would never walk along Water Street, because the smell of fish was so thick in the air that you couldn't get it out of your clothes for days afterward, no matter how long you aired them out.

But the secondary streets were pleasant enough, with their well-tended gardens, the flamboyant blooms splashing everything with color, the rich, shiny green of the leaves making every garden look like Eden. The air was muggy but there was usually a breeze from the sea. All the houses were designed to capture even the slightest breeze, and porches three stories high shaded the wealthier houses along their longest face. It gave them deep shade in the heat of the afternoons, and even now, a bit before noon, many a porch already had slaves setting out iced lemonade and preparing to start the shoo-flies a-swishing.

Small children bounced energetically on the curious flexible benches that were designed for play. Peggy had never seen such devices until she came here, though the bench was simple enough to make—just set a sturdy plank between two end supports, with nothing to brace it in the middle, and a child could jump on it and then leap off as if launched from a sling. Perhaps in other places, such an impractical thing, designed only for play, would seem a shameful luxury. Or perhaps in other places adults simply didn't think of going to so much trouble merely to delight their children. But in Camelot, children were treated like young aristocrats—which, come to think of it, most of them were, or at least their parents wished to pretend they were.

As so often before Peggy marveled at the contradictions: People so tender with their children, so indulgent, so playful, and yet they thought nothing of raising those same children to order that slaves who annoyed them be stripped or whipped, or their families broken up and sold off.

Of course, here in the city few of the mansions had large enough grounds to allow a proper whipping on the premises. The offending slave would be taken to the market and whipped there, so the moaning and weeping wouldn't interfere with conversations in the sitting rooms and drawing rooms of the beautiful houses.

What was the truth of these people? Their love for their children, for king and country, for the classical education at which they excelled, all these were genuine. By every sign they were educated, tasteful, generous, broad-minded, hospitable—in a word, civilized. And yet just under the surface was a casual brutality and a deep shame that poisoned all their acts. It was as if two cities sat on this place. Camelot, the courtly city of the king-in-exile, was the land of dancing and music, education and discourse, light and beauty, love and laughter. But by coincidence, the old city of Charleston still existed here, with buildings that corresponded with Camelot wall for wall, door for door. Only the citizenry was different, for Charleston was the city of slave markets, half-White babies sold away from their own father's household, lashings and humiliations, and, as seed and root and leaf and blossom of this evil town, the hatred and fear of both Blacks and Whites who lived at war with each other, the one doomed to perpetual defeat, the other to perpetual fear of . . .

Of what? What did they fear?

Justice.

And it dawned on her for the first time what she had *not* seen in Fishy's heartfire: the desire for revenge.

And yet that was impossible. What human being could bear such constant injustice and not cry out, at least in the silence of the soul, for the power to set things to rights? Was Fishy so meek that she forgave all? No, her sullen resistance clearly had no piety in it. She was filled with hate. And yet not one thought or dream or plan for retribution, either personal or divine. Not even the hope of emancipation or escape.

As she walked along the streets under the noonday sun, it made her almost giddy to realize what must be going on, and not just with Fishy, but with every slave she had met here in Camelot. Peggy was not able to see everything in their heartfires. They were able to conceal a part of their feelings from her. For it was impossible to imagine that they *had* no such feelings, for they were human beings, and all the Blacks she met in Appalachee had yearnings for retribution, manumission, or escape. No, if she didn't see those passions among the slaves of Camelot, it wasn't because they didn't feel them, it was because they had somehow learned to lie a lie so deep that it existed even in their heartfires.

And that threw everything in doubt. For if there was one thing Peggy had always counted on, it was this: No one could lie to her without her knowing it. It had been that way with her almost since birth. It was one of the reasons people didn't usually like to spend much time around a torch—though few of them could see even a fraction of what Peggy saw. There was always the fear of their secret thoughts being known and exposed.

When Peggy was a child, she did not understand why adults became so upset when she responded to what was in their heartfire rather than the words they were saying to her. But what could she do? When a traveling salesman patted her on her head and said, "I got something for this little girl, I wager!" she hardly noticed his words, what with all that his heartfire was telling her, not to mention her father's heartfire and everybody else nearby. She just naturally had to answer, "My papa's not a fool! He knows you're cheating him!"

But everybody got so upset with her that she learned to keep silent about all lies and all secrets. Her response was to hold her tongue and say nothing at all. Fortunately, she learned silence before she was old enough to understand the truly dark secrets that would have destroyed her family. Silence served her well—so well that some visitors to her father's inn took her for a mute.

Still, she had to converse with local people, and with other children her age. And for a long time it made her angry, how people's words never matched up very well with their desires or memories, and sometimes were the flat opposite. Only gradually did she come to see that as often as not, the lies people told were designed to be kind or merciful or, at the very least, polite. If a mother thought her daughter was plain, was it bad that she lied to the child and told her that she loved how her face brightened up when she smiled? What good would it have done to give her true opinion? And the lie helped the child grow up more cheerful, and therefore more attractive.

Peggy began to understand that what made a statement good was rarely dependent on whether it was true. Very little human speech was truthful, as she knew better than anyone else. What mattered was whether the deception was kindly meant or designed to take advantage, whether it was meant to smooth a social situation or aggrandize the speaker in others' eyes.

Peggy became a connoisseur of lies. The good lies were motivated by love or kindness, to shield someone from pain, to protect the innocent, or to hide feelings that the speaker was ashamed of. The neutral lies were the fictions of courtesy that allowed conversations to proceed smoothly without unnecessary or unproductive conflict. How are you? Just fine.

The bad lies were not all equal, either. Ordinary hypocrisy was annoying but did little harm, unless the hypocrite went out of his way to attack others for sins that he himself committed but concealed. Careless liars seemed to have no regard for truth, and lied from habit or for sport. Cruel liars, though, sought out their target's worst fears and then lied to make them suffer or to put them at a disadvantage; or they gossiped to destroy people they resented, often accusing them falsely of the sins the gossips themselves most wished to commit. And then there were the professional liars, who said whatever was necessary to get others to do their will.

And despite Peggy's gifts as a torch—and no ordinary torch at that, able merely to catch a glimpse of a child inside the womb—even she often had trouble discerning the motive behind a lie, in part because there were often many motives in conflict. Fear, weakness, a desire to be liked—all could produce lies that in someone else might come from ruthlessness or cruelty; and within their heartfire, Peggy could not easily see the difference. It took time; she had to understand the pattern of their lives to find out what sort of soul they had, and where the lies all seemed to lead.

So many questions were posed by every lie she was told that she despaired of answering any but the most obvious. Even when she knew the truth that someone was lying to conceal, what was that truth? The mother who thought her daughter was ugly might be lying when she told the girl that her smile made her pretty—but in fact the mother might be wrong, and in fact her lie might be true in the eyes of another observer. Most "truths" that people believed in, and therefore which they contradicted with their lies, were not objectively true at all. The *real* truth—how things are or were or would become—was almost unknowable. That is, people often knew the truth, but they just as often "knew" things that were not true, and had no reliable way to tell the difference. So while Peggy could always see what the person believed was true while they told their lies, this did not mean that Peggy therefore knew the *real* truth.

After years of sorting out the lies and realizing that the lies often told more truth than the "truth" that the lies concealed, Peggy finally came to the conclusion that what she needed was not a better sense of truth, but simply the skill to hear a lie and react to it as if she knew nothing else.

It was after she ran away from home and went to Dekane that, under the tutelage of Mistress Modesty, she learned the balancing act of hearing both the words and the heartfire, and yet letting her voice, her face, her gestures show only the response that was appropriate for the words. She might sometimes make use of the hidden knowledge she saw in their heartfires, but never in such a way that they would realize she knew their deepest secrets. "Even those of us who are not torches have to learn those skills," said Mistress Modesty. "The ability to act as if you did not know what you know perfectly well is the essence of courtesy and poise." Peggy learned them right along with music, geography, history, grammar, and the classics of philosophy and poetry.

But there was no balancing act with the slaves here. They were able to hide their hearts from her.

Did they know she was a torch, and so hid deliberately? That was hardly likely—they could not *all* have such a sense of her hidden powers. No, their secret dreams were hidden from her because they were also hidden from the slaves themselves. It was how they survived. If they did not know their own rage, then they could not inadvertently show it. Slave parents must teach this to their children, to hide their rage so deeply that they couldn't even find it themselves.

And yet it was there. It was there, burning. Does it turn their hearts to ash, gradually growing cold? Or to lava, waiting to erupt?

The Ashworth house wasn't the largest or the most elegantly finished, but then it didn't need to be, since they could take up residence on at least a half-dozen huge estates all over the Crown Colonies. So the house in town could be relatively modest without loss of prestige.

Even so, the signs of true wealth were there. Everything was perfectly maintained. The bell gave off a musical tone. The street door opened noiselessly on its hinges. The floor of the lower porch did not creak, it was that solidly built—even the porch! And the furniture showed no sign of weathering—obviously it must be carried in whenever the weather went bad, either that or replaced every year. The perfection of detail. The ostentation of people with unlimited money and impeccable taste.

The slave who opened the door for her and ushered her into the room was a wiry, middle-aged man who fit his livery as if he had been born in it and it had grown along with him. Or perhaps he shed it from time to time like a snake, revealing a perfect new costume underneath. He said nothing and never looked at her. She spoke her own name when he opened the door; he stepped back and let her in. By his manner, by the most subtle of gestures, he showed her when she should follow him, and where she should wait.

In his wordlessness she was free to search his heartfire without distraction, and now that she was aware, she could search for the missing part. For it *was* missing: the offended dignity, the anguish, the fear, the rage. All gone. Only service was in his thoughts, only the jobs he had to do, and the manner in which he had to do them. Intense concentration on the routine of the house.

But it was impossible. He could not conduct his life with such intense singularity of thought. No one could. Where were the distractions? Where were the people he liked, or loved? Where was his humanity?

Had the slaveowners succeeded in this place? Had they torn the very life out of the hearts of the slaves? Had they succeeded in making these people what they always claimed they were—animals?

He was gone, and so dim was his heartfire that she had trouble tracking him through the house. What was his name? Was even his name hidden? No, there it was—Lion. But that was only a house name, given to him when he arrived here. Apparently it pleased Lord and Lady

Ashworth to name their slaves for noble animals. How could such a transient name be the one contained in his heartfire?

There was a deep name hidden somewhere in him. As there must be in Fishy, too—some name deeper than Ugly Baby. And where the deep name was hidden, there she would find the true heartfire. In Fishy, in Lion, in all the Blacks whose hands did the labor of this city.

"Miz Larner," said a soft voice. A woman this time, old and wrinkled, her hair steel-gray. *Her* costume hung on her like a sack on a fencepost, but that did not reflect ill on the house—no clothing could look right on such a wizened frame. Peggy wasn't sure whether it spoke well of the family that they kept such an old slave as part of the household, or whether it suggested that they were squeezing the last ounce of service out of her.

No, no, don't be cynical, she told herself. Lady Ashworth is the president of Lap-Rip, publicly committed to putting limits on slavery. She would hardly let this old woman guide company through the house if she thought anyone could possibly find a negative implication in it.

The old woman moved with excruciating slowness, but Peggy followed patiently. She was called Doe in this house, but to Peggy's great relief, there seemed to be no dimming or hiding of her heartfire, and it was easy to find her true name, an African word that Peggy could hear in her mind but wouldn't know how to form with her lips. But she knew what the name meant: It was a kind of flower. This woman had been kidnapped by raiders from another village only days before her planned wedding, and was sold three times in as many days before seeing her first White face, a Portuguese ship captain. Then the voyage, her first owner in America, her struggle to learn enough English to understand what she was being commanded to do. The times she was slapped, starved, stripped, whipped. None of her White masters had ravished her, but she had been bred like a mare, and of the nine children she bore, only two had been left with her past their third birthday. Those were sold locally, a girl and a boy, and she saw them now and then, even today. She even knew of three of her grandchildren, for her daughter had been a virtual concubine to her master, and . . .

And all three of the grandchildren were free.

Astonishing. It was illegal in the Crown Colonies, yet in this woman's heartfire Peggy could see that Doe certainly believed that it was true.

And then an even bigger surprise. Doe herself was also free, and had been for five years. She received a wage, in addition to a tiny rent-free room in this house.

That was why her heartfire was so easily found. The memory of bitterness and anger was there, but Lord Ashworth had freed her on her seventieth birthday.

How wonderful, thought Peggy. After fewer than six decades of slavery, when she had already lived longer than the vast majority of slaves, when her body was shriveled, her strength gone, *then* she was set free.

Again, Peggy forced herself to reject cynicism. It might seem meaningless to Peggy, to free Doe so late in her life. But it had great meaning to Doe herself. It had unlocked her heart. All she cared about now was her three grandchildren. That and earning her wage through service in this house.

Doe led Peggy up a wide flight of stairs to the main floor of the house. Everyone lived above the level of the street. Indeed, Doe led her even higher, to the lavish second story, where instead of a drawing room Peggy found herself being led to the porch and, yes, the cane chairs, the pitcher of iced lemonade, the swaying shoo-flies, the slaveboy with a fan almost the size of his own body, and, standing at a potted plant with a watering can in her hand, Lady Ashworth herself.

"It's so kind of you to come, Miz Larner," she said. "I could scarcely believe my good fortune, when I learned that you would have time in your busy day to call upon me."

Lady Ashworth was much younger and prettier than Peggy had expected, and she was dressed quite comfortably, with her hair pinned in a simple bun. But it was the watering can that astonished Peggy. It looked suspiciously like a tool, and watering a plant could only be construed as manual labor. Ladies in slaveholding families did not do such things.

Lady Ashworth noticed Peggy's hesitation, and understood why. She laughed. "I find that some of the more delicate plants thrive better when I care for them myself. It's no more than Eve and Adam did in Paradise—they tended the garden, didn't they?" She set down the can, sat gracefully on a cane chair beside the table with the pitcher, and gestured for Peggy to be seated. "Besides, Miz Larner, one ought to be prepared for life after the abolition of slavery."

Again Peggy was startled. In slave lands, the word *abolition* was about as polite as some of the more colorful expletives of a river rat.

"Oh, dear," said Lady Ashworth, "I'm afraid my language may have shocked you. But that *is* why you're here, isn't it, Miz Larner? Don't we both share the goal of abolishing slavery wherever we can? So if we succeed, then I should certainly know how to do a few tasks for myself. Come now, you haven't said a word since you got here."

Peggy laughed, embarrassed. "I haven't, have I? It's kind of you to be willing to see me. And I can assure you that ladies of stature in the United States are not up to their elbows in wash water. Paid servants do the coarser sort of work."

"But so much more expensively," said Lady Ashworth. "They expect their wages in cash. We don't use much money here. It's all seasonal. The French and English buyers come to town, we sell our cotton or tobacco, and then we pay all the tradesmen for the year. We don't carry money with us or keep it around the house. I don't think we'd keep many *free* servants with such a policy."

Peggy sighed inwardly. For Lady Ashworth's heartfire told such a different story. She watered her own plants because the slaves deliberately overwatered the most expensive imports, killing them by degrees. Some imaginary shortage of cash had nothing to do with keeping free servants, for the well-to-do families always had money in the bank. And as for abolition, Lady Ashworth loathed the word as much as any other slaveholder. For that matter, she loathed Peggy herself. But she recognized that some limitation on slavery would have to be achieved in order to placate public opinion in Europe and the United States, and all that Lady Ashworth ever intended to allow Lap-Rip to accomplish was the banning of slavery in certain regions of the Crown Colonies where the land and the economy made slavery unprofitable anyway. Lady Ashworth had always had success in convincing Northerners that she was quite radical on slavery, and expected to do as well with Peggy.

But Peggy was determined not to be treated with such contempt. It was a simple matter to find in Lady Ashworth's heartfire some of her more recent mistreatment of her slaves. "Perhaps instead of wielding the watering can," said Peggy, "you might show your commitment to abolition by bringing back the two slaves you have standing stripped in chains without water to drink in the hot sun of the dockyard."

Lady Ashworth's face showed nothing, but Peggy saw the rage and fear leap up within her. "Why, Miz Larner, I do believe you have been doing some research."

"The names and owners of the slaves are posted for all to see," said Peggy.

"Few of our Northern visitors pry into our domestic affairs by visiting our disciplinary park."

Too late did Peggy realize that the guards at the disciplinary yard— hardly a "park"—would never have let her inside. Not without a letter of introduction. And Lady Ashworth *would* inquire who it was who provided a Northern radical like Peggy with such an entree. When she found that there was no such letter and Peggy had made no such visit, she would think—what? That Peggy was secretly a torch? Perhaps. But more likely she would think that one of the household Blacks had talked to Peggy. There would be punishments for the only two Blacks that Peggy had had contact with: Doe and Lion. Peggy looked into the futures she had just created and saw Lady Ashworth hearing Doe's confession, knowing perfectly well that the old woman was lying in order to protect Lion.

And what would Lady Ashworth do? Lion, refusing to confess, would be whipped and, in the futures in which he survived the whipping, sold west. Doe would be turned out of the house, for even though she had not given Peggy a bit of information, she had proven she was more loyal to a fellow Black than to her mistress. As a free black of advanced age, Doe would be reduced to living from scraps provided by the charity of other slaves, all of whom would be opening themselves to charges of stealing from their masters for every bit of food they gave to Doe.

Time to lie. "Do you think that you're the only . . . abolitionist . . . living in Camelot?" said Peggy. "The difference is that some of the others are sincere."

At once Lady Ashworth's heartfire showed different futures. She would now be suspicious of the other ladies in Lap-Rip. Which of them had exposed Lady Ashworth's hypocrisy by speaking to Peggy, or writing to her, about the Ashworth slaves now being disciplined?

"Did you come to my house to insult me?"

"No more than I came to be insulted," said Peggy.

"What did I do to insult you?" said Lady Ashworth. What she did not say, but what Peggy heard just as clearly as her words, was that it was impossible for Lady Ashworth to insult Peggy, for Peggy was nobody.

"You dared to claim that you share the goal of abolishing slavery wherever you can, when you know perfectly well that you have no intention of living for even a single day of your life without slavery, and that your entire effort is merely to pacify Northerners like me. You are part of your husband's foreign-relations strategy, and you are as committed to preserving slavery in the New Counties as anyone else in the Crown Colonies."

At last the façade of cheerfulness cracked. "How dare you, you priggish little nobody? Do you think I don't know your husband is a common tradesman with the name of Smith? No one ever heard of your family, and you come from a mongrel country that thinks nothing of mixing the races and treats people of quality as if they were the common scum of the street."

"At last," said Peggy, "you have consented to deal with me honestly."

"I don't consent to deal with you at all! Get out of my house."

Peggy did not budge from her seat. Indeed, she picked up the pitcher of lemonade and poured herself a tall glass. "Lady Ashworth, the need for you to create the illusion of gradual emancipation has not changed. In fact, I think you and I have a lot more to talk about now that we're not lying to each other."

It was amusing to watch Lady Ashworth think through the consequences of throwing Peggy out—an event which would undoubtedly get reported all over the north, at least in abolitionist circles.

"What do you want, Miz Larner?" said Lady Ashworth coldly.

"I want," said Peggy, "an audience with the King."

⊠ 3 ⊠

Painted Birds

JEAN-JACQUES AUDUBON SOON forgot the strangeness of painting from a live bird and concentrated on colors and shapes. Arthur and Alvin both sat in the grass behind him, watching the goose come to life on the paper. To Arthur it was a kind of miracle. A dab here, a dab there, a streak, colors blending sometimes, sharp-edged in other places. And from this chaos, a bird.

From time to time the model grew weary. Arthur jumped up from the grass and spoke to the geese, and soon another took the place of the first, as close a match as he could find. Jean-Jacques cursed under his breath. "They are not the same bird, you know."

"But they're alive," said Arthur. "Look at the eyes."

Jean-Jacques only grunted. For the bird did look alive on the paper. Arthur whispered about it to Alvin, but Alvin's reply gave him no satisfaction. "How do you know he didn't make the dead birds look just as alive in his paintings?"

At last the painting was done. Jean-Jacques busied himself with putting away his colors and brushes, until Arthur called out to him, rather angrily. "Look here, Mr. Audubon!"

Jean-Jacques looked up. The goose was still there, not posed anymore, but still on the ground, gazing intently at Arthur Stuart. "I'm finish with the goose, you can let it go." He turned back to his work.

"No!" Arthur Stuart shouted.

"Arthur," said Alvin softly.

"He's got to watch," said Arthur.

Sighing, Jean-Jacques looked up. "What am I watching?"

The moment Audubon's eyes were on him, Arthur clapped his hands and the goose ran and clumsily staggered into the air. But as soon as its wings were pulling against the air, it changed into a beautiful creature, turning the powerful beats of its wings into soaring flight. The other geese also rose. And Jean-Jacques, his weariness slipping from him, watched them fly over the trees.

"What grace," said Jean-Jacques. "No lady ever dances with so much beauty."

At that Arthur charged at him, furious. "That's right! Them living birds are prettier than any of your damned old paintings!"

Alvin caught Arthur by the shoulders, held him, smiled wanly at Jean-Jacques. "I'm sorry. I never seen him act so mad."

"Every painting you ever made killed a bird," said Arthur. "And I don't care how pretty you paint, it ain't worth stopping the life of any of them!"

Jean-Jacques was embarrassed. "No one say this to me before. Men shoot their guns all the time, birds die every day."

"For meat," said Arthur. "To eat them."

"Does he believe this?" Jean-Jacques asked Alvin. "Do you think they are hungry and shoot the birds for food? Maybe they are stuffing it for trophy. Maybe they are shooting for *fun,* you angry boy."

Arthur was unmollified. "So maybe they're no better than you. But I'd rather cut off my hand than kill a bird just to make a picture of it."

"All these hours you watch me paint, you admire my painting, no? And now you choose this moment and tout á coup you are angry?"

"Cause I wanted you to see that bird fly. You painted it but it could still fly!"

"But that was because of your talking to the bird," said Jean-Jacques. "How can I know such a boy as you exist? I am oughting to wait for some boy to come along and make the bird pose? Until then I draw trees?''

''Who asked you to paint birds?''

''Is this the question you wanted to ask me?'' said Jean-Jacques.

Arthur stopped short. ''No. Yes. The way you stuffed them birds back in the shop, that showed me you *know* the birds, you really see them, but then how can you kill them? You ain't hungry.''

''I am often hungry. I am hungry right now. But it is not the bird I want to eat. Not goose today. What beautiful gooses. You love them flying, and I love them flying, but in France nobody ever sees these birds. Other birds they see, not the birds of America. Scientists write and talk about birds but they see only sketches, bad printing of them. I am not very good painter of people. Most of the people I do not like, and this makes my paintings not pretty to them. My people look like they are dead—etouffé—avec little glass eyes. But birds. I can paint them to be alive. I can find the colors, I see them there, and put them on the paper. We print, and now the scientist know, they open my book, *voilà* the American bird they never see. Now they can think about bird and they *see* them. God lets you to talk to birds, angry boy. He lets me to paint them. I should throw away this gift of God except today, when you are here to help me?''

''It ain't your gift when it's the bird as dies for it,'' said Arthur Stuart.

''All creatures die,'' said Jean-Jacques. ''Birds live the lives of birds. All the same. It is a beautiful life, but they live in the shadow of death, afraid, watching, and then, boom! The gun. The talon of the hawk! The paws of the cat. But the bird I kill, I make it into the picture, it will live forever.''

''Paint on paper ain't a bird,'' said Arthur Stuart sullenly.

Jean-Jacques's hand flashed out and gripped Arthur's arm. ''Come here and say that to my picture!'' He forced Arthur to stand over the open sketchbook. ''You make me look at flying gooses. Now you look!''

Arthur looked.

''You see this is beautiful,'' said Jean-Jacques. ''And it teaches. Knowing is good. I show this bird to the world. In every eye, there is my bird. My goose is Plato's goose. Perfect goose. True goose. *Real* goose.''

Alvin chuckled. "We aren't too clear on Plato."

Arthur turned scornfully to Alvin. "Miz Larner taught us all about Plato, lessen you was asleep that day."

"Was this the question you had for Mr. Audubon?" asked Alvin. "Asking why he thinks it's worth killing birds to paint them? Cause if it was, you sure picked a rude way to ask it."

"I'm sorry," said Arthur Stuart.

"And I think he gave you a fair answer, Arthur Stuart. If he was shooting birds and selling them to a poulterer you wouldn't think twice cause it's nature's way, killing and eating. It's all right to shoot a bird so some family can buy the carcass and roast it up and eat it gone. But iffen you just paint it, that makes him a killer?"

"I know," said Arthur Stuart. "I knowed that right along."

"Then what was all this shouting for?" asked Alvin.

"I don't know," said Arthur. "I don't know why I got so mad."

"I know why," said Jean-Jacques.

"You do?" asked Alvin.

"Of course," said Jean-Jacques. "The gooses do not like to die. But they cannot speak. They cannot, how you say, complain. So. You are the interpreter for birds."

Arthur Stuart had no answer for this. They walked in silence for a while, as the road led them to the outlying buildings and then quickly into the city, the ground turning into a cobbled street under them.

"I think of a question for you, King Arthur," said Jean-Jacques at last.

"What," said Arthur, sounding far from enthusiastic.

"The sound you make, no goose ever make this sound. But they understand you."

"Wish you could have heard him when he was younger," said Alvin. "He sounded just like any bird you want."

"He lost this when his voice change? Getting low?"

"Earlier," said Alvin. He could not explain how he changed Arthur Stuart's body so that the Finders couldn't claim him. Though Jean-Jacques seemed a decent enough fellow, it wouldn't be good to have any witness who could affirm that Arthur really was the runaway slave the Finders had been looking for.

"But my question," said Jean-Jacques, "is how you learn this language. You never *hear* this language, so how to learn it?"

"I *do* hear the language," said Arthur. "I'm talking their language right back to them. I just have a really thick human accent."

At this, Jean-Jacques burst out laughing, and so did Alvin. "Human accent," Jean-Jacques repeated.

"It ain't like the geese talk in words anyway," said Arthur. "It's more like, when I talk, I'm making the sound that says, Hi, I'm a goose, and then the rest of it says things like, everything's safe, or, quick let's fly, or, hold still now. Not words. Just . . . wishes."

"But there was a time," said Alvin, "when I saw you talking to a redbird and it told you all kinds of stuff and it wasn't just wishes, it was complicated."

Arthur thought about it. "Oh, that time," he finally said. "Well, that's cause that redbird wasn't talking redbird talk. He was talking English."

"English!" said Alvin, incredulous.

"With a really thick redbird accent," said Arthur. And this time all three of them laughed together.

As they neared Mistress Louder's boardinghouse, they could see a burly man bounding out into the street, then returning immediately through the garden gate. "Is that a man or a big rubber ball?" asked Jean-Jacques.

"It's Mr. Fink," said Arthur Stuart. "I think he's watching for us."

"Or is it Gargantua?" asked Jean-Jacques.

"More like Pantagruel," said Arthur Stuart.

Jean-Jacques stopped cold. Alvin and Arthur turned to look at him. "What's wrong?" asked Alvin.

"The boy knows Rabelais?" asked Jean-Jacques.

"Who's that?" asked Alvin.

"Alvin was asleep that day, too," said Arthur Stuart.

Jean-Jacques looked back and forth between them. "You and you have attend to school together?"

Alvin knew what Audubon must be thinking—that Alvin must be a dunce to have gone to school at the same time as a child. "We had the same teacher," said Alvin.

"And she taught us in the same room at the same time," said Arthur Stuart.

"Only we didn't always get the same lesson," said Alvin.

"Yeah, I got Rabelais and Plato," said Arthur Stuart, "and Alvin married the schoolteacher."

Jean-Jacques laughed out loud. "That is so pleasant! Your wife is a schoolteacher but this slaveboy is the top student!"

"Reckon so, except one thing," said Alvin. "The boy is free."

"Oh yes, I'm sorry. I mean to say, this Black boy."

"Half-Black," Arthur Stuart corrected him.

"Which make you half-White," said Jean-Jacques. "But when I look at you, I see only the Black half. Is this not curious?"

"When Black folks look at me," said Arthur Stuart, "they see only the White half."

"But the secret about you," said Jean-Jacques, "is that deep in your heart, *you know Rabelais*!"

"What does that have to do with Black and White?" asked Alvin.

"It have to do that all this Black and White just make this boy laugh inside. When you are laughing deep down where no one else can see, Rabelais is there. Yes, Arthur Stuart?"

"Rabelais," said Alvin. "Was that the book about the big huge fat guy?"

"So you did read it?"

"No," said Alvin. "I got embarrassed and gave it back to Miz Larner. Margaret, I mean. You can't talk about things like that with a lady!"

"Ah," said Jean-Jacques. "Your schoolteacher began as Miz Larner, but now she is Margaret. Next you will call her 'mama,' n'est-ce pas?"

Alvin got a little tight-lipped at that. "Maybe you French folks like to read nasty books and all, but in America you don't go talking about a man's wife having babies."

"Oh, you plan to get them some other way?" Jean-Jacques laughed again. "Look, Pantagruel has seen us! He is coming to crush us!"

Mike Fink strode angrily toward them. "You know what damn time it is!" he called out.

People nearby looked at him and glared.

"Watch your language," Alvin said. "You want to get fined?"

"I wanted to get to Trenton before nightfall," said Mike.

"How, you got a train ticket?" asked Alvin.

"Good afternoon, Pantagruel. I am Jean-Jacques Audubon."

"Is he talking English?" asked Mike.

"Mike, this is John James Audubon, a Frenchman who paints birds. Jean-Jacques, this is Mike Fink."

"That's right, I'm Mike Fink! I'm half bear and half alligator, and my grandma on my mother's side was a tornado. When I clap my hands it scares lightning out of a clear sky. And if I want a bird painted, I'll pee straight up and turn the whole flock yellow!"

"I tremble in my boots to know you are such a dangerous fellow," said Jean-Jacques. "I am sure that when you say these things to ladies, their skirts fly up and they fall over on their backs."

Mike looked at him for a moment in silence. "If he's making fun of me, Alvin, I got to kill him."

"No, he was saying he thinks you make a fine speech," said Alvin. "Come on, Mike, it's me you're mad at. I'm sorry I didn't get back. I found Arthur Stuart pretty quick, but then we had to stay and help Mr. Audubon paint a goose."

"What for?" asked Mike. "Was the old colors peeling off?"

"No no," said Jean-Jacques. "I paint on *paper*. I make a picture of a goose."

Before Alvin could explain that the former river rat was making a joke, Mike said, "Thanks for clearing that up for me, you half-witted tick-licking donkey-faced baboon."

"Every time you talk I hear how much of English I have yet to learn," said Jean-Jacques.

"It wasn't Mr. Audubon's fault, Mike. It was Arthur Stuart who made us stay while he talked a goose into holding still. So Mr. Audubon could paint a picture without having to kill the bird and stuff it first."

"Well that's fine with me," said Mike. "I'm not all that mad about it."

"You get more mad that this?" asked Jean-Jacques.

"None of you ain't seen me mad," said Mike.

"I have," said Alvin.

"Well, maybe a little bit mad," said Mike. "When you broke my leg."

Jean-Jacques looked at Alvin, seeing him in a new light, if he could break the leg of a man who did indeed seem to be half bear.

"It's Verily who's about ready to explode," said Mike.

"Verily?" asked Alvin, surprised. Verily Cooper hardly ever showed his temper.

"Yeah, he drummed his fingers on the table at lunch and on the porch he snatched a fly right out of the air and threw it at the house so hard it broke a window."

"He did?" asked Arthur Stuart, in awe.

"I said so, didn't I?" said Mike Fink.

"Oh, yeah, I forgot who was talking," said Arthur.

"Arthur and Mr. Audubon are hungry and thirsty," said Alvin. "You think you can take them in and see if Mistress Louder can get them a slab of bread and some water, at least?"

"Water?" said Audubon with a painted expression. "Do you Americans not understand that water can make you sick? Wine is healthy. Beer is good for you as long as you don't mind making urine all the time. But water—you will get, what you call it, the piles."

"I been drinking water all my life," said Alvin, "and I don't get no piles."

"But this mean you are, how you say . . ." Then he rattled off a stream of French.

"Used to it," said Arthur, translating.

"Yes! Yoost a twit!"

"Used. To. It," Arthur repeated helpfully.

"English is the stupidest language on Earth. Except for German, and it is not a language, it is a head cold."

"You speak French?" Alvin asked Arthur Stuart.

"No," said Arthur, as if it were the stupidest idea in the world.

"Well, you understood Mr. Audubon."

"I guessed," said Arthur. "I don't even talk English all that good."

Right, thought Alvin. You can talk English any way you want to. You just *like* to break the rules and sound like this is your first day out of a deep-woods cabin.

"Come on in and get something to eat," said Mike. "And if you won't drink water, Mr. Odd Bone—"

"Audubon," Jean-Jacques corrected him.

"I hope hard cider will do the trick, cause I don't reckon Mistress Louder has anything stronger."

"Can *I* have some hard cider?" asked Arthur Stuart.

"No, but you can have a cookie," said Alvin.

"Hurrah!"

"*If* she offers you one," said Alvin. "And no hinting."

"Mistress Louder always knows what a fellow's hungry for," said Arthur Stuart. "It's her knack."

Jean-Jacques laughed. "The food I am hungry for has never been served in this whole continent!"

"What do you mean?" said Mike Fink. "We got frogs and snails here."

"But you have no garlic."

"We got onions so strong they make you fart blue," said Mike. "And I tasted a Red man's peppercorn one time that made me think I was a fish and I woke up in the river."

"The food of France does nothing so wonderful. It *taste* so good that every day God send a saint down to Paris to bring him his dinner, but what does he know?"

They continued the bragging contest into the kitchen. But Alvin stopped off in the small parlor, where Verily sat comfortably with a book on his lap. He glanced at Alvin and then back down at the book.

"Oh, you're back," said Verily. "I assumed you had been killed and Arthur sold into slavery." He turned a page. "Next time, perhaps." He said it with no expression at all. Mike was right. Alvin had never seen Verily Cooper so mad.

"I'm sorry," Alvin said.

"All right then," said Verily, setting down the book and rising to his feet. "Let's go." Verily walked toward the door.

"This late in the afternoon?" asked Alvin as he passed.

Verily stopped and looked at Alvin in feigned surprise. "Afternoon? So late? I had no idea."

"I said I'm sorry," said Alvin.

"I'm not like Peggy," said Verily. "I can't see your heartfire off in the distance and assure myself that everything's all right. I just sit here waiting."

"I can't believe this," said Alvin. "You sound like a wife."

"I sound angry," said Verily. "I think it's interesting that in your mind this translates as 'sounding like a wife.' "

"Now you sound like a lawyer," said Alvin.

"But you still sound like someone who thinks his life is so much more important than anyone else's that he can worry and inconvenience other people and all will be made right if he just says 'I'm sorry.' "

Alvin was stunned. "How can you say that? You know that's not how I feel."

"That's not what you *say*. But it's how you *act*."

"Sure, yes, maybe I do act like that. I'm on this journey trying to find out what this knack I have is *for*. I was told once that I'm supposed to build a Crystal City only I don't know what it is or how it's made. So I'm flailing around, changing my mind from day to day and week to week because I don't even know where to begin. Some Tennizy town calling itself Crystal City? Or maybe New England, because one of the wisest people I know tells me that's where I'll learn how to create a city?"

"This is not about whether or not you follow my suggestion," said Verily.

"I know what it's about," said Alvin. "Your knack is as remarkable as mine. On top of that you're an educated man. So why are you wandering all over America, following a half-educated journeyman blacksmith who doesn't know where he's going?"

"That is precisely the question I've spent this whole day asking."

"Well, answer it," said Alvin. "Because if you want to be the center of your own life, then get on with it. Go away. The longer you follow me around the more you're going to get caught up in *my* life, and pretty soon all you'll be is the fellow who helped Alvin Smith build him a Crystal City."

"That's if you succeed in building it."

"Now we're to it, ain't we, Very?" said Alvin. "It's worth it to tag along with me iffen I end up building the damn city. But what if I never figure it out? *Then* what's your life about?"

Verily turned his back on Alvin, but he didn't leave the room. He walked to the window. "Now I see," he said.

"See what?"

"I sat here getting angrier and angrier, and I thought it was because you were delaying our journey and hadn't sent word, and I talked myself into resenting the high-handed way you make decisions, but that was nonsense, because I'm free to leave any time. I'm with you by my own choice, and that includes being patient while you figure things out. So why was I angry?"

"Being angry isn't always for a reason that makes sense."

"Do you imagine you have to tell a lawyer that?" Verily laughed grimly. "I see now that I was really angry because I'm not in control of my own life. I've handed it over to you."

"Not to me," said Alvin.

"You're the one leading this expedition."

"You think just because you're not in charge of your own life right now, I must be in charge?" Alvin sat down on the floor and leaned against the wall. "I didn't give myself this knack. I didn't set the Unmaker to trying to kill me a dozen times over while I was growing up. I didn't cause myself to be born where this torch girl could see my future and use my birth caul to save my life every one of those times. I didn't choose to get all caught up with Tenskwa-Tawa, either—I was kidnapped by a bunch of Reds as was in cahoots with Harrison. And when I do make a choice it's liable to blow up in my face. I figured out how to save Arthur from the Finders but what did it cost him? He can't do the voices anymore, not even the true voices of the birds. I'd give anything to put him back to rights, the way he was. And this golden plow, this living plow I found in the fire, that was the worst mistake of all, cause I don't know how to use it or what *it's* for. But I feel like it's got to make sense. There's got to be some purpose behind it. Some plan. Only I can't see what it's supposed to be. Not the future, not the present, not the past. And Margaret's no help neither, cause she sees too many futures and all she cares about is whether I'm dead, as if there's some future in which I don't die. Verily, you feel like you're getting led around on a string, but at least you can look at the other end of the string and see who's holding it."

"You," said Verily.

"And you can take it back if you want. You can go your own way. But me, Verily, who's holding *my* string? And how can I get away?"

Verily sank to his knees in front of Alvin and put his hands on Alvin's shoulders, then pulled him into an embrace. "You need a friend, and I'm nothing but a nag, Alvin."

"You're the friend I need, Verily, as long as you want to be," said Alvin.

They held each other for a long moment, both of them rejoicing in the closeness, and both relieved that they hadn't lost it in the flaring of tempers of two strong-willed men.

"So we stay another night?" asked Verily.

"If Mistress Louder hasn't changed the sheets," said Alvin.

"She hasn't," said Verily. "She said she wouldn't till she saw you ride off."

"So she knew I wouldn't get away today?"

"She wished," said Verily. "You know she's set her cap for you."

"Don't be silly. She's twenty years older than me at least, and I'm a married man."

"Cupid shoots his arrows where they'll cause the most mischief," said Verily.

"She mothers me," said Alvin. "That's all it is."

"To you it feels like mothering," said Verily, "but to her it feels like wifing."

"Then let's get out of here tonight."

"The harm's already done," said Verily, "and she's not going to do anything about it, so why not stay tonight in a familiar bed?"

"And eat familiar food," said Alvin.

"Which I smell right now," said Verily.

"It's not even suppertime," said Alvin.

"How often a woman's love comes out as cookies."

"One more night in Mistress Louder's house," said Alvin.

"You'll always come back here when you're in Philadelphia," said Verily.

"Why, you think I can't turn away from a good meal and a soft bed?"

"I think you can't bear the thought of breaking her heart."

"I thought I was blind to other people's needs and desires."

Verily grinned. "I believe that the person who said that was in a bit of a snit. A rational person would never speak of you that way."

"So we leave for New England in the morning?" said Alvin.

"Unless Arthur Stuart has another errand for us."

"And Verily Cooper, attorney-at-law, comes along with us?"

"You never know when you might need someone to talk you out of jail."

"No more jails for me," said Alvin. "Next time somebody locks me up, I'll be out before they turn around."

"Don't you think it's ironic that you have no idea what you're supposed to do," said Verily, "and yet so many people have gone to so much trouble to prevent you from doing it?"

"Maybe they just don't like my face."

"I can appreciate the sentiment," said Verily, "but I think it's more likely that they fear your power. Once you made that plow, once you set Arthur Stuart free, it became known that such a man as you existed. And evil people naturally assume that you will use that power exactly as they would use it."

"And how is that?"

"The greedy among them think of gold. What vault could keep you out? Since the only thing that keeps them from stealing is that they can't get into the vaults, they can't believe you won't use the power that way. By the same reasoning, the more ambitious of your enemies will imagine you have designs on public power and prestige, and they will try to discredit you in advance by tarring you with whatever charge they think might be believed. The mere fact that you've been tried taints you, even though you were acquitted."

"So you're saying they don't have any more idea what I'm spose to do than I have."

"I'm saying that your chances of never getting locked up again are remote."

"And so that's why you're coming along."

"You can't build your Crystal City from inside a jail, Alvin."

"Verily Cooper, if you think I'm going to believe that's why you're coming with me, think again, my friend."

"Oh?"

"You're coming along because this is the most exciting thing going on and you don't want to miss any of it."

"Exciting? Sitting here all day in the heat while you watch a French-man paint?"

"That's what made you mad," said Alvin. "You wanted to be there yourself to see Arthur talk them birds into posing."

Verily grinned. "Must have been a sight to see."

"For the first couple of minutes, maybe." Alvin yawned.

"Oh, that's right, your life is so boring," said Verily.

"No, I was just thinking that you would have gotten a lot bigger kick out of the way we broke into the taxidermist's shop and set free a bird that wasn't quite dead."

Verily paced around the room, orating. "That's it! Right there! This is intolerable! This is what makes me so angry! Leaving me out of everything fun! This is why you are the most irritating friend a man could have!"

"But Verily, I didn't know when I left the house that anything like that was going to happen."

"That's exactly my point," said Verily. "You don't know what's going to happen, and given what's happened to you your whole life, it is unreasonable—indeed it is unconscionable—for you to presume that any task you set out on will proceed without dangerous and fascinating consequences!"

"So what's your solution?"

Verily knelt before him and rested his hands on Alvin's knees. Nose to nose he said, "Always take me with you, dammit!"

"Even when I have to whip it out and pee into a bush?"

"If I allow any exceptions, then sure as you're born, there'll be a talking badger in the bush who'll clamp his jaws on your pisser and won't let go till you give him the secret of the universe."

"Well, hell, Verily, if that ever happens I'll just have to pee sitting down for the rest of my life, cause I don't know the secret of the universe."

"And *that's* why you've got to keep me with you."

"Why, do *you* know the secret?"

"No, but I can strangle the badger till he lets you go."

"Badgers got powerful claws, Verily. Your legs'd be in shreds in ten seconds. You are such a greenhorn."

"There is no badger, Alvin! This was a hypothetical situation, deliberately exaggerated for rhetorical effect."

"You're spitting right in my face, Very."

"I am with you through it all, Alvin. That's what I'm saying."

"I know, Verily Cooper. I'm counting on you."

✄ 4 ✄

Stirred-Up

IN THE CHEAP boardinghouse where Calvin and Honoré were staying, the kitchen was in the back garden. This was fine with them. Arriving home from a night of carousing, they wanted something to eat but didn't want to call the landlady's attention to their late arrival. This was Camelot, after all, in which men were expected to drink, but only with absolute decorum, and never in a way that would discommode polite ladies.

Most of the food was in the locked pantry inside the house, on the ground floor where the slaves lived. No need to wake them up. The kitchen shed had a little food in it. There was a pot of cheap cooking molasses, some rancid butter, and leftover chickpeas stuck to the pot they had been cooked in. Honoré de Balzac looked at the mess with distaste. But Calvin just grinned at him.

"You're too finicky, Monsieur Haute Société," said Calvin. "This is all we need for a good batch of stirred-up."

"A word that I thank God I am not familiar with."

"It's called stirred-up because you stir it up." In moments Calvin had the stove hot and rancid butter melting in the frying pan. He ladled in some molasses and scraped chickpeas out of the pot, adding them to the mess. Then he stirred.

"See?" he said. "I'm stirring."

"You are stirring side-to-side," said Honoré. "And the mixture is going steadily down in quality. The one thing you are *not* doing is stirring *up*."

"Ain't English funny?" said Calvin.

"The longer I know you, the less sure I am that what you speak is English."

"Well, hell, that's the glory of English. You can speak it ten thousand different ways, and it's still OK."

"That barbarous expression! 'O. K.' What does this mean?"

"Oll Korrect," said Calvin. "Making fun of people who care too much about how words get writ down."

"Now, writing *down*, that makes sense. The ink flows down. The pen points down. Your hideous mixture should be called 'stirred-down.' "

The butter-and-molasses mess was bubbling now. "Nice and hot," said Calvin. "Want some?"

"Only to ward off imminent death."

"This cures not just hunger but the French disease and cholera too, not to mention making mad dogs whimper and run away."

"In France we call it the English disease."

"That bunch of Puritans? How could they catch a disease of coition?"

"They may be pure in doctrine, but they hump like bunnies," said Honoré. "Nine children to a family, or it's a sign God hates them."

"I'm a-feared I done taught you to talk substandard English, my friend." Calvin tasted the stirred-up. It was good. The chickpeas were a little hard, and Calvin suspected that in the darkness he had inadvertently added some fresh insect flesh to the mix, but he'd had enough to drink that he cared less than he might have sober. "Polite people don't say 'hump.' "

"I thought that *was* a euphemism."

"But it's a coarse one. We're supposed to get into fine homes here, but we'll never do it if you talk like that." Calvin proffered the spoon.

Honoré winced at the smell, then tasted it. It burned his tongue. Panting, he fanned his open mouth.

"Careful," said Calvin. "It's hot."

"Thank God the Inquisition didn't know about *you*," said Honoré.

"Tastes good, though, don't it?"

Honoré crunched up some chickpeas in his mouth. Sweet and buttery. "In a crude, primitive, savage way, yes."

"Crude, primitive, and savage are the best features of America," said Calvin.

"Sadly so," said Honoré. "Unlike Rousseau, I do not find savages to be noble."

"But they hump like bunnies!" said Calvin. In his drunken state, this was indescribably funny. He laughed until he wheezed. Then he puked into the pan of stirred-up.

"Is this part of the recipe?" asked Honoré. "The pièce de résistance?"

"It wasn't the stirred-up made me splash," said Calvin. "It was that vinegar you made us drink."

"I promise you it was the best wine in the house."

"That's cause fellows don't go there for wine. Corn likker is more what they specialize in."

"I would rather regurgitate than let the corn alcohol make me blind," said Honoré. "Those seem to have been the two choices."

"It was the only saloon open on the waterfront."

"The only one that hadn't already thrown us out, you mean."

"Are you getting fussy now? I thought you liked adventure."

"I do. But I believe I have now gathered all the material I need about the lowest dregs of American society."

"Then go home, you frog-eating stump-licker."

"Stump-licker?" asked Honoré.

"What about it?"

"You are very, very drunk."

"At least my coat isn't on fire."

Honoré slowly looked down at his coattail, which was indeed smoldering at the edge of the stove fire. He carefully lifted the fabric for closer inspection. "I don't think this can be laundered out."

"Wait till I'm awake," said Calvin. "I can fix it." He giggled. "I'm a Maker."

"If I throw up, will I feel as good as you?"

"I feel like hammered horse pucky," said Calvin.

"That is exactly the improvement I want." Honoré retched, but he missed the pan. His vomit sizzled on the stovetop.

"Behold the man of education and refinement," said Honoré.

"That's kind of an unattractive smell," said Calvin.

"I need to go to bed," said Honoré. "I don't feel well."

They made it to the bushes along the garden wall before they realized that they weren't heading for the house. Giggling, they collapsed under the greenery and in moments they were both asleep.

The sun was shining brightly and Calvin was a mass of sweat when he finally came to. He could feel bugs crawling on him and his first impulse was to leap to his feet and brush them off. But his body did not respond at all. He just lay there. He couldn't even open his eyes.

A faint breeze stirred the air. The bugs moved again on his face. Oh. Not bugs at all. Leaves. He was lying in shrubbery.

"Sometimes I just wish we could build a wall around the Crown Colonies and keep all those meddlesome foreigners out."

A woman's voice. Footsteps on the brick sidewalk.

"Did you hear that the Queen is going to grant an audience to that busybody bluestocking abolitionist schoolteacher?"

"No, that's too much to believe."

"I agree but with Lady Ashworth as her sponsor—"

"Lady Ashworth!"

The ladies stopped their ambulation only a few steps away from where Calvin lay.

"To think that Lady Ashworth won't even invite you to her soirees—"

"I beg your pardon, but I have declined her invitations."

"And yet she'll present this Peggy person—"

"I thought her name was Margaret—"

"But her people call her Peggy, as if she were a horse."

"And where is her husband? *If* she has one."

"Oh, she has one. Tried and acquitted of slave-stealing, but we all know a slaveholder can't get justice in those abolitionist courts."

"How do you find *out* these things?"

"Do you think the King's agents don't investigate foreigners who come here to stir up trouble?"

"Instead of investigating, why don't they just keep them out?"

"Oh!"

The exclamation of surprise told Calvin that he had just been spotted. Even though some control was returning, he decided that keeping his eyes closed and lying very still was the better part of valor. Besides, with his face covered by leaves, he would not be recognizable later; if he moved, they might see his face.

"My laws, this boardinghouse should be closed down. It brings entirely the wrong element into a respectable part of town."

"Look. He has fouled his trousers."

"This is intolerable. I'm going to have to complain to the magistrate."

"How can you?"

"How can I not?"

"But your testimony before the court—how could you possibly describe this wretched man's condition, while remaining a lady?"

"Dear me."

"No, we simply did not see him."

"Oh!"

The second exclamation told Calvin that they had found Honoré de Balzac. It was comforting to know he was not alone in his humiliation.

"Worse and worse."

"Clearly he is no gentleman. But to be out-of-doors without trousers at all!"

"Can you . . . can you see his . . ."

Calvin felt that this had gone far enough. Without opening his eyes, he spoke in a thick Spanish accent, imitating the slavers he had heard on the docks. "Señoritas, this tiny White man is nothing compared to the naked Black men in my warehouse on the Spanish dock!"

Shrieking softly, the ladies bustled away. Calvin lay there shaking with silent laughter.

Honoré's voice emerged from the bushes not far away. "Shame on you. A writer of novels has a brilliant chance to hear the way women really talk to each other, and *you* scare them away."

Calvin didn't care. Honoré could pretend to be a writer, but Calvin didn't believe he would ever write anything. "How did you lose your pants?"

"I took them off when I got up to void my bladder, and then I couldn't find them."

"Were we drunk last night?"

"I hope so," said Honoré. "It is the only honorable way I can think of for us to end up sleeping together under a hedge."

By now they had both rolled out from under the bushes. Squinting, Honoré was staggering here and there, searching for his trousers. He paused to look Calvin up and down. "I may be a little bit nude, but at least I did not wet my trousers."

Calvin found them, hanging on the hedge, wet and stained. Calvin pointed and laughed. "You took them off and *then* you peed on them!"

Honoré looked at his trousers mournfully. "It was dark."

Holding his dirty laundry in front of him, Honoré followed Calvin toward the house. As they passed the kitchen shed, they caught a glare from the tiny old Black woman who supervised the cooking. But that was as much of a rebuke as they would ever hear from a slave. They went in through the ground floor, where Honoré handed his wet trousers to the laundress. "I'll need these tonight before dinner," he said.

Keeping her head averted, the slave woman murmured her assent and started to move away.

"Wait!" cried Honoré. "Calvin's got some just as bad off as mine."

"She can come up and get them later," said Calvin.

"Take them off now," said Honoré. "She will not look at your hairy white legs."

Calvin turned his back, stripped off his pants, and handed them to her. She scurried away.

"You are so silly to be shy," said Honoré. "It does not matter what servants see. It is like being naked in front of trees or cats."

"I just don't like going up to our room without trousers."

"In trousers wet with urine, you will be disgusting. But if we are both naked, everyone will pretend not to have seen us. We are invisible."

"Does that mean you plan to use the front stairs?"

"Of course not," said Honoré. "And I must lead the way, for if I have to climb three flights of stairs looking at your buttocks I will lose the ability to write of beauty for at least a month."

"Why do you think the cook glared at us?" asked Calvin.

"I have no idea, my friend," said Honoré. "But does she need a reason? Of course all the Black people in this place hate all the White people."

"But usually they don't show it," said Calvin.

"Usually the White men wear trousers," said Honoré. "I am quite certain that the slaves all knew we were asleep under the hedge long before we woke up. But they did not cover us or waken us—that is how they show their hatred. By not doing things that no one commanded them to do."

Calvin chuckled.

"Tell me what's funny?" Honoré demanded.

"I was just thinking—maybe it wasn't you what peed on your trousers."

Honoré pondered this for a few moments. "For that matter, my friend, maybe it wasn't you who peed on *yours*."

Calvin groaned. "You are an evil man, Honoré, with an evil imagination."

"It is my knack."

Not till they got to their room and were changing clothes had Calvin's head cleared enough for him to realize the significance of what the ladies were talking about by the hedge. "A schoolteacher abolitionist named Peggy? That's got to be Miz Larner, the schoolteacher Alvin married."

"Oh, my poor Calvin. You went three days without mentioning your brother, and now you have relapsed."

"I been thinking about him ever since we got that letter from Mother telling about the wedding and how the curse was lifted and all. I wonder if he plans on having seven sons." Calvin cackled with laughter.

"If he has such a plan we must find him and stop him," said Honoré. "Two Makers is more than the world needs already. We have no need for three."

"What I'm thinking is we ought to look up this bluestocking abolitionist Peggy and make her acquaintance."

"Calvin, what kind of trouble are you planning to make?"

"No trouble at all," said Calvin, annoyed. "Why do you think I want to cause trouble?"

"Because you are awake."

"She's going to have an audience with the Queen. Maybe we can slip in with her. Meet some royalty."

"Why will she help you? If she is married to Alvin, she must know your reputation."

"What reputation?" Calvin didn't like the direction Honoré's comments were tending. "What do you know about my reputation? I don't even have a reputation."

"I have been with you continuously for months, my friend. It is impossible you do not have a reputation with your family and your neighbors. This is the reputation that your brother's wife would know."

"My reputation is that I was a cute little kid when anybody bothered to notice that I existed."

"Oh no, Calvin. I am quite sure your reputation is that you are envious, spiteful, prone to outbursts of rage, and incapable of admitting an error. Your family and neighbors could not have missed these traits."

After all these months, to discover that Honoré had such an opinion of him was unbearable. Calvin felt fury rise up inside him, and he would have lashed out at Honoré had the little Frenchman not looked so utterly cheerful and open-faced. Was it possible he had not meant to offend?

"You see what I mean?" said Honoré. "You are angry even now, and you resent me. But why? I mean no harm by these observations. I am a novelist. I study life. You are alive, so I study you. I find you endlessly fascinating. A man with both the ambition and the ability to be great, who is so little in control of his impulses that he pisses away his greatness. You are a tiger studying to be a mouse. This is how the world is kept safe from you. This is why you will never be a Napoleon."

Calvin roared in fury, but could not bring himself to strike Honoré himself, who was, after all, the only friend he had ever had. So he smashed the flat of his hand against the wall.

"But look," said Honoré. "It is the wall you hit, and not my face. So I was not entirely right. You do have some self-control. You are able to respect another man's opinion."

"I am not a mouse," said Calvin.

"No no, you did not understand. I said you are studying to be a mouse, not that you have passed your examinations and are now living on cheese. When I hear you go, squeak squeak squeak, I think, What an odd noise to come from a tiger. I have known few tigers in my life. Many mice, but few tigers. So you are precious to me, my friend. I am sad to hear this squeaking. And your sister-in-law, I think all she knows of you is the squeak, that is what I was saying before. That is why I doubt that she will be glad to see you."

"I can roar if I need to," said Calvin.

"Look at how angry you are. What would you do, hit me? That, my dear friend, would be a squeak." Honoré looked at his own naked body. "I am filthy like a wallowing pig. I will order up a bath. You may use the water when I'm done."

Calvin did not answer. Instead he sent his doodlebug over the surface of his own body, ejecting all the dirt and grime, the dried-on urine and sweat, the dust and ashes in his hair. It took only moments, for once he had shown his doodlebug what to do, it could finish on its own without his directing it, just as his hand could keep sawing without him thinking of the saw, or his fingers tie a knot without him even looking at the string.

Honoré's eyes grew wide. "Why have you made your underwear disappear?"

Only then did Calvin realize that every foreign object had been pulverized and ejected from his body. "Who cares? I'm cleaner right now than you'll ever be."

"While you are using your powers to beautify yourself, why not change your odor? To a flower, perhaps. Not a nasturtium—those already smell like unwashed feet. What about a lilac? Or a rose?"

"Why don't I change your nose to a cauliflower? Oops, too late, someone already did."

"Aha, you are insulting me with cabbages." Honoré pulled the string that would ring a bell in the servants' quarters.

Calvin pulled on some clean clothes—cleanish, anyway—and was just leaving the room when a slave arrived in response to Honoré's summons. Honoré was buck naked now, without even shirttails to conceal nature's modest endowment, but he seemed utterly unaware; and, for that matter, the slave might not have seen him, for her gaze never seemed to leave the floor. Honoré was still specifying exactly how many kettles of hot water he wanted in his tub when Calvin started down the stairs and could hear the Frenchman's voice no more.

Lady Ashworth's door was opened by a wiry old slave in close-fitting livery. "Howdy," said Calvin. "I heard tell that my sister-in-law Peggy Smith was visiting here and—"

The slave walked away and left him standing at the door. But the door was still open, so Calvin stepped inside onto the porch. By habit he sent his doodlebug through the house. He could see from the heart-fires where everybody was; unlike Peggy, though, he couldn't see a thing *in* the heartfires, and couldn't recognize anyone in particular. All he knew was a living soul was there, and by the brightness of it, whether it was human or not.

He could guess, though. The heartfire moving slowly up the back stairs must be the slave who had opened the door for him. The heartfire on the porch above Calvin, toward which the slave was moving, had to be Lady Ashworth. Or Lord Ashworth, perhaps—but no, *he* was likely to be as close as possible to the King.

He set his doodlebug into the floor of the upstairs porch, feeling the vibration caused by their talking. With a little concentration, it turned into sound. The slave sure didn't say much. "Gentleman at the door."

"I'm expecting no callers."

"Say he sister be Peggy Smith."

"I don't know anyone by such a . . . oh, perhaps Margaret Larner—but she isn't here. Tell him she isn't here."

The slave immediately walked away from Lady Ashworth. Stupid woman, thought Calvin. I never thought she'd be here, I need to know where she *is*. Don't they teach common civility to folks in Camelot? Or maybe she's so high up in the King's court that she didn't need to show decent manners to common folk.

Well, thought Calvin, let's see what your manners turn into when *I'm* through with you.

He could see the slave's slow-moving heartfire on the back stairs. Calvin walked into the house and found the front stairs, then bounded lightly up to the next floor. The family entertained on this level and the large ballroom had three large French doors opening onto the gallery, where Lady Ashworth was studying a plant, pruning shears in hand.

"That plant needs no pruning," said Calvin, putting on the sophisticated English voice he had learned in London.

Lady Ashworth turned toward him in shock. "I beg your pardon. You were not admitted here."

"The doors were open. I heard you tell your servant to send me away. But I could not bear to leave without having seen a lady of such legendary grace and beauty."

"Your compliments disgust me," she said, her cavalier drawl lengthening with the fervor of her opinion. "I have no patience with dandies, and as for trespassers, I generally have them killed."

"There's no need to have me killed. Your contemptuous gaze has already stopped my heart from beating."

"Oh, I see, you're not flattering me, you're mocking me. Don't you know this house is full of servants? I'll have you thrown out."

"Blacks lay hands on a White man?"

"We always use our servants to take out the trash."

The banter was not engaging even a tiny fraction of Calvin's attention. Instead he was using his doodlebug to explore Lady Ashworth's body. In his peregrinations with Honoré de Balzac, Calvin had watched the Frenchman seduce several dozen women of every social class, and because Calvin was a scientist at heart, he had used his doodlebug to note the changes in a woman's body as her lust was aroused. There were tiny organs where certain juices were made and released into the blood. It was hard to find them, but once found, they could easily be stimulated. In moments, Calvin had three different glands secreting rather strong doses of the juices of desire, and now it was his eyes, not just his doodlebug, that could see the transformation in Lady Ashworth. Her eyes grew heavy-lidded, her manner more aloof, her voice huskier.

"Compared to your grace and beauty I am trash and nothing more," Calvin said. "But I am *your* trash, my lady, to do with as you will. Discard me and I will cease to exist. Save me and I will become whatever you want me to be. A jewel to wear upon your bosom. A fan behind which your beauty may continue unobserved. Or perhaps the glove in which your hand may stay clean and warm."

"Who would ever have guessed that such talk could come from a frontier boy from Wobbish," she said, suppressing a smile.

"What matters isn't where a man is from, but where he's going. I think that all my life was leading to this moment. To this hot day in Camelot, this porch, this jungle of living plants, this magnificent Eve who is tending the garden."

She looked down at her pruning shears. "But you said I shouldn't cut this plant."

"It would be heartless," said Calvin. "It reaches up, not to the sun, but to you. Do not despise what grows for love of you, my lady."

She blushed and breathed more rapidly. "The things you say."

"I came in search of my brother's wife, because I heard she had visited here," said Calvin. "I could have left a card with your servant to accomplish that."

"I suppose you could."

"But even on the harsh cobbles of the street, I could hear you like music, smell you like roses, see you like the light of the one star breaking through on a cloudy night. I knew that in all the world this is the place I had to be, even if it cost me my life or my honor. My lady, until this moment every day of life was a burden, without purpose or joy. Now all I long for is to stay here, looking at you, wondering at the marvels of perfection concealed by the draperies of your clothing, tied up by the pins in your hair."

She was trembling. "You shouldn't talk about such . . ."

He stood before her now, inches from her. As he had seen with Honoré's seductions, his closeness would heighten the feelings within her. He reached up and brushed his fingers gently across her cheek, then her neck, her shoulder, touching only bare skin. She gasped but did not speak, did not take her eyes from his.

"My eyes imagine," he murmured, "my lips imagine, every part of my body imagines being close to you, holding you, becoming part of you."

She staggered, barely able to walk as she led him from the porch to her bedroom.

Besides studying the women's bodies, Calvin had also studied Honoré's, had seen how the Frenchman tried to maintain himself on the brink of ecstacy for as long as possible without crossing over. What

Honoré had to do with self-discipline, Calvin could do mechanically, with his doodlebug. Lady Ashworth was possessed by pleasure many times and in many ways before Calvin finally allowed himself to find release. They lay together on sheets clammy with their sweat. "If this is how the devil rewards wickedness," murmured Lady Ashworth, "I understand why God seems to be losing ground in this world." But there was sadness in her voice, for now her conscience was reawakening, ready to punish her for the pleasure she had taken.

"There was no wickedness here today," said Calvin. "Was not your body made by God? Did not these desires come from that body? What are you but the woman God made you to be? What am I but the man God brought here to worship you?"

"I don't even know your name," she said.

"Calvin."

"Calvin? That's all?"

"Calvin Maker."

"A good name, my love," she said. "For you have made me. Until this hour I did not truly exist."

Calvin wanted to laugh in her face. This is all that romance and love amounted to. Juices flowing from the glands. Bodies coupling in heat. A lot of pretty talk surrounding it.

He cleaned his body again. Hers also. But not the seed he left inside her. On impulse he followed it, wondering what it might accomplish. The idea rather appealed to him—a child of his, raised in a noble house. If he wanted to have seven sons, did it matter whether they all had the same mother? Let this be the first.

Was it possible to decide whether it would be a boy or a girl? He didn't know. Maybe Alvin could comprehend things as small as this, but it was all Calvin could do just to follow what was happening inside Lady Ashworth's body. And then even that slipped away from him. He just didn't know what he was looking for. At least she wasn't already pregnant.

"That was my first time, you know," he said.

"How could it be?" she said. "You knew everything. You knew how to—my husband knows nothing compared to you."

"My first time," he said. "I never had another woman until now. Your body taught me all I needed to know."

He caused the sweat on the sheets to dry, despite the dampness of the air. He rose from the cool dry bed, clean and fresh as he was when he arrived. He looked at her. Not young, really; sagging just a bit; but not too bad, considering. Honoré would probably approve. If he decided to tell him.

Oh, he would tell him. Without doubt, for Honoré would love the story of it, would love hearing how much Calvin had learned from his constant dalliances.

"Where is my sister-in-law?" Calvin asked matter-of-factly.

"Don't go," said Lady Ashworth.

"It wouldn't do for me to stay," said Calvin. "The gossipy ladies of Camelot would never understand the perfect beauty of this hour."

"But you'll come back."

"As often as prudence allows," he said. "For I will not permit my visits here to do you any harm."

"What have I done," she murmured. "I am not a woman who commits adultery."

On the contrary, Calvin thought. You're just a woman who was never tempted until now. That's all that virtue amounts to, isn't it? Virtue is what you treasure until you feel desire, and then it becomes an intolerable burden to be cast away, and only to be picked up again when the desire fades.

"You are a woman who married before she met the love of her life," said Calvin. "You serve your husband well. He has no reason to complain of you. But he will never love you as I love you."

A tear slipped out of her eye and ran across her temple onto her hair-strewn pillow. "He rides me impatiently, like a carriage, getting out almost before he reaches his destination."

"Then he has his use of you, and you of him," said Calvin. "The contract of marriage is well-fulfilled."

"But what about God?"

"God is infinitely compassionate," said Calvin. "He understands us more perfectly than humans ever can. And he forgives."

He bent over her and kissed her one more time. She told him where Peggy was staying. He left the house whistling. What fun! No wonder Honoré spent so much time in pursuit of women.

⚔ 5 ⚔

Purity

PURITY DID HER best to live up to her name. She had been a good little girl, and only got better through her teens, for she believed what the ministers taught and besides, wickedness never had much attraction for her.

But living up to her name had come to mean more to her than mere obedience to the word of God in the Bible. For she realized that her name was her only link back to her true identity—to the parents who had died when she was only a baby, and whose only contribution to her upbringing was the name they gave her.

The name contained clues. Here in Massachusetts, the people mostly hailed from the East Anglian and Essex Puritan traditions, which did not name children for virtues. That was a custom more common in Sussex, which suggested that Purity's family had lived in Netticut, not in Massachusetts.

And as Purity grew older in the orphan house in Cambridge, Reverend Hezekiah Study, now well into his seventies, took notice of her bright mind and insisted, against tradition, that she be given a full education of the type given to boys. Of course it was out of the question for her to enroll at Harvard College, for that school was devoted to training ministers. But she was allowed to sit on a stool in the corridor outside any classroom she wanted, and overhear whatever portion of the lesson was given loudly enough. And they let her have access to the library.

She soon learned that the library was the better teacher, for the authors of the books were helpless to shut her out because of her sex. Having put their best knowledge into print, they had to endure the ignominy of having a woman read it and understand it. The living professors, on the contrary, took notice of when Purity was listening, and most of them used that occasion to speak very quietly, to close the door, or to speak in Latin or Greek, which the students presumably spoke and Purity was presumed not to understand at all. On the contrary, she read Latin and Greek with great fluency and pronounced it better than all but a few of the male students—how else would she have come to the notice of a traditionalist like Reverend Study?—but she began to learn that the professors were rarely as coherent, deep, or penetrating in their thought as the authors of the books.

There were exceptions. Young Waldo Emerson, who had only just graduated from Harvard himself, would have brought her right into his classroom if she had not refused. As it was, she heard every word of his teaching quite clearly, and while he was prone to epigrams as a substitute for analysis, his enthusiasm for the life of the mind was contagious and exhilarating. She knew that Emerson cared much more about being thought to be erudite than actually thinking deeply—his "philosophy" seemed to consist of anything that would be particularly annoying to the powers that be without being so shocking that they would fire him. He got the reputation among the students as an original and a rebel without having to pay the penalty for actually being either.

It was not from Emerson, therefore, but from the library that Purity made the next leap toward understanding the meaning of her name and what it told her about her parents' lives. For it was in a treatise, "On the Care of Offspring of Witches and Heretics," by Cotton Mather that she first came to understand why she was an orphan bearing a Netticut name in a Massachusetts house.

"All children being born equally tainted with original sin from Adam," he wrote, "and the children of fallen parents being therefore not more tainted than the children of the elect, it is unjust to exact from them penalties other than those that naturally accrue to childhood, viz. subjection to authority, ignorance, inclination to disobedience, frequent punishment for inattention, etc.'' Purity read this passage with delight, for after all the constant implication that the children of the orphanage clearly were not as likely to be elect as children growing up with parents who were members of the churches, it was a relief to hear no less an authority than the great Cotton Mather declare that it was unjust to treat one child differently from any other.

So she was quite excited when she read the next sentence, and almost failed to notice its significance. ''To give the children the best chance to avoid the posthumous influence of their parents and the suspicion of their neighbors, however, their removal from the parish, even the colony, of their birth would be the wisest course.''

And the clincher, several sentences later: ''Their family name should be taken from them, for it is a disgrace, but let not their baptismal name be changed, for that name cometh unto them from and in the name of Christ, however unworthy might have been the parents who proffered them up for christening.''

I am named Purity, she thought. A Netticut name, but I am in Massachusetts. My parents are dead.

Hanged as witches or burned as heretics. And more likely, witches, for the most common heresy is Quakerism and then I would not be named Purity, while a witch would try to conceal what he was and would therefore name his children as his neighbors named theirs.

This knowledge brought her both alarm and relief. Alarm because she had to be on constant guard lest she also be accused of witchery. Alarm because now she had to wonder if her ability to sense easily what other people were feeling was what the witchy folk called a ''knack.''

Relief because the mystery of her parents had at last been solved. Her mother had not been a fornicator or adulteress who delivered up the baby to an orphanage with the name pinned to a blanket. Her father had not been carried off as a punishment of God through a plague or accident. Her parents had instead been hanged for witchery, and given what she knew of witch trials, in all likelihood they were innocent.

As Waldo Emerson said in class one day, ''When does a God-given talent cross an imperceptible boundary and become a devilish knack? And how does the devil go about bestowing gifts and hidden powers that, when they were granted unto prophets and apostles in the holy scriptures, were clearly gifts of the Spirit of God? Is it not possible that in condemning the talent instead of the misuse of that talent, we are rejecting the gifts of God and slaying some of his best beloved? Should we not then judge the moral character of the act rather than its extraordinariness?''

Purity sat in the hallway when he said this, grateful that she was not inside the classroom where the young men would see her trembling, would see the tears streaming down her cheeks, and would think her a weak womanly creature. My parents were innocent, she said to herself, and my talent is from God, to be used in his holy service. Only if I were to turn it to the service of Satan would I be a witch. I might be one of the elect after all.

She fled the college before the lecture was over, lest she be forced to converse with someone, and wandered in the woods along the river Euphrates. Boats plied the river from Boston as far inland as their draft would allow, but the boatmen took no heed of her, since she was a land creature and beneath their notice.

If my talent is from God, she thought, then if I stay here and hide it, am I not rejecting that talent? Am I not burying it in the garden, like the foolish servant in the parable? Should I not find the greater purpose for which the talent was given?

She imagined herself a missionary in some heathen land like Africa or France, able to understand the natives long before she learned their language. She imagined herself a diplomat for the Protectorate, using her talent to discern when foreign ambassadors or heads of state were lying and when they were sincere.

And then, in place of imagination, she saw a boy of twelve or so, dark of skin with tight-curled hair, shoot up out of the river not three rods off, water falling off him, shining in the sunlight, his mouth open and laughing, and in midair he sees her, and she can see his face change and in that instance she knows what he feels: embarrassment to be seen buck naked by a woman, the fading remnants of his boisterous fun, and, just dawning under the surface where his own mind couldn't know it yet, love.

Well I never had *that* effect before, thought Purity. It was flattering. Not that the love of a twelve-year-old boy was ever going to affect her life, but it was sweet to know that at the cusp of manhood this lad could catch a glimpse of her and see, not the orphan bluestocking that so disgusted or terrified the young men of Cambridge, but a woman. Indeed, what he must have seen and loved was not a woman, but Woman, for Purity had read enough Plato to know that while wicked men lusted after particular women, a man of lofty aspirations loved the glimpse of Woman that he saw in good women, and by loving the ideal in her helped bring her to closer consonance, like lifting the flat shadow off the road and rejoining it to the whole being who cast it.

What in the world am I thinking about. This child is no doubt every bit as peculiar as I am, him being Black in a land of Whites, as I am an orphan in a land of families and am thought to be the child of witches to boot.

All these thoughts passed through her mind like a long crackle of lightning, and the boy splashed back down into the water, and then near him another person rose, a grown man, heavily muscled in the shoulders and back and arms, and considerably taller than the boy, so that although he didn't jump, when he stood his bare white buttocks showed almost completely above the water, and when he saw where the Black boy was looking, his mouth agape with love, he turned and . . .

Purity looked away in time. There was no reason to allow the possibility of impure thoughts into her mind. She might or might not be one of the elect, but there was no need to drag herself closer to the pit, thus requiring a greater atonement by Christ to draw her out.

"So much for a spot where nobody comes!" the man cried out, laughing. She heard a great splashing, which had to be the two of them coming out of the water. "Just a minute and we'll be dressed so you can go on with your walk, ma'am."

"Never mind," she said. "I can go another way."

But at the moment she took her first step to return along the riverbank, a coarse-looking man with heavy muscles and a menacing cast to his face stepped in front of her. She couldn't help gasping and stepping back—

Only to find that she was stepping on a man's boot.

"Ouch," he said mildly.

She whirled around. There were two men, actually, one of them a dapper but smallish man who looked at her with a candor that she found disturbing. But the man she had stepped on was a tall, dignified-looking man who dressed like a professional man. Not in the jet-black costume of a minister, but not in the earthy "sad" colors of the common folk of New England. No, he dressed like nothing so much as . . .

"An Englishman," she said. "A barrister."

"I confess it, but marvel that you guessed it."

"English visitors come to Cambridge often, sir," she said. "Some are barristers. They seem to have a way of dressing to show that their clothing cost considerable money without ever quite violating the sumptuary laws." She turned around to face the menacing man, unsure whether this Englishman was a match for him.

But then she realized that she had been momentarily deceived by appearances. There was no menace in the rough fellow, no more than in the Englishman. And the other one, the dapper little fellow who was still inspecting her with his eyes, posed no danger, either. It was as if he knew only one way to think of women, and therefore shelved his attitude toward Purity under the heading "objects of lust," but it was a volume that would gather dust before he cared enough to take it down and try to read it.

"We must have frightened you," said the Englishman. "Our friends were determined to bathe, and we were determined to lie on the riverbank and nap, and so you didn't see any of us until you were right among us, and I apologize that you saw two of our company in such a state of deshabille."

"And what, pray, is a state of Jezebel?"

The dapper little fellow laughed aloud, then stopped abruptly and turned away. Why? He was afraid. Of what?

"Pardon my French," said the Englishman. "In London we are not so pure as the gentlefolk of New England. When Napoleon took over France and proceeded to annex the bulk of Europe, there were few places for the displaced aristocracy and royalty to go. London is crawling with French visitors, and suddenly French words are chic. Oops, there I go again."

"You still have not told me what the French word meant. 'Cheek,' however, I understand—it is a characteristic that your whole company here seems to have."

The barrister chuckled. "I would say that it's yourself that takes a cheeky tone with strangers, if it were not such an improper thing to say to a young lady to whom I have not been introduced. I pray you, tell me the name of your father and where he lives so I can inquire after your health."

"My father is dead," she said, and then added, despite her own sense of panic as she did so, "He was hanged as a witch in Netticut."

They fell silent, all of them, and it made her uneasy, for they had nothing like the reaction she expected. Not revulsion at her confession of such indecent family connections; rather they all simply closed off and looked another way.

"Well, I'm sorry to remind you of such a tragic event," said the Englishman.

"Please don't be. I never knew him. I only just realized what his fate must have been. You don't imagine that anyone at the orphanage would tell me such a thing outright!"

"But you are a lady, aren't you?" asked the Englishman. "There's nothing of the schoolgirl about you."

"Being an orphan does not stop when you come of age," said Purity. "But I will serve myself as father and mother, and give you my consent to introduce yourself to me."

The Englishman bowed deeply. "My name is Verily Cooper," he said. "And my company at the moment consists of Mike Fink, who has been in the waterborne transportation business but is on a leave-of-absence, and my dear friend John-James Audubon, who is mute."

"No he's not," said Purity. For she saw in both Cooper and Audubon himself that the statement was a lie. "You really mustn't lie to strangers. It starts things off in such an unfortunate way."

"I assure you, madam," said Cooper, "that in New England, he is and shall remain completely mute."

And with that slight change, she could see in both of them that the statement was now true. "So you choose to be mute here in New England. Let me puzzle this out. You dare not open your mouth; therefore your very speech must put you in a bad light. No, in outright danger, for I think none of you cares much about public opinion. And what could endanger a man, just by speaking? The accent of a forbidden nation. A papist nation, I daresay. And the name being Audubon, and your manners toward a woman being tinged with unspeakable presumptions, I would guess that you are French."

Audubon turned red under his suntan and faced away from her. "I do not know how you know this, but you also must be seeing that I did not act improper to you."

"What she's telling us," said Verily Cooper, "is that she's got her a knack."

"Please keep such crudity for times when you are alone with the ill-mannered," said Purity. "I observe people keenly, that is all. And from his accent I am confident that my reasoning was correct."

The rough fellow, Mike Fink, spoke up. "When you hear a bunch of squealing and snorting, you can bet you're somewhere near a pig."

Purity turned toward him. "I have no idea what you meant by that."

"I'm just saying a knack's a knack."

"Enough," said Cooper. "Less than a week in New England and we've already forgotten all caution? Knacks are illegal here. Therefore decent people don't have them."

"Oh yeah," said Mike Fink. "Except she *does*."

"But then, perhaps she is not decent," said Audubon.

It was Purity's turn to blush. "You forget yourself, sir," she said.

"Never mind him," said Cooper. "He's just miffed because you made that remark about unspeakable presumptions."

"You're travelers," she said.

"John-James paints North American birds with an eye toward publishing a book of his pictures for the use of scientists in Europe."

"And for this he needs a troop along? What do you do, hold his brushes?"

"We're not all on the same errand," said Cooper.

At that moment the two she had seen in the river came out of the bushes, still damp-haired but fully clothed.

"Ma'am, I'm so sorry you had to see so much horseflesh without no horses," said the White one.

The Black one said not a thing, but never took his eyes from her.

"This is Alvin Smith," said Cooper. "He's a man of inestimable abilities, but only because nobody has cared enough to estimate them.

The short one is Arthur Stuart, no kin to the King, who travels with Alvin as his adopted nephew-in-law, or some such relationship."

"And you," said Purity, "have been long enough out of England to pick up some American brag."

"But surrounded by Americans as I am," said Cooper, "my brag is like a farthing in a sack of guineas."

She couldn't help but laugh at the way he spoke. "So you travel in New England with a Frenchman, who is only able to avoid being expelled or, worse, arrested as a spy, by pretending to be a mute. You are a barrister, this fellow is a boatman, as I assume, and the two bathers are . . ." Her voice trailed off.

"Are what?" asked Alvin Smith.

"Clean," she said. Then she smiled.

"What were you going to say?" asked Smith.

"Don't press her," said Cooper. "If someone decides to leave something unsaid, my experience is that everyone is happier if they don't insist on his saying it."

"That's OK," said Arthur Stuart. "I don't think she knows herself what was on her lips to say."

She laughed in embarrassment. "It's true," she said. "I think I was hoping that a jest would come to mind, and it didn't."

Alvin smiled at her. "Or else the jest that did come to mind was of a sort that you couldn't imagine yourself making, and so it went away."

She didn't like the way he looked at her as if he thought he knew all about her. Never mind that she must be looking at him the same way— she *did* know about him. He was so full of confidence it made her want to throw mud on him just to show him he wasn't carried along by angels. It was as if he feared nothing and imagined himself capable of achieving anything. And it wasn't an illusion he was trying to create, either. He really *was* conceited; his attitude reeked of it. His only fear was that, when push came to shove, he might turn out to be even better than he thought himself to be.

"I don't know what I done to rub you the wrong way, ma'am," said Smith, "other than bathing nekkid, but that's how my mama taught me it ought to be done, so my clothes don't shrink."

The others laughed. Purity didn't.

"Want something to eat?" Arthur Stuart asked her.

"I don't know, what do you have?" she said.

His eyes were still focused on her, slightly widened, his jaw just a bit slack. Oh, it was love all right, the swooning moon-in-juning kind.

"Berries," said the boy. He held out his hat, which had several dozen blackberries down in it. She reached in, took one, tasted it.

"Oh no," said Cooper mildly. "You've eaten a berry, so you must spend one month of every year in Hades."

"But these berries are from New England, not hell," she said.

"That's a relief," said Smith. "I wasn't sure where the border was."

Purity didn't know how to take this Smith fellow. She didn't like looking at him. His boldness bothered her. He didn't even seem ashamed that she had seen him naked.

Instead she looked at Cooper. The barrister was a pleasant sight indeed. His manner, his dress, his voice, all belonged to a man that Purity thought existed only in a dream. Why was he different from other men who dressed in such a way?

"You aren't an ordinary lawyer," she said to him.

Cooper looked at her in surprise. And then his surprise turned to dread.

"I'm not," he said.

What was he afraid of?

"Yes he is," said Smith.

"No," said Cooper. "Ordinary lawyers make a lot of money. I haven't made a shilling in the past year."

"Is that it?" asked Purity. It could be. Barristers did seem a prosperous lot. But no, it was something else. "I think what makes you different is you don't think you're better than these others."

Cooper looked around at his companions—the smith, the riverman, the French artist, the Black boy—and grinned. "You're mistaken," he said. "I'm definitely the better man."

The others laughed. "Better at what?" asked Mike Fink. "Whining like a mosquito whenever you see a bee?"

"I don't like bees," said Cooper.

"They like *you*," said Arthur Stuart.

"Because I'm sweet." He was joking, but Purity could see that his fear was growing greater. She glanced around, looking for the source of the danger.

Smith noticed the way she looked around and took it as a sign, or perhaps just a reminder. "Come on now," said Smith. "Time for us to move on."

"No," said Cooper. Purity could see his resolve harden. He wasn't just afraid—he was going to act on his fear.

"What's wrong?" asked Smith.

"The girl," said Cooper.

"What about her?" demanded Arthur Stuart. He spoke so truculently that Purity expected one of the men to rebuke him. But no, he was treated as if his voice had equal weight in the company.

"She's going to get us killed."

Now she understood. He was afraid of *her*. "I'm not," she said. "I won't tell anybody he's a papist."

"When they put your hand on the Bible and swear you to tell the truth?" asked Cooper. "You'd send yourself to hell and deny that you know that he's Catholic?"

"I am not a *good* Catholic," said Audubon modestly.

"Then you go to hell no matter who's right," said Smith. It was a joke, but nobody laughed.

Cooper still held Purity in gaze, and now it was her turn to be afraid. She had never seen such intensity in a man, except a preacher in his pulpit, during the most fiery part of the sermon. "Why are you afraid of me?" asked Purity.

"That's why," said Cooper.

"*What's* why?"

"You know that I'm afraid of you. You know too much about what we're thinking."

"I already told you, I don't know what anybody's thinking."

"What we're *feeling*, then." Cooper grinned mirthlessly. "It's your knack."

"We already said that," said Fink.

"What if it is?" Purity said defiantly. "Who's to say that knacks aren't gifts from God?"

"The courts of Massachusetts," said Cooper. "The gallows."

"So she's got a knack," said Smith. "Who doesn't?"

The others nodded.

Except Cooper. "Have you lost your minds? Look at you! Talking knowledgeably of knacks! Admitting that Jean-Jacques here is French and Catholic to boot."

"But she already knew," said Audubon.

"And that didn't bother you?" said Cooper. "That she knew what she could not possibly know?"

"We all know things we shouldn't know," said Smith.

"But until she came along, we were doing a pretty good job of keeping it to ourselves!" Cooper rounded on Purity, loomed over her. "In Puritan country, people hide their knacks or they die. It's a secret they all keep, that they have some special talent, and as soon as they realize what it is they also learn to hide it, to avoid letting anyone know what it is that they do so much better than other people. They call it 'humility.' But this girl has been flaunting her knack."

Only then did Purity realize what she had been doing. Cooper was right—she had never let anyone see how easily she understood their feelings. She had held it back, remaining humble.

"By this time tomorrow I expect this girl will be in jail, and in a month she'll be hanged. The trouble is, when they put her to the question of other witches she's consorted with, whom do you imagine that she'll name? A friend? A beloved teacher? She seems to be a decent person, so it won't be an enemy. No, it'll be strangers. A papist. A journeyman blacksmith. A barrister who seems to be living in the woods. An American riverman."

"I'd never accuse you," she said.

"Oh, well, since you say so," said Cooper.

Suddenly she was aware of Mike Fink standing directly behind her. She could hear his breathing. Long, slow breaths. He wasn't even worried. But she knew that he was capable of killing.

Smith sighed. "Well, Very, you're a quick thinker and you're right. We can't just go on with our journey as if it were safe."

"Yes, you can," she said. "I don't normally act like this. I *was* careless. In the surprise of meeting you here."

"No," said Cooper, "it wasn't meeting us. You were out here walking alone. Oblivious. Blind and deaf. You didn't hear Al and Arthur splashing like babies in the water. You didn't hear Mike howling miserable river ballads in his high-pitched hound-dog voice.''

"I wasn't singing," said Mike.

"I never said you were," said Cooper. "Miss—what's your name again?''

"She never said," Fink answered.

"Purity," she said. "My parents named me."

"Miss Purity, why after all these years of living in humility are you suddenly so careless about showing your knack?''

"I told you, I wasn't, or I'm not usually, and it's not a knack anyway, it's a talent, I'm simply observant, I—"

"Today," said Cooper. "This hour. Do you think I'm a fool? I grew up in one of the most witch-ridden parts of England. Not because more people had knacks but because more people were watching for them. You don't last an hour if you're careless. It's a good thing you ran into us and not someone you knew. This place is thick with ministers, and you were going to show your knack no matter whom you met."

Purity was confused. Was he right? Was that why she had fled the college, because she knew that her knack could no longer be hidden?

But why couldn't it be hidden now? What was driving her to reveal it?

"I believe you may be right," she said. "I thank you for waking me up to what I was doing. You have nothing to fear now. I'm going to be careful now."

"Good enough for me," said Smith.

"No, it isn't," said Cooper. "Al, I yield to you on most things, but not on something that's going to get us caught up in some witch trial."

Smith laughed. "I've done my time setting around waiting for lawyers. There ain't no jail can hold me or any of my friends."

"Yes, there is," said Cooper. "It's six feet long, and they nail it shut and bury it."

They all looked thoughtful. Except Arthur Stuart. "So what are you going to do to her?" he demanded. "She ain't done nothing wrong."

"She *hain't* done nothing," said Mike Fink.

Arthur looked at the river rat like he was crazy. "How can *you* correct me? You're even wronger than I was!"

"You left out the *h* in *haint*."

"I won't be accused myself, and I won't accuse you," said Purity.

"I think you will," said Cooper. "I think you want to die."

"Don't be absurd!" she cried.

"More specifically, I think you want to be hanged as a witch."

For a moment she remained poised, meaning to treat this idea with the scorn it deserved. Then the image of her parents on a gallows came to her mind. Or rather, she admitted that it was already in her mind, that it was an image that had dwelt with her ever since she made the connections and realized how they had died. She burst into tears.

"You got no right to make her cry!" shouted Arthur Stuart.

"Hush up, Arthur," said Smith. "Verily's right."

"How do you know this?" said Audubon.

"Look at her."

She was sobbing so hard now that she could hardly stand. She felt long, strong arms around her, and at first she tried to flinch away, thinking it was Mike Fink seizing her from behind; but her movement took her closer to the man who was reaching for her, and she found herself pressed against the fine suit of the barrister, his arms holding her tightly.

"It's all right," said Cooper.

"They hanged my mother and father," she said. Or tried to say—her voice could hardly be understood.

"And you just found out," said Cooper. "Who told you?"

She shook her head, unable to explain.

"Figured it out for yourself?" said Cooper.

She nodded.

"And you belong with them. Not with the people who killed them and put you out to an orphanage."

"They had no right!" she cried. "This is a land of murderers!"

"Hush," said Cooper. "That's how it feels, but you know it isn't true. Oh, there are murderers among them, but that's true everywhere. People who are glad to denounce a neighbor for witchcraft—to settle a quarrel, to get a piece of land, to show everyone how righteous and perceptive they are. But most folks are content to live humbly and let others do the same."

"You don't know!" she said. "Pious killers, all of them!"

"Pious," said Cooper, "but not killers. Think about it, just *think.* Every living soul has some kind of knack. But how many get hanged for witchcraft? Some years maybe five or six. Most years none at all. The people don't want to surround themselves with death. It's life that they want, like all good people everywhere.''

"Good people wouldn't take me away from my parents!'' Purity cried.

"They thought they were doing good,'' said Verily. "They thought they were saving you from hell.''

She tried to pull away from him. He wouldn't let her.

"Let me go.''

"Not yet,'' he said. "Besides, you have nowhere to go.''

"Let her go if she wants,'' said Arthur Stuart. "We can get away from here. Alvin can start up the greensong and we'll run like the wind and be out of New England before she tells anybody anything.''

"That ain't the problem,'' said Smith. "It's her. Very's worried about keeping her from getting herself killed.''

"He doesn't need to worry,'' Purity said. This time when she pulled away, Cooper let her. "I'll be fine. I just needed to tell somebody. Now I have.''

"No,'' said Cooper. "It's gone. You're not afraid of death anymore, you welcome it, because you think that's the only way you can get home to your family.''

"How do you know what I think?'' she said. "Is that your knack? I hope not, because you're wrong.''

"I didn't say you were *thinking* those things. And no, that's not my knack at all. But I'm a barrister. I've seen people at the most trying moments of their lives. I've seen them when they've decided to give up and let the world have its way. I recognize that decision when I see it. You've decided.''

"What if I have?'' she asked defiantly. "And anyway I haven't, so it doesn't matter.''

Cooper ignored her. "If we leave her here, she'll die, sooner or later. She'll do it just to prove she's part of her family.''

"No I won't,'' said Purity. "I don't even *know* for sure that that's what happened to them. I think the evidence points that way, but it's a slender arrow indeed.''

"But you want it to be true,'' said Cooper.

"That's silly! Why would I want that!''

Cooper said nothing.

"I don't hate it here! People have been kind to me. Reverend Study arranged to let me use the Harvard library. I get to listen to the lectures. Not that it will ever amount to anything."

Cooper smiled ever-so-slightly.

"Well, what *can* it amount to?" Purity demanded. "I'm a woman. Either I'll marry or I won't. If I marry, I'll be raising children. Maybe I'll teach them to read before they get to school. But I won't be the one who gets to teach them Latin and Greek. They'll get their Caesar and their Tully and their Homer from someone else. And if I don't marry, the best I can hope for is to be kept on as a matron in the orphanage. Children are the only people who'll ever hear my voice."

"Ain't nothing wrong with children," said Arthur Stuart.

"That's not what she means anyway," said Cooper.

"Don't you dare interpret me anymore!" Purity cried. "You think you know me better than you know yourself!"

"Yes, I think I do," said Cooper. "I've been down the same road."

"Oh, were you an orphan? As a barrister, did they make you work with children all the time? Did they make you sit outside the courtroom to plead your case?"

"All these sacrifices," said Cooper, "you'd make them gladly, if you believed in the cause."

"Are you accusing me of being an unbeliever?"

"Yes," said Cooper.

"I'm a Christian!" she said. "You're the heretics! You're the witches!"

"Keep your voice down," said Fink menacingly.

"I'm not a witch!" said Audubon fervently.

"You see?" said Cooper. "Now you *are* accusing us."

"I'm not!" she said. "There's no one here but you."

"You're a woman whose world has just turned upside down. You're the daughter of witches. You're angry that they were killed. You're angry at yourself for being alive, for being part of the very society that killed them. And you're angry at that society for not being worthy of the sacrifice."

"I'm not judging others," she said.

"They were supposed to build Zion here," said Cooper. "The city of God. The place where Christ at his coming could find the righteous gathered together, waiting for him."

"Yes," whispered Purity.

"They even named you Purity. And yet you see that nothing is pure. The people are trying to be good, but it isn't good enough. When Christ comes, all he'll find here is a group of people who have done no more than to find another way to be stubble that he will have to burn."

"No, the virtue is real, the people are good," said Purity. "Reverend Study—"

"Virtue is real outside New England, too," said Verily Cooper.

"Is it?" she asked. "Most people here live the commandments. Adultery is as rare as fish with feet. Murder never happens. Drunkenness can never be seen anywhere except at the docks, where sailors from other lands are permitted—and why should I defend New England to you?"

"You don't have to," said Cooper. "I grew up with the dream of New England all around me. In every pulpit, in every home. When someone behaved badly, when someone in authority made a mistake, we'd say, 'What do you expect? This isn't New England.' When somebody was exceptionally kind or self-sacrificing, or humble and sweet, we'd say, 'He belongs in New England,' or 'He's already got his passage to Boston.' "

Purity looked at him in surprise. "Well, we're not *that* good here."

"I know," said Cooper. "For one thing, you still hang witches and put their babies in orphanages."

"I'm not going to cry again, if that's what you're hoping for," said Purity.

"I'm hoping for something else," said Cooper. "Come with us."

"Verily!" said Smith. "For pete's sake, if we wanted a woman with us we'd be traveling with Margaret! You think this girl's ready to sleep rough?"

"Ain't decent anyway," said Mike Fink. "She's a lady."

"You needn't worry about my going with you," said Purity. "What kind of madman are you? Perhaps I *am* angry and disillusioned about the dream of purity here in New England. Why would I be any happier with you, who aren't even as pure as we are here?"

"Because we have the one thing you're hungry for."

"And what is that?"

"A reason to live."

She laughed in his face. "The five of you! And all the rest of the world lacks it? Why don't they all just give up and die?"

"Few give up living," said Cooper. "Most give up looking for a reason. But some have to keep searching. They can't bear to live without a purpose. Something larger than themselves, something so good that just being a part of it makes everything worthwhile. You're a seeker, Miss Purity."

"How do you know all these things about me?"

"Because I'm a seeker, too. Do you think I don't know my own kind?"

She looked around at the others. "If I were this thing, a seeker, why would I want to be with other seekers? If you're still seeking, it means you haven't found anything, either."

"But we have," said Cooper.

Smith rolled his eyes. "Verily Cooper, you know I still don't have a clue what we're even looking for."

"That's not what I'm talking about," said Cooper. "You're not a seeker, Alvin. You already have your life handed to you, whether you want it or not. And Arthur here, he's not a seeker, either. He's already found what *he* wants."

Arthur hung his head, embarrassed. "Don't you go saying!"

"Just like Mike Fink. They've found *you,* Al. They're going to follow you till they die."

"Or till I do," said Smith.

"Ain't going to happen," said Fink. "I'll have to be dead first."

"You see?" said Cooper. "And Jean-Jacques here, he's no seeker. He knows the purpose of his life as well."

Audubon grinned. "Birds, women, and wine."

"Birds," said Cooper.

"But you're still seeking?" asked Smith.

"I've found you, too," said Cooper. "But I haven't found what *I'm* good for. I haven't figured out what *my* life means." He turned to Purity again. "That's why I knew. Because I've stood where you're standing. You've fooled them all, they think they know you but it just means you've kept your secret, only now you're fed up with secrets and you have to get out, you have to find the people who know why you're alive.''

"Yes," she whispered.

"So come with us," said Cooper.

"Dammit, Very," said Smith, "how can we have a woman along?"

"Why not?" said Cooper. "Quite soon you're going to rejoin your wife and start traveling with her. We can't camp in the woods our whole lives. And Miss Purity can help us. Our painter friend may be happy with what he's accomplished here, but we don't know anything more than we did before we arrived. We see the villages, but we can hardly talk to anyone because we have so many secrets and they're so reticent with strangers. Miss Purity can explain things to us. She can help you learn what you need to learn about building the City of—"

He stopped.

"The City," he finally said.

"Why not say it?" said Purity. "The City of God."

Cooper and Smith looked at each other, and Purity could see that both of them were filled with the pleasure of having understood something. "See?" said Cooper. "We've already learned something, just by having Miss Purity with us."

"What did you learn?" demanded Arthur Stuart.

"That maybe the Crystal City has another name," said Smith.

"Crystal City?" asked Miss Purity.

Cooper looked at Smith for permission. Alvin glanced at each of them in turn, until at last his gaze lingered on Purity herself. "If you think she's all right," said Alvin.

"I know she is," said Cooper.

"Got a couple of minutes?" Alvin asked Purity.

"More like a couple of hours," said Mike Fink.

"Maybe while you talk and talk I bath in the river," said Audubon.

"I'll keep watch," said Fink. "I fell in enough rivers in my time without getting nekkid to do it on purpose."

Soon Purity, Smith, Cooper, and Arthur Stuart were sitting in the tall soft grass on the riverbank. "I got a story to tell you," said Alvin. "About who we are and what we're doing here. And then you can decide what you want to do about it."

"Let me tell it," demanded Arthur Stuart.

"You?" asked Alvin.

"You always mix it up and tell it back end to."

"What do you mean, 'always'? I hardly tell this story to anybody."

"You ain't no Taleswapper, Alvin," said Arthur Stuart.

"And you are?"

"At least I can tell it front to back instead of always adding in stuff I forgot to tell in the proper place."

Alvin laughed. "All right, Arthur Stuart, *you* tell the story of my life, since you know it better than I do."

"It ain't the story of your life anyway," said Arthur Stuart. "Cause it starts with Little Peggy."

" 'Little' Peggy?" asked Alvin.

"That's what her name was *then*," said Arthur.

"Go ahead," said Alvin.

Arthur Stuart looked to the others. Cooper and Purity both nodded. At once Arthur Stuart bounded to his feet and walked a couple of paces away. Then he came back and stood before them, his back to the water, and with boats sailing along behind him, and the summer sun beating down on him while his listeners sat in the shade, he put his hands behind his back and closed his eyes and began to talk.

⚔ 6 ⚔

Names

MARGARET DID NOT waste time worrying about when—or if—her promised audience with the Queen might happen. Many of the futures she found in other people's heartfires led to such a meeting, and many more did not, and in neither case did she see such an audience leading to the prevention of the bloody war she dreaded.

In the meantime, there were plenty of other activities to fill her time. For she was finding that Camelot was a much more complicated place than she had expected.

During her childhood in the North she had learned to think of slavery as an all-or-nothing proposition, and in most ways it was. There was no way to half-permit it or half-practice it. Either you could be bought and sold by another human being or you couldn't. Either you could be compelled to labor for another man's profit under threat of death or injury, or you couldn't.

But there were cracks in the armor, all the same. Slave owners were not untouched by the normal human impulses. Despite the most stringent rules against it, some Whites did become quite affectionate in their feelings toward loyal Blacks. It was against the law to free a slave, and yet the Ashworths weren't the only Whites to free some of their slaves and then employ them—and not all those manumitted were as old as Doe. It might be impossible to attack the institution of slavery in the press or in public meetings, but that did not mean that quiet reforms could not take place.

She was writing about this in a letter to Alvin when someone knocked softly at her door.

"Come in?"

It was Fishy. Wordlessly she entered and handed Margaret a calling card, then left almost before the words "Thank you, Fishy" were out of Margaret's mouth. The card was from a haberdasher in Philadelphia, which puzzled her for a moment, until she thought to turn it over to reveal a message scrawled in a careless childish hand:

Dear Sister-in-law Margaret,
I heard you was in town. Dinner? Meet me downstairs at four.
Calvin Miller

She had not thought to check his heartfire in many days, being caught up in her exploration of Camelot society. Of course she looked for him at once, his distinctive heartfire almost leaping out to her from the forest of flames in the city around her. She never enjoyed looking into his heartfire because of all the malice that was constantly harbored there. Her visits were brief and she did not look deep. Even so, she immediately knew about his liaison with Lady Ashworth, which disgusted her, despite her long experience with all the sins and foibles known to humankind. To use his knack to provoke the woman's lust—how was that distinguishable from rape? True, Lady Ashworth could have shouted for her slaves to cast him from the house—the one circumstance in which slaves were permitted to handle a White man roughly—but Lady Ashworth was a woman unaccustomed to feeling much in the way of sexual desire, and like a child in the first rush of puberty she had no strategies for resistance. Where the patterns of society kept girls and boys from being alone together during that chaotic time, preventing them from disastrous lapses in self-control, Lady Ashworth, as an adult of high station, had no such protection. Her wealth bought her privacy and opportunity without giving her any particular help in resisting temptation.

The thought crossed Margaret's mind: It might be useful to know of Lady Ashworth's adultery.

Then, ashamed, she rejected the thought of holding the woman's sin against her. Margaret had known of other people's sins all her life—and had also seen the terrible futures that would result if she told what she knew. If God had given her this intense knack, it was certainly not so that she could spread misery.

And yet . . . if there was some way that her knowledge of Calvin's seduction of Lady Ashworth might help prevent the war . . .

How bitter it was that the most guilty party, Calvin, was untouchable by shame, and therefore could not have his adultery used against him, unless Lord Ashworth was a champion dueler (and even then, Margaret suspected that in a duel with Calvin, Lord Ashworth would find that his pistol would not fire and his sword would break right off). But that was the way of the world—seducers and rapists rarely bore the consequences of their acts, or at least not as heavily as the seduced and the broken-spirited.

Dinner would be at four o'clock. Only a couple of hours away. Fishy had not waited for a return message, and in all likelihood Calvin wasn't waiting either. Either she would meet him or she would not—and indeed, his heartfire showed him unconcerned. It was only a whim for him to meet her. His purpose was as much to find out who she was as to cling to her skirts in order to get in to see the King.

And even the wish to meet King Arthur contained no plan. Calvin knew Napoleon—this exiled king would not impress him. For a moment Margaret wondered if Calvin planned to kill King Arthur the way he had murdered—or, as Calvin thought of it, *executed*—William Henry Harrison. But no. His heartfire showed no such path in his future, and no such desire in his heart at present.

But that was the problem with Calvin's heartfire. It kept changing from day to day, hour to hour. Most people, limited as they were by the circumstances of their lives, had few real choices, and so their heart-fires showed futures that followed only a handful of probable paths. Even powerful people, like her husband Alvin, whose powers gave him countless opportunities, still had their futures sorted into a wider but still countable number because their character was predictable, their choices consistent.

Calvin, on the contrary, was whim-driven to a remarkable extent. His attachment to this French intellectual had shaped his life lately, because Balzac had a firm character, but once Calvin's futures diverged from Balzac's, they immediately branched and rebranched and forked and sprayed into thousands, millions of futures, none more likely than the others. Margaret could not possibly follow them all and see where they led.

It was in Alvin's heartfire, not Calvin's, that she had seen Alvin's death caused by Calvin's machinations. No doubt if she followed every one of the billion paths of Calvin's future she would find almost as many different ways for Calvin to achieve that end. Hatred and envy and love and admiration for Alvin were the one consistency in Calvin's inconstant heart. That he wished harm for Alvin and would eventually bring it to pass could not be doubted; nor could Margaret find any likely way to prevent it.

Short of killing him.

What is happening to me? she wondered. First I think of extortion by threatening to expose Lady Ashworth's sin, and now I actually think of murdering my husband's brother. Is the mere exposure to Calvin a temptation? Does his heartfire influence mine?

Wouldn't that be nice, to be able to blame Calvin for my own failings?

One thing Margaret was sure of: The seeds of all sins were in all people. If it were not so, how would it be virtue when they refrained from acting on those impulses? She did not need Calvin to teach her to think of evil. She only needed to be frustrated at her inability to change events, at her helplessness to save her husband from a doom that she so clearly saw and that Alvin himself seemed not to care about. The desire to force others to bend or break to her will was always there, usually hidden deeply enough that she could forget she had that wish within her, but occasionally surfacing to dangle the ripe fruit of power just out of her reach. She knew, as few others did, that the power to coerce depended entirely on the fear or weakness of other human beings. It was possible to use coercion, yes, but in the end you found yourself surrounded only by the weak and fearful, with all those of courage and strength arrayed against you. And many of your strong, brave enemies would match you in evil, too. The more you coerced others, the sooner you would bring yourself to the moment of your doom.

It would even happen to Napoleon. Margaret had seen it, for she had examined his hot black heartfire several times when she was checking on Calvin during his stay in France. She saw the battlefield. She saw the enemies arrayed against him. No coercion, not even fueled by Napoleon's seemingly irresistible knack, could build a structure that would last. Only when a leader gathered willing followers who shared his goals could the things he created continue after his death. Alexander proved that when his empire collapsed in fragments after his death; Charlemagne did little better, and Attila did worse—*his* empire evaporated upon his death. The empire of the Romans, on the other hand, was built by consensus and lasted two thousand years; Mohammed's empire kept growing after his death and became a civilization. Napoleon's France was no Rome, and Napoleon was no Mohammed.

But at least Napoleon was trying to create something. Calvin had no intention of building anything. To make things was his inborn knack, but the desire to build was foreign to his nature; the persistence to build was contrary to his temperament. He was weak himself, and fearful. He could not bear scorn; he feared shame more than death. This made him think he was brave. Many people made that mistake about themselves. Because they could stand up to the prospect of physical pain or even death, they thought they had courage—only to discover that the threat of shame made them comply with any foolish command or surrender any treasure, no matter how dear.

Calvin, what can I do with you? Is there no way to kindle true manhood in your fragile, foolish heart? Surely it's not too late, even for you. Surely in some of the million divergent paths of your heartfire there is one, at least, in which you find the courage to admit Alvin's greatness without fearing that others will then scorn you for being weaker. Surely there's a moment when you choose to love goodness for its own sake, and cease to care about what others think of you.

Surely, in any heap of straw, there is one strand which, if planted and tended, watered and nurtured, will live and grow.

* * *

Honoré de Balzac trotted along behind Calvin, growing more annoyed by the moment. "Slow down, girder-legs, you will wear me down to a stub trying to keep up with you."

"You always walk so slow," said Calvin. "Sometimes I got to stride out or my legs get jumpy."

"If your legs are jumpy then jump." But the argument was over—Calvin was walking more slowly now. "This sister-in-law of yours, what makes you think she'll pay for dinner?"

"I told you, she's a torch. The Napoleon of torches. She'll know before she comes downstairs to meet us that I don't have a dime. Or a shilling. Whatever they call it here."

"So she'll turn around and go back upstairs."

"No," said Calvin. "She'll want to meet me."

"But Calvin, my friend, if she is a torch then she must know what is in your heart. Who could want to meet you then?"

Calvin rounded on him, his face a mask of anger. "What do you mean by that?"

For a moment, Honoré was frightened. "Please don't turn me into a frog, Monsieur le Maker."

"If you don't like me, why are you always tagging along?"

"I write novels, Calvin. I study people."

"You're studying me?"

"No, of course not, I already have you in my mind, ready to write. What I study is the people you meet. How they respond to you. You seem to wake up something inside them."

"What?"

"Different things. That is what I study."

"So you're using me."

"But of course. Were you under some delusion that I stayed with you for love? Do you think we are Damon and Pythias? Jonathan and David? I would be a fool to love you like such a friend."

Calvin's expression grew darker yet. "Why would you be a fool?"

"Because there is no room for a man like me in your life. You are already locked in a dance with your brother. Cain and Abel had no friends—but then, they were the only two men alive. Perhaps the better comparison is Romulus and Remus."

"Which one am I?" asked Calvin.

"The younger brother," said Honoré.

"So you think he'll try to kill me?"

"I spoke of the closeness of the brothers, not the end of the story."

"You're playing with me."

"I always play with everybody," said Honoré. "It is my vocation. God put me on the earth to do with people what cats do to mice. Play with them, chew the last bit of life out of them, then pick them up in my mouth and drop them on people's doorsteps. That is the business of literature."

"You take a lot of airs for a writer who ain't had a book printed up yet."

"There is no book big enough to contain the stories that fill me up. But I will soon be ready to write. I will go back to France, I will write my books, I will be arrested from time to time, I will be in debt, I will make huge amounts of money but never enough, and in the end my books will last far longer than Napoleon's empire."

"Or maybe it'll just seem that way to the folks who read them."

"You will never know. You are illiterate in French."

"I'm illiterate in most every language," said Calvin. "So are you."

"Yes, but in the illiteracy competition, I will concede to you the laurels."

"Here's the house," said Calvin.

Honoré sized it up. "Your sister-in-law is not rich, but she spends the money to stay in a place that is respectable."

"Who says she ain't rich? I mean, think of it. She knows what folks are thinking. She knows everything they've ever done and everything they're going to do. She can see the future! You can bet she's invested a few dollars here and there. I bet she's got plenty of money by now."

"What a foolish use of such a power," said Honoré. "The mere making of money. If I could see into another person's heart, I would be able to write the truest of novels."

"I thought you already could."

"I can, but it is only the imagined soul of the other person. I cannot be *sure* that I am right. I have not been wrong yet about anyone, but I am never *sure*."

"People ain't that hard to figure out," said Calvin. "You treat it like some mystery and you're the high priest who has the word straight from God, but people are just people. They want the same things."

"Tell me this list as we go inside out of the sun."

Calvin pulled the string to ring the doorbell. "Water. Food. Leaking and dumping. Getting a woman or a man, depending. Getting rich. Having people respect you and like you. Making other people do what you want."

The door opened. A Black woman stood before them, her eyes downcast.

"Miz Larner or Miz Smith or whatever name she's using, Margaret anyway, she's expecting to meet us downstairs," said Calvin.

Wordlessly the Black woman backed away to let them come in. Honoré stopped in the doorway, took the woman by the chin, and lifted her head till their eyes met. "What do *you* want? In the whole world, what do you want most?"

For a moment the woman looked at him in terror. Her eyes darted left, right. Honoré knew she wanted to look down again, to get back to the safe and orderly world, but she did not dare to turn her face away from him as long as he held her chin, for fear he would denounce her as insolent. And then she stopped trying to look away, but rather locked her gaze on his eyes, as if she could see into him and recognized that he meant her no harm, but only wanted to understand her.

"What do you want?" he asked again.

Her lips moved.

"You can tell me," he said.

"A name," she whispered.

Then she tore herself away and fled the room.

Honoré looked after her, bemused. "What do you suppose she meant by that?" he asked. "Surely she has a name—how else would her master call her when he wanted her?"

"You'll have to ask Margaret," said Calvin. "She's the one who sees what's going on inside everybody's head."

They sat on the porch, watching bees and hummingbirds raid the flowers in the garden. Soon Calvin began to amuse himself by making the bees' wings stop flapping. He'd point to a bee and then it would drop like a stone. A moment later, dazed and annoyed, it would start to buzz again and rise into the air. By then Calvin would be pointing to another bee and making it fall. Honoré laughed because it *was* funny to see them fall, to imagine their confusion. "Please don't do it to the hummingbirds," Honoré said.

He regretted at once that he had said such a foolish thing. For of course that was exactly what Calvin had to do. He pointed. The hummingbird's wings stopped. It plummeted to the ground. But it did not buzz and rise back into the sky. Instead it struggled there, flapping one wing while the other lay useless in the dirt.

"Why would you break such a beautiful creature?" said Honoré.

"Who makes the rules?" said Calvin. "Why is it funny to do it to bees but not to birds?"

"Because it doesn't hurt the bee," said Honoré. "Because hummingbirds don't sting. Because there are millions of bees but hummingbirds are as rare as angels."

"Not around here," said Calvin.

"You mean there are many angels in Camelot?"

"I meant there are thousands of hummingbirds. They're like squirrels they're so common."

"So it is all right to break this one's wing and let it die?"

"What is it, God watches the sparrows and you're in charge of hummingbirds?"

"If you can't fix it," said Honoré, "you shouldn't break it."

Calvin glowered, then pushed himself out of his chair, vaulted the railing, and knelt down by the hummingbird. He fiddled with the wing, trying to straighten it. The bird kept struggling in his grasp.

"Hold still, dammit."

Calvin held the broken wing straight, closed his eyes, concentrated. But the fluttering of the bird kept annoying him. He made an exasperated gesture, as if he were shaking a child, and the bones of the wing crumbled in his fingers. He took his hands away and looked at the ruined wing, a sick expression on his face.

"Is this a game?" asked Honoré. "See how many times can you break the same hummingbird wing?"

Calvin looked at him in fury. "Shut your damn mouth."

"The bird is in pain, Monsieur le Maker."

Calvin leapt to his feet and stomped down hard on the bird. "Now it's not."

"Calvin the healer," said Honoré. Despite the jesting tone he was sick at heart. It was his goading that had killed the bird. Not that there was any hope for it. It was doomed to die as soon as Calvin made it fall from the air. But even that had been partly Honoré's fault for having asked Calvin *not* to do it. He knew, or should have known, that would be a goad to him.

"You made me do it," said Calvin. He couldn't meet Honoré's gaze. This worried Honoré more than a defiant glare would have. Calvin felt shamed in front of his friend. That did not bode well for that friend's future.

"Nonsense," said Honoré cheerfully. "It was your own wise choice. Do not kill bees, for they make honey! But what does a humming bird make? A splash of color in the air, and then it dies, and voilà! A splash of color on the ground. And where is color more needed? The air is full of bright color. The ground never has enough of it. You have made the world more beautiful."

"Someday I'll be sick of you and your sick jokes," said Calvin.

"What's taking you so long? I'm already sick of me."

"But you like your jokes," said Calvin.

"I never know whether I will like them until I hear myself say them," said Honoré.

He heard footsteps inside the house, coming to the door. He turned. Margaret Smith was a stern-looking woman, but not unattractive. Au contraire, she was noticeably attractive. Perhaps some might think her too tall for Honoré's comfort, but like most short men, Honoré had long since had to settle for the idea of admiring taller women; any other choice would curtail too sharply the pool of available ladies.

Not that this one was available. She raised one eyebrow very slightly, as if to let Honoré know that she recognized his admiration of her and thought it sweet but stupid of him. Then she turned her attention to Calvin.

"I remember once," she said, "I saw Alvin heal a broken animal."

Honoré winced and stole a glance at Calvin. To his surprise, instead of exploding with wrath, Calvin only smiled at the lady. "Nice to meet you, Margaret," he said.

"Let's get one thing straight from the start," said Margaret. "I know every nasty little thing you've ever done. I know how much you hate and envy my husband. I know the rage you feel for me at this moment and how you long to humiliate me. Let's have no pretenses between us."

"All right," said Calvin, smiling. "I want to make love to you. I want to make you pregnant with my baby instead of Alvin's."

"The only thing you want is to make me angry and afraid," said Margaret. "You want me to wonder if you'll use your powers to harm the baby inside my womb and then to seduce me the way you did with another poor woman. So let me put your mind at rest. The hexes that protect my baby were made by Alvin himself, and you don't have the skill to penetrate them."

"Do you think not?" said Calvin.

"I know you don't," said Margaret, "because you've already tried and failed and you don't even begin to understand why. As for wanting to seduce me—save those efforts for someone who doesn't see through your pretenses. Now, are we going to dinner or not?"

"*I'm* hungry," said Honoré, desperate to turn the conversation away from the dangerous hostility with which it had begun. Didn't this woman know what kind of madman Calvin was? "Where shall we eat?"

"Since I'm expected to pay," said Margaret, "it will have to be in a restaurant I can afford."

"Excellent," said Honoré. "I am ill at the thought of eating at the kind of restaurant *I* can afford."

That earned him a tiny hint of a smile from the stern Mrs. Smith. "Give me your arm, Monsieur de Balzac. Let's not tell my brother-in-law where we're going."

"Very funny," said Calvin, climbing over the railing and back onto the porch. The edge of fury was out of his voice. Honoré was relieved. This woman, this torch, she must truly understand Calvin better than Honoré did, for Calvin seemed to be calming down even though she had goaded him so dangerously. Of course, if she was protected by hexes that might give her more confidence.

Or was it hexes she was counting on? She was married to the Maker that Calvin longed to be—maybe she simply counted on Calvin's knowledge that if he harmed her or her baby, he would have to face the wrath of his brother at long last, and he knew he was no match for Alvin Maker. Someday he would have it out with him, but he wasn't ready, and so Calvin would not harm Alvin's wife or unborn baby.

Certainly that was the way a rational man would see it.

Calvin tried to keep himself from getting angry during the meal. What good would it do him? She could see everything he felt; yet she would also see that he was suppressing his anger, so even that would do no good. He hated the whole idea of her existence—someone who thought she knew the truth of his soul just because she could see into his secret desires. Well, everyone had secret desires, didn't they? They couldn't be condemned for the fancies that passed through their mind, could they? It was only what they acted on that counted.

Then he remembered the dead hummingbird. Lady Ashworth naked in bed. He stopped himself before he remembered every act that others had criticized—no reason to list the catalogue of them for Margaret's watchful eye. For her to report to Alvin with, no doubt, the worst possible interpretation. Alvin's *spy*—

No, keep the anger under control. She couldn't help what her knack was, any more than Calvin could, or anybody else. She wasn't a spy.

A judge, though. She was clearly judging him, she had said as much. She judged everybody. That's why she was here in the Crown Colonies—because she had judged and condemned them for practicing slavery, even though the whole world had always practiced slavery until just lately, and it was hardly fair to condemn these people when the idea of emancipation was really just some fancy new trend from Puritan England and a few French philosophers.

And he didn't want to be judged by what he did, either. That was wrong, too. People made mistakes. Found out later that a choice was wrong. You couldn't hold that against them forever, could you?

No, people should be judged by what they meant to do in the long run. By the overarching purpose they meant to accomplish. Calvin was going to help Alvin build the Crystal City. That was why he had gone to France and England, wasn't it? To learn how people were gathered to one purpose and governed in the real world. None of this feeble teaching that Alvin did back in Vigor Church, trying to turn people into what they were not and never could be. No, Alvin would get nowhere that way. Calvin was the one who would figure it all out and come back and show Alvin the way. Calvin would be the teacher, and together the brothers would build the great city and the whole world would be ruled from that place, and even Napoleon would come and bow to them, and *then* all of Calvin's mistakes and bad thoughts would be forgotten in the honor and glory that would come to him.

And even if he never succeeded, it was his *purpose* that counted. *That's* who Calvin really was, and that was how Margaret should judge him.

Come to think of it, she had no business judging him at all. That's what Jesus said, wasn't it? Judge not lest ye be judged. Jesus forgave everybody. Margaret should take a lesson from Jesus and forgive Calvin instead of condemning him. If the world had a little more forgiveness in it, it would be a better place. Everybody sinned. What was Calvin's little fling with Lady Ashworth compared to Alvin killing that Slave Finder? What was a dead hummingbird compared to a dead *man*? Margaret could forgive Alvin, but never Calvin, no, because he wasn't one of the favored ones.

People are such hypocrites. It made him sick, the way they were always pretending to be *soooo* righteous. . . .

Except Balzac. He never pretended at all. He was just himself. And he didn't judge Calvin. Just accepted him for the man he was. Didn't compare him with Alvin, either. How could he? They had never met.

The meal was almost over. Calvin had been so busy brooding that he hadn't noticed that he was almost completely silent. But what could he say, when Margaret thought she already knew everything about him anyway?

Balzac was talking to her about the slavegirl who opened the door for them at the boardinghouse. "I asked her what she wanted most in all the world, and she told me what she wanted was a name. I thought people named their slaves."

Margaret looked at him in surprise, and it took a moment for her to respond. "The girl you talked to has two names," she finally said. "But she hates them both."

"Is that what she meant?" asked Balzac. "That she didn't like her name? But that's not the same as wishing she had one."

Again Margaret looked contemplative for a few moments.

"I think you've uncovered something that I was having trouble understanding. She hates her name, and then she tells you she wishes she had one. I can't decipher it."

Balzac leaned over the table and rested his hand on Margaret's. "You must tell me what you are really thinking, madame."

"I am really thinking you should take your hand off mine," said Margaret mildly. "That may work with the women of France, but uninvited intimacies do not work well with me."

"I beg your pardon."

"And I did tell you what I really thought," said Margaret.

"But that is not true," said Balzac.

Calvin almost laughed out loud, to hear him front her so bold.

"Is it not?" asked Margaret. "If so, I am not aware of what the truth might be."

"You got a look in your eyes. Very thoughtful. Then you reached a conclusion. And yet you told me that you can't decipher this girl's wish for a name."

"I said I can't decipher it," said Margaret. "I meant that I can't find her real name."

"Ah. So that means you *have* deciphered *something*."

"I've never thought to look for this before. But it seems that the two names I had for her—the name her mother called her, which was awful, and her household name, which is hardly better; they call her 'Fishy'— neither of those is her true name. But she thinks they are. Or rather, she knows of no other name, and yet she knows there must *be* another name, and so she wishes for that true name, and—well, as you can see, I haven't deciphered anything."

"Your decipherment is not up to your own standard of understanding maybe," said Balzac, "but it is enough to leave me breathless."

On they blathered, Balzac and Mrs. Smith, trading compliments. Calvin thought about names. About how much easier his life might have been if his own name had not been shared with Alvin, save one letter. About how Alvin resisted using the name Maker even though he had earned it. Alvin Smith indeed. And then Margaret—why did she decide to stop being Peggy? What pretension was she nursing? Or was Margaret the true name and Peggy the disguise?

Chatter chatter. Oh, shut up, both of you. "Here's a question," Calvin asked, interrupting them. "Which comes first, the name or the soul?"

"What do you mean?" asked Balzac.

"I mean is the soul the same, no matter what you name it? Or if you change names do you change souls?"

"What do names have to do with . . ." Margaret's voice trailed off. She looked off into the distance.

"I think decipherment happens before our eyes," said Balzac.

Calvin was annoyed. She wasn't supposed to take this seriously. "I just asked a question, I wasn't trying to plumb the secrets of the universe."

Margaret looked at him with disinterest. "You were going to make some foolish joke about giving Alvin the *C* from your name and you could be the one that everybody likes."

"Was not," said Calvin.

She ignored him. "The slaves have names," she said, "but they don't, because the names their masters give them aren't real. Don't you see? It's a way of staying free."

"Doesn't compare with actual freedom," said Calvin.

"Of course it doesn't," said Margaret. "But still, it's more than just a matter of the name itself. Because when they hide their names, they hide something else."

Calvin thought of what he had said to start this stupid discussion. "Their souls?"

"Their heartfires," she said. "I know you understand what I'm talking about. You don't see into them the way I do, but you know where they are. Haven't you noticed that the slaves don't have them?"

"Yes, they do," said Calvin.

"What are you talking about?" said Balzac.

"Souls," said Calvin.

"Heartfires," said Margaret. "I don't know if they're the same thing."

"Doesn't matter," said Calvin. "The French don't have either one."

"Now he insults me and my whole country," said Balzac, "but you see that I do not kill him."

"That's because you've got short arms and you drink too much to aim a gun," said Calvin.

"It is because I am civilized and I disdain violence."

"Don't either of you care," said Margaret, "that the slaves have found a way to hide their souls from their masters? Are they so invisible to you, Calvin, that you haven't ever bothered to notice that their heartfires are missing?"

"They still got a spark in them," said Calvin.

"But it's tiny, it has no depth," said Margaret. "It's the memory of a heartfire, not the fire itself. I can't see anything in them."

"Seems to me that they've found a way to hide their souls from *you*," said Calvin.

"Doesn't he ever listen to anybody?" Margaret asked Balzac.

"He does," said Balzac. "He hears, but he doesn't care."

"What am I supposed to be caring about that I'm not?" asked Calvin.

"What the Black girl said she wished for," said Balzac. "A name. She has hidden away her name and her soul, but now she wants them back and she doesn't know how."

"When did you two figure this out?" asked Calvin.

"It was obvious once Madame Smith made the connection," said Balzac. "But you are the most knowledgeable people I know of, when it comes to hidden powers. How could you not know of this?"

"I don't do souls," said Calvin.

"The powers they bring from Africa work differently," said Margaret. "Alvin tried to figure it out, and so did I, and we think that everybody is born with hidden powers, but they learn from the people around them to use them in different ways. We White people—or at least English people—but Napoleon's like this too, so who knows—we learn to use these powers individually, binding them tightly to some inborn talent or preference or need. A little bit of it we can put outside ourselves, in hexes, but the real power is held in each person. While the Reds, they open their powers to the world around them, becoming less and less alone, more and more tied to the power of nature. It gives them great powers, but cut them off from the natural world and it's gone."

"And Blacks?" asked Balzac.

"They learn to put it into objects, or perhaps they find it there, I don't know. Since I've never done it myself, nor has Alvin, we could only speculate. Some things I've seen in Black folks' heartfires, though—I could hardly believe it. Yet it's so. Arthur Stuart's mother—she had extraordinary power, and by making something, she gave herself wings. She flew.''

Balzac laughed, then realized she wasn't joking or even speaking metaphorically. ''Flew?''

''At least a hundred miles,'' said Margaret. ''Not far enough, not entirely in the right direction, but it was enough to save her baby, though her own strength and life were spent.''

''This Arthur Stuart, why don't you ask *him* how the power of Black people works?''

''He's just a boy,'' said Calvin scornfully, ''and he's half-White anyway.''

''You don't know him,'' said Margaret. ''He doesn't know how the powers of Blacks work because it isn't carried in the blood, it's taught from parent to child. Alvin learned the greensong of the Reds because he became like a child to Tenskwa-Tawa and Ta-Kumsaw. Arthur Stuart grew up with his power shaped into a knack, like Whites, because he was raised among Whites. I think Blacks have a hard time holding on to their African ways. Maybe that's why Fishy can't remember her real name. Someone took her name from her, took her soul, to keep it in hiding, to keep it safe and free. But now she wants it back and she can't get it because she's not African-born, she's not surrounded by a tribe, she's surrounded by beaten-down slaves whose heartfires and names are all in hiding.''

''If they got all these powers,'' said Calvin, ''how come they're slaves?''

''Oh, that's easy,'' said Balzac. ''The ones who capture them in Africa, they are also African, they know what the powers are, they keep them from having the things they need.''

''Blacks against Blacks,'' said Margaret sadly.

''How do you know all that?'' Calvin asked Balzac.

''I was at the docks! I saw the Blacks being dragged off the ships in chains. I saw the Black men who searched them, took away little dolls made of cloth or dung, many different things.''

''Where was I when you were seeing this stuff?''

"Drunk, my friend," said Balzac.

"So were you, then," said Calvin.

"But I have an enormous capacity for wine," said Balzac. "When I am drunk I am at my best. It is the national knack of the French."

"I wouldn't be proud of it if I were you," said Margaret.

"I wouldn't be sanctimonious about our wine, here in the land of corn liquor and rye whiskey." Balzac leered at her.

"Just when I think I might like you, Monsieur Balzac, you show yourself not to be a gentleman."

"I don't have to be a gentleman," said Balzac. "I am an artist."

"You still walk on two legs and eat through your mouth," said Margaret. "Being an artist doesn't give you special privileges. If anything, it gives you greater responsibilities."

"I have to study life in all its manifestations," said Balzac.

"Perhaps that is true," said Margaret. "But if you sample all the wickedness of the world, and commit every betrayal and every harm, then you will not be able to sample the higher joys, for you will not be healthy enough or strong enough—or decent enough for the company of good people, which is one of the greatest joys of all."

"If they cannot forgive me my foibles, then they are not such good people, no?" Balzac smiled as if he had played the last ace in the deck.

"But they do forgive your foibles," said Margaret. "They would welcome your company, too. But if you joined them, you would not understand what they were talking about. You would not have had the experiences that bind them together. You would be an outsider, not because of any act of theirs, but because you have not passed along the road that teaches you to be one of them. You will feel like an exile from the beautiful garden, but it will be you who exiled yourself. And yet you will blame *them*, and call them judgmental and unforgiving, even as it is your own pain and bitter memory that condemns you, your own ignorance of virtue that makes you a stranger in the land that should have been your home."

Her eyes were on fire and Balzac looked at her with rapt admiration. "I always thought I would experiment with evil, and imagine good because it was easier. Almost you convince me I should do it the other way around."

Calvin was not so entranced. He knew that this little sermon was directed at him and he didn't like it. "There's no such secret that the good people know," said Calvin. "They just pretend, to console themselves for having missed out on all the fun."

Margaret smiled at him. "I took these ideas from your own thoughts of only a few minutes ago, Calvin. You know that what I'm saying is true."

"I was thinking the opposite," said Calvin.

"That's what you *thought* you were thinking," said Margaret. "But you wouldn't have had to think such thoughts if that was what you really thought about it."

Balzac laughed aloud, and Calvin joined him—albeit halfheartedly.

"Madame Smith, I could have labored all my days and never thought of a conversation in which someone was able to deliver such a sentence and have it mean anything at all. 'That's what you thought you were thinking.' Delicious! 'You would not think these thoughts if you really thought what you think you thought.' Or was it 'thought you think.' ''

"Neither one," said Margaret. "You are already preparing to misquote me."

"I am not a journalist! I am a novelist, and I can improve any speech."

"Improve this," said Margaret. "You two play your foolish games— Calvin playing at being powerful, Monsieur de Balzac playing at being an artist—but around you here is real life. Real suffering. These Black people are as human as you and me, but they give up their heartfires and their names in order to endure the torment of belonging to other people who despise and fear them. If you can dwell in this city of evil and remain untouched by their suffering, then it is you who are the trivial, empty people. You are able to hold on to your names and heartfires because they aren't worth stealing."

With that she rose from the table and left the restaurant.

"Do you think we offended her?" asked Calvin.

"Perhaps," said Balzac. "But that concerns me a great deal less than the fact that she did not pay."

As he spoke, the waiter was already approaching them. "Do the gentlemen wish to pay in cash?"

"It was the lady who invited us," said Balzac. "Did she forget to pay?"

"But she did pay," said the waiter. "For her own meal. Before you sat down, she wrote us her check."

Balzac looked at Calvin and burst out laughing. "You should see your face, Monsieur Calvin!"

"They can arrest us for this," said Calvin.

"But they do not wish to arrest a French novelist," said Balzac. "For I would return to France and write about their restaurant and declare it to be a house of flies and pestilence."

The waiter looked at him coldly. "The French ambassador engages us to cater his parties," he said. "I do not fear your threat."

A few moments later, up to his arms in dishwater and slops, Calvin seethed in resentment. Of Margaret, of course. Of Alvin, whose fault it was for marrying her. Of Balzac, too, for the cheerful way he bantered with the Black slaves who would otherwise have done all the kitchen work they were doing. Not that the Blacks bantered back. They hardly looked at him. But Calvin could see that they liked hearing him from the way more and more of them lingered in the room a little longer than their jobs required. While *he* was completely ignored, carrying buckets of table scraps out to be composted for the vegetable garden, emptying pails of dishwater, hauling full ones from the well to be heated. Heavy, sweaty labor, filth on his hands, grime on his face. He thought last night's urine-soaked sleep was as low as he could get in his life, but now he was doing the work of slaves while slaves looked on; and even here, there was another man that they all liked better than him.

Calvin returned to the kitchen just as a Black man was carrying a stack of clean plates to put back on the shelves. The Black man had just a trace of a smile on his face from something Balzac had said, and it was just too much after all that had happened that night. Calvin got his bug inside the dishes and cracked them all, shattered them in his arms. Shards sprayed out everywhere.

The crashing sound immediately brought the White chef and the overseer, his short, thick rod already raised to beat the slave; but Balzac was already there, throwing himself between the slave and the rod. And it was, truly, a matter of throwing himself, for the slave and the overseer were both much taller than Balzac. He leapt up and fairly clung to the slave like a child playing pick-a-pack.

"No, monsieur, do not strike him, he was innocent. I carelessly bumped into him and dropped all the plates on the floor! I am the most miserable of men, to take a dinner I could not pay for and now I have break all these plates. It is my back that deserves the blows!''

"I ain't going to whip no White man like a buck," said the overseer. "What do you think I am?"

"You are the arm of justice," said Balzac, "and I am the heart of guilt."

"Get these imbeciles out of my kitchen," said the chef.

"But you are French!" cried Balzac.

"Of course I am French! Who would hire an English cook?"

Immediately Balzac and the chef burst into a torrent of French, some of which Calvin understood, but not enough to be worth trying to hear any more of it. Balzac had taken all the fun out of it, of course, and the slaves were looking at him—sidelong, lest they be caught staring at a White man—as if he were God himself come to lead them out of captivity. Even when Calvin was annoyed and tried to get even a little, it ended up making Balzac look good and Calvin look like nothing.

Lead them out of captivity. God himself. His own thought of a moment before echoed in his mind. Margaret says they've lost their names and their heartfires. She hates slavery and wants it done away. They need someone to get their souls back and lead them out of captivity.

Balzac can't do that for them. What is he? A prawn of a Frenchman with ink on his fingers. But if I free the slaves, what will Alvin be then, compared with me?

For a moment he thought of striking the overseer dead and getting the slaves to run. But where would they run? No, what was needed was a general uprising. And without souls, the Blacks could hardly be expected to have the gumption for any kind of revolt.

So that was the first order of business. Finding souls and naming names.

7

Accusation

ALVIN DIDN'T EXACTLY doze off while Arthur Stuart told the story of his life. But his mind did wander.

He couldn't help hearing how Arthur Stuart's voice didn't change when he spoke. No one else would have remarked upon it, but Alvin still remembered how, when Arthur Stuart was younger, he could mimic other folks' voices perfectly. No matter how high or low the voice, no matter what accent or speech impediment it had, no matter how whispery or booming it might be, it came easily from the boy's mouth.

And then came the Slave Finders, with a sachet containing pieces of Arthur's hair and body taken when he was first born. They had the knack of knowing when a person matched up with a sachet, and there was no hiding from them, they could smell like bloodhounds. So Alvin took the boy across the Hio River, and there on the Appalachee side he made a change in the deepest heart of the tiniest parts of Arthur's body. Not a large change, but it was enough that Arthur no longer matched up with his own sachet. Alvin took him down under the water to wash away the last traces of his old skin. And when he came up out of the water, Arthur was safe. But he had lost his knack for doing voices.

Ain't that the way of it? thought Alvin. I try to help, and I take away as much as I give. Maybe that's how God set up the world, so nobody could get no special advantages. You get a miracle and you lose something ordinary that you miss from then on. Some angel somewhere measures out the joy and misery, and whatever your portion, you get it no matter what you do.

Suddenly Alvin was filled with loneliness. Silly to feel that way, he knew, what with these good companions alongside him. But somewhere down south there was his wife who was also his teacher and his guardian, the bright pair of eyes that watched him from infancy on, even though she was scarcely more than a baby herself when she started. Margaret. And in her womb, the start of the next generation. Their firstborn daughter.

And, thinking of them, he began to seek for them. He wasn't like Margaret, able to leap from heartfire to heartfire with a thought, able to see just by having the wish to see. He had to send his doodlebug out, fast, faster, racing across the map of America, down the coast, passing heartfires of every living thing, through fields and bright green forests, over rivers, across the wide Chesapeake. He knew the way and never got lost. Only in the city of Camelot itself did he have to search, looking for the paired heartfires that he knew so well, that he sought out every night.

Found. Mother and the tiny heartfire of their developing daughter. He could not see into heartfires the way Margaret could, but he could see into the body. He could tell when Margaret was speaking but had no notion what was said. He could hear the heartbeat, feel the breathing, tell if she was upset or calm, but he could not know why.

She was eating. She was tense, her muscles held rigid, her attitude wary. Two companions at dinner. One of them unfamiliar to him. The other . . .

What was Calvin doing across a table from Margaret?

At once Alvin did a closer check on his wife and baby. Nothing interfering with the baby in the womb—her heartbeat was regular, she showed no distress.

Of course not. Why should he even imagine that Calvin posed any threat to his family? Calvin might be a strange boy, plagued with jealousy and quick to wrath, but he wasn't a monster. He didn't hurt people, beyond hurting their feelings. No doubt his fear came from Margaret's constant warnings about how Calvin was going to get him killed someday. If he posed any danger to Margaret or the baby, she'd know long beforehand and would take steps to stop him.

Calvin and Margaret dining together. That bore thinking about. He could hardly wait for Margaret to get some time alone and write to him.

Then he got to thinking about Margaret and how he missed her and what it might be like, the two of them settling down without feeling the weight of the world on their shoulders, spending their time raising children and working to make a living. No Unmaker to be watched for and fended off. No Crystal City to be built. No horrible war to be avoided. Just wife, children, husband, neighbors, and in time grandchildren and graveyards, joy and grief, the rising and falling floods and droughts of the river of life.

"You fall asleep, Alvin?" asked Verily.

"Was I snoring?" asked Alvin.

"Arthur finished his tale. Your life story. Weren't you listening?"

"Heard it all before," said Alvin. "Besides, I was there when it happened, and it wasn't half so entertaining to live through as the tale Arthur makes of it."

"The question is whether Miss Purity wants to be one of our company," said Verily.

"Then why are you asking *me?*" said Alvin.

"I thought you might help us listen to her answer."

Alvin looked at Purity, who blushed and looked away.

Arthur Stuart glared at Verily. "You accusing Miss Purity of lying?"

"I'm saying," said Verily, "that if she believed your story, then she might fear the great power that Alvin has within him, and so she might give the answer that she thinks will keep her safe, instead of the answer that corresponds to her true inclinations."

"And I'm supposed to know whether she's telling the truth or not?" asked Alvin.

"Her heart isn't made of wood," said Verily, "so *I* can't tell if it beats faster or slower when she answers."

"She's the one with the knack to tell what people feel," said Alvin. "Margaret's the one as sees into folks' heartfire. Me, I just fiddle with stuff."

"You are too modest," said Purity, "if what your disciples say is true."

That perked Alvin right up. "Disciples?"

"Isn't that what you are? The master and his disciples, wandering about in the wilderness, hoping to recruit another."

"To me it looks more like a lost man and his friends, who are willing to be lost with him till he finds what he's looking for," said Alvin.

"You don't believe that," said Purity.

"No," said Alvin. "They're my friends, but that's not why they're here. They're fellow dreamers. They want to see the Crystal City as much as I do, and they're willing to travel hundreds of miles to help me find it."

Purity smiled faintly. "The Crystal City. The City of God. I wonder who it is you'll end up hanging, since you can't very well hang witches."

"Don't plan on hanging anybody," said Alvin.

"Not even murderers?" said Purity.

Alvin shrugged. "They get themselves hung no matter where they go."

"Once you have the gallows, you'll find new reasons to hang people from it."

"Why are you being so spiteful?" asked Verily. "New England hasn't added a capital crime in the two hundred years since it was founded. And some former capital crimes haven't led to the gallows in a century. You have no reason to think that a decent society will go mad with the power to kill."

"New England didn't need new reasons," said Purity, "because it had such a fine catchall. No matter what someone did, if you want him dead, he's a witch."

"I wouldn't know," said Verily.

"You said it yourself," said Purity. "Everyone has a knack. They hide it out of fear and call it humility. But if someone wants to kill a man, he only has to detect his knack and denounce him for it. So anyone can be killed at any time. Who needs new laws, when the old ones are so broad?"

"Did you become this cynical in the past few hours?" asked Verily. "Or have you always taken the lowest possible view of human life?"

"Human life is wicked to the core," said Purity, "and only the elect of God are lifted above human wickedness and caught up into the goodness of heaven. To expect wickedness from human beings is the best way I know of to avoid surprises. And when I am surprised, it's always pleasantly."

"Ask her the question and have done," said Alvin.

"And if I say I don't want to travel with you?" said Purity.

"Then we'll travel on without you," said Alvin.

"Doing me no harm?" asked Purity.

Verily Cooper laughed. "Even if we wanted to, Alvin wouldn't let us. When a bee stings him, he puts the stinger back in it, heals it up, and sends it on its way."

"Then my answer is no," said Purity. "People will be looking for me by now. If you want to be safe from inquiries, you'd best let me go and be about your business."

"No," said Arthur Stuart. "You got to come with us."

"And why should I?" asked Purity. "Because you spin a good tale?"

"I told you the truth and you know it," said Arthur.

"Yes," said Purity, softening. "You did believe every word you said. But it has no bearing on me. I have no part in what you're trying to do."

"Yes, you do!" cried Arthur Stuart. "Didn't you get the point of my story? Somebody's in charge of all this. Somebody gave Alvin the powers he's got. Somebody led his family to Horace Guester's roadhouse, so Little Peggy would be in place to watch over him. Why did my mother fly so near to that place, so I'd be there waiting when Alvin came back? And Mike Fink, and Verily Cooper—how did they get to meet up with him? Don't tell me it was chance cause I don't believe in it."

"Nor do I," said Purity.

"So whoever led us to Alvin, or him to us, that's who led you here today. You could have walked anywhere. We could have been anywhere on the river, bathing. But here we were, and here you came."

"I have no doubt that we were brought together," said Purity. "The question is, by whom?"

"I don't know as it's a who," said Alvin. "Arthur thinks God's in charge of all this, and I don't doubt but what God has his eye on the whole world, but that don't mean he's spending extra time looking out for me. I got a feeling that knacks get drawn together. And the power I was born with, it's right strong, and so it's like a magnet, it just naturally grabs hold on other strong people and links them up. It's not like good folks are the only ones as get drawn to me. Seems like I get more than my share of the other kind, too. Why would God send *them* to me?''

Arthur Stuart didn't seem to be swayed by Alvin's argument. Clearly they'd been down this road before. "God brings some, and the other one brings the others."

"They just come natural," said Alvin, "both kinds. Don't go guessing what God's doing, because them as tries to guess always seems to get it wrong."

"And how would you know they was wrong," said Arthur, "lessen you thought you had a scope on God's will!" He sounded triumphant, as if he had at last landed a blow on the body of Alvin's argument.

"Cause it works out so bad," said Alvin. "Look at this place. New England's got everything going for it. Good people, trying to serve God as best they can. And they do, mostly. But they figured that God wanted them to kill everybody as used a knack, even though they never found out how to tell if knacks came from God or the devil. They just called all knacks witchcraft and went off killing folks in the name of God. So even if they got all the rest of God's will just right, look what they done to Miss Purity here. Killed her folks and got her brought up in an orphanage. It don't take a scope on God's will to know New England ain't got it figured out yet."

"You sound like professors arguing over an obscure point of Latin grammar, when the passage itself is a forgery," said Purity. "Whether I was led to you by God or nature or Satan himself, it doesn't change my answer. I have no business with you. It's here that my destiny lies. Whatever I am and whatever happens to me, my story begins and ends with the . . . with New England."

"With the courts of New England," said Verily.

"So you say," said Purity.

"With the gallows of New England," Verily insisted.

"If God wills," said Purity.

"No," said Verily, "you'll meet the gallows only if *you* will it."

"On the contrary," said Purity. "Meeting you has been the most important lesson of my life. Until I met you, until I heard your story, I was sure my parents could not really have been witches and therefore a great injustice was committed. I didn't really believe that witches existed. But I have seen now that they do. You have powers far greater than God meant anyone but a prophet or apostle to have, Mr. Smith, and you have no qualms about using them. You are going about gathering disciples and planning to build a city. You are Nimrod, the mighty hunter against the Lord, and the city you mean to build is Babel. You want it to lift mankind above the flood and take men into heaven, where they will be as God, knowing all things. You are a servant of the devil, your powers are witchery, your plans are anathema, your beliefs are heresy, and if my parents were one-tenth as wicked as you, they deserved to die!''

They all stared at her in silence. Arthur Stuart had tears streaking his cheeks.

Finally Alvin spoke—to the others, not to her. "Best be on our way, boys," he said. "Arthur, you run and tell Audubon to dry off and get dressed."

"Yes, sir," said Arthur quietly, and he was gone.

"Aren't you even going to argue with me?" asked Purity.

Alvin looked quizzically at her for a moment, then walked away toward where Mike Fink had gone to stand watch. Only Verily Cooper remained.

"So you admit that what I said is true," said Purity.

Verily looked at her sadly. "What you said is false as hell," said Verily. "Alvin Maker is the best man I know in all the world, and there's no trace of evil in him. He's not always right, but he's never wrong, if you understand what I'm saying."

"That is just what I'd expect a demon to say of his master the devil."

"There," said Verily. "What you just said. That's why we're giving up on you."

"Because I dare to name the truth?"

"Because you've latched on to a story that can capture everything we say and do and turn it into a lie."

"Why would I do that?" asked Purity.

"Because if you don't believe these stupid lies about us, then you have to admit that they were wrong to kill your parents, and then you'd have to hate them, and they're the only people that you know. You'd be a woman without a country, and since you're already a woman without a family, you can't let go of them.''

"See how the devil twists my love for my country and tries to turn it against me?'' said Purity.

Verily sighed. "Miss Purity, I can only tell you this. Whatever you do in the next few hours and days, I expect you'll have plenty of chance to judge between Alvin Smith and the law of New England. Somewhere inside you there's a place where truth is truth and lies get shed like raindrops off oil. You look in that place and see which is acting like Christ.''

"Christ is just as well as merciful,'' said Purity. "Only the wicked claim that Christ is only forgiving. The righteous remember that he denounced the unrepented sin, and declared the truth that everlasting fire awaited those who refused to choose righteousness.''

"He also had sharp words for hypocrites and fools, as I recall,'' said Verily.

"Meaning that you think I'm a hypocrite?''

"On the contrary,'' said Verily. "I think you're a fool.''

She slapped his face.

As if she hadn't touched him, he went on in a mild tone of voice. "You've been made foolish by the harm that's been done to you, and by the fact that the wickedness of this place is so small compared to its goodness. But that doesn't mean it isn't real, and hasn't poisoned you, and won't kill you in the end.''

"God dwells in New England,'' said Purity.

"He visits here as he visits all places, and I dare say he finds much to be glad of in these farms and villages. A garden of the soul. But still aslither with snakes, like every other place.''

"If you plan to kill me,'' said Purity, "you'd better do it quick, because I'm going now to denounce you and send them after you.''

"Then be off,'' said Verily. "They'll either find us or they won't, depending on what Alvin decides. And if they do find us, keep this in mind: All he wants is for people to have a chance at happiness. Even you.''

"My happiness doesn't depend on a witch!''

"Does so," said Verily. "But up to now, the witches it depended on were dead."

Tears appeared in her eyes; her face reddened; she would have slapped him again except she remembered that it did no good. Instead she turned and ran from him into the woods, almost bumping into Alvin and Mike Fink, who were returning along the path. A moment later she was gone.

"I think you lost, Very," said Alvin. "Or was that your plan?"

"She's not at her best," said Verily. He looked from Mike to Arthur to Alvin. "Well, is it time for us to put on seven-league boots?"

Alvin grinned at him. "Wouldn't you rather we tied you to the mast as we sailed on past the siren?"

Verily was startled. "What do you mean by that?"

"I mean that I saw how you were looking at her. She struck something in you."

"Of course she did," said Verily. "She's been strangled by the need to hide her very considerable knack, and now she finds that her parents were killed for the same cause. She has to distinguish between herself and those who knowingly do witchcraft. She has to draw the line of virtue and stand on the right side of it without denying what she is and what she knows. I lived that life, except that my parents were fortunate enough to stay alive. I understand something of what she's going through."

"Inconvenient time for her to come to her crisis of faith, don't you think?" said Alvin.

"Don't make more of this than it is," said Verily. "As I told her, if she denounces us the authorities will either find us or not, depending on what *you* decide."

Mike snorted. "That's an easy one."

At that moment Arthur Stuart and a dripping, somewhat-dressed Audubon appeared. "She's gone," Arthur Stuart said.

"That is good, the way I am dress," said Audubon.

"She's gone to report us," said Mike Fink, "and here we are jawing."

"It's up to Alvin whether we run or wait," said Verily. "She might not denounce us."

"But then she might," said Mike. "And if she does, let's not be here.'' But Verily and Alvin were looking at each other, deciding some question that the others hadn't heard.

"Is there some reason," Alvin asked, "why I might choose to let them find us?"

Still Verily declined to answer.

"To save her," said Arthur Stuart.

Now they all looked at Arthur. He looked at Alvin, just as intently as Verily had the moment before. Alvin had the distinct impression that he was supposed to understand some unspoken explanation.

"How would it save her, for us to be caught?" asked Alvin.

"Because the way she's acting," said Arthur Stuart, "she's going to get herself killed. Unless we save her."

Mike Fink came between them. "Let me get this straight. You want *us* to get locked up and tried as witches so we can save *her*?"

"How would us getting locked up help her?" said Alvin.

"How many birds can I paint in jail?" asked Audubon.

"You wouldn't stay in jail long," said Verily. "Witch trials are notoriously quick."

"What is it about a woman that makes *her* life worth the lives of four men and a boy?" demanded Mike.

Verily laughed in exasperation. "What are you thinking, Mike? This is Alvin Smith. The Maker of the Golden Plow. How long do you suppose he'd let us wait in jail?"

"You really don't want to leave her behind, do you, Very?" said Alvin. "Or you neither, Arthur Stuart, is that right?"

"Sure is," said the boy.

"That's right," said Verily.

"Goodness gracious," said Mike sarcastically. "Is this love we're talking about?"

"Who's in love?" demanded Arthur.

"Verily Cooper's in love with Miss Purity," said Mike Fink.

"I don't think so," said Verily.

"He must be," said Mike, "because he's let her go off to denounce us to the authorities and he wants us to get arrested because he thinks that'll make her feel bad and she'll change her mind about us and she'll recant her testimony against us and then she'll decide to come along with us. Which is a fine plan, except for the part where we get hung and she kneels at the foot of the gallows weeping her poor little eyes out she feels so bad.''

Arthur Stuart looked at Verily, calculation in his eyes. ''You think we might change her mind about us by getting arrested?'' he asked.

''Mike is wrong, it's not pity I'm counting on,'' said Verily. ''It's fear.''

''Fear of what?'' asked Alvin.

''Fear of the working of the law. Right now she believes the law is just and therefore we and her parents deserve to die. She'll change her mind quick enough when she sees how witch trials go.''

''You've made a pretty long chain out of one link,'' said Mike.

''Give her a chance,'' said Arthur Stuart.

Alvin looked at Arthur, then at Verily. Who ever would have thought this man and this boy would be rivals in love? ''Might be worth a try,'' said Alvin.

''If they arrest me they'll take my paintings and destroy them,'' said Audubon.

''I'll keep you and your paintings safe,'' said Alvin.

''And if they kill you,'' said Audubon, ''what will happen to my paintings?''

''I won't care,'' said Alvin.

''But I will!''

''No you won't,'' said Arthur Stuart. ''Cause if Alvin gets killed, so will you.''

''That is my point!'' cried Audubon. ''Let us run away! This green-song that you speak of, for hiding in the forest while running very fast. Sing!''

''What I got in mind,'' said Alvin, ''is more like a saunter on the riverbank. And remember, all of you—confess to nothing. No witch-craft. No knacks. Don't even admit to being French, John James.''

''I ain't going to lie under oath,'' said Arthur Stuart.

''Don't lie, just refuse to answer,'' said Alvin.

''That's when they torture you,'' said Verily. ''When you refuse to say yes or no.''

''Well, they *hang* you when you say yes,'' said Alvin, ''and I ain't heard of them just letting you go if you deny it.''

''If you don't answer, you can die without ever going to trial.''

Alvin began to chuckle. "Well, now I get it. You *want* to go to trial. This ain't about Purity or being in love or any such thing. You want to take on the witch laws."

"Well *I* don't," said Mike Fink. "I sure don't have to answer under oath when someone asks me if I ever served Satan."

"It seems to me," said Alvin, "that if you want to have your day in court, Verily, you ought to do it as a lawyer, and not as a defendant."

"And you oughtn't to drag along folks as don't want to stand trial," said Mike.

"Not that any harm would come to any of us," said Alvin.

Audubon threw his arms heavenward. "Listen to him! Alvin has the . . . *hubris.* He think he can save everybody."

"I can," said Alvin. "That's just a fact."

"Then let's stay around and save *her,*" said Arthur Stuart. "We don't have to get arrested to do that."

"I want to do more than save her body from death," said Verily.

"Please don't tell us what more you want to do to her body," said Audubon.

Verily ignored him. "I want her to learn the truth about her parents and about herself. I want her to be proud of her knack. I want her to come join us in building the Crystal City."

"Those are all good things to want," said Alvin. "But just at this moment I have a keen memory of the months I spent in jail back in Hatrack River, and I got to say I don't wish even an hour in such a place for any of this company."

"Yes! The wisdom of Solomon!" cried Audubon.

"Which ain't to say I don't see your point, too, Very," said Alvin. "And as for you, Arthur Stuart, I can see as how a young man like you sees a damsel walking straight to the dragon's lair and he's plain got to draw his sword."

"What are you talking about?" asked Arthur.

"Saint George," said Alvin. "And the dragon."

"The boy will not let me to kill birds," said Audubon, "but *dragons.*"

Mike Fink looked puzzled. "Ain't no dragons around here."

"Fall in line behind me," said Alvin, "and say nothing, and touch nothing, and don't stray from the path I mark."

"So you'll leave her to their mercy," said Verily.

"I promise you, Very," said Alvin, "you'll get everything you want."

Verily nodded. Alvin looked at Arthur Stuart, wordlessly making him the same promise, and the boy also nodded.

They all lined up behind him on the riverbank. Alvin started off walking, then picked up his pace, jogging along, then loping, then flat-out running. At first the others worked hard at it, but then they began to hear a kind of music, not with instruments, not the kind you sing or dance to, but the sound of wind in leaves and birds singing, the chatter of squirrels and the buzz of insects, the high white sizzle of sunlight striking the dew on the leaves, the languid rush of water vapor distilling into the air. The sound of their footfalls merged with the music and the world around them turned into a blur of green, which contained every leaf, every tree, every bit of earth, and made them all one thing; and the runners were part of that one thing, and their running was part of the song, and the leaves parted to let them pass, and the air cooled them and the streams bore them over without their feet getting wet and instead of growing legsore or ribstitched they felt exhilarated, full of the life around them. They could run like that forever.

Then, moments later, the greensong began to fade. The trees narrowed to a strip of wood along the river. Cultivated fields held a muted music, low tones of thousands of identical lives. Buildings broke the song entirely, gaps of silence that were almost painful. They staggered, felt the pounding of their feet on the ground, which was hard now, and the branches snagged at them as they passed. They cantered, jogged, walked, and finally stopped. As one they turned away from the fields and buildings, away from the city of Boston with the tall masts of the ships in the harbor rising higher than the buildings, and faced upriver, to the place through which the song had carried them.

"Mon dieu," said Audubon. "I have flied on angel wings."

They stood in silence for a while longer. And then Arthur Stuart spoke.

"Where's Alvin?" he said.

Alvin wasn't there. Mike scowled at Verily Cooper. "Now look what you've done."

"Me?" said Verily.

"He sent us off and stayed behind to get arrested," said Mike. "I'm sworn to protect him and then you get him to do something like this."

"I didn't ask him to do this alone," said Verily.

Arthur Stuart started walking up the path, back into the woods.

"Where are you going?" asked Verily.

"Back to Cambridge," he said. "It can't be that far. The sun's hardly moved in the sky."

"It's too late to stop Alvin from doing this," said Mike.

Arthur looked back at him like he was crazy. "I know that," he said. "But he expects us to go back and help."

"How do you know this?" asked Audubon. "He tell you what he plan to do?"

"He told all of us," said Arthur. "He knows Verily wants to have a witch trial. So, Alvin's decided he'll be the witch. Verily gets to be the lawyer. And the rest of us have to be witnesses."

"But the girl will denounce us, too," said Audubon.

Verily nodded. "That's right," he said. "Yes, that's right. So the three of you, I want you to wait in the woods until I come fetch you."

"What's the plan?" asked Mike.

"I won't find that out till I talk to Alvin," said Verily. "But remember this: The only charge that matters in a witch trial is, Did Satan rule you? So that's the only question you answer. Nothing about knacks or hidden powers. Just about Satan. You never saw him, you never talked to him or any demons, he never gave you anything. Can you all swear to that truly?"

They all laughed and agreed they could.

"So when it's time to testify, that's the only question you answer. For the rest, you just look stupid."

"What about me?" said Audubon. "I was baptized Catholic."

"You can talk about that, too," said Verily. "You'll see. If I'm half the lawyer I trained to be, none of this will ever come to trial." He joined Arthur on the path. "Come along. It's legal work now. And if everything comes out right, we'll have Alvin free and Miss Purity as a traveling companion."

"I don't want to travel with her!" said Mike. "Look at the trouble she's already caused us!"

"Trouble?" said Verily. "I've been stupefied with boredom in New

England. Everything's so peaceful here. Everything runs smoothly, most disputes are settled peacefully, neighbors pretty much get along, people are happy an extraordinary proportion of the time. I'm a lawyer, for heaven's sake! I was about to lose my mind!''

At first Reverend Study was dismissive. "I can understand your being fascinated with the idea of witches, but it's from the past, my dear Purity.''

"They bragged about it," said Purity. "I didn't ask them.''

"That's just it, you see," said the minister. "They're not from New England, and those from outside tend to mock our stricter adherence to scripture. They were having fun with you.''

"They were not," said Purity. "And if you refuse to help me, I'll go straight to the tithingmen myself.''

"No no," said Study. "You mustn't do that.''

"Why not? A woman's testimony is valid in court. Even an orphan, I think!''

"It's not a matter of—Purity, do you realize the trouble you are heading into with these wild charges?''

"They're not wild. And I know what you're trying so hard not to say—that my parents were hanged as witches.''

"What!" said Study. "Who told you such a thing! Who is spreading such slanders!''

"Are you saying it's not so?''

"I have no idea, but I can't imagine it's true. There hasn't been a witch trial in this part of New England for . . . for much longer than you've been alive.''

"But the trial wasn't here," said Purity. "It was in Netticut.''

"Well, that's a bit of a reach, don't you think? Why Netticut?''

"Reverend Study, the longer we talk, the farther these men will flee. And one of them is a papist, a Frenchman, brought here under false pretenses. They've been pretending he was mute.''

Reverend Study sighed.

"I can see you have no respect for me, just like the others," said Purity.

"Is that what this is about? Trying to earn respect?''

"No, it's not!''

"Because this is not the way to do it. I remember the Salem trials. Well, not that I remember them myself, I wasn't even here, but the shame of that city still endures. So many killed on the testimony of a group of hysterical girls. The girls were left unpunished, you know. They lived out their lives, however their consciences let them do it, because it was impossible for an earthly judge to know which charges were malicious and which were the product of self-delusion and mob mentality.''

"I am neither a group nor hysterical.''

"But such charges do provoke a certain skepticism.''

"That's nonsense, Reverend Study. People believe in witchcraft. Everyone does. They check for it at the borders! They preach—no, *you* preach against it in meetings!''

"It's all so confusing. What I preach about is the attempt to use hidden powers. Even if they exist, they should not be used to gain advantage over one's neighbor, or even to gain good fame among one's friends. But the formal charge of witchcraft, that requires allegations of contact with Satan, of maleficence. Depending on who the interrogators are, there may be questions about witches' sabbaths, there will be naming of names. These things get out of hand.''

"Of course they'll lie about Satan. They never said anything about Satan to me.''

"There. It's not witchcraft, you see?''

"But isn't that just what we expect?'' said Purity. "Don't we *expect* a witch to lie?''

"That's what happened at Salem!'' cried Study. "They started interpreting denials as lies, as attempts to cover up Satan's penetration of the community. But later it was discovered, it was realized, that there had never been any witchcraft at all, and that the confessions they got were all motivated by a selfish desire to save one's own life, while the only ones hanged were those who refused to lie.''

"Are you saying that you believe the Bible is wrong when it says we shall not suffer a witch to live?''

"No, no, of course if you actually find a witch, then you must . . . act, but—''

"I have found a witch, Reverend Study. Please summon the tithing-men to help me obey the Lord's injunction in the Bible.''

Sick at heart, Reverend Study rose to his feet. "You leave me no choice."

"As they left *me* no choice."

Study stopped at the door and spoke without facing her. "Do you not understand that many long-pent resentments can be released by this sort of thing?"

"These men are intruders here. What resentments can anyone have against them? The judges will be honest. My testimony will be honest."

Study leaned his head into the doorjamb and almost whispered his answer. "There *have* been rumors. About you."

Purity felt a thrill of fear and joy run through her body, making her tremble for a moment. Her guess was right. Her parents *did* die for witchcraft, just as she figured. "All the more reason, then, for me to prove myself loyal to the scripture and an enemy to Satan."

"Fire burns all hands that touch it."

"I serve God, sir. Do you?"

"Sometimes God is best served by obeying his more merciful statements. Judge not lest ye be judged. Think of that before you point a finger." Then he was gone.

Purity waited alone in Reverend Study's office. His library, really, it was so stacked and shelved with books. How did he get so many? Had he really read them all? Purity had never had an opportunity to study the titles. Sets of pious literature, of course. Collections of noted sermons. Scriptural commentary. Law books? Interesting—had he thought of studying law at some time? No, it was ecclesiastical law. With several books on the prosecution of witches, the investigation of witches, the purification of witches. Reverend Study might pretend to have no concern with such matters, but he *owned* these books, which meant that at some time he must have planned to refer to them. He had not been "here" during the witch trials in Salem, which were the last held in eastern Massachusetts. That could mean he hadn't been born yet—how long ago were they?—at least a century, perhaps half again that long. But he had been involved in witch trials somewhere. Yes, he knew and cared very much about these things.

She held the book *On the Investigation of Witchcraft, Wizardry, and Other Satanic Practices* but could not bring herself to open it. She heard that they used to torture the accused. But that must not be the way of it today. The laws were strict that a person could not be forced to incriminate himself. Ever since the United States were formed from the middle colonies and put that rule into their Bill of Rights, the same principle had been given force of law in New England as well. There would be no torture.

The book fell open in her hands. Could she help it? It fell open to a particular place which had been well-thumbed and much underlined. How to put the question to a witch who is with child.

Was my mother pregnant with me when she was arrested and tried?

The child is innocent before the law, being unborn and thus untouched by original sin. Original sin inheres to the child only upon birth, and therefore to take any action which might harm the unborn infant would be like punishing Adam and Eve in the garden before the fall: an injustice and an affront to God.

I gave my mother a little longer life. I saved her by being—yes, my very name—by being pure, unstained, untouched by original sin. How many weeks, how many months did I give to her?

Or did she think of this as torture, too? Had my father already been hanged as she languished in prison, awaiting her own trial as she grieved for him and for the child in her womb, doomed to be an orphan? Would she rather have died? Did she wish she didn't have a child?

She should have thought of that before she partook of forbidden practices. "Knacks" they called them in the wicked parts of the land. God-given gifts, that journeyman blacksmith called them, as he attempted to deceive her. But the true nature of Satan's false gifts would soon come clear. The "knacks" these witches use, they come from Satan. And because I know I have never had truck with Satan, then the small talents I have can't possibly be a hidden power. I'm just observant, that's all. I don't turn iron into a golden plow, like the one Arthur Stuart told about—a plow that dances around because it's possessed by evil spirits like the Gadarene swine.

She trembled with uncontainable excitement. Fear is what it felt like, though she had nothing to fear. It also felt like relief, like she was receiving something long waited for. Then she realized why: Her mother named her Purity to help her keep herself unstained by sin. Today she had faced the temptation of Satan in the form of that wandering blacksmith and his troupe of lesser witches, and for a moment she felt such terrible desires. The barrister was so attractive to her, that half-Black imp was so endearing, and Alvin himself now seemed sufficiently modest and self-effacing, and his dream of the City of God so real and desirable, that she longed to join with them.

That had to be how her mother was seduced by the devil! Not understanding, not being warned, she fell into the trap. Perhaps it was Purity's father who seduced her mother, just the way Verily Cooper had been calling to Purity on the riverbank today, evoking strange feelings and longings and whispering inside her mind that this was love. It had to be the devil making her think such thoughts. Married to a witch! Trapped just as her mother had been! Oh my Father which art in heaven, I thank thee for saving me! I am a sinner like all others, but oh, if thou hast chosen me to be among thy elect, I shall praise thy name forever!

She heard the hurried footsteps on the stairs. She closed the book and replaced it on the shelf. When the door opened, Reverend Study and the tithingmen found her sitting on a side chair, her eyes closed, her hands clasped in her lap, the classic pose of the soul who refused to be touched by the evils of the world.

Reverend Study declined to go with them to catch the witches. Well, too bad for him, Purity thought. Let others of stronger heart do what must be done.

Horses would do little good on the river road. One of the tithingmen, Ezekial Shoemaker, took a group of grim-looking men on horseback to try to block escape downriver, while the other, Hiram Peaseman, kept his men with Purity as they walked the path that the witches must have taken.

"Why are you so certain they went downriver?" asked Peaseman, a stern-looking man who, until now, had always made Purity somewhat afraid.

"They said they were bound for Boston no matter what I chose to do."

"If they're witches, why wouldn't they lie to throw us off?"

"Because at the time," she said, "they thought to persuade me to join them."

"Still don't mean they weren't lying," said Peaseman.

"They told many a lie, I assure you," said Purity, "but they spoke the truth when they said they were bound for Boston."

Peaseman fixed his icy gaze upon her. "How do you know that wasn't a lie as well?"

For a moment Purity felt the old fear come over her. Had she revealed her hidden power?

And then her new confidence returned. It wasn't a hidden power. "I'm very observant," she said. "When people lie, they show it by little things."

"And you're never wrong?" asked Peaseman.

They had stopped walking now, and the other men were also gathered around her.

She shook her head.

"Only God is perfect, miss," said one of the other men.

"Of course you're right," said Purity. "And it would be pride in me to say I was never wrong. What I meant was that if I've been wrong I didn't know it."

"So they might have lied," said Peaseman, "only they did a better job than others."

Purity grew impatient. "Are you really going to stand here, letting the witches get away, all because you don't know whether to believe me or not about which way they were going to walk? If you don't believe me, then you might as well doubt everything I said and go back home!"

They shuffled their feet a little, some of them, and none spoke for a moment, until Peaseman closed his eyes and spoke what was on their minds. "If they be witches, miss, we fear they lay a trap for us, into which you lead us, all unwitting."

"Have you no faith in the power of Christ to protect you?" asked Purity. "I have no fear of such as they. Satan promises terrible power to his minions, but then he betrays them every time. Follow me if you dare." She strode forth boldly on the path, and soon heard their footsteps behind her. In moments they were all around her, then ahead of her, leading the way.

That's why she was last to see why they were stopping not fifty rods along the river path. There sat Alvin Smith on a fallen tree, leaning up against a living one, his hands clasped behind his head. He grinned at her when she emerged from the crowd. "Why, Mistress Purity, you didn't need to come and show me the road to Boston, or to trouble these men to help me on my way.''

"He's the chief witch," said Purity. "His name is Alvin Smith. His companions must be nearby."

Alvin looked around. "Companions?" He looked back at her, seeming to be puzzled. "Are you seeing things?" He asked the men: "Does this girl see things what ain't there?"

"Don't be deceived," said Purity. "They're hereabouts."

"Am I remembering aright, or did she just call me a witch a minute ago?" asked Alvin.

"She did, sir," said Peaseman. "And as one of the tithingmen of Cambridge village, it's my duty to invite you back to town for questioning."

"I'll answer any questions you have for me," said Alvin. "But I don't see why I should go back instead of furthering my journey."

"I'm not the law, sir," said Peaseman. "Not the judge anyway. I'm afraid we need to bring you one way or another."

"Well, let's choose the one way and not the other," said Alvin. "On my own two feet, unbound, in free acceptance of your hospitable invitation."

A faint smile touched Peaseman's lips. "Yes, that's the way we prefer, sir. But you'll forgive us if we have to bind you so you can't get away."

"But I give you my word," said Alvin.

"Forgive us, sir," said Peaseman. "If you're acquitted, you'll have my apology. But we have to wonder if the accusation be true, and if it be, then bound is safer for all, don't you think?"

In answer, Alvin held his hands forward, offering to be bound. Peaseman was not to be tricked, however, and tied Alvin's hands behind his back.

"That's not a good rope," said Alvin.

"It's a good one I bet," said Peaseman.

"No, it won't hold a knot," said Alvin. "Look." He shook his hands lightly and the knot slipped right off the rope.

Peaseman looked dumbly at the rope, which now dangled limp from his hand. "That was a good knot."

"A good knot on a bad rope is no better than a bad knot," said Alvin. "I think it was old Ben Franklin what said that first. In *Poor Richard.*"

Peaseman's face went a little darker. "You'll do us the favor of not quoting that wizard's words."

"He wasn't no wizard," said Alvin. "He was a patriot. And even if he were as wicked as . . . as the pope, the words are still true."

"Hold still," said Peaseman. He tied the knot again, tighter, and then redoubled it.

"I'll try to hold my hands still so it don't slip off," said Alvin.

"He's toying with you," said Purity. "Don't you see this is his hidden power? Don't you know the devil when you see him?"

Peaseman glared at her. "I see a man and a rope that don't hold a knot. Who ever heard of the devil giving a man the power to untie knots? If that were so, how would ever a witch be hung?"

"He's mocking you," Purity insisted.

"Miss, I don't know how I offended you," said Alvin. "But it's a hard enough thing for a traveler to be named for a witch, without being accused of causing everything that happens. If one of these men loses his footing and falls into the river, will that be my doing? If someone's cow sickens somewhere in the neighborhood, will it be blamed on me?"

"You hear his curses?" said Purity. "You'd best all look to your cattle, and step careful all the way home."

The men looked from one to another. The rope slipped off Alvin's hands and fell onto the ground. Peaseman picked it up; the knot had already loosened visibly.

"I give you my word not to flee," said Alvin. "How would I get away from so many men even if I had a mind to? Running would do me no good."

"Then why did your companions flee?" demanded Purity.

Alvin looked at the men with consternation. "I got no one with me, I hope you can all see that."

Purity grew angry. "You had them, four of them, three men and a half-Black boy who you saved from slavery by changing his nature, and another one a French painter who's a papist pretending to be mute, and a riverman who tried to kill you and you used your powers to take a tattooed hex right off his skin, and the last was an English barrister."

"Excuse me, miss, but don't that sound more like a dream than an actual group of folks what might be traveling together? How often do you see barristers from England with country boys like me?"

"You killed a man with your knack! Don't deny it!" cried Purity, furious, near tears at his obvious lies.

Alvin looked stricken. "Is it murder I'm charged with now?" He looked at the men again, showing fear now. "Who am I supposed to have killed? I hope I'll have a fair trial, and you have some witnesses if I'm to stand for murder."

"No one's been murdered here," said Peaseman. "Miss Purity, I'll thank you to keep silent now and let the law take this man."

"But he's lying, can't you see?" she said.

"The court can decide the truth."

"What about the plow? The Black boy told how this man made a golden plow that he carries with him always, but doesn't show to anyone, because it's alive and his very companions saw it move of itself. If that's not proof of Satanic power, what is?"

Peaseman sighed. "Sir, do you have a plow like the one she describes?"

"You can search my sack," Alvin answered. "In fact, I'd take it kindly if someone would carry it along, as it has my hammer and tongs, which is to say it holds my livelihood as a journeyman smith. It's yonder on the far side of the fallen maple."

One of the men went and hefted the bag.

"Open it!" cried Purity. "That's the one the plow was in."

"Ain't no plow in that sack, gold or iron or bronze or tin," said Alvin.

"He's right," said the man with the sack. "Just hammer and tongs. And a loaf of dry bread."

"Takes an hour of soaking before it can be et," said Alvin. "Sometimes I think my tongs might soften up faster than that old hardtack."

The men laughed a little.

"And so the devil deceives you bit by bit," said Purity.

"Let's have no more of that talk," said Peaseman. "We know you accuse him, so there's no need to belabor it. There's no plow in his sack and if he walks along peaceful, there's no need to tie him."

"And thus he leadeth them carefully down to hell," said Purity.

Peaseman showed wrath for the first time, walking boldly to her and looking down at her from his looming height. "I say enough talk from you, miss, while we lead the prisoner back to Cambridge. Not one of us likes to hear you saying *we* are deceived by Satan."

Purity wanted to open her mouth and berate all the men for letting this slick-talking "country bumpkin" win them over despite her having named him for a servant of hell. But she finally realized that she could not possibly persuade them, for Alvin would simply continue to act innocent and calm, making her look crazier and crazier the angrier she got.

"I'll stay and search for the plow," she said.

"No, miss, I'd be glad if you'd come along with us now," said Peaseman.

"Someone needs to look for it," she said. "His confederates are no doubt skulking nearby, waiting to retrieve it."

"All the more reason that I won't let you stay behind alone," said Peaseman. "Come along now, miss. I speak by the authority of the village now, and not just by courteous request."

This had an ominous ring to it. "Are you arresting *me*?" she asked, incredulous.

Peaseman rolled his eyes. "Miss, all I'm doing is asking you to let me do my work in the manner the law says I should. By law and common sense I can't leave you here exposed to danger, and with a prisoner who can't be tied I need to keep these men with me." Peaseman looked to two of his men. "Give the young lady your arms, gentlemen."

With exaggerated courtesy, two of the men held their arms to her. Purity realized that she had little choice now. "I'll walk of myself, please, and I'll hold my tongue."

Peaseman shook his head. "That was what I asked many minutes and several long speeches ago. Now I ask you to take their arms and argue no further, or the next step will not be so liberal."

She hooked her hands through the crooks of their elbows and miserably walked along in silence, while Alvin talked cheerily about the weather, walking freely ahead of her on the path. The men laughed several times at his wit and his stories, and with every step she tasted the bitterness of gall. Am I the only one who knows the devil wears a friendly face? Am I the only one who sees through this witch?

⚔ 8 ⚔

Basket of Souls

"WHAT IS IT that you think you're looking for?" asked Honoré. They had spent the heat of the day on the docks and were dripping with sweat. It was getting on toward evening without a sign of relief from the heat.

"Souls," said Calvin. "In particular, the theft of souls."

They stood in the scant shade of a stack of empty crates, watching as a newly arrived ship was moored to the dock. Honoré sounded testy. "*If* the transaction I saw on the docks has something to do with missing heartfires—which are *not* souls as the priests describe them—then it was not theft at all. The dolls were freely given."

"Sometimes theft doesn't look like theft. What if they think they're lending them, but they can't get them back? What about that?"

"And what if you are getting us in the path of something dangerous? Did you think of *that*?"

Calvin grinned. "We can't get hurt."

"That statement is so obviously false that it is not worth answering," said Honoré.

"I don't think you understand what I can do," said Calvin.

A gangplank was run up from the dock to a gap in the ship's gunwale.

"These are a filthy-looking crew, don't you think? Portuguese, perhaps?"

"If I decide you and I aren't going to get hurt, we won't," said Calvin.

"Oh, so you can read minds like your sister-in-law?"

"Don't have to read minds when you can melt the knife right out of a man's hand."

"But Monsieur le Genius, not all knives are seen in advance."

"I see 'em."

"Nothing ever surprises you?"

Before Calvin could get farther than the first sound of the word *nothing*, Honoré slapped him on the back of the head. Calvin staggered forward and whirled around, holding his neck. "What the hell do you think that proved!"

"It proved that you *can* be harmed."

"No, it proved you can't be trusted."

"You see my point?" said Honoré. "It is when you feel safe that you are most vulnerable. And since you are stupid enough to feel safe all the time, then you are vulnerable all the time."

Calvin's eyes became narrow slits. "I didn't feel safe all the time. I felt safe with *you*."

"But lately we have been together all the time." Honoré grinned again. "You *are* safe from me. I am not the proud owner of any useful knack and I carry no weapon and I am too busy studying humanity to bother harming any individual human. But being safe *from* me does not mean you are safe *with* me."

"Don't lecture me, you French fart."

"You praise me too much. Garlic, wine, onion soup, rich cheese, these combine to make the fart française the best of all possible farts. Voltaire said so."

Calvin didn't laugh. "Look," he said. "Look at that slave. Got nothing to do."

"You have a sharp eye. He is waiting."

"Is he your man?"

"I observe what men *do*. I do not pretend to be able to tell whether two Black men, one seen from behind, the other from the face, both from a distance, and their clothes identical to the costume of half the slaves in Camelot, are in fact the same man.''

''You saying it's him?''

Honoré sighed. ''I say I cannot tell.''

''Then just say it. Don't get into those damned fancy orations.''

Honoré ignored him. Staggering and squinting, their backs bent, their eyes searching, the first Blacks were appearing on the deck. ''It *is* a slave ship.''

''Well we knew that,'' said Calvin.

''We 'knew' it about three other ships today that had no slaves aboard.''

''We knew this was a slave ship because look at the White men on the deck with padded sticks. They wouldn't need those to load crates.''

''If only I were as clever as you,'' said Honoré.

The Black they had been looking at before, who might or might not be the one Honoré had seen taking puppets, came forward with two buckets of water and a basket. His head down, so as not to look any of the White dockworkers in the eye, he said something to the dock foreman, who waved him over to the foot of the gangplank.

''No, you dumb buck!'' The foreman's voice carried clear over to where Calvin and Honoré were waiting. ''Wait back there! If you start backing them up on the gangplank then they crowd each other right off into the water! Stupid, stupid, stupid.'' By the time he was through with his list of stupids, the Black man with the buckets had bowed and ducked his head long enough to get to the indicated waiting place.

''He knew,'' said Honoré.

''What did he know?''

''He knew where to stand,'' said Honoré. ''He was already walking there before the man pointed.''

''Why would he get the foreman angry?''

''He got the foreman to think he was stupid,'' said Honoré.

''The foreman started out thinking he was stupid. They think *all* Black people are stupid.''

''Do they?'' said Honoré. ''They think some are more stupid than others.''

The first slaves, hobbled and joined by ankle chains, staggered and clanked down the gangplank, then headed straight for the water. There was a great deal of spilling and quiet cursing from the waterboy. Calvin used his doodlebug to get a closer view. Sure enough, each slave was handing over some small item, made of scraps of cloth and splinters of wood and bits of iron.

"He's our man," said Calvin. "But what made you think those were dolls they were handing over?" asked Calvin.

"I got a good look at only one. It was larger than the others. It was a doll."

"Well the others aren't."

"But they are something, am I right?"

"Oh, they're something all right. Wish I could ask them what it is. How they get powers into those things."

"What *are* they, if they aren't dolls?"

"They're nothing. I mean they don't look like anything. Knotted cloth, strings, threads, iron, wood, bits of this and that. No two alike."

"Ah, for the knack of your brother's wife."

"We'll find out soon enough."

"But is it not ironic that we spend all day watching and waiting, and now that we have found this man, we still have no idea what he's doing, but *she* already knows?"

"What makes you think she knows anything?" demanded Calvin.

"Because she can see into that man's heartfire. She has watched us all day, and the moment we saw *him,* she could hop over and look inside him and know it all."

"Damn," said Calvin, looking at Honoré with annoyance. "Don't go telling me you can *feel* when she's looking at you?"

"I didn't have to *feel* anything," said Honoré. "I knew she would because she was curious. She would see in our heartfires that we were going to search for this man, so she would watch us. Obvious."

"To you."

"Of course to me. I am the world's leading authority on the behavior of human beings."

"In your opinion."

"But you see, I am the kind of man who always thinks he is the best in the world at whatever he does. So are you. It is one of the ways we are alike."

Calvin grinned. "Damn right."

"The difference between us is that I am correct in that opinion."

Calvin's eyes squinted again. "Someday I'm not going to pretend I think you're joking when you say things like that."

"What will you do to punish me, make me wake up under a hedge with a terrible headache and my clothing covered with urine?"

The women were coming down now, naked to the waist and roped, not chained together, though the ropes had chafed their wrists and ankles enough to draw blood.

"Your brother's wife already knows the name of this bringer of water, and where he lives, and what he had for breakfast," said Honoré.

"Yeah, well, we'll know soon enough."

"Do you think he won't notice two White men following him?"

Calvin grinned wickedly. "Like I said, I can do everything that needs doing. I can follow him without him seeing us or knowing he was followed."

"Using your doodoobug?"

"Doodlebug."

"But you do not know all the hidden powers this Black man might have. How do you know he won't catch your doodlebug and hold it captive?"

Calvin started to scoff at this idea, but then grew solemn. "You know, I'd be a fool to think he's not dangerous just cause he acts dumb around the foreman."

"You are learning to be suspicious! I am proud of you!"

"But my doodlebug doesn't have to ride inside him or anything like that."

"Good," said Honoré. But he could see that Calvin was worried now.

Every single one of the newly arrived slaves had something to give the man. The women were not as trusting as the men. They didn't have them in their hands or the scant clothing they wore—they spat these things from their mouths into the dipper. "Some of them have two," said Calvin. "Two thingamajigs." When there was something in the dipper, the waterboy always put it into the right-hand bucket. He was building up quite a collection in there.

Last in line were a dozen or so good-sized children, looking far more terrified and weak than the adults. None of them had anything for the waterboy.

"The women who had two," said Honoré.

"Yes," said Calvin. "For the children."

In the midst of serving them, the waterboy clumsily knocked over the right-hand bucket, spilling water over the hot boards of the dock. He served the rest of the children from the other one. When the last was served, they saw why he had spilled the important pail, for one of the sailors snatched up the bucket that still had water and dashed it onto the back of the last child. This was uproariously funny to the White stevedores. While they laughed, the waterboy knelt, scooped everything out of the other bucket, and tucked it into the small basket he carried.

He wasn't home free, though. The foreman stopped him just as he started away from the dock. "What you got in *that*?" he demanded, pointing at the basket.

"I don't know what my master put there," said the waterboy.

"I know one thing he better put there," said the foreman.

The two men looked at each other in grim silence for a long time, until finally the waterboy grinned and rolled his eyes and reached into the basket. "I so stupid, boss, I so stupid, I plumb forget." He took out a coin and offered it to the foreman.

"Where's the rest?" asked the foreman.

"That all he give me," said the waterboy.

"Come on, Denmark," said the foreman.

"Ah," whispered Honoré. "We have learned his name."

"Better be his name," said Calvin. "He sure as hell ain't no Scandinavian."

"Tell you what," said the foreman. "I'll tell him you give me one penny and see what he says."

"But I give you a shilling," said Denmark.

"You think he'll believe that, if I tell him otherwise?"

"You get me a whipping, that don't get you no more money," said Denmark.

"Get the hell off my dock," said the foreman.

"You a kind man, boss," said Denmark, bowing and nodding as he backed away. Then he turned his back and picked up the buckets again, but before he could stand up the foreman planted a foot on his backside and sent him sprawling on the dock. The stevedores and sailors laughed. But the slaves lined up for inspection by the customs officers, they didn't laugh. And Denmark himself, when he got up from the dock his face didn't show much amusement. But Calvin and Honoré could see how he composed himself, putting on a silly grin before he turned around. "You a funny man, boss," said Denmark. "You always make me laugh."

With exaggerated care, Denmark picked up the buckets without turning his back to the foreman. And he made a show of stopping and looking behind him a couple of times to make sure no one had snuck up to kick him again. His clowning kept the White man laughing even after he was gone.

Through it all, the newly arrived slaves didn't take their eyes off him.

"He is showing them how to survive here," said Honoré.

"You mean get a White man mad? That's smart."

"He is not a stupid man," said Honoré. "He is a clever man. He shows the others that they must act stupid and make the White man *laugh*. They must make the White man feel amusement and contempt, for this will keep Whites from feeling fear and anger."

"Probably," said Calvin. "Or maybe he just gets his butt kicked now and then."

"No," said Honoré. "I tell you I am the authority on human nature. He does this on purpose. After all, he is the one who gathers up their souls."

"I thought you said these weren't their souls at all."

"I changed my mind," said Honoré. "Look at them. The soul is missing now."

They looked at the Blacks in their chains and ropes, while the customs inspectors prodded them, stripped them, checked their body orifices, as if they were animals. They bore it easily. The looks of fear that they had worn as they emerged into sunlight were gone now. Gone also was the intensity with which they had gazed after Denmark as he carried away their tokens, or whatever they were. They really did seem like animals now.

"They been emptied, all right," said Calvin. "They all had heartfires getting off the boat, strong ones, but now they're all slacked back like a fire settled down to coals."

"They knew," said Honoré. "The were ready before they got off the boat. How did they know?"

"Maybe that's one of the things Margaret can tell us later," said Calvin.

"If she ever speaks to us again," said Honoré.

"She'll speak to us," said Calvin. "She's a nice person. So she'll start feeling guilty about sticking us for the price of the meal last night."

"They knew," said Honoré. "And they all consented. They gave away their souls into his hands."

"What I want to know," said Calvin, "is where he keeps them and what he does with them."

"Then we must go to your sister-in-law and ask her, since you are certain she will speak to us."

Calvin glared at him. "I'm already following him. He can't see my bug."

"Or he does not *show* you that he sees," said Honoré.

"I been doing this longer than you have. I *know*."

"Then why are you trembling?" said Honoré.

Calvin whirled on him, backing him against the crates. "Because I'm barely stopping myself from making your heart . . . stop . . . beating."

Honoré looked surprised. "Did you lose your sense of humor under the hedge?"

Calvin backed away, only slightly mollified. "One thing you ain't is funny," said Calvin.

"But if I practice, perhaps I will *become* funny."

"*I'm* the funny one," said Calvin. He backed off, leaving Honoré room to stand without pressing his body against the crates. "Or did *you* lose *your* sense of humor under the hedge?"

"We are both funny fellows," said Honoré. "Let's follow the man with a basket of souls. I have to know what he does with them."

"He's going through a door."

"Where?"

"In Blacktown," said Calvin. "There's junk hanging all over the place. Only one other heartfire in the house." He whistled. "That's *bright*."

"What's bright?" asked Honoré.

Calvin didn't answer.

Honoré leaned closer to him. "It's not fair not to tell me."

Calvin looked at him stupidly. "Tell you what?"

Margaret sat at her writing table, composing her daily letter to Alvin. She never mailed them. She could have, since she always knew where he was and where he was going. But why make him find post offices in every town he visited? Better to wait until the last hours before sundown. Whatever he was doing, he'd pause and let his thoughts turn to her. More to the point, he would send out his doodlebug to watch her. He could not read her thoughts, but he could see how her arms moved, her fingers; he could find the pen, the paper. She dipped it into ink only so that she could look back and see what she had written. She knew that he could see the words she formed on paper as clearly as if he were looking over her shoulder. She would ask questions; when they were half-formed, she would find the answer in his memory.

It was a lopsided arrangement, she knew. She could see his inmost thought, even the feelings he was scarcely aware of himself. She could see his choices unfold before him, could see them narrow again as he chose. He had no secrets from her. She, on the other hand, could keep anything secret that she chose, except for the condition of her body. He could reassure her that the baby was doing well; he could worry about her working too hard. But her thoughts remained closed to him. It hardly seemed fair.

And yet Alvin didn't mind—honestly didn't mind at all, never even seemed to notice. She knew there were several reasons for this. First, Alvin was an open fellow, not given to keeping secrets. He could keep them, of course, but once he trusted someone, he told the whole story, leaving nothing out, whether it reflected badly on him or not. Sometimes it sounded to others like boasting, when the things he had done were quite remarkable. But it was neither boasting nor confession. He simply reported what was in his memory. So it was no burden to him to have her see into his heartfire so readily.

A second reason for his lack of resentment, however, troubled her: He simply didn't care. He didn't mind that she knew his secrets, and he also didn't mind that he didn't know hers. He might be more inquisitive! Did this mean he didn't love her? Did it betray some fundamental selfishness? No, Alvin was generous of spirit. He simply wasn't all that curious about the minutiae of her thoughts. He was content to know what she told him. He trusted her. That's what it was, trust, not a lack of love.

The third reason, and probably the most important, was also the least satisfying. Alvin accepted everything about Margaret as a given, as part of the natural world around him. Though he didn't learn of it till later, she had watched over him through his entire childhood and saved his life many times. She had taught him, disguised as an older spinster schoolmarm. As the sun had shone on him every day, so had her care for him. He took her for granted. Having her inside his mind was as natural as breathing.

I am not even the weather in his life. I am more like the climate. No, more like the calendar. There are holidays, but the rest of the time he loses track, knowing the days will pass one by one whatever he names them.

Mustn't think that way. Write.

Dearest Alvin, I miss you now more than ever. Calvin is such an unpleasant boy, the opposite of you, and yet when I hear his voice it reminds me of yours.

Only the letters were not really written out so nicely. As soon as she saw that he understood, she would cease writing a word and skip ahead. The letter really began more like this: DA, I miss now mor. C is such an unpl boy, the opp of y&yet wh I hear hi voi it rem me of yo.

It was hard to imagine anyone else making sense of these scraps of words, scrawled in a child's printed hand instead of Margaret's elegant script, since printing was easier for Alvin to detect from a distance.

She kept writing: I think you're a fool to stay in that jail a single night. Walk out of it, gather up your companions, and come home. I don't much care for Mistress Purity. She has some good futures but they're not likely, and there's great harm possible, too, if you stay and win her away from New England.

His question: So it can be done?

Yes but . . .

Does she hang if we don't take her?

Margaret knew that a truthful answer would leave Alvin no choice but to stay.

Death isn't the worst thing in the world, she wrote. We're all going to do it, and if she's hanged as a witch it has a very good chance of leading to the repeal of the death penalty for witchery, and a much higher standard for conviction. So her death does much good.

In Alvin's mind she saw the immediate answer but she had known it already, known it without looking, for it was in his character: Let's try to achieve that same end without letting them dangle her.

By telling him the truth she had guaranteed that he would linger in that jail.

She wrote: Wasn't last year's imprisonment and trial enough of that for one lifetime?

He ignored her, and framed a question in his mind: Calvin? What does he want?

To be you, she wrote. Or, failing that, to destroy everything you ever accomplish. He seduced a fine lady by giving her irresistible lust. Can you do that?

His reply: Never thought of that. Want me to?

No!!!! Not while you're not here in the flesh, you torturer.

I'm going to be tortured.

They're just going to run you. You'll enjoy the exercise.

The conversation would have gone on for a while, but there came an urgent knock at her door.

Someone knocking, she wrote.

Then she looked for heartfires just outside her door and found one. Fishy.

"Come in?"

"Two White man downstairs a-see you, ma'am."

Visitors, she wrote.

She looked for heartfires downstairs, but found only one man there to visit her.

Honoré de Balzac, she wrote. Calvin's partner in debauch. Must go down. Tomorrow?

And his answer: Tomorrow. Always. I love you.

Feeling a lump in her throat, Margaret folded up the paper and put it away. There were still many inches on the page to write more letters to Alvin.

Downstairs, Balzac bounded up from his chair. He was as jumpy as a frog on a frying pan.

"Monsieur Balzac," Margaret began.

"You must to help me with Calvin," said Balzac, his excellent English collapsing just a little. "Where is he?"

"I don't know," said Margaret. "He's not here, if that's what you mean."

"But he is here, Madame. He is here but he is not here. Look!"

When she looked where he pointed, she was surprised to see that Calvin was indeed there, sitting on a wooden plank bench, bouncing mindlessly, his eyes staring off into space. How could she not have noticed he was with Balzac when she looked for heartfires before coming downstairs?

Because his heartfire wasn't there. Or rather, it was a mouse-sized heartfire, and there was no future in it, only a sort of numb awareness of the present. As if Calvin were looking at his own actions through peripheral vision.

As if Calvin were one of the slaves.

But no. The slaves of Camelot still had their heartfires. Weak ones, with their true names lost to them, their passions damped and gone, their futures channeled into a few narrow paths. More, certainly, than was left with Calvin. He kept his name, but very little else. And as for future and past, they were a thick fog. Shimmers and shadows appeared, but she could make no sense of them. Most particularly, Margaret could not see anything about where his doodlebug was.

"Let's take my dear brother-in-law out into the garden for our chat," said Margaret.

Balzac nodded, clearly relieved that she had so readily grasped the situation.

The garden lay in the hot deep shadow the house cast in the afternoon. With no one nearby to overhear, Margaret listened as Balzac poured out his story; even as he spoke, she followed the same events in his memory. The day on the docks; the unloading of the slaves; the waterboy named Denmark; the little bits of knotted this-and-that which were handed over or spat into the dipper; Calvin following Denmark with his doodlebug.

"I warned him," said Balzac. "He wouldn't listen."

"He never has," said Margaret.

"Never?" asked Balzac. "I thought you hadn't met him till this week."

"It is my misfortune to be deeply acquainted with everyone I meet," said Margaret. "Calvin is not a prudent man. Nor are you."

"As a pebble is to the moon, so is my imprudence compared to Calvin's," said Balzac.

"When you're dying of the disease that you call 'English' and the English call 'French,' when your mind is failing you, when you are blind and decaying, you will not be able to remember thinking of your imprudence as a slight thing," said Margaret.

"Mon dieu," said Balzac. "Have I heard my fate?"

"A very likely ending to your life," said Margaret. "Many paths lead there. But then, there are also many paths on which you are more prudent with the company you keep."

"What about luck?" asked Balzac.

"I'm not much of a believer in luck," said Margaret. "It wasn't luck that lost our friend Calvin his soul."

"How *could* it be lost, if the devil already had it?" Balzac was only half joking.

"What do I know of souls?" said Margaret. "I've been trying to understand what it is that the slaves in this city have given up. In Appalachee they don't do this, and I wonder if it's because they have some hope of escape. Whereas here, hope is nonexistent. Therefore, to remain alive, they must hide from their despair."

"Calvin wasn't despairing."

"Oh, I know," said Margaret. "Nor did he provide his captor with bits of string and whatnot. But then, those devices may be the Blacks' way of accomplishing what Calvin can do on his own, by his inborn knack: to separate some part of himself from his body."

"I am persuaded. But what part? And how can we get it back?"

Margaret sighed. "Monsieur Balzac, you seem to think I am a better person than I really am. For I am still quite uncertain whether I wish to help Calvin recover himself." She looked at Calvin's empty face. A fly landed on his cheek and walked briefly into and out of his nostril. Calvin made no move to brush it away. "The slaves function better than this," said Margaret. "And yet he seems not to be suffering."

"I understand," said Balzac, "that the better one knows Monsieur Calvin, the more one may wish to leave him in this docile state. But then, you must consider a few other things."

"Such as?"

"Such as, I am no blood kin of this man, and feel no responsibility for him. You, however, are his sister-in-law. Therefore, I can and will walk away from this garden without him. What will you do with the body? It still breathes—there are those who might criticize you for burying it, though I would never speak ill of you for such a decision."

"Monsieur Balzac, you should consider a few things yourself."

"Such as?" Balzac echoed her with a smile.

"Such as, you have no idea how much of our conversation Calvin is overhearing, however inattentive he might seem. The slaves hear what is said to them. Furthermore, there is no place on this earth where you could go that Calvin could not find you to wreak whatever vengeance he might wish to exact from you."

Balzac deflated slightly. "Madame, you have caught me in my deception. I would never leave my dear friend in such a state. But I hoped that a threat to leave you responsible for him might persuade you to help me save him, for I have no idea how to find where his soul is kept, or how to free it if I find it."

"Appeals to decency work much better with me than threats of inconvenience."

"Because you are a woman of virtue."

"Because I am ashamed to appear selfish," said Margaret. "There is no virtue that cannot be painted as a vice."

"Is that so? I have never found a need to do that. Painting vices as virtues, now, that is my expertise." Balzac grinned at her.

"Nonsense," said Margaret. "You name virtues and vices for what they are. That is your knack."

"I? Have a knack?"

"What were the last things Calvin said?"

Balzac held still a moment, his eyes closed. "In Blacktown," he said. " 'Junk hanging all over the place,' he said. Oh, and a moment before that he mentioned going through a door. So perhaps that's inside. Yes, in a house, because I remember him saying, 'Only one other heartfire in the house.' And then the last thing he said was, 'That's *bright.*' "

"A light," said Margaret. "A house with one other heartfire in it. Besides the one belonging to this Denmark fellow. And something bright. And then he was taken."

"Can you find it?" asked Balzac.

Margaret didn't answer. Instead she looked doubtfully at Calvin. "Do you suppose he's incontinent?"

"Pardon?" asked Balzac.

"I'm speculating on the best place to take him. I think he should stay with you."

"Why am I not surprised?"

"If he has trouble dealing with urination and defecation, I believe it will cause less scandal for you to help him."

"I admire your prudence," said Balzac. "I suppose I must also provide him with food and drink."

Margaret opened the purse tucked into her sleeve and handed a guinea to Balzac. "While you tend to his physical needs, I will find his doodlebug."

Balzac tossed the guinea into the air and caught it. "Finding it is one thing. Will you bring it back?"

"That is beyond my power," said Margaret. "I carry well-made hexes, but I don't know how to make them. No, what I will do is find where he is and discover who is detaining him. I suspect that in the process I will find the souls of the slaves of Camelot. I will learn how the thing is done. And when I am armed with information . . ."

Balzac grimaced. "You will write a treatise on it?"

"Nothing so useless as that," said Margaret. "I'll tell Alvin and see what he can do."

"Alvin! Calvin's life depends upon the brother he hates above all other persons on earth?"

"The hate flows in only one direction, I fear," said Margaret. "Despite my warnings, Alvin seems unable to realize that the playmate of his childhood has been murdered by the man who usually dwells in this body. So Alvin insists on loving Calvin."

"Doesn't it make you weary? Being married to such a lunatic?"

Margaret smiled. "Alvin has made me weary all my life," she said.

" 'But' . . . no, let me say it for you . . . 'But the weariness is a joy, because I have worn myself out in his service.' "

"You mock me."

"I mock myself," said Balzac. "I play the clown: the man who pretends to be so sophisticated that he finds kindly sentiment amusing, when the reality is that he would trade all his dreams for the knowledge that a woman of extraordinary intelligence felt such sentiments for him.''

''You create yourself like a character in a novel,'' said Margaret.

''I have bared my soul to you and you call me false.''

''Not false. Truer than mere reality.''

Balzac bowed. ''Ah, madame, may I never have to face critics of such piercing wisdom as yourself.''

''You are a deeply sentimental man,'' said Margaret. ''You pretend to be hard, but you are soft. You pretend to be distant, but your heart is captured over and over again. You pretend to be self-mockingly pretentious, when in fact you know that you really are the genius that you pretend to be pretending to be.''

''Am I?'' asked Balzac.

''What, haven't I flattered you enough?''

''My English is not yet perfect. Can the word 'flattery' be used with the word 'enough'?''

''I haven't flattered you at all,'' said Margaret. ''On every path of your future in which you actually begin to write, there comes from your pen such a flood of lives and passions that your name will be known for centuries and on every continent.''

Tears filled Balzac's eyes. ''Ah, God, you have given me the sign from an angel.''

''This is not the road to Emmaus,'' said Margaret.

''It was the road to Damascus I had in mind,'' said Balzac.

She laughed. ''No one could ever strike you blind. You see with your heart as truly as I do.''

Balzac moved closer to her, and whispered. No, he formed the words with his lips, counting on her to understand his heart without hearing the sound. ''What I cannot see is the future and the past. Can I have my freedom from Calvin? I fear him as I fear no other living man.''

''You have nothing to fear from him,'' said Margaret. ''He loves you and wants your admiration more than that of any man but one.''

''Your husband.''

''His hatred for Alvin is so intense he has no real hate left over for you. If he lost your admiration, it would be a mere fleabite compared to losing hope of Alvin's respect.''

"And what is that compared to my fleabite? A bee sting? A snake-bite? An amputation?"

Margaret shook her head. "Now you *are* reaching for flattery. Take him home, Monsieur Balzac. I will try to find his heartfire somewhere in a house in Blacktown."

❈ 9 ❈

Witch Hunt

HEZEKIAH STUDY COULD not concentrate on the book he was trying to read, or the sermon he needed to write, or even on the pear he knew he ought to eat. There were several bites taken out of it, and he knew he must be the one who had taken them, but all he remembered was fretful, wandering thoughts about everything. Purity, you young fool. He'll come now, don't you know? He'll come, because he always comes, and because your name is on it, and he knows who you are, oh yes, he knows you, he wants your life, he wants to finish the job he started before you were born.

This is how he spent the afternoon, until at last a breeze arose, rattling the papers pinned under the paperweight on his writing desk. A breeze, and a shadow of cloud that dimmed the light in the room, and then the sound he had been waiting for: the trot-trot-trot of a horse drawing a little shay behind it. Micah Quill. Micah the Witcher.

Hezekiah rose and walked to the window. The shay was only just passing on the street below; Hezekiah caught but a glimpse of the face in profile, from above. So sweet and open, so trustworthy—Hezekiah had once trusted it, believed the words that came out of the shyly smiling mouth. "God will not permit the innocent to be punished," said that mouth. "Only the Lord Savior was foreordained to suffer innocently." The first of a thousand lies. Truth flowed to Micah Quill, was sucked in and disappeared, and emerged again looking ever so much like it used to, but changed subtly, at the edges, where none would notice, so that simple truth became a complicated fabric indeed, one that could wrap you up so tightly and close you off from the air until you suffocated in it.

Micah Quill, my best pupil. He has not come to Cambridge to visit his old schoolmaster, or hear the sermons he now preached on Sundays.

Leaning out his window, Hezekiah saw the shay stop at the main entrance of the orphanage. How like Micah. He does not stop for refreshment after his journey, or even to void his bladder, but goes instead directly to work. Purity, I cannot help you now. You didn't heed my warning.

Purity came into the room, relieved to see that the witcher was not some fearsome creature, some destroying angel, but rather was a man who must have been in his forties but still had the freshness of youth about him. He smiled at her, and she was at once relaxed and comfortable. She was much relieved, for she had feared the torment of conscience it would cost her, to have Alvin Smith, who seemed such a nice man, examined and tried by some monster. Instead the proceeding would be fair, the trial just, for this man had no malice in him.

"You are Purity," said the witcher. "My name is Micah Quill."

"I'm pleased to meet you," said Purity.

"And I to meet you," said Quill. "I came the moment your deposition was sent to me. I admire your courage, speaking up so boldly against a witch so dire."

"He made no threat to me," said Purity.

"His very existence is a menace to all godly souls," said Quill. "You could feel that, even if he uttered no threat, because the spirit of Christ dwells in you."

"Do you think so, sir?" asked Purity.

Quill was writing in his book.

"What do you write, sir?"

"I keep notes of all interviews," said Quill. "You never know what might turn out to be evidence. Don't mind me."

"It's just that . . . I wasn't giving my evidence yet."

"Isn't that silly of me?" said Quill. "Please, sit down, and tell me about this devil-worshiping slave of hell."

He spoke so cheerfully that Purity almost missed the dark significance of the words. When she realized what he had said, she corrected him at once. "I know nothing of what or how the man worships," said Purity. "Only that he claims to have a witchy knack."

"But you see, Miss Purity, such witchy knacks are given to people only because they serve the devil."

"What I'm saying is I never saw him worship the devil, nor speak of the devil, nor show a sign of wishing to serve him."

"Except for his knack, which of course *does* serve the devil."

"I never actually saw the knack, either, with my own eyes," said Purity. "I just heard tales of it from the boy who traveled with him."

"Name the boy," said Quill, his pen poised.

"Arthur Stuart."

Quill looked up at her, not writing.

"It *is* a joke, sir, to name him so, but the joke was made years ago by those who named him, I do not jest with you now."

He wrote the name.

"He's a half-Black boy," she began, "and—"

"Singed in the fires of hell," said Quill.

"No, I think he's merely the son of a White slave owner who forced himself on a Black slave girl, or that's the implication of the story I was told."

Quill smiled. "But why do you resist me?" he said. "You say he's half-Black. I say this shows he was singed by the fires of hell. And you say, no, not at all—and then proceed to tell me he is the product of a rape of a Black woman by a White man. How could one better describe such a dreadful conception than by saying the child was singed in the fires of hell? You see?"

Purity nodded. "I thought you were speaking literally."

"I am," said Quill.

"I mean, that you literally meant that the boy had been to hell and burned there a little."

"So I say," Quill said, smiling. "I don't understand this constant insistence on correcting me when we already agree."

"But I'm not correcting you, sir."

"And is that statement not itself a correction? Or am I to take it some other way? I fear you're too subtle for me, Miss Purity. You dazzle me with argument. My head spins."

"Oh, I can't imagine you ever being confused by anybody," said Purity, laughing nervously.

"And again you feel the need to correct me. Is something troubling you? Is there some reason that you find it impossible to feel comfortable agreeing with me?"

"I'm perfectly comfortable to agree with you."

"A statement which, while sweet of sentiment, does constitute yet another disagreement with my own prior statement. But let us set aside the fact that you are unable to accept a single word I utter at face value. What puzzles me, what I must have your help to clarify, is the matter of some missing information, and some extra information. For instance, your deposition includes several extraneous persons whom no one else has seen. To wit: a lawyer named Verily Cooper, a riverman named Mike Fink, and a half-Black boy named Arthur Stuart."

"But I'm not the only one who saw them," said Purity.

"So the deposition is wrong?"

"I never said in the deposition that I was the only one who saw them."

"Excellent! Who else was there at this witches' sabbath?"

"What witches' sabbath?" Purity was confused now.

"Did you say you stumbled upon this coven of witches as they frolicked naked on the banks of the river?"

"Two of them were bathing, but I saw no sign of anything more dire than that."

"So to you, when witches cavort naked before your eyes, it is innocent bathing?"

"No, I just . . . I never thought of it as a . . . it wasn't a worship of any kind."

"But the tossing of the child toward heaven—a Black child, no less— and the way the naked man laughed at you, unashamed of his nakedness . . ."

Purity was sure she had neither spoken of nor written down any such description. "How could you know of that?"

"So you admit that you did not include this vital evidence in your deposition?"

"I didn't know it *was* evidence."

"Everything is evidence," said Quill. "Beings who frolic naked, laugh at Christians, and then disappear without a trace—which part of this experience would not be evidence? You must leave nothing out."

"I see that now," said Purity. "I reckon I didn't know what a witches' sabbath might look like, so I didn't know when I saw it."

"But if you didn't know, why would you denounce them?" asked Quill. "You haven't brought a false accusation, have you?"

"No, sir! Every word I said was true."

"Oh, and what about the words you did *not* say?"

Purity was even more confused. "But if I didn't say them, how can I know which words they are?"

"But you know them. We just discovered them. The fact that it was a pagan bacchanal, with a naked man molesting a naked boy before your eyes—"

"Molest! He only tossed him in the air as a father might toss his own child, or an older brother might toss a younger."

"So you think this might be incest as well?" asked Quill.

"All I ever thought was to report what they said of themselves, that Alvin Smith is the seventh son of a seventh son, with all the knacks that such men are prone to have."

"So you believe the words of the devil concerning this?" asked Quill.

"The words of what devil?"

"The devil who spoke to you and told you that knacks just happen to come to seventh sons of seventh sons, when in fact witchcraft can only be practiced by those who have given themselves over to the service of Satan."

"I didn't understand that," said Purity. "I thought it was the use of hidden powers that was the crime, all by itself."

"Evil is never all by itself," said Quill. "Remember that when you testify you will take an oath with your hand on the sacred scripture, the very word of God under your hand, which is the same as holding Christ by the hand, for he is the very Word. You will give oath to tell the truth, the *whole* truth. So you must not attempt to withhold any more information as you have been doing.''

''But I've withheld nothing! I've answered every question!''

''Again she must contradict the servant of God even when he speaks the plain truth. You withheld the information about pederasty, about the witches' sabbath, about incest—and you attempted to pretend that this Alvin's hidden powers came naturally from the order in which he was born within his family, even though it is impossible for any such devilish power to come from nature, for nature was born in the mind of God, while witchy powers come from the anti-Christ. Don't you know that it is a terrible sin to bear false witness?''

''I do know it, and I told the truth as I understood it.''

''But you understand it better now, don't you?'' said Quill. ''So when you testify, you will speak truly, won't you, and name things as they truly were? Or do you intend to lie to protect your witch friends?''

''My—my *witch friends*?''

''Did you not swear that they were witches? Are you recanting that testimony?''

''I deny that they were friends of mine, not that they were witches.''

''But your deposition,'' said Quill. ''You seem to be retreating from that document as fast as you can.''

''I stand by every word in it.''

''And yet you claim these men were not your friends? You say that they pleaded with you to go with them as they continued their wicked journey through New England. Is this something they would ask of a stranger?''

''It must be so, since I was a stranger to them, and they asked me.''

''Beware of a defiant tone,'' said Quill. ''That will not help your cause in court.''

''Am I in court? Have I a cause there?''

''Haven't you?'' said Quill. ''The only thing standing between you and the gallows is this deposition, your first feeble attempt to turn away from evil. But you must understand that the love of Christ cannot protect you when you half-repent.''

''Turn away from evil? I have done no evil!''

''All men are evil,'' said Quill. ''The natural man is the enemy of God, that's what Paul said. Are you therefore better than other people?''

"No, I'm a sinner like anyone else."

"So I thought," said Quill. "But your deposition shows that these men called you by name and begged you to go with them. Why would they do that, if they did not count you among their number, as a fellow witch?"

Purity was stunned. How could this have happened? She was the accuser, wasn't she? And yet here she sat denounced by a witcher. "Sir, is it not as likely to be a sign that I was *not* among their number, and that they wished to persuade me?"

"But you do not describe a scene of seduction," said Quill. "You do not tell us how the devil stood before you, his book open, waiting to write your name in it the moment you say that you consent."

"Because he did not do that," said Purity.

"So it was *not* a seduction, and the devil did *not* entice you to love and serve him."

Purity remembered how she felt in the presence of Verily Cooper, the desires that washed over her when she saw how handsome he was, when she heard the clear intelligence of his speech.

"You are blushing," said Quill. "I see that the spirit of God is touching you with shame at what you have withheld. Speak, and clear your conscience."

"I didn't think it was anything," said Purity. "But yes, I did for a moment feel enticed by one of Alvin's companions, the lawyer named Verily Cooper. I thought of it only as the feelings a girl my age might easily have toward a handsome man of good profession."

"But you did not have those feelings toward a man of good profession," said Quill. "You had them toward a man that you yourself have called a witch. So now the picture is almost complete: You came upon a witches' sabbath, unspeakable incestuous debauchery taking place between a naked man and a naked boy on the riverbank, and another witch caused you to feel sexual desire for him, and then they invite you to join them on their evil passage through New England, and at the end of this you dare to tell me they had *no* reason to think you might go along with them?"

"How can I know what reasons they had?"

Quill leaned across the table, his face full of love and sympathy toward her. "Oh, Miss Purity, you don't have to hide it any longer. You have kept the secret for so long, but I know that long before you were brought to that witches' sabbath, you were keeping your powers hidden, the powers the devil gave you, concealing them from everyone around you, but secretly using them to gain advantage over your neighbor."

Tears started flowing down Purity's cheeks. She couldn't help it.

"Doesn't it feel better to tell the truth? Don't you understand that telling the truth is how you say no to Satan?"

"Yes, I have a knack," said Purity. "I have always been able to sense what a person feels, what they're about to do."

"Can you tell what *I* am about to do?"

Purity searched his face, searched her own heart. "Sir, I truly do not know you."

"Thus the devil leaves you to fend for yourself in the hour of your need. Oh, Miss Purity, the devil is a false friend. Reject him! Turn away from him! Cease this pretense!"

"What pretense? I have confessed all!"

"Again she contradicts me. Don't you understand that as long as you are contradicting me, the spirit of the devil is in you, forcing you to contend against those who serve God?"

"But I don't know what more to confess."

"Who told you the witches' sabbath was to be held there on the riverbank that day?"

"No one told me," said Purity. "I told you, I was walking along the path."

"But is it your custom to walk along the river at that time of day?"

"No. No, I just read something in the library that made me think."

"What was it you read?"

"Something about . . . witchcraft."

Quill nodded, smiling. "Now, didn't that feel better?"

Purity did not know what it was that should have felt better.

"You were thinking of your evil pact with Satan, and suddenly you found yourself walking along the river. Perhaps you flew, perhaps you walked—I hardly think that matters, though it is possible you flew without knowing that you flew—most people fly to the witches' sabbath, often upon a broom, but I will not deny that some might walk. However it happened, you suddenly found yourself in the midst of a debauch so foul it shocked even a hardened witch such as yourself, and you longed to be cleansed of your deep wickedness, for having met souls even more lost than you, you remembered to fear God and so you came back with a story. It was still full of lies and you still left out much, but the key was there: You said the word *witch,* and you named a name. That is the beginning of redemption, to name the sin and repudiate the seducer.''

Though many of his statements were not at all the way she remembered it happening, nevertheless, the end of his statement was true. How could she not have seen it before? She was led there, and probably by the devil. And hadn't she be filled with such terrible emotions that they had to warn her to be careful or she'd get herself denounced as a witch? Yes, she was one of them, they recognized her as one of them, and instead of accusing them, she should have accused herself. The beginning of redemption. ''Oh, I want to have the love of God again. Will you help me, Mr. Quill?''

He leaned forward and kissed her on the cheek. ''Miss Purity, I come to you with the kiss of fellowship, as the Saints greeted each other in days of old. Deep inside you is a Christian soul. I will help you waken the Christian within you, and get shut of the devil.''

Weeping now, she clutched his hands within hers. ''Thank you, sir.''

''Let us begin in earnest, then,'' said Quill. ''In your fear you first named only strangers, people passing through. But you have been a witch for many years, and it is time for you to name the witches of Cambridge.''

She echoed him stupidly. ''Witches of Cambridge?''

''It's been many, many years since this part of Massachusetts has had a witch trial. Witchery and witchism are thick here, and with your repentance we have a chance to root them out.''

''Witchism?''

''The belief system surrounding witchery, which protects it and allows it to flourish. I'm sure you've heard these lies. The claim that knacks are natural or even a gift from God—this clearly is a satanic lie designed to keep people from getting rid of witchcraft. The claim that knacks don't exist—absurdly, that is what many supposedly wise men claim!—that also provides a shelter under which the covens can remain safe to work their evil. It is well known that while many witchists are simply echoing the beliefs of strong-willed people around them, others are secret witches, pretending to disbelieve in witchery even as they practice it. These are terrible hypocrites who must be exposed; and yet often they are the most attractive or interesting of the witchists, keeping you from recognizing their true nature. Can you think of any who speak this way?''

''But I can't imagine any of them are witches,'' said Purity.

''That's not for you to decide, is it?'' said Quill. ''Name the names, and let me examine them. If they're witches, I'll have it out of them eventually. If they're innocent, God will preserve them and they'll go free.''

''Then let God show them to you.''

''But I am not the one being tested,'' said Quill. ''You are. This is your chance to prove that your repentance is real. You have denounced the stranger. Now denounce the snake in our own garden.''

She imagined herself naming names. Whom would she denounce? Emerson? Reverend Study? These were men she loved and admired. There was not witchery in them, nor witchism either.

''All I know of witchcraft is my own knack,'' she said. ''That and the men I already denounced.''

Suddenly tears appeared in Quill's eyes. ''Now Satan fears that his whole kingdom in this land is in jeopardy, and he terrifies you and forbids you to speak.''

''No sir,'' said Purity. ''Honor forbids me to name those who are not witches and who to my knowledge have done only good in the world.''

''So you are the judge?'' whispered Quill. ''You dare to speak of honor? Let God judge them; you have only to name them.''

Now she remembered Reverend Study's admonition. Why did I ever speak at all? Is this where it always leads? I cannot be considered pure unless I falsely accuse others?

''There are no other witches but myself, as far as I know,'' she said.

''I ask for witchists, too, remember,'' said Quill. ''Come now, child, don't fall back into the cruel embrace of Satan out of a misplaced sense of loyalty. If they are Christians, Christ will keep them safe. And if they are not Christians, then do you not better serve them and the world at large by exposing them for what they are?''

''You twist everything I say,'' she said. ''You'll do the same to them.''

"I twist things?" said Quill. "Are you now *denying* your confession of witchcraft?"

For a moment she wanted to say yes, but then remembered: The only people ever hanged as witches were those who confessed and then either did more witchcraft—or recanted their confession.

"No sir, I don't deny that I'm a witch. I just deny that I ever saw anyone from Cambridge do anything that I might call witchery or even ... witchism."

"It's not a good sign when you lie to me," said Quill. "I believe you attend a class taught by one Ralph Waldo Emerson."

"Yes," she said, hesitantly.

"Why are you so reluctant to tell the truth? Is Satan stopping your mouth? Or is that how these other witches punish you for your honesty, by stopping up your mouth when you try to speak? Tell me!"

"Satan isn't stopping my mouth, nor any witch."

"No, I can see the fear in your eyes. Satan forbids you to confess the names, and even frightens you into denying that he is threatening you. But I know how to get you free of his clutches."

"Can you drive out the devil?" she asked.

"Only you can drive out the devil within you," said Quill, "by denouncing Satan and those who follow him. But I will help you shake off the fear of Satan and replace it with the fear of God by mortifying the flesh."

Now she understood. "Oh, please sir, in the name of God, I beg you, do not torture me."

"Oh really," he said impatiently. "We're not the Spanish Inquisition, now, are we? No, the flesh can be mortified better through exhaustion than through pain." He smiled. "Oh, when you're free of this, when you can stand before this community of Saints and declare that you have named all of Satan's followers here, how happy you will be, filled with the love of Christ!"

She bowed her head over the table. "Oh God," she prayed, "what have I done? Help me. Help me. Help me."

Waldo Emerson saw the men at the back of the classroom. "We have visitors," he said. "Is there something in the teachings of Thomas Aquinas that I can explain to you, goodmen?"

"We're tithingmen of the witch court of Cambridge," they said.

Waldo's heart stopped beating, or so it seemed. "There is no witch court in Cambridge," he said. "Not for a hundred years."

"There's a witch girl naming other witches," said the tithingman. "The witcher, Micah Quill, he sent us to fetch you for examination, if you be Ralph Waldo Emerson."

The students sat like stones. All but one, who rose to his feet and addressed the tithingmen. "If Professor Emerson is accused of witchery then the accuser is a liar," he said. "This man is the opposite of a witch, for he serves God and speaks truth."

It was a brave thing the boy had done, but it also forced Emerson's hand. If he did not immediately surrender himself, the tithingmen would be taking along two, not just one. "Have done," Waldo told his students. "Sit down, sir." Then, walking from his rostrum to the tithingmen, he said, "I'm happy to go with you and help you dispel any misconception that might have arisen."

"Oh, it's no misconception," said the tithingman. "Everyone knows you're a witchist. It's just a matter of whether you do so as a fool or as a follower of Satan."

"How can everyone know that I'm a thing which I never heard of until this moment?"

"That's proof of it right there," said the tithingman. "Witchists are always claiming there's no such thing as witchism."

Waldo faced his students, who had either turned in their seats to face him, or were standing beside their chairs. "This is today's puzzle," he said. "If the act of denial can be taken as proof of the crime, how can an innocent man defend himself?"

The tithingmen caught him by the arms. "Come along now, Mr. Emerson, and don't go trying any philosophy on us."

"Oh, I wouldn't dream of it," said Waldo. "Philosophy would be wasted against such sturdy-headed men as you."

"Glad you know it," said the tithingman proudly. "Wouldn't want you thinking we weren't true Christians."

They had Alvin in irons, which he thought was excessive. Not that it was uncomfortable—it was a simple matter for Alvin to reshape the iron to conform with his wrists and ankles, and to cause the skin there to form calluses as if they had worn the iron for years. Such work was so long-practiced that he did it almost by reflex. But the necessity to be inactive during the hours when he could be observed made him weary. He had done this before—and without the irons—for long weeks in the jail in Hatrack River. Life was too short for him to waste more hours, let alone days or weeks, growing mold in a prison cell and weighed down by chains, not when he could so easily free himself and get on about his business.

At sundown, he sat on the floor, leaned back against the wooden side wall of the cell, and closed his eyes. He sent out his doodlebug along a familiar path, until he found the dual heartfire of his wife and the unborn daughter that dwelt within her. She was already heading for her writing table, aware through long custom that because Alvin was farther east, sundown came earlier to him. She was always as impatient as he was.

This time there was no interruption from visitors. She commiserated with him about the chains and the cell, but soon got to the matter that concerned her most.

"Calvin's doodlebug has been stolen," she said. "He had sent it forth to follow the man who collects the names and some part of the souls of Blacks arriving at the dock." She told him of Calvin's last words to Balzac before all his will seemed to depart from his body. "First, I must know how much of his soul remains with his body. It is different from the slaves, for he seems to hear nothing and has to be led. His bodily functions also are like an infant's, and Balzac and their landlord are equally disgusted at the result, though the slaves clean him without complaint. Is this reversible? Can we communicate with him to learn his whereabouts? I have searched this city all the way up the peninsula, and find no collection of heartfires and no sign of Calvin's. It has been hidden from me; I pray it is not hidden from you."

Alvin had no need to write or even formulate his answers. He knew that she could find all his ideas in his heartfire moments after he thought of them and they fell into his memory. The kidnapped doodlebug—Alvin had never worried about that. His fears had always been that something awful might happen to his body while he wandered. But in his experience, his body remained alive and alert, and whenever anything in his environment changed—his eyes detecting movement, his ears hearing some unexpected sound—his attention would be drawn back into his body.

His attention, and therefore his doodlebug. That's what the doodlebug was, really—his full attention. That's what was missing from Calvin. Even when things happened around his body, happened *to* his body, he could not bring his attention back to it. His body was no doubt sending him frantic signals demanding his attention.

The slaves, on the other hand, couldn't possibly have surrendered their attention to the man named Denmark. What they gave up was their passion, their resentment, their will to freedom. And their names.

That was an important conclusion: There was no reason to think that this Denmark fellow had Calvin's name. In fact, what he probably had was a net of hexwork that contained the free portion of separated souls. He might not even be aware that Calvin's doodlebug had got inside. The hexes caught him automatically, like the workings of an engine. The hexwork also served to hide the soulstuff that it contained. Calvin could not see out, and could not be seen inside.

But the hexes could be seen. Margaret could not possibly find them, since she saw only heartfires, and if a man knew how to hide heartfires from her, he could certainly hide his own heartfire so she could not discover the man who knew the secret.

"Is he hiding from me?" she wrote.

He doesn't know you exist. He's hiding from everybody.

"How could Calvin be captured, when he didn't make the little knotted things the slaves made?"

I don't know the workings of Black powers, but my guess is that each slave put his own name and all his fears and hatred into the knotwork. They needed the knots in order to lift this part of their souls out of their bodies. Calvin needed no such tool.

"They had to do a Making?" she wrote.

Yes, he thought, that's what it was. A Making. Whether it was the power of Whites or Reds or Blacks, that's what it came down to: connecting yourself to the world around you by Making. Reds made the connection directly—that connection *was* their Making, the link they forged between man and animal, man and plant, man and stone. Blacks made artifacts whose only purpose was power—poppets and knotted strings. Whites, however, spent their lives making tools that hammered, cut, tore at nature directly, and only in the one area that they called their knack did they truly make that link. Yet they did make that connection. They were not utterly divorced from the natural world. Though Alvin could imagine such men and women, never feeling that deep, innate connection, never seeing the world change by the sheer action of their will in harmony with that part of nature. How lonely they must be, to be able to shape iron no other way than with hammer and anvil, fire and tongs. To make fire only by striking flint on steel. To see the future only by living day to day and watching it unfold one path at a time. To see the past only by reading what others wrote of it, or hearing their tales, and imagining the rest. Would such people even know that nature was as alive and responsive as it is? That hidden powers move in the world—no, not just *in* the world, they *move* the world, they *are* the world at its foundation? How terrible it would be, to know and yet not touch these powers at any point. Only the bravest and wisest would be able to bear it. The rest would have to deny the hidden powers entirely, pretend they did not exist.

And then he realized: That's what the witchcraft laws *are*. An attempt to shut off the hidden powers and drive them away from the lives of men.

"At least the witchcraft laws admit that hidden powers exist," wrote Margaret.

With that, Alvin realized the full import of what Verily was attempting. It would be good to strike down the witchery laws, but only if it led to an open acknowledgment that knacks were good or evil only according to the use made of them.

"Verily's strategy is to make the whole idea of witchcraft look foolish."

Well, it *is* foolish, thought Alvin. All the images of the devil that he had heard of were childish. What God had created was a great Making that lived of itself and contained lesser beings whom he tried to turn into friends and fellow Makers. The enemy of that was not some pathetic creature giving a few lonely, isolated people the power to curse and cause misery. The enemy of Making was Unmaking, and the Unmaker wore a thousand different masks, depending on the needs of the person he was attempting to deceive.

I wonder what form the Unmaker takes to bring this witcher fellow along?

"Some men need no deception to serve him," wrote Margaret. "They already love his destructive work and engage in it freely of their own accord."

Are you speaking of this Quill fellow? Or of Calvin?

"No doubt they both believe they serve the cause of Making."

Is that true, Margaret? Aren't you the one who told me that however much a man might lie to himself, at the core of him he knows what he truly is?

"In some men the truth lies hidden so deeply that they see it again only at the last extremity. Then they recognize that they have known it all along. But they see the truth only at the moment when it is too late to seize upon it and use it to save themselves. They see it and despair. That is the fire of hell."

All men deceive themselves. Are we all damned?

"They cannot save themselves," she wrote. "That does not mean they cannot be saved."

Alvin found that comforting, for he feared his own secrets, feared the place in himself where he had hidden the truth about his own motives when he killed the Finder who murdered Margaret's mother. Maybe I can open up that door and face the truth someday, knowing that I might still be saved from that hard sharp blade when it pierces my heart.

"Calvin's need for redemption is more dire than yours right now."

I'm surprised you want to save him. You're the one who tells me he'll never change.

"I tell you I've seen no change in any of his futures."

I'll search for him. For the hexes that hide him. I can see what you cannot. But what about Denmark? Can't you find him when he walks the streets, and learn the truth?

"He is also guarded. I can find him on the street, and his name is carried with him, so he hasn't parted with that part of his heartfire. Nevertheless, he has no knowledge, no memory of where he takes the knotwork and whom he gives it to. There are blank places in his memory. As soon as he leaves the docks with a basket of souls, he remembers nothing until he wakes up again. I could follow him, with eyes instead of doodlebug. . . ."

No! No, don't go near him! We know nothing of the powers at work here. Stay away and cease to search. Who knows but what some part of yourself goes forth from your body, too, when you do your torching? If you were captive as well it would be too much for me to bear.

"We are all captives, aren't we?" she wrote. "Even the baby in my womb."

She is no captive. *She* is home in the place she wants most to be.

"She chooses me because she knows no other choice."

In due time she'll eat of the fruit of the tree of knowledge of good and evil. For now, she is in the garden. You are paradise. You are the tree of life.

"You are sweet," she wrote. "I love you. I love you."

His own love for her swept over him, filling his eyes with tears and his heart with longing. He could see her set down the pen. No more words would appear on the paper tonight.

He lay there, sending forth his doodlebug. He found Purity easily. She was awake in her cell, weeping and praying. He stifled the vindictive thought that a sleepless night was the least she owed him. Instead, he entered her body and found where the fluids were being released that made her heart beat faster and her thoughts race. He watched her calm down, and then kindled the low fires of sleep in her brain. She crawled into bed. She slept. Poor child, he thought. How terrible it is not to know what your life is for. And how sad to have found such a destructive purpose for it.

Verily Cooper left Arthur Stuart, Mike Fink, and John-James Audubon in a small clearing in a stand of woods well north of the river and far from the nearest farmhouse. Arthur was making some bird pose on a branch—Audubon discoursed about the bird but it never made it into Verily's memory. It was a daring thing he was going to try. He had never knowingly attempted to defend a man he knew was guilty. And Alvin was, under New England law, guilty indeed. He had a knack; he used it.

But Verily thought he knew how witch trials were run. He had read about them in his mentor's law library—surreptitiously, lest anyone wonder why he took interest in such an arcane topic. Trial after trial, in England, France, and Germany, turned up the same set of traditional details: curses, witches appearing as incubi and succubi, and the whole mad tradition of witches' sabbaths and powerful gifts from the devil. Witchers asserted that the similarity of detail was proof that the phenomenon of witchcraft was real and widespread.

Indeed, one of their favorite ploys was to alarm the jury with statements like, "If this has all been happening under your very noses in this village, imagine what is happening in the next village, in the whole county, all over England, throughout the world!" They were forever citing "leading authorities" who estimated that, judging from the numbers of known witches actually brought to trial, there "must be" ten thousand or a hundred thousand or a million witches.

"Suspect everybody," they said. "There are so many witches it is impossible that you don't know one." And the clincher: "If you ignore small signs of witchcraft then you are responsible for permitting Satan to work unhindered in the world."

All this might have had some meaning if it weren't for one simple fact: Verily Cooper had a knack, and he knew that he had never had any experience of Satan, had never attended a witches' sabbath, had not left his body and wandered as an incubus to ravish women and send them strange dreams of love. All he had done was make barrels that held water so tightly that the wood had to rot through before the joints would leak. His only power was to make dead wood live and grow under his hands. And he had never used his knack to harm a living soul in any way. Therefore, *all* these stories had to be lies. And the statistics estimating the number of uncaught witches were a lie based upon a lie.

Verily believed what Alvin believed: that every soul was born with some connection to the powers of the universe—perhaps the powers of God, but more likely the forces of nature—which showed up as knacks among Europeans, as a connection to nature among the Reds, and in other strange ways among the other races. God wanted these powers used for good; Satan would of course want them used for evil. But the sheer possession of a knack was morally neutral.

The opportunity was here not just to save Purity from herself, but also to discredit the entire system of witch trials and the witchery laws themselves. Make the laws and the witnesses so obviously, scandalously, ludicrously false that no one would ever stand trial for the crime of witchcraft again.

Then again, he might fail, and Alvin would have to get himself and Purity out of jail whether she liked it or not, and they'd all hightail it out of New England.

Cambridge was a model New England town. The college dominated, with several impressive buildings, but there was still a town common across from the courthouse, where Alvin was almost certainly imprisoned. And, to Verily's great pleasure, the witcher and the tithingmen were running both Alvin and Purity. A crowd surrounded the common—but at a safe distance—as Alvin was forced to run around in tight circles at one end of the meadow and Purity at the other.

"How long have they been at it?" Verily asked a bystander.

"Since before dawn without a rest," said the man. "These are tough witches, you can bet."

Verily nodded wisely. "So you know already that they're both witches?"

"Look at 'em!" said the bystander. "You think they'd have the strength to run so long without falling over if they weren't?"

"They look pretty tired to me," said Verily.

"Ayup, but still running. And the girl's a brought-in orphan, so it's likely she had it in her blood anyway. Nobody ever liked her. We knew she was strange."

"I heard she was the chief witness against the man."

"Ayup, but how would she know about the witches' sabbath iffen she didn't go to it her own self, will you tell me that?"

"So why do they go to all this trouble? Why don't they just hang her?"

The man looked sharply at Verily. "You looking to stir up trouble, stranger?"

"Not I," said Verily. "I think they're both innocent as you are, sir. Not only that, but I think you know it, and you're only talking them guilty so no one will suspect that you also have a knack, which you keep well-hidden."

The man's eyes widened with terror, and without another word he melted away into the crowd.

Verily nodded. It was a safe enough thing to charge, if Alvin was right, and all folks had some kind of hidden power. All had something to hide. All feared the accusers. Therefore it was good to see this accuser charged right along with the man she accused. Hang her before she accuses anybody else. Verily had to count on that fear and aggravate it.

He strode out onto the common. At once a murmur went up—who was the stranger, and how did he dare to go so close to where the witcher was running the witches to wear them down and get a full confession out of them?

"You, sir," said Verily to the witcher. He spoke loudly, so all could hear. "Where is the officer of the law supervising this interrogation?"

"I'm the officer," said the witcher. He spoke just as loudly—people usually matched their voices to the loudest speaker, Verily found.

"You're not from this town," Verily said accusingly. "Where are the tithingmen!"

At once the dozen men who had formed watchful rings around both Alvin and Purity turned, some of them raising their hands.

"Are you men not charged with upholding the law?" demanded Verily. "Interrogation of witnesses in witch trials is to take place under the supervision of officers of the court, duly appointed by the judge or magistrate, precisely to stop *torture* like this from taking place!"

The word *torture* was designed to strike like a lash, and it did.

"This is not torture!" the witcher cried. "Where is the rack? The fire? The water?"

Verily turned toward him again, but stepped back, speaking louder than before. "I see you are familiar with *all* the methods of torture, but running them is one of the cruelest! When a person is worn down enough, they'll confess to . . . to *suicide* if it will end the torment and allow them to rest!"

It took a moment for the surrounding crowd to understand the impossibility of a confession of suicide, but he was rewarded with a chuckle. Turn the crowd; everyone who ended up on the jury would know of what was said here today.

Because the tithingmen were looking away, both Alvin and Purity had staggered and dropped to their knees. Now they both knelt on all fours in the grass, panting, heads hanging like worn-out horses.

"Don't let them rest!" the witcher cried frantically. "You'll set the whole interrogation back by hours!"

The tithingmen looked to their rods and switches, which they used to goad the runners, but none moved toward the two victims.

"At last you remember your duty," said Verily.

"You have no authority here!" cried the witcher. "And I *am* an officer of the court!"

"Tell me then the name of the magistrate here in Cambridge who appointed you."

The witcher knew he'd been caught exceeding his authority, since he had none until the local judge called for his services, and so he did not answer Verily's challenge directly. "And who are *you*?" the witcher demanded. "From your speech you're from England—what authority do *you* have?"

"I have the authority to demand that you be clapped in irons yourself if you cause these two souls to be tortured for one more moment!" cried Verily. He knew the crowd was spellbound, watching the confrontation. "For I am Alvin Smith's attorney, and by torturing my client without authority, you, sir, have broken the Protection Act of 1694!" He flung out an accusing finger and the witcher visibly wilted under his accusation.

Verily was growing impatient, however, for the plan wasn't to win a petty victory here on the common. Was Purity so tired she couldn't lift her head and see who was speaking here?

He was about to launch into another tirade, during which he would wander closer to Purity and stand her up to face him if need be, but finally she recognized him and eliminated the need.

"That's him!" she cried.

The witcher sensed salvation. "Who? Who is he?"

"The English lawyer who was traveling with Alvin Smith! He's a witch too! He has a knack with wood!"

"So he was also at the witches' sabbath!" cried the witcher. "Of course Satan quotes the law to try to save his minions! Arrest that man!"

Verily immediately turned to the crowd. "See how it goes! Everyone who stands up for my client will be accused of witchcraft! Everyone will be clapped into jail and tried for his life!"

"Silence him!" cried the witcher. "Make him run along with the others!"

But the tithingmen, who reluctantly took Verily by the elbows because he *had* been accused, had no intention of doing any more running, now that it had been called torture and declared to be illegal. "No more running today, sir,'' said one of them. "We'll have to hear from the judge before we let you do such things again."

As a couple of tithingmen helped Purity stagger toward the courthouse, she whimpered when she came near Verily. "Don't bring me near him," she said. "He casts spells on me. He wants to come to me as an incubus!"

"Purity, you poor thing," Verily said. "Hear yourself spout the lies this witcher has taught you to tell."

"Speak no word to her!" cried the witcher. "Hear him curse her!"

To the tithingmen, Verily wryly muttered, "Did that sound like a curse to you?"

"No muttering! Keep still!" screamed the witcher.

Verily answered the witcher loudly. "All I said was, to a man with a hammer everything looks like a nail!"

Some people understood at once and chuckled. But the witcher was not one for irony. "A satanic utterance! Hammers and nails! What have you cursed me with? Confess your meaning, sir!"

"I mean, sir, that to those who *profit* from *witch trials,* every word sounds like a curse!"

"Get him out of here with his filthy lies and innuendoes!"

The tithingmen dragged him and Alvin off to the courthouse, to cells far from each other, but they were near each other several times, and though they didn't speak, they traded glances, and Verily made sure Alvin saw him grinning from ear to ear. This is working exactly as I wanted, Verily was saying.

Alone in his cell, though, Verily lost his smile. Poor Purity, he thought. How deeply had this witcher twisted her mind? Was her integrity so tied up in knots that she was no longer capable of seeing how she was being manipulated? Somewhere along the line, she had to realize that the witcher was using her.

Let it be soon, thought Verily. I don't want Alvin to have to wait long in this jail.

Hezekiah Study had already packed his bag for an extended stay with his niece in Providence when he heard the shouting on the common and leaned out his window to listen. He watched the English lawyer embarrass Micah Quill, manipulating the master manipulator until Hezekiah wanted to cheer. His heart sank when Purity denounced the lawyer—and, indeed, she *had* spoken of a lawyer in Alvin Smith's party right from the start—but the lawyer managed to plant seeds of doubt in every onlooker's mind all the same. To Hezekiah Study, it was the first time he'd ever seen the early stages of a witch trial without dread and despair seizing his heart. For the English lawyer was grinning like a schoolboy who doesn't mind the punishment because it was worth it to put the rock through the schoolmaster's window.

He's in control of this, thought Hezekiah.

His better sense—his bitter experience—answered: No one's ever in control of a witch trial except the witchers. The man is grinning now, but he'll not grin in the end, with either the rope around his neck or his decency stripped from him.

Oh, God, let this be the day at last when the people finally see that the only ones serving the devil at these trials are the witchers!

And when his prayer was done, he came away from the window and unpacked his bag. Come what may, this trial was going to be fought with courage, and Hezekiah Study had to stay. Not just to see what was going to happen, but because this young lawyer would not stand alone. Hezekiah Study would stand with him. He had that much hope and courage left in him, despite all.

⚔ 10 ⚔

Captivity

CALVIN DIDN'T NOTICE, at first, that he was trapped. With his doodlebug he followed Denmark into Blacktown, the section of Camelot devoted to housing skilled slaves whose services were being rented out, or where trusted slaves who were running errands for out-of-town landlords found room and board. Blacktown wasn't large, but it spilled over its official borders, as one warehouse after another had rooms added on upper floors—illegally and without registration—and where slaves came and went.

It was into one such warehouse just outside Blacktown that Denmark went and Calvin followed. Rickety stairs inside the building led to an attic story filled with an incredible array of junk. Boards, bits of furniture, strap and scrap iron, old clothes, ropes, fishnets, and all sorts of other random items dangled from hooks in the ceiling joists. At first he was puzzled—who would spend the time to bind all these things together?—but then he realized what he was seeing: larger versions of the knotwork that Denmark had collected from the newly arrived slaves.

He was about to return to his body and tell Honoré what he had found and where it was, when suddenly the junk parted and Calvin saw a dazzling light. He exclaimed about it, then moved closer and saw that it was made of thousands and thousands of heartfires, held within a net which hung, of course, from a hook in the ceiling.

What kind of net could hold souls? He moved closer. The individual heartfires were much tinier than those he was used to seeing. As so often before, he wished he could see into them the way torches did. But they remained a mystery to him.

His vision, though, could see what Margaret's never could: He could see the stout web of knotted cords that held the heartfires. On closer examination, though, he saw that each heartfire danced like a candle flame above one of the little bits of knotwork that he and Honoré had watched Denmark collect from the arriving slaves. So the web probably wasn't hexy at all.

With that, Calvin drew back, expecting to return instantly to his body to speak to Honoré. He even started to speak. But his mouth didn't move. His eyes didn't see. He remained where he was, looking at the heartfires with his doodling sight instead of gazing out of his eyes at the street.

No, that wasn't so. He was vaguely aware of the street, as if seeing it out of the corners of his eyes. He could hear sounds, too, Honoré's voice, but when he tried to listen, he kept getting distracted. He couldn't pay attention to Honoré, couldn't focus on what his eyes were seeing. He kept coming back here to the knots and the net, no matter how hard he tried to tear himself away. He could feel his legs moving, as if they were someone else's legs. He could tell that Honoré's voice was becoming agitated, but still he couldn't make out what was being said. The sounds entered his mind, but by the time the end of a word was said, Calvin had lost his hold on the beginning of it. Nothing made sense.

Now with sick dread he realized that Honoré's warning had been well placed. This net was designed to catch and hold souls, or bits of souls, anyway, and keep anyone from finding them. Calvin had sent a bit of his own soul into the net, and now he couldn't get out.

Well, that's what *they* thought. Nets were made of cord; cord was made of threads wound and twisted; threads were spun from fibers. All of these were things that Calvin well understood. He set to work at once.

*   *   *

Denmark Vesey scowled at Gullah Joe, but the old witchy man didn't even seem to notice. White men had been known to step back a bit when they saw Denmark passing by with such a look on his face. Even the kind of White men who liked to goad Blacks, like those men on the dock today, they wouldn't mess with him when he wore that scowl on his face. He only let them push him around today because he had to show the new slaves how to keep White folks happy. But he still felt the rage and stored it up in his heart.

Not that he felt the kind of fury that filled that net of souls hanging up not ten paces away. That's because Denmark wasn't no man's slave. He wasn't even fully Black. He was the son of one of those rare slave-owners who felt some kind of fatherly responsibility toward the children he sired on his Black women. He gave freedom to all his half-Black bastards, freedom and a geography lesson, since every one of them was named for a European country. Few of them stayed free, though, if they once strayed from Mr. Vesey's plantation near Savannah. What difference did it make being free, if you had to live among the slaves and work among them and couldn't leave any more than the slaves did?

It made a difference to Denmark. He wasn't going to stick around on the plantation. He figured out what letters were when he was still little and got hold of a book and taught himself to read. He learned his numbers from his father's cousin, a French student who lived on the plantation to hide out because he took part in an anti-Napoleon rally at the university. The boy fancied himself some kind of hero of the oppressed, but all Denmark cared about was learning how to decode the mysteries that White people used to keep Black folks down. By the time he was ten, his father had him keeping the books for the plantation, though they had to keep it secret even from the White foreman. His father would pat his head and praise him, but the praise made Denmark want to kill him. "Just goes to show your Black mama's blood can't wipe out *all* the brains you get from a White papa." His father was still sleeping with his mother and getting more babies on her, and he knew she wasn't stupid, but he still talked like that, showing no respect for her at all, even though *her* children were smarter than the dim-witted little White weaklings that Father's *wife* produced.

Denmark nursed that anger and it kept him free. He wasn't going to end up on this plantation, no sir. The law said that there wasn't no such thing as a free Black man in the Crown Colonies. One of Denmark's own brothers, Italy, had been seized as a runaway in Camelot, and Father had to lay some stripes on Italy's back before the law would let up and go away. But Denmark wasn't going to get caught. He went to his father one day with a plan. Father didn't like it much—he didn't want to have to go back to doing his own books—but Denmark kept after him and finally went on strike, refusing to do the books if Father didn't go along. Father had him back in the fields under the overseer for a while, but in the end he didn't have the heart to waste the boy's talents.

So when Denmark was seventeen, his father brought him to Camelot and set him up with letters of introduction that Denmark had actually written, so the hand would always match. Denmark went around pretending to be a messenger for his absentee owner, soliciting bookkeeping jobs and copy work. Some White men thought they could cheat him, getting him to work but then refusing to pay the amount agreed on. Denmark hid his anger, then went home and in his elegant hand wrote letters to an attorney, again using his father's name. As soon as the White men realized that Denmark's owner wasn't going to let them get away with cheating him, they generally paid up. The ones that didn't, Denmark let the matter drop and never worked for them again. It wasn't so bad being a slave when your owner was yourself and stood up for you.

That went on till his father died. Denmark was full grown and had some money set by. No one knew his father in Camelot so it didn't matter he was dead, as long as nobody went back to Savannah to try to follow up on something Denmark wrote in his father's name. Not that Denmark didn't worry for a while. But when it became clear that it was all going well, he started to fancy himself a real man. He decided to buy himself a slave of his own, a Black woman he could love and get children from the way his father did.

He chose the one he wanted and had an attorney buy her for him, then went to pick her up in the name of his father. But when he got her home and she found out that a Black man had bought her, she near clawed his eyes out and ran out screaming into the neighborhood that she wasn't going to be no slave to a Black man. Denmark chased her down, getting no help from the other residents of Blacktown—that was when he realized they all knew he was free and resented him for it. It all came down to this, from his woman and from his neighbors: They hated being slaves, hated all White people, but more than anyone or anything else they hated a free buck like him.

Well, let them! That's what he thought at first. But it grew so he could hardly bear the sight of his woman, chained to the wall in his tiny room, cursing him whenever he came home. She kept making dolls of him to try to poison him, and it made him good and sick more than once. He didn't know a thing about poppeting. He'd spent all his effort learning the White man's secrets and knew nothing about what Black folks did. He came to the day when he realized he had nothing. He might fool White folks into letting him keep the results of his own labor, but he was never going to be White. And Black folks didn't trust him because he didn't know their ways, either, and because he acted so White and kept a slave.

Finally one day he knelt down in front of his woman and cried. What can I do to make you love me? She just laughed. You can't set me free, she said, cause Black folks are never free here. And you can't make me love you cause I never love him as owns me. And you can't sell me cause I tell my new master about you, see if I don't. All you can do is die when I make you a right poppet and kill it dead.

All that hate! Denmark thought that rage was the ruling principle of his own life, but it was nothing compared to what slaves felt. That was when Denmark realized the difference between free and slave—freedom stole hate away from you, and made you weaker. Denmark hated his father, sure, but it was nothing compared to his woman's hate for him.

Of course he had to kill her. She'd laid it out so plain, and it was clear he wasn't going to change her mind. It was just a matter of time before she killed him, so he had to defend himself, right? And he owned her, didn't he? She wouldn't be the first Black woman killed by her master.

He hit her in the head with a board and knocked her cold. Then he bundled her into a sack and carried her down to the dock. He figured to hold her under the water till she drowned, then pull her out of the sack and let her float so it didn't look like murder. Well, he had her under the water all right, and she wasn't even struggling inside the sack, but it was like a voice talking in his mind telling him, You killing the wrong one. It ain't the Black woman killing you, it's the White folks. If it wasn't for the White folks, you could marry this girl and she be free beside you. They the ones she wants to kill, they the ones you ought to kill.

He dragged her out of the water and revived her. But she wasn't right after that. It might have been the blow to the head or it might have been the water she took on and the time she spent not breathing, but she walked funny and didn't talk good and she didn't hate him anymore, but everything he loved about her was dead. It was like he was a murderer after all, but the victim lived in his house and bore him a baby.

Oh, Denmark, he was a sad man all the time after that. The joy of fooling White folks was gone. He got sloppy with his work, doing it late, and his customers stopped hiring him—though of course they thought it was his White master they were firing. The Black people around him hated him too, for what he done to his woman, and he had to watch all the time to keep them from getting any of his hair or fingernails or toenails, or even his spit or his urine. Cause they would have killed him with that, if they could.

His son Egypt got to be four years old and Denmark prenticed him to a Black harness maker. Had to do all kinds of pretending, of course, that it was a White man who owned the boy and wanted him trained to be useful on his plantation, and it cost nine pounds a year, which was most of what Denmark was earning these days, but the paperwork went well enough, and even though Egypt was treated like a slave, he was learning a trade and there'd come a day when Denmark would tell him the truth. You free, boy, he'd say that day. Egypt Vesey, no man owns you. Not me, not nobody.

When Egypt was gone, the last light went out of the boy's mama. The day Denmark saw his woman drinking varnish, he knew he had to do something. Stupid as she had become, she hated her life and hated him. He agreed with her. Maybe he hated himself even more than she did. Hated everything and everybody else, too. It was chewing him up inside.

That was when he met Gullah Joe. Joe came to him. Little Black man, he suddenly appeared right in front of Denmark when he was in the dirt garden peeing. He wasn't there, and then he was, holding a crazy-looking umbrella all a-dangle with strange knots and bits of cloth and tin and iron and one dead mouse. "Stop peeing on my foot," said Gullah Joe.

Denmark didn't have much to say. Piss just dried right up when Gullah Joe said so. Denmark knew he must be the witchy man they were always threatening him with. "You come to kill me, witchy man?" Denmark said.

"Might," said Gullah Joe. "Might not."

"Maybe you best just do it," said Denmark. "Cause if you don't, what if I kill *you*?"

Gullah Joe just grinned. "What, you hit me with a board, put me in a sack, drown me till I can't walk or talk right?"

Denmark just started to cry, fell to his knees and begged Gullah Joe to kill him. "You know what I am! You know I'm a wicked man!"

"I'm not God," said Gullah Joe. "You gots to go see him preacher, you want somebody send you to hell."

"How come you talk so funny?"

"Cause I not no slave," said Gullah Joe. "I from Africa, I don't like White man language, I learn it bad and I don't care. I say *people* talk real good." Then he let loose a string of some strange language. It went on and on, and turned into a song, and he danced around, splashing up the mud from Denmark's pissing all over his bare feet while he sang. Denmark felt every splash as if he'd been kicked in the kidneys. By the time Gullah Joe stopped singing and dancing, Denmark was lying on the ground whimpering, and there was blood leaking out of him instead of piss.

Gullah Joe bent over him. "How you feel?"

"Fine," Denmark whispered. " 'Cept I ain't dead yet."

"Oh, I don't want you dead. I make up my mind. You be fine. Drink this."

Gullah Joe handed him a small bottle. It smelled awful, but there was alcohol in it and that was persuasive enough. Denmark drank the whole bottle, or at least he would have, if Joe hadn't snatched it out of his hands. "You want to live forever?" Gullah Joe demanded. "You use up all my saving stuff?"

Whatever it was, it worked great. Denmark bounded to his feet. "I want more of that!" he said.

"You never get this again," said Gullah Joe. "You like it too good."

"Give it to my woman!" cried Denmark. "Make her well again!"

"She sick in the brain," said Gullah Joe. "This don't do no good for brain."

"Well then you go on and kill me again, you cheating bastard! I'm sick of living like this, everybody hate me, I hate myself!"

"I don't hate you," said Gullah Joe. "I got a *use* for you."

And ever since then, Denmark had been with Gullah Joe. Denmark's money had gone to supporting both him and Gullah Joe, and to accomplish whatever Joe wanted done. Half Denmark's day was spent taking care of new-arrived slaves, gathering their names and bringing them home to Joe.

The whole idea of taking names came from Denmark's woman. Not that she thought of it. But when Denmark rented the warehouse and brought Gullah Joe and the woman both to live there, Gullah Joe asked her what her name was. She just looked at him and said, "I don' know, master." It was a far cry from what she used to say to Denmark, back before he made her stupid. In those days she'd say, "Master never know my name. You call me what you want, but I never tell my name."

Well, when Gullah Joe asked Denmark what the woman's name was, and Denmark didn't know, why, you might have thought Joe had eaten a pepper, the way he started jumping around and howling and yipping. "She never told her name!" he cried. "She kept her soul!"

"She kept her *hate*," said Denmark. "I tried to *love* her and I don't even know what to call her except Woman."

But Gullah didn't care about Denmark's sad story. He got to work with his witchery. He made Denmark catch him a seagull—not an easy thing to do, but with Joe's Catching Stick it went well enough. Soon the seagull's body parts were baked, boiled, mixed, glued, woven, or knotted into a feathered cape that Gullah Joe would throw over his head to turn himself into a seagull. "Not really," he explained to Denmark. "I still a man, but I fly and White sailor, he see gulls." Joe would fly out to slaveships coming in to port in Camelot. He'd go down into the hold and tell the people they needed to get their name-string made before they landed, and give it to the half-Black man who gave them water.

"Put hate and fear in name-string," he said to them. "Peaceful and happy be all that stay behind. I keep you safe till the right day." Or that was what he told Denmark that he said. Few of the arriving slaves spoke any English, so he had to explain it to them in some African language. Or maybe he was able to convey it all to them in knot language. Denmark wouldn't know—Gullah Joe wouldn't teach him what the knotwork meant or how it worked. "You read and write White man talk," Gullah Joe said. "That be enough secret for one man." Denmark only knew that somehow these people knew how to tie bits of this and that with scraps of string and cloth and thread and somehow it would contain their name, plus a sign for fear and a sign for hate. Even though he couldn't understand it, the knotted name-strings made Denmark proud, for it proved that Black people knew how to read and write back in Africa, only it wasn't marks on paper, it was knots in string.

Besides gathering the names of the newly arrived slaves, Denmark helped collect the names of the slaves already in Camelot. Word spread among the Blacks—Denmark only had to pass along a garden fence with an open basket, and Black hands would reach out and drop name-strings into the basket. "Thank you," they said. "Thank you."

"Not me," he would answer. "Don't thank *me*. I ain't nobody."

Came a day not long ago when they had all the slaves' names, and Gullah Joe sang all night. "My people happy now," he said. "My people got they happy."

"They're still slaves," Denmark pointed out.

"All they hate in there," said Gullah Joe, pointing at the bulging net.

"All their hope, too," said Denmark. "They got no hope now either."

"I no take they hope," said Gullah Joe. "White man take they hope!"

"They all stupid like my woman," said Denmark.

"No, no," said Gullah Joe. "They smart. They wise."

"Well, nobody knows it but you."

Gullah Joe only grinned and tapped his head. Apparently it was enough for Joe to know the truth.

There was one person who wasn't happy, though. Oh, Denmark was glad enough to have a purpose in his life, to have Black people look at him with gratitude instead of loathing. But that wasn't the same as being happy. His woman was still before him every day, lurching through her housework, mumbling words he could barely understand. Gullah Joe saw that his people weren't unhappy anymore. But Denmark saw that the happiest people were the Whites. He heard them talking.

"You see how docile they are?"

"Slavery is the natural state of the Black man."

"They don't *wish* to rise above their present condition."

"They are content."

"The only place where Blacks are angry is where they are permitted to live without a master."

"The Black man cannot be happy without discipline."

And so on, throughout the city. White people came to Camelot from all over the world, and what they saw was contented slaves. It persuaded them that slavery must not be such a bad thing after all. Denmark hated this. But Gullah Joe seemed not to care.

"Black man day come," said Gullah Joe.

"When?"

"Black man day come."

That was why Denmark Vesey was scowling at Gullah Joe today, as the old witchy man carried the basket of name-strings through the knot-work that guarded the place. All these happy slaves. Was Denmark Vesey the only Black man in Camelot who lived in hell?

Gullah Joe pulled the net open and started to pour in the new name-strings. At that moment, cords along the bottom of the net began to pop open, one by one, as if someone were cutting them. Name-strings dropped out, at first a few, then dozens, and then the whole net opened up and the name-strings lay heaped on the floor.

"What did you *do*?" asked Denmark.

Gullah Joe did not answer.

"Something wrong?" asked Denmark.

Gullah Joe just stood there, his hands upraised. Denmark walked through the hanging junk, circling around until he could see Joe's face. He was frozen like a statue—a comic one, with eyes wide and teeth exposed in a grimace, like the minstrels in those hideous shows that White actors did with their faces painted Black.

This wasn't just a net giving way. Someone or something *had* broken open the net and spilled the name-strings onto the floor. If it had the power to do that, it had the power to hurt Gullah Joe, and that's what seemed to be happening.

What could Denmark do? He knew nothing about witchery. Yet he couldn't let anything happen to Joe. Or to the name-strings, for that matter, for the name of every slave in Camelot was spilled here. Yet if Denmark walked within the charmed circle that Joe had shown him, wouldn't he be in the enemy's power, too?

Maybe not if he didn't stay long. Denmark ran and leapt, knocking Joe clear out of the circle. They both sprawled on the floor, leaving a dozen large charms swaying and bumping each other.

Gullah Joe didn't show any sign of being hurt. He leapt up and looked frantically around him. "Get up by damn! A broom! A broom!"

Denmark scrambled to his feet and ran for the broom.

"Two broom! Quick!"

In moments the two of them were standing just outside the circle, reaching the brooms inside to sweep the name-strings outside in great swaths.

"Fast!" cried Joe. "He take apart you broom you go slow!"

Denmark hadn't thought he was going any slower than Joe, but then he realized that the end of the broomstick nearest his body was holding almost still as he levered the broom to sweep out name-strings. No sooner had he thought of this than the broomstick rocketed straight at him like a bayonet, ramming him in the stomach just under the breastbone. Denmark dropped like a rock, the breath knocked out of him. And when he did manage to take in a great gasp of air, he immediately vomited.

A few minutes later, Gullah Joe was bending over him. "You got you air? He not hurt you bad. He no see you, or you dead man."

"Who?" asked Denmark.

"You think I know?"

"You talk like you know everything," said Denmark.

"When I know, I say I know. This one, he a bad devil. He wander like stray dog, come passing through, he see all the names, devil eat name like food, like cake, taste him sweet. He come in my circle and now he get caught, he no come out. So he mad, him! Tear up net. Tear up name, kill me if he can. But I stop him."

"I helped."

"Yes, you knock me down, very smart."

"Why you holding still like that?"

"See me knotty hair? She wiggle, he get inside, he break me in bits."

Denmark had long wondered why Gullah Joe had braided his hair with ribbons and scraps. It wasn't decoration, it was protection—as long as the knotted braids weren't wiggling.

"So that hair keep out the devil?"

Joe flipped his braids boastfully. "Hair, she keep him out of *me*." Then he pointed at the dangling charms that used to ring the net of name-strings. "These charm, they keep him in my circle." Joe grinned. "It got him."

"What you want him for?" asked Denmark. "Can you ask him for wishes or something?"

Gullah Joe looked at him like he was stupid. "You live White too long, boy, it make you strange."

"I thought maybe it was like a genie or something."

"You no ask devil help you, he help you be dead, that be his help you." Gullah Joe began walking around, looking at the dangling charms hanging elsewhere in the room. "You get me that one, that one, that one."

Denmark, being tall, had no trouble unhooking the charms Joe indicated. Soon they had a new circle created, just like the other one, only when you looked close there were no two charms alike. It seemed not to matter. In a few more minutes they gathered the name-strings from the floor, piled them in another net, and hoisted them off the floor in the midst of the charmed circle.

"Now nobody see them again, they safe, they don't get lost, they don't get found."

"So we beat the devil this time," said Denmark.

Gullah Joe shook his head sadly. "No, he tear one up. He pick that one, he tear her up, he break the string, she name be fly off somewhere."

"Lost?"

"Oh, she name try to get home, she try so hard." Gullah Joe sighed. "Some name she strong, but she blind, no find the way. Some name see the way, but she no fly, she fade away. This one, she strong, she bright, maybe she get home."

"Which one was it?"

"You think I tell she name? Call that name to *me*? You think I be so bad? No sir. I no say she name, I be pray that name find that girl, she a good one. Why he pick her?"

"Don't ask me," said Denmark. "I don't know why anybody picks anybody."

"No, he go to her, he know her. He know her. That devil, he been walking Camelot street, him. That devil, be maybe him a man. Be maybe him a White man." Gullah Joe smiled. "Be maybe him soul fly, get caught here, but he body be somewhere."

Denmark thought about this. A White man somewhere with his soul trapped outside his body. "You thinking maybe we ought to find him?"

"How much him I catch here?" Gullah Joe asked. "Black people soul, I take name, I take anger, I take sad, all the rest stay body. But the White man, how much he send out, how much he give me?" He went to his table, where a hundred secrets sat in jars and little boxes. He opened one, then another, rejecting each until he found a box with a fine white powder in it. He grinned and picked up a pinch of it between his fingers. Then he walked to the edge of the original circle, where the devil-man was trapped. He parted his fingers as he blew the powder sharply. The fine grey dust quickly filled the exact dimensions of the circle, swirling right up to the edges but never drifting out. Denmark saw a tiny light, like a mosquito with a firefly's tail, changing colors as it darted about within the cloud.

"That's him?" asked Denmark.

"He got him power," said Gullah Joe, his voice filled with awe.

"How can you tell?"

"You so far off, you see him, right?"

"Sure, I saw him. Like a firefly."

Gullah Joe laughed. "You so blind! He like a star. Bright star. We got trouble in this circle. He be find a way out. And then he be mad."

"Then let's get out of here," said Denmark. "I don't want him clipping me open like that net."

"No problem," said Gullah Joe.

"You mean you can keep him from getting out?"

"I got my best circle hold him. She strong enough? I don't know.

But I don't got no better, so . . . maybe we dead, maybe we safe.'' Gullah Joe shrugged. ''No problem.''

''Well it matters to me!'' cried Denmark.

''Be maybe you better go,'' said Gullah Joe, grinning. ''You go find out what house got him a man, him eyes open, nobody inside.''

''White man?''

''You think Black man break a name-string?'' asked Gullah Joe contemptuously.

''Not all Black men be good,'' said Denmark.

''Black men all be on our side,'' said Gullah Joe.

Denmark laughed rudely. ''That the stupidest thing you said since I know you.''

Gullah Joe looked at him oddly. ''I know what I know.''

''Oh, they on your side now, Joe, cause you got their name-strings in a bag, you keeping them happy. But that don't mean they on your side, you fool. White master got them all so scared they want to please him, like little puppy dogs. They not telling *now* cause what if the White man take their soul? But they ain't on your *side*. They on their master's side.''

''You think you the only smart man?'' asked Joe, annoyed.

''I seen it a thousand times. Blacks betraying Blacks, each time hoping the master will like them better than the other slaves, treat them good. You watch.''

''I be do this long time, lots of year now,'' said Gullah Joe. ''Black people know what I got here, they never turn against me.''

''Then how did this White devil find out where you were?''

Joe's eyes grew wide at the question. Then he grinned at Denmark. ''You show them the way.''

''I did not,'' said Denmark. ''I wore that memory net you made me, nobody find anything about you from me!''

''He no look in your *head*, my net make it empty in there. This devil follow your *feet* till he come in right behind you.''

''How do you know that?''

''I know what I know,'' said Gullah Joe, for about the thousandth time since Denmark had known him. ''I see him come in.''

''You're lying,'' said Denmark. ''If you seed him come in you would have told me.''

"I feel him. I feel him hot eyes looking. I feel them charm dance, I feel them charm shake."

"Then why didn't you stop him?"

Gullah Joe grinned. "Be maybe I think he no find name-string. Be maybe I think circle keep him out."

"Be maybe you full of shit," said Denmark. "You didn't know he was here till the net started popping. He probably followed *you* inside the circle."

Gullah Joe thought about that. "Better us find him body."

"So you ain't going to admit he took you by surprise," said Denmark testily. "You got to keep pretending you see all, you know all."

"I no see *all*," said Gullah Joe. "I see more than you."

"*Some*times."

"You see so good? Then you go out and use you eyes and you mouth and you ears, you find out where they be this empty White man body without no soul."

Denmark laughed bitterly. "That be every White man I know of."

Gullah Joe ignored his remark. "You find him, and then we make him soul go back in him."

"You can do that?"

Gullah Joe shrugged. "Maybe."

"So what if it doesn't work?"

"Then he body die," said Gullah Joe. "Body him not last long time it got no soul in."

"What the hell did you just say?" asked Denmark. "All these slaves, they be dying without their souls?"

"Black people still got they soul!" said Joe impatiently. "Only White man put him soul out like this. Soul no come home, he body, she think she dead, she be rotting."

"So if he don't find his way home, his body's going to die?"

"No, she don't die, him body. That body rot, she turn to bone, she turn to dust, but she still be alive cause that soul, she can't find that body no more, she never go home."

"So he's walking around dead already," said Denmark. "All right then, why look for him?"

"Body rotting alive, that too slow. He do mischief." Gullah Joe grinned and held up a huge knife. "Better us get him out of here."

"How, by killing his body?"

"Kill?" Gullah Joe laughed. "We got to bring him body here, put she inside the circle. Soul go back in body, then he leave my house."

"Won't that make him stronger, to have body and soul together again?" asked Denmark. "You want him out wandering around, knowing what we got going here?"

"Maybe that happen if we put him *whole* body in the circle," said Gullah Joe, laughing.

"I thought you said—"

"We put in just him head," said Gullah Joe. "Then we all be safe. That soul got to go into that head. But he go in, he drop dead!"

Denmark laughed. "I got to see that." Then his face grew grim. "Course you know, you talking about killing a White man."

Gullah Joe rolled his eyes. "They plenty White man. You find him."

In the early evening, Margaret took a turn around the block. Hot as it was, she couldn't have hoped to get to sleep tonight if she hadn't taken some exercise. And the air, though at street level it was charged with the smell of fish and horse manure, was not as stale as the air inside the house. Alvin had assured her that most of the time smelly air was still just air and it did no harm to breathe it. Better the smell than the mold indoors. When he tried to tell her all the nasty living creatures that inhabited every house, no matter how clean or well-swept, Margaret had to make him stop. Some things were better not to know.

She was coming back down the long side of the house when she heard the sound of someone whimpering off in the garden. There was but one heartfire there, one she knew well—the slave called Fishy. But Margaret almost didn't recognize her, because her heartfire had been transformed. What was the difference? A tumult of emotions: rage at every insult done her, grief at all that she had lost. And deep down, where there had been nothing at all, now Margaret found it: Fishy's true name.

Njia-njiwa. The Way of the Dove. Or the Dove in the Path. It was hard for Margaret to understand, because the concept was a part of both. A dove seen in the midst of its flight in the sky, which also marks the path of life. It was a beautiful name, and in the place where her name was kept, there also was the love and praise of her family.

"Njia-njiwa," said Margaret aloud, trying to get her mouth and nose to form the strange syllables: *N* without a vowel, as a syllable by itself. Nnn-jee-yah. Nnn-jee-wah. She said it aloud again.

The whimpering stopped. Margaret stepped around a bush and there was Fishy—Njia-njiwa—cowering where the foundation of the house next door rose out of the earth. Fishy's eyes were wide with fright, but Margaret could also see that her hands were formed into claws, ready to fight.

"You stay away from me," said Fishy. It was a plea. It was a warning.

"You got your name back," said Margaret.

"How you know that? What you do to me? You a witchy woman?"

"No, no, I did nothing to you. I knew your name was lost. How did you get it back?"

"He cut me loose," said Fishy with a sob. "All of a sudden I feel myself go light. Down on a breeze. I can't even stand up. I know my name's flying only I can't call it home cause I don't *know* it. I thought I was going a-die. But it do come home and then it all come back to me." Fishy shuddered, then burst into tears.

Margaret didn't need an explanation. She saw it now in Fishy's memory. "Every vile thing that your master has done to you. Every insult by every White person. The happy life with your mama that got taken away. No wonder you wanted to kill somebody." Margaret stepped closer. "And yet you didn't. All that fire inside you, and all you did was come out into the garden and hide."

"When she find out I didn't do my work she going a-beat me," said Fishy. "She going a-beat me bad, only this time I don't know if I can take it. She not so strong, ma'am. I take the stick outen her hand, I beat her *back,* how she going a-like that, you think?"

"It wouldn't feel good, Njia-njiwa."

The girl winced at the sound of her name and wept again. "Oh, Mama, Mama, Mama."

"You poor thing," said Margaret.

"Don't you pity me, you White woman! I clean your filth just like all the rest!"

"Good people clean up after the people they love," said Margaret.

"It isn't the cleaning that you mind, it's being forced to do it for people you don't love."

"People I hate!"

"Fishy, would you rather I call you by that name?"

"Don't you go saying my true name no more," said Fishy.

"All right, then. How about this? How about if I say I had you helping me today, and I pay your mistress a little to compensate for having taken you away from your duties?"

Fishy looked at her suspiciously. "Why you do that?"

"Because I *do* need your help."

"You don't have to pay for that," said Fishy. "I be a slave, ain't you heard?"

"I don't want your labor," said Margaret. "I want your *help*."

"I don't got no help for White folks," said Fishy. "It be all I can do not to kill you right now."

"I know," said Margaret. "But you're strong. You'll contain these feelings. It's good to have your name back. It's as if you weren't alive before, and now you are."

"This ain't no life," said Fishy. "I got no hope now."

"Now is when your hope begins," said Margaret. "This thing you've done, you and the other slaves, giving up your names, your anger—it makes it safer for you, yes, it makes it easier, but you know who else it helps? Them. The White people who own you. Look at the other slaves, now that you have your anger back. See what they look like to the master."

"I know how they look," said Fishy. "They look stupid."

"That's right," said Margaret. "Stupid and contented."

"I ain't going a-look stupid no more," said Fishy. "She going a-see it in my eyes, how much I hate her. She going a-beat me all the time now."

"I can't help you with that right now," said Margaret. "I'd buy you away from her if I could, but I haven't that much money. I might rent your services, though, so you don't have to spend time with your mistress until you've got these feelings under control."

"I never going a-*control* these feelings! Hate just going a-get bigger and bigger till I kill somebody!"

"That's how it feels now, but I assure you, slaves in other cities, in other places, nobody takes their pride and hides it away, but they learn, they watch, they wait.''

''Wait for what? Wait to die.''

''Wait for hope,'' said Margaret. ''They don't *have* hope, but they hope for hope, for a reason to hope. And in the meantime, there are many White men and women like me, who hate the whole idea of slavery. We're doing all we can to set you free.''

'' 'All you can' ain't worth nothing.''

Margaret had to admit the truth of what she said. ''Fishy, I fear that you're right. I've been trying to do it with words alone, to persuade them, but I fear that they're never going to change until they're made to change. I fear that it will take war, bloody terrible war between the Crown Colonies and the United States.''

Fishy looked at her strangely. ''You telling me there be White folks up North, they willing to fight and die just to set Black folks free?''

''Some,'' said Margaret. ''And many more who are willing to fight and die in order to break the back of King Arthur, and others who would fight to show that the United States won't get pushed around by anybody, and—why should you care why they fight? If the war comes, if the North wins, then slavery will end.''

''Then bring on that war.''

''Do you want it?'' asked Margaret, curious. ''How many White people should die, so you can be free?''

''All of them!'' cried Fishy, her voice full of loathing. Then she softened. ''As many as it takes.'' And then she wept again. ''Oh, sweet Jesus, what am I? My soul so wicked! I going to hell!''

Margaret knelt beside her, facing her, and dared now to lay her hand gently on Fishy's shoulder. The girl did not recoil from her, as she would have earlier. ''You will not go to hell,'' said Margaret. ''God sees your heart.''

''My heart be full of murder all the time now!'' said Fishy.

''And yet your hand is still the hand of peace. God loves you for choosing that, Fishy. God loves you for living up to your true name.''

The movement was slight, but it was real, as Fishy leaned a little closer to Margaret, accepting her touch, and then her embrace, until she wept into Margaret's shoulder. ''Let me stay with you, ma'am,'' whispered Fishy.

"Come with me to my room, then," said Margaret. "I hope you don't mind going along with me in some lies."

Fishy giggled, though at the end it was more of a sob than a laugh. "Around here, ma'am, if folks got they mouth open, if they ain't eating then they lying."

11

Decent Men

SO THIS WAS what it came to, after all these years at the bar, as lawyer and as judge: John Adams had to sit in judgment in Cambridge over a witch trial. Oh, the ignominy of it. For a time he had been something of a philosopher, and caused an international incident over his involvement in the Appalachee Revolution. He had spoken for union between New England and the United States, daring the Lord Protector to arrest him for treason. He had called for a ban on trade with the Crown Colonies as long as they trafficked in slaves, at the very time that his fellow New Englanders were loudly calling for the right to enter into such trade. There wasn't a question of import in New England since the 1760s that John Adams hadn't been a part of. He had even founded a dynasty, or so it seemed, now that his boy John Quincy was governor of Massachusetts and chairman of the New England Council. And for the past fifteen years he had distinguished himself as a jurist, winning at last the love of his fellow Yankees when he refused an appointment to the Lord Protector's Bench in England, preferring to remain ''among the free men of America.''

And now he had to hear a witch trial. The toadlike witcher, Quill, had come to see him when he arrived in Cambridge last night, reminding him that it was his duty to uphold the law—as if John Adams needed prompting in his duty from the likes of Quill. "I have not exceeded the law in any respect," said Quill, "as you'll see even from the testimony of the witches, unless they lie."

"God help us if a witch should tell a lie," John had murmured. Quill missed the irony entirely and took the answer as an affirmation. Well, that was fine. John didn't mind if he went away happy, as long as he went away.

John should have died last year, when he got the grippe. He had it on the best authority that the Boston papers had all planned on a double-page spread for his obituary. That was precisely the space devoted to the eulogy of the last Lord Protector to shuffle off his mortal coil. It was good to be considered at a level with rulers and potentates, even though he had never quite succeeded in joining New England to the United States, making it impossible for him to play a role in that extraordinary experiment. Instead he remained here, among the good people of New England, whom he truly loved like brothers and sisters, even though he longed now and then to see a face that didn't look like every other face.

Witch trials, though—it was an ugly thing, a holdover from medieval times. A shame on the face of New England.

But the law was the law. An accusation had been made, so a trial would have to be held, or at least the beginning of one. Quill would have his chance to get some poor wretch hanged—if he could do it without violating the prerogatives of the bench or pushing the powers of the law beyond their statutory and natural limits.

Now at breakfast John Adams sat with his old pupil, Hezekiah Study. *I adhere to a double standard,* John admitted to himself. *Quill's visit to me last night I thought highly improper. Hezekiah's visit, equally intended to influence my judgment in this case, I plan to enjoy. Well, any fool can be consistent, and most fools are.*

"Cambridge is not what it used to be," said John to Hezekiah. "The students don't wear their robes."

"Out of fashion now," said Hezekiah. "Though if anyone had known you were coming, they might have put the robes back on. Your opinion on the subject is well known."

"As if these boys would so much as part their hair for a relic like me."

"A holy relic, sir?" asked Hezekiah.

John grimaced. "Oh, so I'm to be called 'sir' by you?"

"I was your student. You gave me Plato and Homer."

"But you wanted Aristophanes, as I recall." John Adams sighed. "You must realize, all my peers are dead. If I'm to have anyone on this earth call me John, it will have to be a friend who once called me 'sir' because of my seniority. We should have a new social rule. When we reach fifty, we're all the same age forever."

"John, then," said Hezekiah. "I knew God had heard my prayer when I learned that it was you and no other who drew this case."

"One judge is coughing his life out into bloody handkerchiefs and the other is burying his wife, and you think this is how God answers your prayers?"

"You weren't due, and here you are. A witch trial, sir. John."

"Oh, now you've knighted me. Sir John." He wanted to laugh at the idea of his ever being the answer to someone's prayer. Since his own prayers seemed rarely to be answered, it wouldn't be quite fair of God, would it, to play him as the prize in someone else's game of piety.

"I know how you feel about witches," said Hezekiah.

"You also know how I feel about the law," said John. "I may disbelieve in the crime, but that doesn't mean I'll have any bias in the handling of the case." Oh, let's stop the pretense that the question has come up casually. "What's your interest in it? Didn't you used to defend these cases, back when you were a lawyer?"

"I was never a good one."

John heard the pain in his voice. Still haunted after all these years? "You were an excellent lawyer, Hezekiah. But what is a lawyer against a superstitious, bloody-minded mob?"

Hezekiah smiled wanly. "I assume you know that the blacksmith's lawyer was arrested last night."

Quill hadn't seen fit to mention this little ploy, but John had learned it from the sheriff. "I can see it now. Lawyer after lawyer steps forth to defend this man, only to be accused, each in turn, and locked away. Thus the trial continues till all the lawyers are in jail."

Hezekiah smiled. "There are those who would regard that as the best of all possible outcomes."

John chuckled with him, then sighed. "Don't worry, Hezekiah. I won't have defense attorneys locked up in order to bolster the witchers' case. You shouldn't be talking to me about this, though."

"Oh, I knew what you'd do about that," said Hezekiah. "If Quill thought he could get away with *that*—well, you'll see when you meet the lawyer. He has Quill by the character!"

"That would be a slippery place to try to hold him."

"No, it wasn't the lawyer. It was another matter I wanted to bring to your attention."

"Bring it in open court then, Hezekiah."

"I can't. And it's not evidentiary, anyway."

"Then tell me afterward."

"Please don't torment me, friend," said Hezekiah. "I wouldn't attempt anything unethical. Trust me enough to hear me out."

"If it's about the case . . ."

"It's about the accuser. . . ."

"Who will also be a defendant in her own trial."

"She'll not be tried," said Hezekiah. "She's cooperating with Quill. So this can have no compromising effect on an action in court."

"Don't blame Quill for *her*. She came up with this accusation on her own."

"I know, sir. John. But she's not your normal accuser. Her parents were hanged for witches when she was a newborn. Indeed, her father took the drop, as they say, before she was even born, and her mother but weeks afterward. She found it out only a few days ago, and it put her in such a state that—"

"That she brought false accusation against a stranger?" John grimaced. "You have a fleck of yolk on your chin."

Hezekiah dabbed at it with his napkin. "I think the accusation is not false," said Hezekiah.

John glared at him. "I'm glad you didn't say anything to compromise this blacksmith's case."

"I don't mean that it's objectively true, I mean that she's being forthright. Her intent is pure. She believes the charge."

John rolled his eyes. "So how many should I hang for one girl's superstition?"

Hezekiah looked away. "She's not superstitious, sir. She's a sweet girl, good-hearted, and very bright. She's been studying with me, and sitting in on lectures."

"Oh, right. The girl and her professors. That's why Harvard got raided by the tithingmen and half the faculty hauled off for questioning."

"She didn't initiate that, sir. She refuses to accuse any but the original defendants."

"Till that rope-happy ghoul runs her into the ground."

"You should have heard the blacksmith's lawyer accuse Quill of using torture. Out on the common in front of everybody." Hezekiah smiled at the memory. "He held the strings and Quill danced for the crowd."

John liked the image as much as Hezekiah did, but he was a judge, and the first skill he had perfected was the ability to remain solemn and suppress even so much as a twinkle in his eye. "So you're here to tell me that this girl, this Purity, means well as she tries to get this young man hanged."

"I mean to say it isn't a case of vengeance for spurned love, or any such thing as are usually at the heart of witch trials."

"Then what is it? Since we both know . . ." John glanced around and lowered his voice. ". . . that the one certainty in this trial is that there *are* no witches."

"The boy was full of brag about some knack or other. All she knows is what he told her, or someone in his party. But she believed it. She's doing this because she *must* believe in the law that hanged her parents. If she did not believe that the law was right, then the sheer injustice of it would drive her mad."

"Oh, now, Hezekiah. 'Drive her mad'? Have you been reading sensational novels?"

"I mean it quite literally. She has a deep faith in the goodness of our Christian community. If she thought her parents were falsely accused and hanged for it—"

"Who were her parents? Is it a case I . . ." And then, doing the arithmetic in his head—the girl's age, that many years ago—he realized whose daughter she was. "Oh, Hezekiah. *That* case?"

Tears spilled from Hezekiah's eyes. "What I wanted you to know, John, was that the one who seems to be the accuser is merely the last victim of that wretched affair."

John answered gently. "New England is a lovely place, Hezekiah. We have our share of hypocrisy, of course, but generally we face up to our sins and the frailty of human nature, and confess our wrongs right smartly. But this one—how did it ever go that far?"

"You didn't see what I saw, John," said Hezekiah.

"No, don't tell me. You need no excuse, my friend. You stood alone."

"I couldn't . . . I could not . . ."

John laid his hand over Hezekiah's. "Thus we take a good breakfast and render it indigestible," he said. "Come, now, there's no blame attached to you."

"Oh, but there is."

"So you're defending her, to make up for it?"

Hezekiah shook his head. "I've looked after her all her life. It's my penance. To stay here, in obscurity. There's blood on my hands. I won't have more. The young lawyer who's languishing in the jail, he's the one. When you let him out, when he defends his friend, see if he doesn't give you a way to resolve the whole matter. All I ask is that you not bring charges against the accuser."

"This English barrister can do it, but not you?"

"I took a vow most solemnly before heaven."

"And deprived the New England bar of an honest man. The bench as well. You should be in robes like mine, my friend."

Hezekiah brusquely wiped the tears from his cheeks. "Thank you for seeing me, John. And for treating me as a friend."

"Now and always, Hezekiah. Will I see you at the trial?"

"How could I bear that, John? No. God bless you, John. He brought you here, I know it. Yes, I know you think God is a watchmaker who installed an infinite spring—"

"A quotation I never said, though it's much attributed to me—"

"I heard the words from your lips."

"Stir your memory, and you'll recall that I was quoting the line in order to refute it! I'm no deist, like Tom Jefferson. That's *his* line. It's the only God he's willing to worship—one who has closed up shop and gone away so there's no risk of Tom Jefferson being contradicted when he spouts his nonsense about the 'rational man.' Him and his wall of separation between church and state—such claptrap! Such a wall serves only those who want to keep God on the far side of it, so they can divide up the nation without interference.''

"I'm sorry to have brought your old nemesis into this.''

"You didn't,'' said John. "*I* did. Or rather, *he* did. You'd think that he'd stop getting under my skin, but it galls me that *his* little country is going to be part of the United States, and mine isn't.''

"Isn't *yet*,'' said Hezekiah.

"Isn't in my lifetime,'' said John, "and I'm selfish enough to wish I could have lived to see it. The United States needs this Puritan society as a counter-influence to Tom Jefferson's intolerantly secular one. Mark my words, when a government pretends that it is the highest judge of its own actions, the result is not freedom as Jefferson says, but chaos and oppression. When he shuts religion out of government, when men of faith are not listened to, then all that remains is venality, posturing, and ambition.''

"I hope you're wrong about that, sir,'' said Hezekiah. "Many of us look to the United States as the next stage of the American experiment. New England has come this far, but we are stagnant now.''

"As this trial proves.'' John sighed. "I wish I *were* wrong, Hezekiah. But I'm not. Tom Jefferson claims to stand for freedom, and charges me with trying to promote some kind of theocracy or aristocracy. But there is no freedom down his road.''

"How can we know that, sir?'' said Hezekiah. "No one has ever been down this road?''

"I have,'' said John, and regretted it at once.

Hezekiah looked at him, startled, but then smiled. "No matter how precise your imagination, sir, I doubt it will be accepted as evidence.''

But it wasn't imagination. John had *seen*. Had seen it as clearly as he saw Hezekiah standing before him now. It was a sort of vision that God had vouchsafed to him all his life, that he could see how power flowed and where it led, in groups of men both large and small. It was a strange and obscure sort of vision, which he could not explain to anyone else and had never tried, not even to Abigail, but it allowed him to chart a course through all the theories and philosophies that swirled and swarmed throughout the British colonies. It had allowed him to see through Tom Jefferson. The man talked freedom, but he could never quite bring himself to free his slaves. Abolitionists criticized him for hypocrisy, but they missed the point. He wasn't a lover of freedom who had neglected to free his slaves; he was a man who loved to control other people, and did it by talking about freedom. Jefferson had stood naked in front of the world when he tried to silence his critics with the Alien and Sedition Acts almost as soon as Appalachee won its freedom from the Crown. So much for his love of freedom—you could have freedom of speech as long as you didn't use it to oppose Jefferson's policies! Yet as soon as the acts were repealed—after years of hounding Jefferson's enemies into silence or exile—people still talked about him as the champion of liberty!

John Adams knew Tom Jefferson, and that's why Tom Jefferson hated John Adams, because John really was what Jefferson only pretended to be: a man who loved freedom, even the freedom of those who disagreed with him. Even Tom Jefferson's freedom. It made them unequal in battle. It handed the victory to Jefferson.

"Are you all right, sir?" asked Hezekiah.

"Just fighting over old battles in my mind," said John. "It's the problem with age. You have all these rusty arguments, and no quarrel to use them in. My brain is a museum, but alas, I'm the only visitor, and even I am not terribly interested in the displays."

Hezekiah laughed, but there was affection in it. "I would love nothing better than to visit there. But I'm afraid I'd be tempted to loot the place, and carry it all away with me."

To John's surprise, Hezekiah's words brought tears to his eyes. "Would you, Hezekiah?" He blinked rapidly and his eyes cleared. "You see, now, you've moved this old man with your kindness. You found the one bribe I'm susceptible to."

"It wasn't flattery, sir."

"I know," said John. "It was honor. May God forgive me, but I've never been able to purge my heart of the desire for it."

"There's no sin in it, John. The honor of good men is won only by goodness. It's how the children of God recognize each other. It's the feast of love.''

''Maybe God *did* bring me here,'' said John. ''In answer to my own prayers.''

''Maybe that's how God works,'' said Hezekiah. ''We pray for a messenger from God—who knows but what the messenger also prayed for a place to take his message?''

''What does that make me, an angel?''

''Wrestle with Jacob. Smite his thigh. Leave him limping.''

''Once your allusions were all to Homer and the Greek playwrights.''

''It's the Bible now,'' said Hezekiah. ''I have more to fear from death than you do.''

''But longer to wait before it comes,'' said John ruefully.

Hezekiah laughed, shook John's hand, and left the table. John sat back down, tucked in, and finished. The meeting had been more emotional than John had expected, or than he cared for, truth be known. Emotions had a way of filling you up and then what did you do with them? You still had to go on about your life.

Except for Hezekiah Study. He had *not* gone about his life. His life had ended, all those years ago, back in Netticut, on the end of a couple of ropes.

And my life? When did it end? Because it has ended, I see that now. I'm like Hezekiah. I took a turn, or didn't take a turn; I stopped, or failed to stop. I should have been something else. I should have been president of a fledgling nation of free men. Not a judge at a witch trial. Not a stout little man eating the dregs of his breakfast alone at table in a boardinghouse in Cambridge, waiting for Tom Jefferson, damn him, to die, so I can have the feeble satisfaction of outliving that bastard son of Liberty.

Oh, Tom. If only we could have been friends, I could have changed you, you could have changed me, we could have become in reality the statesmen you pretend to be and I wish I were.

Purity could hardly sleep all night. It was unbearable, yesterday, the running, running, running. And yet she bore it. That's what surprised her. She sweated and panted but she kept on and on and on, and all the while she ran there was a kind of music in the back of her mind. As soon as she tried to listen to it, to find the melody of it, the sound retreated and all she could hear then was the throbbing of her pulse in her head, her own panting, her feet thudding on the grassy ground. But then she'd stagger a few steps and the music would come back and it would sustain her and . . .

She knew what it was. Hadn't Arthur Stuart talked about how Alvin could run and run with the greensong he learned from that Red prophet? Or was it Ta-Kumsaw himself? It didn't matter. Alvin was using his witchery to sustain her and she wanted to scream at him to stop.

But she had learned a little between yesterday and today. Quill had taught her. Everything she said got twisted. She had never mentioned Satan, had never even thought of him, but somehow her meeting with Alvin and his friends on the banks of the river had turned into a witches' sabbath, and Alvin swimming in the river with Arthur Stuart had been turned into incestuous sodomy. And she finally realized what should have been obvious all along—what Reverend Study had tried to warn her about—that whatever fault there might be in Alvin Smith, it was nothing compared to the terrible evil that resulted from denouncing him as a witch. What would happen if she cried out what was in her heart? "Stop it! Stop witching me to keep running!" It would only make things worse.

Is this what happened to my parents?

Gradually, as the day wore on, she had begun to notice something else. It was Quill who was filled with fear and rage, his mind alert to take anything that happened and turn it into proof of the evil he was looking for. Quill looked at Purity with fascination and loathing, a combination she found fearful and disturbing. But Alvin Smith, he was as cheerful toward her today as he ever was on the riverbank. Not a complaint toward her for getting him locked up. And yes, he used his witchery, or so it seemed to her, but he did it out of genuine kindness toward her. That was the truth—by her own knack she knew it. He was a little impatient with her, but he bore her no ill will.

Now, as the day of her testimony loomed, she did not know what to do. If she bore witness against Alvin now, telling the simple truth, Quill would make it seem as though she was holding back. She could imagine the questioning. "Why are you refusing to mention the witches' sabbath?" "There was no witches' sabbath." "What about the naked debauchery between this man and this half-White boy who is said to be as it were his own son?" "They played in the river, that's all." "Ah, they *played* in the river, a naked man, a naked boy, they sported in the river, is that your testimony?" Oh, it would be awful, every word twisted.

Simpler by far to confess to a lesser crime: I made it up, Your Honor, because they frightened me by the riverbank and I wished them to see what it felt like. I made it up because I had just learned my parents were hanged for witchcraft and I wanted to show how false accusations are too readily believed.

She had almost resolved on this course of action when the key turned in the lock and the door opened and there stood Quill, his face warm and smiling, filled with love. To her it looked like hate, and now she could see what somehow had eluded her before: Quill wanted her to die.

How could she have missed it? It was her knack, to see what people intended, what they were about to do. Yet she saw no further than his smile the first time they met, saw nothing but his genuine love and sympathy and concern for her. How could her knack have failed her?

Was it what Quill had said to her, in one of his many rambling discourses on Satan? That Satan was not loyal and did not uphold his disciples?

Why, then, would she see the truth now?

Or was it the truth? Was Satan now deceiving her into thinking she saw hatred where love truly existed?

There was no way out of this circle of doubt. There was no firm ground to hold to. Alvin Smith, who admitted to witchery, was kind and forgiving to her though she did him great harm. Quill, who was the servant of God in opposing witchery, twisted every word she said to make her bear false witness against Smith and his friends. And now he seemed to want her to hang. That was how it *seemed*. Could the truth be so simple? Was it possible that things were exactly as they seemed?

"I know what you're thinking," said Quill softly.

"Do you?" she murmured.

"You're thinking that you want to recant your testimony against Alvin Smith and make the whole trial go away. I know you're thinking that because everybody does, just before the trial."

She said nothing. For she could sense the malice coming from him like stink from an untended baby.

"It wouldn't go away," said Quill. "I already have your testimony under oath. All that would happen is that perjury would be added to your crimes. And worse—having repented, you would be seen to have returned to Satan, trying to conceal his acts. Indeed, you already seemed to be concealing the other witches in Cambridge. You could not have expected to protect your friends and incriminate only the strangers, could you? Were you that naive? Were you so caught up in the snares and nets of Satan that you believed you could hide from God?"

"I've hidden nothing." Even as she said it, she knew the futility of denial.

"I have here a list of the professors and lecturers at Cambridge who are known to create an atmosphere of hostility toward faith and piety in their classrooms. You are not alone in denouncing them—my colleagues and I have compiled this list over a period of years. Emerson, for instance, scoffs at the very idea of the existence of witches and witchery. You like Emerson, don't you? I've heard that you were especially attentive in spying outside his classroom."

"It wasn't spying, I was given the right to listen," said Purity.

"You heard him," said Quill. "But my question is, did you see him? At a witches' sabbath?"

"I never saw a witches' sabbath, so how could I have seen him at one?"

"Don't chop logic with me," whispered Quill. "The syllogism is false because your testimony has been false. You told me about one witches' sabbath yourself."

"I never did."

"The debauchery," he whispered. "The crimes against nature."

She looked him boldly in the face, seeing his lust for her blood so strongly depicted in the fire of his face, the tension of his body that she would not have needed a knack to detect it. "You are the one who hates nature," she said. "You are the enemy of God."

"Feeble. I advise against your using that line in court. It will only make you look stupid and I answer it so easily."

"You are the enemy of goodness and decency," she said, speaking more boldly now, "and insofar as God is good, you hate God."

"Insofar as? The professors have taught you well. I think your answer, despite your attempts to deceive, has to be 'yes' to the question of whether you saw Emerson at a witches' sabbath."

"I say no such thing."

"I say that by using professorial language in the midst of a satanic denunciation of my role in God's service, your true spirit, held a helpless prisoner by Satan, was trying to send me a coded message denouncing Emerson."

"Who would believe such nonsense?"

"I'll say it in a way the court can understand," said Quill. He checked off Emerson's name. "Emerson, yes. One of Satan's spies, caught. Now look at the other names."

"Coded message," she said contemptuously.

"What you don't understand is that your very sneer shows your contempt for holiness. You hate all things good and decent, and your scornfulness proves it."

"Go away."

"For now," said Quill. "Your arraignment is this morning. The judge wants to hear you when Alvin Smith makes his plea."

But she was not fooled. Her knack was too trustworthy for her to doubt what she saw now.

"You're such a bad liar, Quill," she said. "The judge never needs to have a witness at the arraignment. I'll be there because I'm to be arraigned as well."

Quill was face-to-face with her again at once. "Satan whispered that lie to you, didn't he."

"Why would you say that?"

"I saw it," he said. "I saw him whisper to you."

"You're insane."

"I saw you looking at me, and in a sudden moment you were told something that you hadn't known before. Satan whispered."

Had he seen it? Was it his knack to see other knacks working?

No. It was his knack to find the useful lie hidden inside every useless truth. He had simply seen the transformation in her facial expression when she understood the truth about his intentions.

"Satan has never told me anything," she said.

"But you already told me about your knack," he answered with a smile. "Don't recant—it will go hard with you."

"Maybe I have a talent for seeing other people's intentions," she said defiantly. "That doesn't mean it comes from Satan!"

"Yes," he said. "Use that line in court. Confess your sin and then deny that it's a sin. See what happens to you under the law." He reached out and touched her hand, gently, caressingly. "God loves you, child. Don't reject him. Turn away from Satan. Admit all the evil you have done so you can prove you have left it behind you. Live to let your womb bear children, as God intended. It's Satan, not God, who wants you twitching at the end of a rope."

"Yes," she said. "That much is true. Satan your master wants me dead."

He winked at her, got up, and went to the door. "That's good. Keep that up. That'll get you hanged." And he was gone, the door locked behind him.

She shook with cold as if it weren't summer with the heat already oppressive this early in the morning. Everything was clear to her now. Quill came here ready to do exactly what he had done—take a simple accusation of the use of a knack, and turn it into a story about Satan and gross perversions. He knew he had to do this because honest people never told stories about Satan. He knew that she would not name others she saw at witches' sabbaths because there were never any such conclaves, and all such denunciations had to be extracted through whatever torture the law would allow. Witchers did what Quill did because if they did not do it, no one would ever be convicted of trafficking with Satan.

This was how her parents died. Not because they really did have knacks that came from Satan, but because they would not play along with the witchers and join them in persecuting others. They would not confess to falsehood. They died because the City of God tried so hard to be pure that it created its own impurity. The evil the witchers did was worse than any evil they might prevent. And yet the people of New

England were so afraid that they might not live up to the ideals of Puritanism that they dared not speak against a law that purported to protect them from Satan.

I believed them. They killed my parents, raised me as an orphan, tainted with the rumor of evil, and instead of denouncing them for what they had done to me, I believed them and tried to do the same thing to someone else. To Alvin Smith, who did me no harm.

Purity threw herself to her knees and prayed. O Father in heaven, what have I done, what have I done.

Alvin finished the piss-poor breakfast they served to prisoners in the jail, then lay back on his cot to survey the people that he cared about. Far away in Camelot, his wife and their unborn daughter thrived. In Vigor Church, his mother and father, his brothers and sisters, all were doing well, none sick, none injured. Nearby, Verily was being let out of his cell. Alvin tracked him for a while, to be sure that he was being released. Yes, at the door of the courthouse they turned him loose to go find his own breakfast.

Out on the riverbank, Arthur Stuart and Mike Fink were fishing while Audubon was painting a kingfisher in the early-morning light. All was well.

It was only by chance that Alvin noticed the other heartfires converging on the river. He might not even have noticed them, in his reverie about eating fish just caught from the river, roasted over a smoky fire, except that something was wrong, some indefinable change in the world his doodlebug passed through. A sort of shimmering in the air, a feeling of something that loomed just out of sight, trembling on the verge of visibility.

Alvin knew what he was seeing. The Unmaker was abroad in the world.

Why was the Unmaker coming out in the open with the tithingmen? There had been no sign of the Unmaker lingering around Quill, who was clearly a lover of destruction.

Of course the very question contained its own answer. The Unmaker didn't have to emerge where people served its cause willingly, knowingly. Eagerly. Quill wasn't like Reverend Thrower. He didn't have to be lied to. He loved being the serpent in the garden. He would have been disappointed if he couldn't get the part. But the tithingmen were decent human beings and the Unmaker had to herd them.

Which was, quite literally, what it was doing. Quill had asked them to go searching for a witches' sabbath. They set out with no particular destination, except a vague idea that since Purity had spoken of encountering Alvin's party on the riverbank, that might be a good area to explore. Now, whenever they turned away from Arthur and Mike and Jean-Jacques, they stepped into the Unmaker's influence and they became uneasy, vaguely frightened. It made them turn around and walk quite briskly the other way. Closer to Alvin's friends.

Well, thought Alvin, this looks like a much better game if played by two.

His first thought was to bring up a fog from the river, to make it impossible for them to find their way. But he rejected this at once. The Unmaker could herd them whether they could see their way or not. The fog would only make it look more suspicious-sounding, more like witchery, when they recounted their story later. Besides, fog was made of water, and water was the element the Unmaker used the most. Alvin wasn't altogether certain that his control was so strong, especially at a distance, that he could count on keeping the Unmaker from subverting the fog. Someone might slip and die, and it would be blamed on witchery.

What did the tithingmen care about? They were good men who served their community, to keep it safe from harm and to keep the peace among neighbors and within family. When a couple quarreled, it was a tithingman who went to them to help them iron it out, or to separate them for a time if that was needed. When someone was breaking the sumptuary laws, or using coarse language, or otherwise offending against the standards that helped them all stay pure, it was a tithingman who tried, peacefully, to persuade them to mend their ways without the need of dire remedies. It was the tithingmen who kept the work of the courts to a minimum.

And a man didn't last long as a tithingman in a New England town if he fancied himself to be possessed of some sort of personal authority. He had none. Rather he was the voice and hands of the community as a whole, and a soft voice and gentle hands were preferred by all. Anyone who seemed to like to boss others about would simply be overlooked when the next round of tithingmen were chosen. Sometimes they realized that they hadn't been called on for many years, and wondered why; some even humbly asked, and tried to mend their ways. If they never asked, they were never told. What mattered was that the work be done, and done kindly.

So these were not cudgel-wielding thugs who were being herded toward the riverbank. Not like the Finders who came after Arthur Stuart back in Hatrack River, and were perfectly happy to kill anyone who stood violently against them. Not even like Reverend Thrower, who was somewhat deceived by the Unmaker but nevertheless had a zeal to pursue "evil" and root it out.

How could Alvin turn good men away from an evil path? How could he get them to ignore the Unmaker and take away its power to herd them?

Alvin sent his doodlebug into the village of Cambridge. Into the houses of families, listening for voices, voices of children. He needed the sound of a child in distress, but quickly realized that in a good Puritan town, children were kindly treated and well watched-out-for. He would have to do a little mischief to get the sound.

A kitchen. A three-year-old girl, watching her mother slice onions. The mother leaned forward on her chair. It was a simple matter for Alvin to weaken the leg and break the chair under her. With a shriek she fell. Alvin took care to make sure no harm befell her. What he wanted was from the child, not from her. And there it was. The girl cried out : "Mama!"

Alvin captured the sound, the pattern of it in the air. He carried it, strengthened it, the quivering waves; he layered them, echoed them, brought some slowly, some quickly in a complicated interweave of sound. It was very hard work, and took all his concentration, but finally he brought the first copy of the girl's cry to the tithingmen.

"Mama!"

They turned at once, hearing it as if in the near distance, and behind them, away from the river.

Again, fainter: "Mama!"

At once the tithingmen turned, knowing their duty. Searching for witches was their duty, but the distress of a child calling for her mother clearly was more important.

They plunged right into the Unmaker, and of course it chilled their hearts with fear, but at that moment Alvin brought them the girl's cry for yet a third and last time, so when fear struck them, instead of making them recoil it made them run even faster toward the sound. The fear turned from a sense of personal danger into an urgent need to get to the child because something very bad was happening to her—their fear became, not a barrier, but a spur to greater effort.

For a while the Unmaker tried to stay with them, trying out other emotions—anger, horror—but all its efforts worked against its own purpose. It couldn't understand what Alvin was relying on: the power of decent men to act against their own interest in order to help those who trusted them. The Unmaker understood how to make men kill in war. What it could not comprehend was why they were willing to die.

So the tithingmen hunted fruitlessly in the woods and meadows, trying to find the girl whose voice they had heard, until finally they gave up and headed into town to try to find out which child was missing and organize a search. But all the children were in their places, and, despite some misgivings—they had all heard the voice, after all—they went about their ordinary business, figuring that if there needed to be a witch hunt, tomorrow would do as well as today.

On the riverbank, Arthur and Mike and Jean-Jacques had no idea that the Unmaker had been stalking them.

In his cell, Alvin wanted only to lie back and sleep. That was when the sheriff came for him, to bring him into the court for his arraignment.

Verily had only a few minutes to confer with Alvin before the arraignment began, and always with the sheriff present, so there couldn't be much candor—but such was the rule with witch trials, so no potions or powders could be passed between them, or secret curses spoken. "No matter how it seems, Alvin, you must trust me."

"Why? How is it going to seem?"

"The judge is John Adams. I've been reading his writings and his court cases, both as lawyer and as judge, since I first began the study of law. The man is decent to the core. I had no knowledge of his ever doing a witch trial, though, and so I had no idea of his position on them. But when I came out of jail this morning, I was met by a fellow who lives here—''

"No need for names," said Alvin.

Verily smiled. "A fellow, I say, who's made some study of witch law—in fact that's his name, Study—and he tells me that Adams has never actually rendered a verdict in a witchery case."

"What does that mean?"

"There's always been some defect in the witchers' presentation and he's thrown the whole thing out."

"Then that's good," said Alvin.

"No," said Verily. "That's bad."

"I'd go free, wouldn't I?"

"But the law would still stand."

Alvin rolled his eyes. "Verily, I didn't come back here to try to reform New England, I came in order to—"

"We came to help Purity," said Verily. "And all the others. Do you know what it would mean, if the law itself were found defective? Adams is a man of weighty reputation. Even from the circuit bench of Boston, his decisions would be looked at carefully and carry much precedence in England as well as in America. The right decision might mean the end of witch trials, here as well as there."

Alvin smiled thinly. "You got too high an opinion of human nature."

"Do I?"

"The law didn't make witch trials happen. It was the hunger for witch trials that got them to make up the law."

"But if we do away with the legal basis—"

"Listen, Verily, do you think men like Quill will flat-out disappear just cause witchery ain't there to give them what they want? No, they'll just find another way to do the same job."

"You don't know that."

"If it ain't witchcraft, they'll find new crimes that work just the way witchcraft does, so you can take ordinary folks making ordinary mistakes or not even mistakes, just going about their business, but suddenly the witcher, he finds some wickedness in it, and turns everything they say into proof that they're guilty of causing every bad thing that's been going wrong."

"There's no other law that works that way."

"That's because we *got* witch laws, Very. Get rid of them, and people will find a way take all the sins of the world and put them onto the heads of some fellow who's attracted their attention and then destroy him and all his friends."

"Purity isn't evil, Alvin."

"Quill is," said Alvin.

The sheriff leaned down. "I'm trying not to listen, boys, but you know it's a crime to speak ill of a witcher. This Quill, he takes it as evidence that Satan's got you by the short hairs, begging your pardon."

"Thank you for the reminder, sir," said Verily. "My client didn't mean it quite the way it sounded."

The sheriff rolled his eyes. "From what I've seen, it doesn't matter much how it sounds when you say it. What matters is how it sounds when Quill repeats it."

Verily grinned at the sheriff and then at Alvin.

"What are you smiling at?" asked Alvin.

"I just got all the proof I need that you're wrong. People don't like the way the witch trials work. People don't like injustice. Strike down these laws and no one will miss them."

Alvin shook his head. "Good people won't miss them. But it wasn't good people as set them up in the first place. It was scared people. The world ain't steady. Bad things happen even when you been careful and done no wrong. Good people, strong people, they take that in stride, but them as is scared and weak, they want somebody to blame. The good people will think they've stamped out witch trials, but the next generation they'll turn around and there they'll be again, wearing a different hat, going by a different name, but witch trials all the same, where they care more about getting somebody punished than whether they're actually guilty of anything."

"Then we'll stamp them out again," said Verily.

Alvin shrugged. "Of course we will, once we figure out what's what and who's who. Maybe next time the witchers will go after folks with opinions they don't like, or folks who pray the wrong way or in the wrong place, or folks who look ugly or talk funny, or folks who aren't polite enough, or folks who wear the wrong clothes. Someday they may hold witch trials to condemn people for being Puritans."

Verily leaned over and whispered into Alvin's ear. "Meaning no disrespect, Al, it's your wife who can see into the future, not you."

"No whispering," said the sheriff. "You might be giving me the pox." He chuckled, but there was just a little bit of genuine worry in his voice.

Alvin answered Verily out loud. "Meaning no disrespect, Very, it don't take a knack to know that human nature ain't going to change anytime soon."

Verily stood up. "It's time for the arraignment, Alvin. There's no point in our talking philosophy before a trial. I never knew till now that you were so cynical about human nature."

"I know the power of the Unmaker," said Alvin. "It never lets up. It never gives in. It just moves on to other ground."

Shaking his head, Verily led the way out of the room. The sheriff, tightly holding the end of Alvin's chain, escorted him right after. "I got to say, I never seen a prisoner who cared so little about whether he got convicted or not."

Alvin reached up his hand and scratched the side of his nose. "I'm not all that worried, I got to admit." Then he put his hand back down.

It wasn't till they were almost in the courtroom that the sheriff realized that there was no way the prisoner could have got his hand up to his face with those manacles on, chained to his ankle braces the way they were. But by then he couldn't be sure he'd actually seen the young fellow scratch his nose. He just thought he remembered that. Just his mind playing tricks on him. After all, if this Alvin Smith could take his hands out of iron manacles, just like that, why didn't he walk out of jail last night?

12

Slaves

"YOU MUST TAKE care of him," said Balzac.

"In a boardinghouse for ladies?" asked Margaret.

Calvin stood there, his unblinking gaze focused on nothing.

"They have servants, no? He is your brother-in-law, he is sick, they will not refuse you."

Margaret did not have to ask him what had precipitated his decision. At the French embassy today Balzac received a letter from a Paris publisher. One of his essays on his American travels had already appeared in a weekly, and was so popular that the publisher was going to serialize the rest of them and then bring them out as a book. A letter of credit was included. It was enough for a passage home.

"Just when you start earning money from your writing about America, you're going to leave?"

"Writing about America will pay for leaving America," said Balzac. "I am a novelist. It is about the human soul that I write, not the odd customs of this barbaric country." He grinned. "Besides, when they read what I have written about the practice of slavery in Camelot, this will be a very good place for me to be far away."

Margaret dipped into his futures. "Will you do me one kindness, then?" she asked. "Will you write in such a way that when war comes between the armies of slavery and of liberty, no government of France will be able to justify joining the war on the side of the slave-holders?"

"You imagine my writing to have more authority than it will ever have."

But already she saw that he would honor her request, and that it would work. "You are the one who underestimates yourself," said Margaret. "The decision you made in your heart just now has already changed the world."

Tears came to Balzac's eyes. "Madame, you have give me this unspeakable gift which no writer ever get: You tell me that my imaginary stories are not frivolous, they make life better in reality."

"Go home, Monsieur de Balzac. America is better because you came, and France will be better when you return."

"It is a shame you are married so completely," said Balzac. "I have never loved any woman the way I love you in this moment."

"Nonsense," said Margaret. "It is yourself you love. I merely brought you a good report of your loved one." She smiled. "God bless you."

Balzac took Calvin's hand. "It does me no good to speak to him. Tell him I did my best but I must to go home."

"I will tell him that you remain his true friend."

"Do not go too far in this!" said Balzac in mock horror. "I do not wish him to visit me."

Margaret shrugged. "If he does, you'll deal with him."

Balzac bowed over her hand and kissed it. Then he took off at a jaunty pace along the sidewalk.

Margaret turned to Calvin. She could see that he was pale, his skin white and patchy-looking. He stank. "This won't do," she said. "It's time to find where they've put you."

She led the docile shell of a man into the boardinghouse. She toyed with the idea of leaving him in the public room, but imagined what would happen if he started breaking wind or worse. So she led him up the stairs. He climbed them readily enough, but with each step she had to pull him on to the next, or he'd just stand there. The idea of completing the whole flight of stairs in one sweep was more than his distracted attention could deal with.

Fishy was in the hall when Margaret reached her floor. Margaret was gratified to see that as soon as Fishy recognized who it was, she shed the bowed posture of slavery and looked her full in the eye. "Ma'am, you can't bring no gentleman to this floor."

Margaret calmly unlocked her door and pushed Calvin inside as she answered. "I can assure you, he's not a gentleman."

Moments later, Fishy slipped into the room and closed the door behind her. "Ma'am, it's a scandal, She throw you out." Only then did she look at Calvin. "What's wrong with this one?"

"Fishy, I need your help. To bring this man back to himself." As briefly as she could, she told Fishy what had happened with Calvin.

"He the one send my name back to me?"

"I'm sure he didn't realize what he was doing. He's frightened and desperate."

"I don't know if I be hating him," said Fishy. "I hurt all the time now. But I know I be hurting."

"You're a whole woman now," said Margaret. "That makes you free, even in your slavery."

"This one, he gots the power to put all the names back?"

"I don't know."

"The Black man who take the names, I don't know his name. Be maybe I know his face, iffen I see him."

"And you have no idea where they take the names?"

"Nobody know. Nobody *wants* to. Can't tell what you don't know."

"Will you help me find him? From what Balzac said, he lurks by the docks."

"Oh, it be easy a-find him. But how you going a-stop him from killing you and me and the White man, all three?"

"Do you think he would?"

"A White woman and a White man who know that he gots the names? He going a-think I be the one a-tell you." She drew a finger across her throat. "My neck, he cut that. Stab you in the heart. Tear him open by the belly. That's what happen to the ones who tell."

"Fishy, I can't explain it to you, but I can assure you of this—we will *not* be taken by surprise."

"I druther be surprise iffen he kill us," said Fishy. She mimed slitting her own throat again. "Let him sneak up behind."

"He won't kill us at all. We'll stand at a distance."

"What good that going a-do us?"

"There's much I can learn about a man from a distance, once I know who he is."

"I still gots a room to finish cleaning."

"I'll help you," said Margaret.

Fishy almost laughed out loud. "You the strangest White lady."

"Oh, I suppose that would cause comment."

"You just set here," said Fishy. "I be back soon. Then I be on your half-day. They have to let me go out with you."

Denmark spent a fruitless morning asking around about a White man who suddenly went empty. He'd knock on a door, pretending to be asking for work for a non-existent White master—just so the slave who talked to him had a story to tell when somebody asked them who was at the door. The slaves all knew who Denmark was, of course—nobody was more famous among the Blacks of Camelot than the taker of names. Unless it was Gullah Joe, the bird man who flew out to the slaveships. So there wasn't a soul who didn't try to help. Trouble was, all these people with no name, they had no sharp edge to them. They vaguely remembered hearing this or that about a White man who was sick or a White man who couldn't walk, but in each case it turned out to be some old cripple or a man who'd already died of some disease. Not till afternoon did he finally hear a story that sounded like it might be what he needed.

He followed the rumor to a cheap boardinghouse where yes, indeed, two White men had shared a room, and one of them, the Northerner, had taken sick with a strange malady. "He eat, he drink, he pee, he do all them thing," said the valet who had cared for their room. "I change him trouser three times a day, wash everything twice a day." But they had left just that morning. "French man, he gots a letter, he pack up all, take away that empty man, now they be both all gone."

"Did he say where he taking the sick man?" asked Denmark.

"He don't say nothing to me," said the valet.

"Does anybody know?"

"You want me to get in trouble, asking question from the White boss?"

Denmark sighed. "You tell him that Frenchman and that Northerner, they owe my master money."

The valet looked puzzled. "Your master dumb enough a-lend them money?"

Denmark leaned in close. "It's a lie," he said. "You *say* they owe my master money, then the White boss tell you where they gone off to."

It took a moment, but finally the valet understood and retreated into the house. When he came back, he had some information. "Calvin, he the sick man, he gots a sister-in-law here. At a boardinghouse."

"What's the address?"

"White boss don't know."

"White boss hoping for a bribe," said Denmark.

The valet shook his head. "No, he don't know, that the truth."

"How'm I going to find her with no address?"

The valet shrugged. "Be maybe you best ask around."

"Ask what? 'There's a woman with a sick brother-in-law named Calvin and she living in a boardinghouse somewhere.' That get me a lot of results."

The valet looked at him like he was crazy. "I don't think you get much that way. I bet you do better, you tell them her name."

"I don't *know* her name."

"Why not? I do."

Denmark closed his eyes. "That's good. How about you tell me that name?"

"Margaret."

"She got her a last name? White folks has a last name every time."

"Smith," said the valet. "But she don't look big enough for smith work."

"You've *seen* her?" asked Denmark.

"Lots of times."

"When would you see her?"

"I run messages to her and back a couple of times."

Denmark sighed, keeping anger out of his voice. "Well now, my friend, don't that mean you know where she lives?"

"I do," said the valet.

"Why couldn't you just tell me that?"

"You didn't be asking where she live, you ask for the *address*. I don't know no number or letter."

"Could you lead me there?"

The valet rolled his eyes. "Sixpence to the White boss and he let me take you."

Denmark looked at him suspiciously. "You sure it ain't tuppence to the White boss and the rest to you?"

The valet looked aggrieved. "I be a Christian."

"So be all the White folks," said Denmark.

The valet, all anger having been stripped from him long ago, had no chance of understanding pointed irony. "Of course they be Christian. How else I learn about Jesus 'cept from them?"

Denmark dug a sixpence out of his pocket and gave it to the valet. In moments he was back, grinning. "I gots ten minutes."

"That time enough?"

"Two blocks over, one block down."

When they got to the door of Margaret Smith's boardinghouse, the valet just stood there.

"Step aside so I can knock," said Denmark.

"I can if you want," said the valet. "But I don't see why."

"Well if I don't knock, how'm I going to find out if she be in?"

"She ain't in," said the valet.

"How you know that?"

"Cause she over there, looking at you."

Denmark turned around casually. A White woman, a White man, and a Black servant girl were across the street, walking away.

"Who's looking at me?"

"They *was* looking," said the valet. "And I know she can tell you about that Calvin man."

"How do you know that?"

"That be him."

Denmark looked again. The White man was shuffling along like an old man. Empty.

Denmark grinned and gave another tuppence to the valet. "Good job, when you finally got around to telling me."

The valet took the tuppence, looked at it, and offered it back. "No, it be sixpence the White boss want."

"I already paid the sixpence," said Denmark.

The valet looked at him like he had lost his mind. "If you done that, why you be giving me more? This tuppence not enough anyway." Huffily, he handed the coin back. "You crazy." Then he was gone.

Denmark sauntered along, keeping them in sight. A couple of times the slave girl looked back and gazed at him. But he wasn't worried. She'd know who he was, and there was no chance of a Black girl telling this White lady anything about the taker of names.

"That him," said Fishy. "He take the names."

Margaret saw at once in Denmark's mind that he could not be trusted for a moment. She had been looking for him, and he had been looking for her. But he had a knife and meant to use it. That was hardly the way to restore Calvin's heartfire.

"Let's go down to the battery. There are always plenty of people there. He won't dare harm a White man in such a crowd. He doesn't want to die."

"He won't talk to you, neither," said Fishy. "He just watch."

"He'll talk to me," said Margaret. "Because you'll go ask him to."

"He scare me, ma'am."

"Me too," said Margaret. "But I can promise you, he won't harm you. The only one he wants to hurt is Calvin here."

Fishy looked at Calvin again. "Look like somebody done hurt him most all he can be hurt till he be dead." Then she realized what she had said. "Oh."

"This name-taker, Denmark Vesey, is quite an interesting fellow. You know that he isn't a slave?"

"He free? Ain't no free Blacks in Camelot."

"Oh, that's the official story, but it isn't so. I've already met another. A woman named Doe. She was given her freedom when she became too old to work."

"They turn her out then?" demanded Fishy, outraged.

"Careful," said Margaret. "We're not alone here."

Fishy at once changed her demeanor and looked down at the street again. "I seen too many damn cobblestones in my life."

"They didn't turn her out," said Margaret. "Though I have no doubt there are masters cruel enough to do so. No, she has a little room of her own and she eats with the others. And they pay her a small wage for very light work."

"They think that make up for taking her whole life away from her?"

"Yes, they think it does. And Doe thinks so, too. She has her name back, and I suppose she has reason enough to be angry, but she's happy enough."

"Then she a fool."

"No, she's just old. And tired. For her, freedom means she doesn't have to work anymore, except to make her own bed."

"That won't be enough for me, Miz Margaret."

"No, Fishy, I'm quite sure it won't. It shouldn't be enough for anyone. But don't begrudge Doe her contentment. She's earned it."

Fishy looked back and became agitated. "He coming closer, ma'am."

"Only because he's afraid of losing track of us in the crowd." Margaret steered Calvin toward the seawall. Out in the water they could see the fortresses: Lancelot and Galahad. Such fanciful names. King Arthur indeed. "Denmark Vesey is free and he earns his living by keeping the account books of several small businesses and professional offices."

"A Black man know his numbers?"

"And his letters. Of course he pretends that he works for a White man who really does the work, but I doubt any of his clients are fooled. They maintain the legal fiction so that nobody has to send anyone to jail. They pay half what they would for a White man, and he gets paid far more than he needs to live in Blacktown. Clever."

"And he take the names."

"No, actually, he collects them, but he takes them somewhere and gives them to someone else."

"Who?"

Margaret sighed. "Whoever it is, he knows how to shut me out of just that part of Denmark's memory. That's never happened to me before. Or perhaps I simply didn't notice it. I must have skimmed past this man's heartfire before, searching for the taker of names, but because only part of his memory was hidden, I would never have noticed." Then she thought a little more. "No, I daresay I never looked in his heartfire, because he has his name, and so his heartfire burns brightly enough that

I would have assumed he was a White man and not looked at all. He was hidden right out in the open.''

"You a witchy woman, ain't you, ma'am?''

"Not in the sense that White folks use the word,'' said Margaret. "I don't do any cursing, and what hexes I have to protect me, those were made by my husband, I do no such work. What I am is a torch. I see into people's heartfire. I find the paths of their future.''

"What you see in my future?''

"No, Fishy,'' said Margaret. "You have so many paths open before you. I can't tell you which one you'll take, because it's up to you.''

"But that man, he don't kill me, right?''

Margaret shook her head. "I don't see any paths right now where that happens. But I don't tell futures, Fishy. People live and die by their own choices.''

"Not even your own future? Your husband?''

Margaret grimaced. "I did try to get my husband to change his life. You see, on every path where he doesn't get killed sooner, he ends up dying because of the betrayal of his own brother.''

Fishy took only a moment to realize the connection. "Be maybe you don't mean *this* brother?''

"No, I *do* mean this brother.''

"Then why you not let that name-taker man cut his throat?''

"Because my husband loves him.''

"But he going a-kill him!''

Margaret smiled wanly. "Isn't that the strangest thing?'' she said. "Knowing the future doesn't change a man like my husband. He does what's right no matter where the road leads.''

"He *always* do what's right?''

"As much as he understands it. Most of the time he tries to do as little as possible. He tries to learn, and then teach. Not like Denmark Vesey. He's a man who *acts*.'' Margaret shuddered. "But not wisely. Cleverly, yes, but not wisely, and not kindly, either.''

"He squatting under that tree yonder.''

"Now is the time, Fishy. Go to him, tell him I want to talk to him.''

"Oh, Miz Margaret, you sure he don't hurt me?''

"He'll think you're pretty.'' Margaret touched her arm. "He'll think you're the most beautiful woman he's ever seen.''

"You joking now."

"Not at all. You see, you're the first free Black woman he's known."

"I not free."

"He bought a slave once. Hoping to make her his wife. But she was so ashamed of being owned by a Black man that she threatened to expose his ability to read and write and tell the authorities that he's a free Black in Camelot."

"What he do?"

"What do you think?"

"He kill her."

"He tried. At the last moment he changed his mind. She's still his slave, but she's crippled. Mind and body."

"You didn't have to tell me that story," said Fishy. "I wasn't going to let him talk love to me. He scare me too bad."

"I just thought you should know."

"Well, you know what? It take away some of my scared, knowing that about him."

It stabbed Margaret to the heart, watching the smiling girl change before she turned around and walked among the Whites promenading on the battery. The smile fled; her eyelids half closed; she bent her shoulders and looked down as she made her way, not directly toward Denmark, but off at an angle. After a short time she doubled back and came to him from another way. Very good, thought Margaret. I didn't think to tell her to do that, but it keeps it from being obvious to on-lookers that I sent her to fetch Denmark.

Fishy handled it deftly. My mistress want a-talk to you. What about? My mistress want a-talk to you. No matter what he said, she answered like a parrot. Maybe he knew she was pretending or maybe he thought she was stupid and stubborn, but either way, it got him up and walking, following Fishy's roundabout course as she walked two paces ahead of him. They couldn't walk side by side, or it would seem to White folks that they were promenading, and it would be taken as outrageous mock-ery. Instead it was obvious she was leading him, which meant they were on an errand for their master, and all was well with the world.

"What you want to talk about?" Denmark asked her, keeping his head downcast. But in the tone of his voice she could hear his hostility toward her.

"You're looking for me," she said.

"Am not," he said.

"Oh, that's right. It's Calvin you're looking for."

"That his name?"

"His name won't give you any power over him greater than what you already have."

"I got no power over nobody."

Margaret sighed. "Then why do you have a knife in your pocket? That's against the law, Denmark Vesey. You have other hidden powers. You're a free Black in Camelot, doing account books for—let's see, Dunn and Brown, Longer and Ford, Taggart's grocery—"

"I should have knowed you been spying on me." There was fear in his voice, despite his best effort to sound unconcerned. "White ladies got nothing better to do."

Margaret pressed on. "You found out where I lived because the valet at Calvin's former boardinghouse led you. And you have a woman at home whose name you never utter. You nearly drowned her in a sack in the river. You're a man with a conscience, and it causes you great pain."

He almost staggered from the blow of knowing how much she knew about him. "They hang me, a Black man owning a slave."

"You've made quite a life for yourself, being a free man in a city of slaves. It hasn't been as good for your wife, though, has it?"

"What you want from me?"

"This isn't extortion, except in the mildest sense. I'm telling you that I know what and who you are, so that you'll understand that you're dealing with powers that are far out of your reach."

"Sneakiness ain't power."

"What about the power to tell you that you have it in you to be a great man? Or to be a great fool. If you make the correct choice."

"What choice?"

"When the time comes, I'll tell you what the choice is. Right now, you have no choice at all. You're going to take me and Calvin and Fishy to the place where you keep the name-strings."

Denmark smiled. "So they still some things you don't know."

"I didn't say I knew everything. The power that hides the names also hides from me your knowledge of where they are."

"That be the truth, more than you know," said Denmark. "I don't even know myself."

Fishy scoffed aloud at that. "This ain't no White fool you can play games with."

"No, Fishy," said Margaret, "he's telling the truth. He really doesn't know. So I wonder how you find your way back?"

"When it time for me to go there, I just wander around and pretty soon I be there. I walk in the door and then I remember everything."

"Remember what?"

"How do I know? I ain't through that door."

"Powerful hexery," said Margaret, "if hexery it be. Take me there."

"I can't do that," said Denmark.

"How about if I cut off your balls?" asked Fishy cheerfully.

Denmark looked at Fishy in wonder. He'd never heard a Black woman talk like that, right out in public, in front of a White.

"Let's hold off on the mutilation, Fishy," said Margaret. "Again, I think Denmark Vesey may be telling me the truth. He really can't find the place unless he goes there alone."

Denmark nodded.

"Well, then. I think we have no further business together," said Margaret. "You can go now."

"I want that man," said Denmark. He glanced at Calvin.

"You'll never have him," said Margaret. "He has more power than you can imagine."

"Can't be that much," said Denmark. "Look at him, he's empty."

"Yes, he was taken by surprise," said Margaret. "But you won't hold him for long."

"Long enough," said Denmark. "His body starting to rot. He be dying."

"You have till the count of three to walk away from me and keep on walking," said Margaret.

"Or what?"

"One. Or I'll call out for you to take your filthy paws off of my body."

Denmark at once backed away. There could be no charge more sure of putting Denmark on the end of a rope without further discussion.

"Two," said Margaret. And he was gone.

"Now we lost him again," said Fishy.

"No, my friend, we've got him. He's going to lead us right where we want to go. He can't hide from me." Margaret made a slow turn, taking in the view. "Today, I think it's worth it to splurge on a carriage ride."

Margaret led Fishy and Calvin to the row of waiting carriages. It took Margaret lifting his foot and Fishy pulling him up to get Calvin's uncaring body into the coach. The moment Calvin was settled in his seat, Fishy started to get down.

"Please, stay inside with me," said Margaret.

"I can't do that."

As if he were part of their conversation, the White driver opened the sliding window between his seat and the interior of the carriage. "Ma'am," he said, "you from the North, so you don't know, but around here we don't let no slaves ride in the carriage. She knows it, too—she's got to step out and walk along behind."

"She has told me of this law and I will gladly obey it. However, my brother-in-law here is prone to get rather ill during carriage rides, and I hope you understand that if he vomits, *I* am not prepared to hold a bag to catch it."

The driver considered this for a moment. "You keep that curtain closed, then. I don't want no trouble."

Fishy looked at Margaret, incredulous. Then she leaned over and pulled the drapes closed on one side of the coach while Margaret closed them on the other. Once they were closed off from public view, Fishy sat on the padded bench beside Calvin and grinned like a three-year-old with a spoon full of molasses. She even bounced a little on the seat.

The window opened again. "Where to, ma'am?" asked the driver.

"I'll know it when I see it," Margaret said. "I'm quite sure it's in Blacktown, however."

"Oh, ma'am, you oughtn't to go up there."

"That's why I have my brother-in-law with me."

"Well, I'll take you up there, but I don't like it."

"You'll like it better when I pay you," said Margaret.

"I'd like it better iffen you paid me in advance," said the driver.

Margaret just laughed.

"I meant to say half in advance."

"You'll be paid upon arrival, and that, sir, *is* the law. Though if you'd like to throw me out of your carriage, you are free to summon a constable. You can ask him about having a slave seated in your carriage, too, while you're at it."

The driver slammed the window shut and the carriage lurched forward, quite roughly. Fishy whooped and nearly fell off her seat, then sat there laughing. "I don't know how come you White folks don't ride like this all the time."

"Rich people do," said Margaret. "But not all White people are rich."

"They all richer than me," said Fishy.

"In money, I'm quite sure you're right." And then, because she was enjoying Fishy's delight, she also bounced up and down on her seat. The two of them laughed like schoolgirls.

Denmark felt the knife in his pocket like a two-ton weight. It was a terrible thing he'd been planning to do, killing a helpless man like that, and it was made all the worse by the fact that White lady knew he meant to do it. He was used to being invisible, White people paying him no mind except now and then to give him a little random trouble. But this woman, her idea of trouble was specific. She knew things about him that nobody knew, not even Gullah Joe. She scared him.

So he was glad to get away, glad to wander the streets of Blacktown until he came upon a door and suddenly he knew this was the one, though he couldn't have said how he knew, or why he didn't remember it from before. He set his hand on the knob and it opened easily, without a key. Once he was inside and the door shut behind him, he remembered everything. Gullah Joe. The struggle over the name-strings. No wonder he was supposed to kill that White man! The thing he did, unraveling some poor slave's name and cutting it loose to wander who knows where. . . .

But he did know where. He whooped with laughter. "Gullah Joe, you won't believe it! I met the Black girl what got her name cut loose by the devil you caught!"

Gullah Joe glared at him. "Be maybe you not shouting me business so all can hear it in the street, they."

"She goes by the name Fishy," said Denmark, close enough that he didn't have to shout. "I don't think it was no accident that White boy cut *her* name loose, cause she be rented out to his sister-in-law."

"I think you telling me you find this White man?"

"I did, but he ain't dead yet."

Gullah Joe slapped the table hard. Denmark was startled and his jocular mood fell away. "You lose you courage?"

"She knew I was coming," said Denmark.

"A woman, she!"

"She got him down to the battery, all them White folks around, you think I'm going to show that knife, let alone cut a White boy with it?"

"Boy? This White man be maybe him a child?"

"No, he a man, but he be young. Bet he don't shave." Denmark remembered how Calvin looked. So empty. Like his woman. That White witch knew all about her.

Against his will, Denmark looked for her. There she was, mending clothes in a corner. She didn't look up. It took all her concentration just to get the needle into and out of the cloth. She used to be hot-hearted like that Fishy girl. Maybe I could have won her over fairly, if I tried. If I set her free. But I had to control her, didn't I? Just like a White man. I was *master*.

"How he be?" demanded Gullah Joe.

"Who?"

"The devil him body!"

"He pretty far gone, Gullah Joe."

"Not far enough." Gullah Joe glanced over to the circle that contained the captive. Denmark saw that it was twice as thick with knotwork charms as it had been when he left early in the morning.

"He been trying to escape?"

"Be maybe he already escape, him."

"Well, if he did, wouldn't we know it? Wouldn't you be dead?"

"Be maybe he learn too much," said Gullah Joe. "Look! Look a-that."

Though there was not a touch of a breeze in the attic, one of the charms suddenly swayed, then bounced up and down.

"He doing that?" asked Denmark.

Gullah Joe looked at him with scorn. "No, fool, they cockroaches in the charm, they be making her bounce."

"How can he do that if you got him captive?"

Gullah Joe might have had an answer, but at that moment they both heard the door opening downstairs. Gullah Joe seemed to leap straight up in the air, and Denmark was about to let out an exclamation when Joe shook his head violently and covered his own mouth with his hand as a sign for silence.

Denmark leaned over close. "I thought you said nobody could get in here."

There were footsteps on the stairs. No effort was being made to muffle them, either. Clump, clump, clump. Slow progress, many feet.

Finally Denmark realized what he was hearing. "It's her," he whispered. "She brought him here."

Her voice wafted up the stairs. "Indeed I did," she said. "Step aside, Denmark Vesey. It's Gullah Joe I need to talk to."

Gullah Joe danced around his desk like a child desperate to pee. Nobody had ever pierced his defenses so easily. No one had ever called him by name when he didn't want them to. Whoever this was had to be so powerful that Gullah Joe hardly knew what charms to try. She had already passed by some of his most powerful ones.

Denmark saw the witchy man's desperation and realized that this situation was definitely not under control.

"Calvin!" cried Margaret. "Can you hear my voice?"

They were near the top of the stairs, now, able to peer around in the attic and see all the hanging charms. The White woman, the White man, and the slave girl Fishy.

Margaret was listening for an answer. To her surprise, it came from the man beside her.

"I hear you," said Calvin. But his voice was soft, his manner distracted.

"I've brought your body near to your doodlebug, Calvin," she explained.

Calvin's mouth mumbled a reply. "Get me out of here," he said, his voice flat.

"Kill him now," said Gullah Joe. "He body, she calling back him soul. Kill him!"

Denmark picked up a much larger knife than the one he had concealed in his pocket. "You keep him back," he said to Margaret.

She ignored him completely, and instead began to lead Calvin closer to the large concentration of charms.

"Stop, you! Don't take him there!" Gullah Joe threw a handful of powder at her, but it blew away from her in a sudden breeze and ended up stinging his eyes and making him weep. "How you do that witchery!"

She ignored him, and parted the charms to push Calvin through.

"Oh, yes," said Calvin, now sounding more like himself, though not quite that cocky yet. "This is right. Bring me home."

"Stop him!" screamed Gullah Joe.

Denmark lunged between the charms and the White man, his knife drawn.

Margaret immediately shoved Calvin hard, forcing him and Denmark both to stumble and fall into the midst of the circle that contained Calvin's doodlebug.

Gullah Joe howled in fury and threw himself to the floor.

"I have a problem, here, Margaret."

It was quite likely the thing Calvin would have said. It had his intonation. And it was certainly true. Unfortunately, the voice was coming out of Denmark Vesey's mouth.

"What's your problem, Calvin?" she asked.

"I can't get back into my body," he said. "So I'm glad you tossed in a spare."

"That's not a spare body, somebody's using it," Margaret said.

"You think I don't know that? But I can't get into my own body and I can't talk without I got one."

Margaret walked over to Gullah Joe. "What's wrong? Why can't he get back into his body?"

"Cause she be half-dead, she! Look a-him, he steal my friend body him!"

"Your body is dying," Margaret said to Calvin. "Denmark said something about that before. You're rotting."

"Give back him body!" cried Gullah Joe.

"Then help me get him back into his own body!"

"How I do that!" said Gullah Joe. "He dead man in him grave!"

"He is *not*," said Margaret. "Calvin, you have to heal your body."

"I don't know how," said Calvin. "I never tried to raise the dead."

"You're not dead," said Margaret. "Look, your chest is rising and falling."

"All right, I'm trying, but it's not like a cut finger, I don't know what to—"

"Wait!" Abruptly, Margaret turned around, walked over to Gullah Joe, and dragged him to his feet. "You know!" she shouted. "Tell me!"

"What I know?" said Gullah Joe, feigning helpless misery. "You the witchy woman, you break down all this charm, you."

Gullah Joe smiled and shrugged. Margaret recognized the expression, the gesture. It was the way slaves told their masters to go to hell. She looked into his heartfire and saw many things. But all his lore was hidden from her.

"You know how to heal him," Margaret said, looking him in the eyes, her breath on his face. "You've captured souls before, and you know how to put them back."

Gullah Joe just folded his arms and stared off into space.

"Excuse me, Miz Margaret," said Fishy. She pushed past Margaret and, placing her left hand on Gullah Joe's right cheek, with her right hand she slapped his other cheek with such force that blood shot right out of his mouth. "Talk to the nice lady!" screamed Fishy in Gullah Joe's face. "She be no enemy, you hear me?"

"Him scare me!" cried Gullah Joe, pointing at Calvin on the floor. "Get him out on that body!"

Fishy laid another slap on him, this time so hard that Gullah Joe fell over, his arms pinwheeling, his long knotted braids flopping away from his body. Some charm must have come loose this time, because suddenly more of his mind opened up to Margaret. She didn't need him to tell her now. She opened two little jars on Joe's big table, got two solid pinches of powder, one from each, then strode to the charm circle where Calvin lay and threw the powder out over him.

She thought of Antigone as she did it, spreading dirt on her brother's corpse despite the edict of Creon forbidding it. Am I ritually burying my husband's brother? If I thought Alvin might be saved by letting him die . . . but I'd lose Alvin. This is his beloved little brother that he played with half his growing-up years. If he dies it can't be by my hand, even indirectly. It would destroy my life with Alvin, and wouldn't necessarily save his. In Alvin's heartfire, which she spent a moment checking, there was no path that did not lead to Calvin's treachery. As long as the boy is alive, Alvin isn't safe.

And yet it was for love of Alvin that she didn't let him die. The powders drifted down onto Calvin's body, got sucked in through his nostrils, and almost at once he became more animated. He sat up. "I'm so damn hungry," he said.

Gullah Joe screamed. "No! Go back! Get out of here!"

Calvin rose to his feet. "This the bastard trapped me here outside my body?"

"It was an accident," said Margaret. "Don't harm him."

Calvin reached up, then winced and stumbled.

"Heal yourself!" cried Margaret again.

Calvin stood there, apparently trying something that no one else could see. "I'm getting better by the second," he said. "Just having my bug back in my body, it's healing me by itself."

At that moment, Fishy screamed. Margaret whirled around, and there was Denmark, knife in hand, staggering toward Calvin, brandishing the blade. Fishy leapt onto his back, tugging on the knife arm, and finally toppling the two of them onto the floor.

In the meantime, Calvin wasn't swaying anymore. He was steady on his feet, and when he turned around to face Denmark, he had the presence of mind to heat the knife so hot that Denmark screamed and flung it from him. "You got into my body!" Denmark screamed at Calvin, but now he was holding his burned hands limply in front of him. "I be wearing your castoff!"

Calvin seemed not even to notice Denmark. It was Gullah Joe he was looking for. "You lousy bastard, you filthy trap-laying witch!" he cried. "Where are you!"

At that moment a seagull started fluttering frantically around the room. Before it could find an open window, Calvin pointed at it and it dropped to the floor. In the instant, the bird disappeared and Gullah Joe lay there where it had been. Calvin advanced toward him, and the look of hate and rage on his face was terrible to behold.

"Calvin, stop it!" cried Margaret. "It was an accident! They caught you in a snare but they had no idea it was you, and when they realized your powers they had no choice but to keep you confined for fear of whatever vengeance you might take.''

Calvin regarded her in silence for a moment, then turned back to the circle he had been in. He yanked all the charms from the ceiling until the circle didn't exist anymore. Gullah Joe's weeping was the only sound they could hear. But when Calvin walked over to the lesser circle and began pulling down those charms too, Joe began to shout at him. ''Leave that alone! I begging you! You turn them loose like that, some of names never find they way home to they body!''

Calvin paid no attention to him. He tore the charms from the ceiling and then opened the new net, this time by hand, scattering the name-strings all over the attic floor.

''Don't hurt them,'' Gullah Joe pleaded, weeping. ''Stop him, Denmark!''

But Denmark was sitting on the floor, weeping.

''Tear up the name-strings,'' cried Fishy. ''Give the slaves back their anger!''

Calvin looked over at Fishy and smiled nastily. ''What good does anger do for anybody?''

Then, savagely, furiously, with the power of his mind alone he unmade all the knotted strings until they lay in tatters. They all watched the seething pile of name-strings as bits of this and that flew upward from the untangling mass. And then all lay still, the bits and pieces commingled.

Now that the deed was done, Gullah Joe stopped remonstrating with Calvin. He looked up toward the invisible sky beyond the ceiling that crouched overhead. ''Go home to you body, you! All you name go home!'' Then he sank to his knees, weeping.

''What are you crying for,'' demanded Calvin. He looked at Denmark, too, who was only just beginning to dry his eyes.

''You too strong a wind for me,'' said Gullah Joe. ''Oh, my people, my people, go home!''

Calvin lurched toward him a couple of steps, then fell to the floor. ''I'm dying, Margaret,'' he said. ''My body's too far gone.''

''He be dying, that save me the trouble of killing him,'' said Denmark. ''All we done for our people, he just undid it all.''

"No!" cried Fishy. "He be setting us free! All our rage tied up in that net, that be the bad jail of all. We be slaves then, right down to the heart. Give up ourself so we can hide? From what? The worst thing already happen, when we give you our name-string."

Margaret knelt beside Calvin's body. "You have to heal yourself," she kept murmuring to him.

"I don't know where to start," Calvin whispered. "I'm filled with corruption clear through."

"Alvin!" cried Margaret desperately. "Alvin, look! Look at me! See what's happening here!" She rose to her feet and began forming letters in the air. H-E-L-P. C-A-L-V-I-N. H-E-A-L H-I-M! "Look at me and save his life, if you want him to live!"

"What you do in the air, you?" asked Fishy. "What you waving at?"

"My husband," said Margaret. "He doesn't see me." She turned to Gullah Joe. "Is there something you can do to help all those lost names return home?"

"Yes," said Joe.

"Then take your friend Denmark and go do it."

"What are *you* going to do" asked Denmark sullenly.

"I'm going to try to get my husband to heal his brother. And if he can't, then I'm going to hold Calvin's hand while he lies dying."

Calvin let out a deep moan of despair. "I ain't ready to die!" he said.

"Ready or not, you'll have to do it sometime," Margaret reminded him. "Heal yourself, as best you can," she told him. "You're supposed to be a Maker, aren't you?"

Calvin laughed. Weak and bitter, the sound of that laughter. "I spend my whole life trying to get out from under Alvin. Now the one time I need him, it's the only time he isn't right there under foot."

In the ensuing silence, Gullah Joe's voice came, soft and low. "They do it, them," he said. "They finding the way back."

"Then you'd better go out into the street and spread the word through the city," said Margaret. "They're filled with rage long pent up. You have to keep them from rising up in a fruitless rebellion as soon as all their strong passions come back." They did nothing. "Go!" she shouted. "I'll take care of Calvin here."

Gullah Joe and Denmark staggered out into the street, going from house to house. Already the sound of moaning and singing could be heard all over the city. In Blacktown, they collared every black person they could find and explained it to them as best they could, then sent them out with the warning: Contain your anger. Harm no one. They'll destroy us if we don't keep to that. The taker of names says so. We're not ready yet. We're not ready yet.

Inside the warehouse attic, Margaret and Fishy were reduced to mopping Calvin's brow as he lay delirious in his fever-racked stupor. Body and soul were together again, but only, it seemed, in time to die.

After a while a third pair of hands joined them. A Black woman who moved slowly, hesitantly. Her speech was slurred when she asked a question or two; it was hard to understand her. Margaret knew at once who she was. She laid her hand on the Black woman's hand; on the other side of her, Fishy did the same. "You don't gots to work today," said Fishy. "We take care of him."

But the woman acted as if she didn't understand. She kept on helping them take care of Calvin as if she had some personal stake in keeping him alive. Or maybe she was simply loving her neighbor as herself.

☙ 13 ❧

Judgment Day

JOHN ADAMS DIDN'T even bother to seat himself comfortably on the bench. It was supposed to be routine. Quill would read out the charge. The young lawyer for the defense would plead his client guilty or not. They'd be back out the door in a few minutes.

It started right. Quill read the charge. It was the normal collection of allegations of dealings with Satan, and as it became clear it was more a peroration than a simple reading of charges, John gaveled him down. "I think we've heard all the charges and you've moved on to opening arguments, Mr. Quill."

"For a full understanding of the charges, Your Honor, I—"

"I have a full understanding of the charge, as does the defendant," said John. "We'll hear your elaboration of the particulars at a later time, I'm sure. How does the defendant answer to the charges?"

Verily Cooper rose from his chair, his movement smooth, a perfect gentleman. By contrast, the lanky smith seemed to unfold himself, to come out of the chair like a turtle out of its shell. His chains clanked noisily.

"Alvin Smith, how do you plead?" asked John.

"Not guilty, Your Honor."

Alvin sat back down, and John started to announce the schedule for tomorrow, when the trial would begin. Then he noticed that Cooper was still standing.

"What is it, Mr. Cooper?"

"I believe it is customary to hear motions."

"Peremptory motions to dismiss are never granted in witch trials," John reminded him.

Cooper just stood there, waiting.

"All right, let's have your motion."

Cooper approached the bench with several petitions written out in an elegant hand.

"What is all this?" demanded Quill.

"It seems," said John, "that the defendant has some interesting requests. All right, Mr. Cooper. Relieve Mr. Quill's curiosity and read out your motions."

"First, the defense requests that since the prosecution intends to prosecute a witness named in the records of the parish as Purity Orphan on the same evidence as my client, the trials be joined."

"That's ridiculous," said Quill. "Purity is our prime witness and the defense knows it."

John was amused by Cooper's maneuver, and he enjoyed seeing Quill's outrage. "Are you saying, Mr. Quill, that you are *not* planning to try Mistress Purity on the basis of the same evidence?"

"I'm saying it's irrelevant to this trial."

"I believe that Mistress Purity should have the rights of a defendant in this courtroom," said Cooper, "since the evidence she gives here should not then be able to be turned against her in her own trial."

Before Quill could answer, John asked him sharply, "Mr. Quill, I'm inclined to grant this motion, unless you are prepared to grant an irrevocable dismissal of all charges against Mistress Purity that might arise from her testimony in this trial."

Quill was speechless, but only for a moment. It was easy to guess what he was thinking during his hesitation: Was it more important to keep the trials separate, or to be able to try Purity at all? "I have no intention of dismissing on a confessed witch."

John banged his gavel. "Motion granted. Is Mistress Purity in the court?"

A timid, weary-looking young woman rose from her place behind the prosecutor's bench.

"Mistress Purity," said John, "do you consent to a joint trial? And, if you do, do you consent to having Mr. Verily Cooper represent you and Alvin Smith together?"

Quill objected. "Her interests are different from those of Alvin Smith!"

"No, they're not," said Purity. Her voice was surprisingly bold. "I consent to both, sir."

"Take your place at the defense table," said John.

They waited while she seated herself on the other side of Verily Cooper. John gave them a moment or two to whisper together. It was Quill who broke the silence. "Your Honor, I feel I must protest this irregular procedure."

"I'm sorry to hear that you feel that way. Let me know if the feeling becomes irresistible."

Quill frowned. "Very well, Your Honor, I *do* protest."

"Protest noted. Note also, however, that the court takes exception to the practice of deceiving a witness into testifying in someone else's trial, only to find his own testimony used against him in his own trial. I believe this is standard in witch trials."

"It is a practice justified by the difficulty of obtaining evidence of the doings of Satan."

"Yes," said John. "That well-known difficulty. So much depends upon it, don't you think? Next motion, Mr. Cooper."

"I move that because Mr. Quill has openly and publicly violated the laws against extracting testimony under torture, all evidence obtained from interrogation of either of my clients during and after that torture be barred from these proceedings."

Quill bounded to his feet. "No physical pain was inflicted on either defendant, Your Honor! Nor was there threat of such pain! The law was strictly adhered to!"

Quill was right, John knew, according to more than a century of precedents since the anti-torture law was adopted after the Salem debacle. The witchers all made sure they didn't cross the line.

"Your Honor," said Cooper, "I submit that the practice of running an accused person until a state of utter exhaustion is reached is, in fact, torture, and that it is well known to be such and falls under the same strictures as the forms of torture specifically banned by the statute."

"The statute says what it says!" retorted Quill.

"Watch your temper, Mr. Quill," said John. "Mr. Cooper, the language of the statute is clear."

Cooper then read off a string of citations from contract law dealing with attempts to skirt the letter of a contract by devising practices that were not specifically banned but that clearly defied the fair intent of the contract. "The principle is that when a practice is engaged in solely in order to circumvent a legal obligation, the practice is deemed to be a violation."

"That is contract law," said Quill. "It has no bearing."

"On the contrary," said Cooper. "The anti-torture law is a contract between the government and the people, guaranteeing the innocent that they will not be forced by torture into giving false testimony against themselves or others. It is the common practice of witchers to use methods of torture invented after the writing of the law and therefore not enumerated in it, but having all the same pernicious effects as the prohibited practice. In other words, the common practice of running a witness in a witch trial is designed to have precisely the same effect as the tortures specifically prohibited: to extract testimony of witchcraft regardless of whether such testimony is supported by other evidence."

Quill ranted for quite a while after that, and John let him have his say, while the court reporter scribbled furiously. Nothing that Quill was saying would make the slightest difference. John knew that in terms of truth and righteousness, Cooper's position was true and righteous. John also knew that the legal issue was nowhere near as clear. To drag precedents from contract law into witchery law, which was a branch of ecclesiastical law, would expose John to charges that he had wilfully sown confusion, for where would such a practice stop? All the legal traditions would be hopelessly commingled, and then who could possibly learn enough law to practice in any court? It would be an outrageously radical step. Not that John worried about being criticized or censured. He was old, and if people chose not to follow his precedent, so be it. No, the real question was whether it was right to risk damaging the entire system of law in order to effect a righteous outcome in witchery cases.

When Quill wound down, John hadn't yet made up his mind. "The court will take this motion under advisement and announce a decision at a later point, if it isn't mooted by one of the other motions."

Cooper was clearly disappointed; Quill was not much relieved. "Your Honor, even to consider this motion is—"

John gaveled him to silence. "Next motion, Mr. Cooper."

Cooper arose and began a string of citations of obscure cases in English courts. John, having the advantage of the written motion in front of him, enjoyed watching Quill come to realize what Cooper was setting up. "Your Honor," Quill finally said, interrupting Cooper. "Is counsel for the defense seriously suggesting that the interrogator be barred from giving testimony?"

"Let's hear him out and see," said John.

"Therefore, Your Honor," said Cooper, "the interrogators in witch trials, being without exception professionals whose employment depends, not on finding truth, but on obtaining guilty verdicts, are interested parties in the action. There is no record of a witcher in the last hundred years ever finding, upon interrogation, that a person charged with witchcraft was not guilty. Furthermore, there is a consistent pattern of witchers expanding upon testimony; there are only two cases in which charges of Satanic involvement were present in the original testimony, and both those cases were found to be deliberate falsifications. The pattern is clear: All legitimate witch trials begin with no evidence of anything beyond the use of a knack. Testimony concerning Satan only shows up when the interrogator arrives, and then comes into court in only two ways: through the interrogator's own testimony contradicting a witness or defendant who denies that Satan was involved, or through testimony from witnesses who confess to Satanic involvement as part of a confession that is taken as repentance, following which charges are dismissed. In short, your Honor, the historical record is clear. Evidence of Satanic involvement in all witch trials in New England is produced by the witchers themselves and those who, in fear of death, bend to their will and produce the only kind of confession that the witchers will accept."

"He's asking this court to deny the very basis of witchcraft law!"

cried Quill. "He's asking this court to contradict the clear intent of Parliament and the Massachusetts assembly!"

John almost laughed aloud. Cooper was audacious in the extreme. He wasn't just trying to get this case thrown out without a trial, he was demanding that John rule in such a way as to make it almost impossible to hold a witch trial ever again. If, that is, John's decision was accepted as a valid precedent.

It came down to this thought: He's giving me a chance to do something brilliant in the last years of my life.

"Your charge is of serious malfeasance on the part of Mr. Quill," said John. "If I were to sustain this motion, I would have no choice but to revoke Mr. Quill's license and institute charges of perjury against him, just to start with."

"I have acted according to the best traditions of my profession!" cried Quill. "This is an outrage!"

"Nevertheless," said John, "these charges are of so grave a nature as to call into question the entire proceeding against Mr. Smith and Mistress Purity. For I have a feeling that if I were to grant either of these two motions, your next motion would be for a strict reading of the witchcraft laws."

"It would, Your Honor," said Cooper.

"Strict reading is what *I'm* asking for!" cried Quill.

"You're asking for a strict reading of the anti-torture law," said John. "The courts have long been aware that a strict reading of the witchcraft law requires that for a conviction there must be evidence not only of the use of hidden powers, but also that such powers originate from the influence and power of Satan."

"That is not a requirement, it is a stipulation!" Quill shouted.

"Do not shout at me, Mr. Quill," said John. "Justice may be blind, but she is not deaf."

"I beg your pardon."

"No matter how it exercises your temper, Mr. Quill, it is long established that a strict reading of the traditional text of the witchcraft laws leads to the conclusion that the involvement of Satan is not stipulated but rather must be proved. That the possession of an extraordinary ability is not prima facie evidence of Satanic involvement, and that this specifically arises from the tradition of ecclesiastical law, which must always leave room for the possibility of a miracle enacted by faith in Jesus Christ and the intervention of heaven.''

''Is it the defense's theory that these two witches have been working miracles by the power of Christ?'' Quill said it as if it were the most absurd thing ever heard. But then the words hung in the air, unanswered, undisputed, and the effect was the opposite of what Quill intended. John knew that one of the main points taken from the courtroom today would be the possibility that people with the power of God in them might be charged with witchcraft if witchers had their way.

Good work, Mr. Cooper.

''It is the decision of this court that the motions raised by the defense must be decided before the trial can proceed. Therefore, I order the bailiff to send the jury home and to clear the courtroom, lest the discussion of evidence that is about to take place influence the eventual trial. We reconvene at noon. I recommend that everyone take an early dinner, because I intend to resolve these matters before we adjourn this evening.''

Bang with the gavel, and John got up from the bench and almost danced back to the robing room. Who would have thought that a nasty little witch trial would suddenly take on such proportions? John had dismissed charges based on faultiness of evidence in both the witch trials he had presided over before, but in those cases it was because of contradiction within a witness's testimony, and it created no precedent. Cooper had created a far more potent situation, in which granting either of his evidentiary motions could destroy the witch laws, making them unenforceable. And given the political climate in New England, there was little chance of a legislature reinstating them, not without strict safeguards that would remove all the little tricks from the witchers' arsenal. What they did in England, of course, might be quite different. But if John knew his son Quincy, the Massachusetts assembly would act immediately and before Parliament even discussed the issue, the law in New England would be established. Parliament would then be in the awkward position of having to repudiate an ecclesiastical law set forth in New England, the place where Christian life was regarded as being most pure. There was a good chance that it could all be ended, right here, today.

John sat in the plush chair, almost lost in the cushions, for it had been designed for larger men than he. He closed his eyes and smiled. God had a role for him to play, after all.

Purity had no idea what Verily Cooper's plan was. All she knew was that Quill hated it, and if Quill hated it, she had to like it. Besides, she could see plainly that Verily Cooper had no ill intent toward her, nor Alvin, though he was in chains because of her. Still, it wasn't easy for her to sit beside these men that she had accused. If she had known when she made her charges where they would lead . . . She tried to explain this to them.

"We know that," said Verily Cooper. "Don't think twice about it."

"Where's the food?" said Alvin. "We only got a little while to eat."

"I don't know why you're helping me," said Purity.

"He's not," said Alvin. "He's trying to change the world."

"Alvin has trouble with authority," said Verily. "He doesn't like it when somebody else is in charge."

"I want somebody to be in charge of getting me something to eat. This table is starting to look mighty tasty."

At that point the bailiff approached and asked them if they wanted to eat down in the jail, separately, or right there at the defense table, with a picnic lunch donated by several of the ladies of Cambridge, including his own wife.

"What extraordinary kindness," said Verily.

The bailiff grinned. "My wife was on the commons yesterday. She thinks you're Galahad. Or Percival."

"Will you thank her for me? For all of us?"

Soon the table was spread with bread, cheese, and summer fruit, and Alvin set to eating like a teenager. Purity had a much harder time working up an appetite, though once she had the taste of pears and cheese in her mouth, she found she was hungrier than she had thought.

"I don't know," said Purity, "why you should ever forgive me."

"Oh, we forgive you," said Alvin. "We more than forgive you. Verily, here, he's downright obsessed with you."

Verily only smiled, his eyes twinkling. "Alvin's feeling out of sorts," he said. "He doesn't like jails."

"Have you been in jail before?" asked Purity.

"He was acquitted of all charges," said Verily. "Proving that I'm a clever lawyer."

"Proving I was innocent," said Alvin. "An advantage I don't have this time."

Only now did Verily show annoyance. "If you think you're guilty, why did you plead innocent?" he said sharply.

"I'm not guilty of witchcraft," said Alvin. "Under a 'strict reading' or whatever. But the things Mistress Purity said about me, well, you and I both know they're true." As if to demonstrate it, he peeled the manacle from his right hand like it was made of clay.

Purity gasped. She had never seen such power. Even hearing Arthur Stuart's account on the riverbank, she had not realized how effortlessly Alvin worked his will with iron. No incantations, no sign of strain.

"Mistress Purity is startled," said Verily.

"What do you think?" said Alvin. "Should I spread some iron on this bread and eat it?"

"Don't be a show-off," said Verily.

Alvin leaned back in his chair and ate a thick slab of bread and cheese—a posture he could not have assumed while manacled. His mouth full, he talked anyway. "I reckon you needed to remember, Mistress Purity, that what you said about me was true. Don't you go blaming yourself for telling the truth."

Purity found herself on the verge of tears. "The whole world's awry," she said.

"True," said Alvin, "but in different ways in different places. Which is what makes traveling worthwhile."

"I know you only mean good for me, both of you. Though you're annoyed with each other. I don't know why."

"Verily Cooper thinks he's in love with you," said Alvin.

Purity didn't know what to say to that. Nor did Verily, who was blushing as he ate a slice of pear. He didn't contradict Alvin, though.

"Not that I don't approve of Verily falling in love," said Alvin, "and my wife tells me you're a good girl, loyal and smart and patient and all the other virtues that a wife of Mr. Cooper has to have."

"I didn't know that I had met your wife, sir," said Purity.

"You haven't," said Alvin. "Don't you remember what Arthur told you about her?"

"That she was a candle."

"Torch," said Alvin.

"We don't hear much about knackery here in New England. Except as it pertains to disposing of the bodies of downer animals."

Verily laughed aloud. "I told you she had a sense of humor, Al."

She allowed herself a small smile.

"Let's just say that Margaret thinks you're worth the trouble of my staying in jail a couple of nights," said Alvin.

"You sustained me while we were running yesterday, didn't you?"

Alvin shrugged. "Who knows how tough you are? At some point, everybody gives in and says what the questioner wants to hear."

"I'd like to think I could withstand torture as well as the next person," said Purity.

"That's my point," said Alvin. "Nobody can withstand it, if the questioner knows what he's doing. The body betrays us. Most people never find that out because they're never asked a question that matters. And those that are, most give the answer the questioner wants without a lick of torture. It's only the strong ones, the most stubborn ones as gets tortured."

"Mr. Cooper," said Purity, "I hope you don't think I'm giving any stock to Mr. Smith's jests about your feelings toward me."

Verily smiled at her. "You don't know me, so I can hardly expect you to welcome such an idea."

"On the contrary," said Purity, "I know you very well. I saw you in court today, and on the commons, too. I know the kind of man you are."

"You don't know he farts in his sleep," said Alvin.

Purity looked at him, appalled. "Everyone does," she answered, "but most people find no need to mention it during meals."

Alvin grinned at her. "Just didn't want this to turn into a love feast. Not while my lawyer here is trying to burn down the barn to kill the fleas."

Verily's face darkened. "It's not 'fleas' when innocent people die, and others become perjurers out of fear."

"How much justice will be done when judges go striking down laws whenever some lawyer gives them half an excuse?"

"That's theory," said Verily. "When the practice of the law leads to injustice, then the law must change."

"That's what Parliament is for," said Alvin. "And the assembly."

"What politician would dare announce that he was in favor of witchcraft?"

The argument might have gone on, but at that moment the door of the courtroom opened and Hezekiah Study came in. He gave no greeting, but stalked down the aisle straight to a chair directly behind the defense table. He spoke only to Verily Cooper.

"Don't do it," said Hezekiah Study.

"Don't do what?"

"Don't take on the witchers," he said. "Try the case. Or better yet, if your client really has the knack he's charged with, shed the chains and begone with you."

Only then did Hezekiah notice the manacle lying warped and deformed in Alvin's lap. Alvin grinned at him and mashed the last hunk of bread and cheese into his mouth all at once.

"Pardon me, sir, but who are you?" asked Verily Cooper.

"This is Reverend Study," said Purity. "He advised me not to charge Alvin with witchcraft. I wish I'd listened to him then."

"You'll wish you had listened to me now," said Hezekiah.

"The law is on my side," said Verily.

"No, it isn't," said Hezekiah. "Nothing is on your side."

"Sir, I know my case, and I know the law."

"So did I," said Hezekiah. "I tried the same strategy."

Now Verily was interested. "You're a lawyer, sir?"

"I *was* a lawyer. I gave it up and became a minister."

"But you lost a witch trial, I take it?"

"I tried to use the strict reading you're going for," said Hezekiah. "I tried to show that the testimony of the witcher was tainted. Everything you're doing."

"And it failed?" asked Verily.

"What do you do," asked Hezekiah, "when the witcher calls *you* to the stand?"

Verily stared at him in silence.

"The witcher can call my lawyer?" asked Alvin.

"It's ecclesiastical law," said Hezekiah. "The law is older than advocacy. There is no privilege unless you're an ordained minister."

"So they called you," said Purity. "But what did you say?"

"I could only tell the truth," said Hezekiah. "I had seen my clients use their knacks. Harmless! A gift of God, I said it, but there was my testimony." Tears flowed down his cheeks. "That's what hanged them."

Purity was weeping also. "What were their knacks?"

"Who?" asked Alvin.

"My mother and father," said Purity, looking at Hezekiah for confirmation.

He nodded and looked away.

"What did they die for?" asked Purity. "What was their crime?"

"Your mother could heal animals," said Hezekiah. "That's what killed her. A neighbor with an old quarrel waited too long, called her too late, and his mule died, so he said that by the power of Satan she cursed the animals of all those who didn't please her."

"And my father?"

"He could draw a straight line."

The words hung there for a moment.

"That's *all?*" asked Alvin.

"On paper. In the soil. Truer than a surveyor. His fences were the marvel of the neighborhood. He won the plowing prize every year at the parish fair. No one could cut so straight a furrow. His wife always made him cut the fabric when she was sewing. People remembered his knack when his wife was on trial, and he admitted it readily, seeing no harm in it, since it neither harmed others nor gave him any advantage. Except at the fair."

Purity could hardly talk for weeping. "That's why they died?"

"They died for envy," said Hezekiah, "and for the bloodlust of the witcher, and for the incompetence and arrogance, the *pride* of their attorney who called himself their friend but dared to put their lives at risk in a larger cause. I could have won them a banishment. They were well-liked and the trial was unpopular. The witcher was willing to dicker. But I had a cause." He gripped Purity's hands. "I can't let this man do the same to you! I've spent my life trying to keep you from the same fate, because they marked you, don't think they haven't. Quill knows who you are. Because of you, they couldn't hang your mother until you were born, and the outrage built and built among the people. There was a strong sentiment to break them out of jail. But the witchers called in the authorities and they guarded the hangings. And then they sent you away, so as not to remind the people of the outrage that had been done against you. To this day, God help the witcher who comes through that part of Netticut, because the people know the truth there.''

''Then it was a victory of sorts,'' said Purity quietly. ''They didn't die for nothing.''

''They *died*,'' said Hezekiah. ''Their accusers were ostracized until they moved away, but they're still alive, aren't they? The witchers lost a lot of prestige, but they're still in the witch business, aren't they? That feels like dying for nothing to me.''

''It's a different trial,'' said Verily. ''And a different judge.''

''He's an honorable man, bound by law,'' said Hezekiah. ''Don't think he isn't.''

''Honorable men aren't bound by bad laws,'' said Verily.

Alvin laughed, a little nastily. ''If that's so, how you going to tell the honorable ones from the dishonorable? Who's bound by law at all, since every law is bad at one time or another?''

''Whose side are you on?'' Verily asked testily.

''I'm supposed to build a city,'' said Alvin. ''And if I don't build it on law, what am I going to build it on? Even Napoleon makes laws that bind him, because if you don't then there's no order, it's chaos all the way down.''

''So you'd rather hang?''

Alvin sighed and held up the twisted manacle. ''I'm not going to hang.''

''But someone will,'' said Verily. ''If not this year then next, or the year after. Someone will hang. You said so yourself.''

''Let witch trials fade out by themselves,'' said Alvin.

''The way slavery's fading?'' Verily answered mockingly.

The door opened again. People were beginning to return. The bailiff came back to clean up the meal. ''You didn't eat much,'' said the bailiff.

''*I* did,'' said Alvin.

Hezekiah and Purity still held hands across the railing separating spectators from the court. ''Beg pardon,'' said the bailiff. ''She's a defendant now. I don't want to put her in chains, but she's not allowed to touch folks beyond the rail.''

Hezekiah nodded and withdrew his hands.

The bailiff left with the picnic basket. Alvin wrapped the manacle around his wrist again. Purity couldn't resist touching it. It was hard again. As hard as iron.

Quill came back into the courtroom smiling.

Purity turned and whispered to Hezekiah. ''You're wrong, you know,'' she said. ''It wasn't you that hanged them.''

Hezekiah shook his head.

''I never knew them, but I sit now where they sat, though guiltier, because I'm the one who leveled the charge. And I tell you, they knew who their friends were.''

''I was no friend to them.''

''They knew who their friends were,'' said Purity, ''and I know who their friends were. All may have been outraged, but they let the hanging take place. You alone followed me or found me here. You alone took care to raise me in safety. You gave years of your life to their child. That is a true friend.''

Hezekiah buried his face in his hands. His shoulders shook, unable to bear what she had placed upon them. Absolution was a heavier burden, for the moment, than guilt.

Quill rose to his feet the moment John Adams called the court to order.

''Your Honor, I have a motion.''

''Out of order,'' said John.

''Your Honor, I think all can be settled when we call Mr. Verily Cooper to the stand! This is ecclesiastical law and there is no—''

John banged the gavel again and again until Quill fell silent.

''I said your motion was out of order.''

''There are precedents!'' said Quill, seething with fury.

''On the contrary,'' said John. ''Your motion may be in order when we resume the trial of Alvin Smith and Purity Orphan. But at the moment, this is a hearing on a motion, and in this procedure I am the questioner. There are no sides and no attorneys, only my own pursuit of information to allow me to reach a conclusion. So you will take your seat until I call you for questioning. You are the equal of all other persons in this court. You have no standing to make a motion of any kind. Is that clear to you at last, Mr. Quill?''

"You exceed your authority, Your Honor!''

"Bailiff, bring manacles and leg irons. If Mr. Quill speaks again, they are to be placed upon him to remind him that he has no authority in this courtroom during this hearing.''

White-faced and trembling, Quill sat down.

The hearing went quite smoothly for quite a while. John questioned Purity first. She described the nature of the charges she originally made, and then told how Quill had deformed them, turning harmless frolicking in the river into an incestuous orgy, and a peaceful conversation on the riverbank into a witches' sabbath. He asked her about the professors from the college, and she affirmed that she had never mentioned them and only found out they were being questioned when Quill demanded that she denounce them, Emerson in particular.

Then the professors were brought forward, one at a time, to recount the experience of being questioned by Quill. Each one stated that he had been led to believe that others had confessed and implicated them, and that their only hope was to confess and repent. All denied being the one who confessed.

Then John turned to Quill.

"Aren't you going to question *him* first?'' Quill said, pointing to Alvin.

"Have you forgotten whose hearing this is?'' asked John.

"I just want to hear whether *he* denies the witchcraft charges!''

"You'll find that out in the trial,'' said John, "since the accused can be called to give testimony against themselves in witch trials.''

"You're favoring him,'' said Quill.

"You're testing my patience,'' said John. "Put your hand on the Bible and take your oath.''

Quill complied, and the questioning began. Quill answered scornfully, denying that he had deceived anyone. "She's the one who talked of Satan. I had to stop my ears, she spoke of him so lovingly. She wanted carnal knowledge of him. She even told me that Satan had instructed her to lie and say I made up the story, but I was not afraid because I knew that in *lawful* courts, my testimony would have greater trust than hers.''

John listened to Quill calmly enough, as his testimony grew nastier and nastier. "These professors behave exactly as one would expect a conclave of wizards to behave," said Quill. "I wouldn't have questioned them if the girl hadn't denounced them. She thought better of it at once, of course, and tried to deny it, but I knew what she had told me, and it was enough. They deny that they confessed, but several of them did, as my depositions to the court affirm."

John picked up a pile of affidavits from the bench. "I do have those depositions and I've read them all."

"So you know the truth, and this whole hearing is a travesty."

"If it is," said John, "it follows the script you wrote."

"I wrote no script for *this*," said Quill. "I expected this court to function like a proper witch trial."

"But Mr. Quill, this is not a witch trial. This is a hearing on a motion. You seem unable to grasp that. This proceeding has been entirely proper. And I am ready now with my ruling on the motion."

"But you haven't questioned Alvin Smith!"

"All right," said John. "Mr. Smith, how are you today?"

"Tired of being in chains, Your Honor," said Alvin, "but otherwise in good condition."

"You ever have any dealings with Satan?"

"I'm not sure who you're referring to," said Alvin.

John was surprised. He was expecting a simple 'no.' "Satan," he said. "The enemy of God."

"Why, if Satan means an enemy of God, I've had dealings with a fair number in my time, including Mr. Quill here."

"Your Honor!" cried Quill.

"Sit down, Mr. Quill," said John. "Mr. Smith, you seem to be deliberately misunderstanding my question. Don't try my patience, please. Satan, as generally conceived, is a supernatural being. You've been accused of getting powers from him and obeying his commands. Did you get any hidden powers from Satan, or obey him?"

"No sir," said Alvin.

"More to the point," said John, "did you ever tell Purity Orphan that you had dealings with Satan, or could she ever have seen you in the presence of Satan?"

"If you mean the bright red fellow with the claws of a bear and cloven hooves and horns on his head,'' said Alvin, ''I've never seen him or heard from him. He's never even sent me a note. I have *smelled* him, but only when I was alone with Quill.''

John shook his head. ''I don't think you're taking this proceeding seriously.''

''No sir,'' said Alvin, ''I admit that I am not.''

''And why is that? Don't you understand that your life may hinge upon the outcome of this hearing?''

''It doesn't,'' said Alvin.

Cooper tried to shush him.

''And why do you believe that you're safe, regardless of the outcome of this hearing?''

Alvin rose to his feet and pulled the manacles off his wrists as easily as he might have pulled off mittens. He shook his feet and the ankle braces clanked on the floor. ''Because I got the knack I was born with. As far as I know, it's God, not Satan, who creates us, and so whatever knack I have came from God. I try to use it kindly and decently. One thing I never do is try to use my knack to force someone else to do something against their will. But you and my lawyer here, you seem determined to force the people of New England to get rid of their witchery laws whether they want to or not. Mr. Quill is a lying snake, but you don't strike down all the laws just to catch a few liars.''

Verily Cooper rested his head on the desk. John, who was trembling at the sight of such obvious supernatural powers, could see that to Verily Cooper this was old news.

Alvin was still talking. ''I was willing to stick it out and see how you two twisted up the laws without actually breaking too many of them, but my wife needs me right now, and I'm not wasting another minute here. When I got time I'll come back and you and I can talk this out, Your Honor, because I think you're an honorable man. But for the present, I've got somewhere else to be.''

Alvin started toward the door at the back of the court.

Quill jumped to his feet and tried to stop him. His hands slid off Alvin as if he'd been greased. ''Stop him!'' Quill cried. ''Don't let him go!''

''Bailiff,'' said John. ''Mr. Smith seems to be escaping.''

Alvin turned around and faced the judge. ''Your Honor, I thought this wasn't my trial. I thought this was a hearing on a motion. You don't need me here.''

Verily stood up. "Alvin, what about Purity?"

"She ain't going to hang," said Alvin. "By the time you're through, she'll probably be Queen of England."

"Wait just a minute, Alvin," Verily said. He turned to face John Adams. "Your Honor, I ask the court to release my client on his own recognizance, with his promise to appear in court in the morning."

John understood what he was asking, and decided to grant it. The escape would be turned into a legal release. "The defendant's presence not being necessary at this hearing, and with proof positive that the defendant's compliance with his imprisonment up to this point has been entirely voluntary, the court deems him worthy of our trust. Released on his own recognizance, to appear in court at ten in the morning tomorrow."

"Thank you, Your Honor," said Alvin.

"An outrage!" cried Quill.

"Sit down, Mr. Quill," said John Adams. "I'm ready to rule on the motion."

Quill slowly sat down as the door closed behind Alvin Smith.

"Your Honor," said Verily Cooper. "I must apologize for my client's behavior."

"Sit down, Mr. Cooper," said John. "I have my rulings. Mr. Smith's point was well taken. It is not the place of the court to destroy the law in order to achieve justice. Therefore both motions are denied."

Quill flung his arms out wide. "Praise God!"

"Not so fast, Mr. Quill," said John. "This hearing is not over."

"But you've ruled."

"During the process of this hearing, I have heard substantial evidence of misconduct by those officers called interrogators or witchers. The appointment of these witchers is in the hands of the ecclesiastical authorities, who have delegated that responsibility to an examining board of experts on witchery, who are responsible for making sure that witchers are fully trained. However, the actual license to interrogate and serve as an officer of the court is issued by the governor upon a swearing-in by a judge. This license is required for an interrogator to have standing in a civil court and call a witch trial. The licenses of all witchers fall under the law that governs the licensing of all government officials not specified in any particular act. Under that law, your license can be suspended upon a finding by a judicial officer of the level of magistrate or higher that you have used your office against the interests of the people of the commonwealth. I so find. Mr. Quill, I hereby declare your license and the license of all other interrogators in the commonwealth of Massachusetts and in the judicial circuit of New England to be suspended.''

"But you can't—you—"

"Furthermore, I declare all interrogations made under these licenses to be suspended as well. I order that no judicial proceeding may continue until and unless hearings are held that substantiate the evidence under the normal rules of evidence in the civil courts, which are the courts that have jurisdiction over licensing. If you or any other witchcraft interrogator cannot demonstrate that the evidence you have given in court meets the standard of evidence in the civil courts, the suspension of your license may not be lifted. And as long as your license is suspended, no officer of the law in New England is permitted to arrest, imprison, confine, arraign, or try any person on the orders of an interrogator; and since the law requires that a witcher be the prosecutor at any witch trial in New England, I order that no witch trial may be held in New England until and unless an interrogator in possession of a valid license is available to prosecute.''

The words flowed out of John like water from a spring. He felt as though he were singing. Alvin Smith's point had been well taken. But in the moment when he realized that, for honor's sake, he would have to deny Cooper's clever motions, a new path opened up in his mind and he saw how he could put a stop to witch trials, not by using judicial precedent to destroy the law, but by using another law to trump it.

"I declare this hearing adjourned.'' He banged the gavel. Then he banged it again. "I call the court to order in the matter of the commonwealth versus Alvin Smith and Purity Orphan. This being a witch trial, we may not proceed without the presence of an interrogator with a valid license. Is there an interrogator with such a license in the courtroom?''

John looked at Quill cheerfully. "You, sir, seem to be sitting at the prosecutor's table. Have you such a license?''

Quill saw the handwriting on the wall. "No, Your Honor.''

"Well,'' said John. "As there seem to be no other candidates for the role of interrogator present, I have no choice but to find that this trial is improper and illegal. I dismiss the charges. The defendants are free to go. Mr. Smith is not obligated to return to court. Court is adjourned.''

Quill rose shakily to his feet. ''If you think you can get away with this, you're wrong, sir!''

John ignored him and walked away from the bench.

Quill shouted after him. ''We'll get new licenses! See if we don't!''

But John Adams knew something that Quill had forgotten. Licenses were issued only on the authority of the governor. And John was pretty sure that Quincy would not issue any licenses until the Assembly of Massachusetts had plenty of time to write a new witch law that eliminated the office of interrogator and required the normal rules of evidence to hold sway, including the right of the defendant not to be compelled to testify. The churches had the right, of course, to hold witch trials any time they wanted, but the maximum penalty in the ecclesiastical courts was excommunication from the congregation. And they used *that* power against people who didn't attend church often enough.

When the door of the robing room had closed behind him, John couldn't help it. He danced a little jig all around the room, singing a childish ditty as he did.

Then he remembered what he had seen Alvin Smith do, and his mood sobered at once.

He sat in the plush chair and tried to understand what he had seen. John had never believed in knacks that defied natural law, but now he realized that he had come to believe this, not because they didn't exist, but because no one would dare to use such powers in New England, where you could hang for it. The witch laws were wrong, not because such powers were wholly imaginary, but because they didn't necessarily come from Satan. Or did they? Had he crippled the witchcraft laws at the very moment when he had proof that they were necessary?

No. Cooper might not have prevailed with his motions, but his point was well taken. It was only the falsified testimony of the witchers that showed any involvement of Satan with knacks. Without the witchers, knacks were just inborn talents. That some of them were extraordinary did not mean that the possessor of such a knack was either evil or good. Nor was there any evidence that the witch laws had ever been used against people whose hidden powers were truly dangerous. It was obvious that if Alvin Smith had not wished to be confined, no jail could have held him. Therefore only those whose knacks were relatively mild and harmless could ever have been convicted and hanged. It was a law that did nothing it was intended to do. It protected no one and harmed many. It would be good to be rid of it.

In the meantime, though, there was Alvin Smith. What a strange young man! To walk away from his own trial because he thought his lawyer was going to get him off by hurting society at large—was he really that altruistic? Did the good of the people mean more to him than his own good name? For that matter, why had he stayed? John knew without asking. Just as Hezekiah had begged him not to let any harm come to Purity, so also had Alvin stayed for the trial specifically in order to link Purity's fate to his own. But no matter what happened, Purity wasn't going to hang. Alvin had the power to see to that.

But that wasn't enough for Verily Cooper. Saving his friend, saving this girl, that wasn't enough. He had to save everybody. John understood the impulse. He had it himself. He had been thwarted in it, and it hurt him to fail. Not like it hurt Hezekiah Study, of course. But at long last, Cooper had brought them both a chance to redeem their past failures. It was a good gift. Cooper might be too clever for his own good, but he used it in a good cause, which was more than could be said for many clever men.

Knacks. Alvin Smith could shed iron like melting butter. What is my knack? Do I have one? Perhaps my knack is just to hold on my course whether it seems to be taking me anywhere or not. Stubbornness. That could be a gift of God, couldn't it? If so, I daresay I've been blessed with far more than my share. And when God judges me someday, he'll have to admit I didn't bury my talent. I shared it with everyone around me, much to their consternation.

John Adams had a good laugh about that, all by himself.

⚑ 14 ⚑

Revolt

NO SOONER WAS Alvin out of the courtroom than he began to run, long loping strides that would carry him to the river. No greensong helped him at first, for the town was too built up. Yet he was scarcely wearied when he reached the place where Arthur, Mike, and Jean-Jacques were just awakening from their late-afternoon naps. For a moment they wanted to show him what Jean-Jacques had painted, but Alvin had no time for that.

"I was in court and I couldn't pay attention to half that folderol, and my mind wandered to Margaret and there she was, her heart beating so fast, I knew something was wrong. She was spelling big letters in mid-air. Help. And I looked around her and there was Calvin lying on the floor of an attic in Camelot, and he's in a bad way."

Jean-Jacques was all sympathy. "You must feel so helpless, to be so far away."

Mike Fink hooted with laughter. "Alvin ain't all that helpless wherever he is."

"It means we're going to part company with you, Jean-Jacques," Alvin said. "Or rather, some of us are. Arthur, you're coming with me."

Arthur, who had been on tenterhooks waiting to hear the plan, now grinned and relaxed.

"Mike, I'd appreciate it if you'd go on into town and meet Very. He'll have that Purity girl with him, I reckon, or I'll be surprised if he don't. So if you'd tell him that he and you and her and Jean-Jacques here, you should all head for the border of New Amsterdam. I figure we can join up in Philadelphia when I'm done with whatever it is Margaret wants me to do."

"Where?" asked Mike. "Philadelphia's a big place."

"Mistress Louder's rooming house, of course."

"What if she don't got room?"

"Then leave word with her where you'll be. But she'll have room." Alvin turned again to Jean-Jacques. "It's been a pleasure, and I'm proud to know a man with such a knack for painting, but I'm taking Arthur and we got nobody to hold the birds still for you now."

"So what I do now?" said Jean-Jacques. "I make you angry when I kill the bird and stuff it. My career is over if I do not kill the bird."

Alvin looked at Arthur Stuart. "I got to tell you, Arthur, I got no problem with him killing a bird now and then for the sake of folks studying his paintings."

Arthur stood there looking down at the ground.

"Arthur, it ain't like I got a lot of time here," said Alvin.

Arthur looked up at Jean-Jacques, then at Alvin. "I just got to know one thing. Does a bird have a soul?"

"Am I a, how you say, théologien?"

"I just—if a bird dies, when it dies, when you kill it, what happens to it? Is it completely dead? Or is there some part of it that . . ."

Arthur stood there with tears beading up on his cheeks. Alvin reached out to hug him, but Arthur pulled away. "I ain't asking for a hug, dammit, I'm asking for an answer!"

"I don't know about that," said Alvin. "What I see is like a little fire inside every living thing. Humans got a big bright one, most of them anyway, but there's fire like that in every animal. The plants, too, only the fire is spread out all through the plant, not just in one place like it is with the animals. Margaret sees something like that, she says, only she don't catch much more than a glimpse of what's in the animals, like the shadow of a fire, if you get my drift. Now is that heartfire a soul? I don't know. And what happens to it after a body dies? I don't know that either. I know it ain't in the body anymore. But I know sometimes the heartfire can leave the body. Happens when I'm doodle-bugging, part of it goes out of me. Does that mean that when the body's dead the whole thing can go? I don't know, Arthur. You're asking me what I can't tell you.''

"But it might, you can say that, can't you? It might live on, I mean if humans do it, then birds might too, right? Their heartfires may be smaller but that don't mean they'll burn out when they die, does it?''

"I reckon that's good thinking," said Alvin. "I reckon if anybody lives on after death—and I think they do, mind you, I just ain't seen it—then why not birds? Heartfire is heartfire, I should think, lessen somebody tells me different. Is that good enough?''

Arthur Stuart nodded. "Then you can kill a bird now and then, if you got to.''

Jean-Jacques bowed in salute to Arthur. "I think, Mr. Stuart, that this was the question you really wanted to ask me from the start. Back in Philadelphia.''

Arthur Stuart looked a little embarrassed. "Maybe it was. I wasn't sure myself.''

Alvin rubbed Arthur's tight-curled hair. Arthur ducked away. "Don't treat me like a baby.''

"You don't like it, get taller," said Alvin. "Long as you're shorter than me, I'm going to use your head to scratch an itch whenever I feel like it." Alvin touched the brim of his hat in salute to Mike and Jean-Jacques. "I'll see you in Philadelphia, Mike. And Jean-Jacques, I hope to see you again someday, or at least to see your book.''

"I promise you your own copy," said Jean-Jacques.

"I don't like this," said Mike. "I should be with you.''

"I promise you, Mike, I'm not the one in danger down there.''

"It's a blame fool thing to do!" said Mike.

"What, leave you behind?''

"Healing Calvin.''

Alvin understood the love that prompted these words, but he couldn't leave the idea unanswered. "Mike, he's my brother.''

"I'm more brother to you than he ever was," said Mike.

"You are now," said Alvin. "But there was a time when he was my dearest friend. We did everything together. I have no memories of my childhood without him in them, or scarcely any.''

"So why doesn't he feel that way?''

"Maybe I wasn't as good a brother to him as he was to me,'' said Alvin. "Mike, I'll come back safe.''

"This is as crazy as it was you going back to jail.''

"I walked out when I needed to,'' said Alvin. "And now I've got to get moving. I need you to get Jean-Jacques out of New England without getting deported as a Catholic, and Verily and Purity need somebody who isn't ga-ga with love to make sure they eat and sleep.''

Arthur Stuart solemnly shook hands with Mike and Jean-Jacques. Alvin hugged them both. Then they took off at a jog, the man leading, the boy at his heels. In a few minutes the greensong had them and they fairly flew through the woods along the river.

"He's coming,'' said Margaret.

"Where he be, you say?'' asked Gullah Joe.

Outside, they heard the sound of galloping horses. The singing and wailing from the slave quarters had grown more intense as the sun set and darkness gathered.

"I can't tell,'' said Margaret. "He's in the midst of the music. Running. He moves like the wind. But it's such a long way.''

"We tell folks what you say,'' said Denmark, "but this be too hard for them. The anger, it come so fast to them. I hear some talking about killing their White folks tonight in their beds. I hear them say, Kill them the White babies, too, the children. Kill them all.''

"I know,'' said Margaret. "You did your best.''

"They be other ones, too,'' said Gullah Joe. "No name come back a-them. Empty like him. More empty. They die. He kill them.''

Margaret looked down at Calvin's body. The young man's breath was so shallow that now and then she had to check his heartfire just to see if he was alive. Fishy and Denmark's woman were tending him now, so Margaret could rest, but what good did washing him do? Maybe they were keeping the fever down. Maybe they were just keeping him wet. They certainly weren't keeping him company, for he had lapsed into unconsciousness hours ago and all his futures had come down to just a handful that didn't lead to a miserable death here, tonight, in this place.

"Why he no fix up, him?" asked Gullah Joe. "He strong."

"Strong but ignorant," said Margaret. "My husband tried to teach him, but he refused to learn. He wanted the results without practicing the method."

"Young," said Gullah Joe.

"I learned when I was young," said Denmark.

"You never be young," said Gullah Joe.

Denmark grimaced at that. "You right, Gullah Joe."

"Your wife," said Margaret.

Denmark looked at the slave woman he had bought and ruined. "She never let me call her that."

"She never told you her name, either," said Margaret.

Denmark shook his head. "I never call her by no slave name. She never tell me her true name. So I got no name for her."

"Would you like to speak that name? Don't you think that in her present state, she'd like to hear someone call her by name?"

"When she be in her right mind she don't want me to," said Denmark.

"Slavery makes people do strange things," said Margaret.

"I never was a slave," said Denmark.

"You were, all the same," said Margaret. "They fenced you around with so many laws. Who is more a slave than the man who has to pretend he's a slave to survive?"

"That didn't make me do *that* to her."

"I don't know," said Margaret. "Of course you made your own choices. You tried to find a wife in just the way your father did—you bought one. Then you found yourself in a corner. You thought murder was your only hope. But at the last moment you couldn't do it."

"Not the last moment," said Denmark. "The moment after."

"Yes," said Margaret. "Almost too late."

"Now I live with her every day," said Denmark. "Now who own who?"

"All that anger outside—what if they kill? Do you think they're murderers?"

"You think they not?" asked Denmark.

"There has to be something between murder and innocence. I've seen the darkest places in everyone's heartfire, Denmark. There's no one who doesn't have memories he wishes he didn't have. And there are crimes that arise from—from decent desires gone wrong, from justified passions carried too far. Crimes that began only as mistakes. I've learned never to judge people. Of course I judge whether they're dangerous or not, or whether they did right or wrong, how can anyone live without judging? What I mean is, I can't condemn them. A few, yes, a few who love the suffering of others, or who never think of others at all, worthless souls that exist only to satisfy themselves. But those are rare. Do you even know what I'm talking about?"

"I know you scared," said Denmark. "You talk when you scared."

"We're safe enough here," said Margaret. "I'm just . . . what you did to your wife, Denmark. Do you think I haven't thought of doing that to someone? An enemy? Someone who I know will someday cause the death of the person I love most, the person I've loved my whole life, from childhood up. I know that desperate feeling. You have to stop him. And then you see the chance. He's helpless. All you have to do is let nature take its course, and he's gone."

"But you call your husband," said Denmark. "You wave your arms and make letters in the air. Somehow he see that."

"So I chose to do the right thing," she said.

"Like me," said Denmark.

"But maybe I chose too late," she said.

Denmark shrugged.

"Maybe. It ain't all work out yet."

"All these people thirsting for vengeance. What will they choose? When will it be too late for them? Or just in time?"

A new sound. Marching feet. Margaret ran to the window. The King's Guard, marching in Blacktown.

"Damn fool they," said Gullah Joe. "What we do here in Blacktown? Who we hurt? They scared of *us,* they no remember they gots them Black people hate them, in they house, they wait down the stair, White man sleep, up the stair they go, cook she got she knife, gardener he got he sickle, butler he break him wine bottle, he got the glass, the edge be sharp. When they blood paint the walls, when they body empty, who the Black man put on that tall hat? Who the Black woman wear the bloody dress?"

The images were too terrible for Margaret to bear. She had already seen them herself, in the blazing heartfires of angry slaves. What Gullah Joe imagined, she had seen down ten thousand paths into the future. Until Calvin tore up the name-strings, that future hadn't shown up anywhere. She couldn't predict it. Calvin had the power to change everything without warning. Margaret was unaccustomed to surprise. She didn't know how to deal with a situation that she hadn't had time to watch and think about.

She walked away, into a corner of the room. She began to pray.

But she couldn't keep her mind on the words of her prayer. She kept thinking of Calvin. As if she didn't have enough to worry about. Wasn't it just like Cal? Set loose forces that could cause the deaths of thousands of people, and he was going to lie there dying through it all.

As for Gullah Joe and Denmark, she hadn't the heart to tell them, but the likeliest future, whether the slave revolt happened or not, was that the King and his men would be looking for the person who planned the revolt. It had to be a conspiracy. It couldn't be mere chance that in the morning the entire slave population of Camelot was docile, and suddenly by nightfall they were keening and howling in every house. There had to be a plot. There had to be a signal given. It wasn't hard to find slaves who, under torture, would mention the taker of names. And others who would point him out. The mastermind of the conspiracy, that's what they'd call him. They'd call it Denmark Vesey's War, as if it was war to have families murdered in their sleep, and then every third slave in Camelot hanged in retribution, while Denmark Vesey himself would be drawn and quartered, and the pieces of him hung on poles in Blacktown, lest anyone forget.

She hadn't the heart to tell him that. Nor did it matter, in the end, for one thing was certain in Denmark's heartfire: If this happened to him, he would believe that he deserved it, for the sake of what he did to his woman.

Calvin. Again he kept intruding in her thoughts. Something about Calvin. What? He can't heal himself, so what is he good for?

For something that he *does* know how to do.

Margaret got up from her prayer and rushed to Gullah Joe. "You've done this before, Gullah Joe. I've heard the stories, I've seen them in the slaves' memories, legends of the zombi, the walking dead."

"I no do that," said Gullah Joe.

"I know, you don't do it on purpose, but there he is, dead but alive. There must be something you have, something in your tools, your powders, that can wake him up. Just for a little while."

"Wake him up, then he die faster," said Gullah Joe.

"I need him. To save the people he did this to."

"He no heal him own body," said Gullah Joe scornfully.

"Because he doesn't know how. But he can do *something*."

Gullah Joe got up and went to his jars. Soon he had a mixture—a dangerous one, to judge from the way he never let any of the powders touch his skin and looked away when mixing so as not to breathe in any of the dust. When it was mixed, he poured it through a hole in a small bellows, then plugged the hole tightly. Even at that, he wetted down cloths for the rest of them to breathe through, in case any dust got loose in the air.

Then he took the bellows, put the end in one of Calvin's nostrils, then waxed the other nostril closed. "You," he said to Denmark. "Hold him mouth closed."

"No," said Denmark. "I can't do that. That too much like drowning him."

"I'll do it," said Margaret.

"What you tell husband then, this go bad?"

"It's my fault anyway," said Margaret. "I told you to do it."

"I do it, ma'am," said Fishy. "I do this."

Margaret stepped back. Fishy got one hand under Calvin's jaw and the other atop his head.

"I say go, you close him tight the mouth," said Gullah Joe.

Fishy nodded.

"Go."

She clamped Calvin's mouth shut. Calvin feebly resisted, desperate for breath. Nothing came in except a thin stream of air around the nipple of the bellows. Gullah Joe slammed the bellows together just as Calvin inhaled desperately. A cloud of dust emerged from around the bellows. Gullah Joe was ready for it. He picked up a bucket of water and doused Calvin with it, catching and settling the dust at the same time.

Calvin jerked and twitched violently. Then he sat up, pulling away from Fishy's grip, tearing the bellows and the wax out of his nostrils. Then he choked and coughed, trying to clear his lungs.

He looked no healthier. Indeed, patches of his skin were sloughing off, sliding like rotten fruit thrown against a window. But he was alert.

"Calvin, listen to me," Margaret said.

Calvin only choked and gasped.

"The slaves are about to revolt. It has to be stopped. Alvin's too far away, I need your help!"

Calvin wept. "I can't do nothing!"

"Wake up!" Margaret shouted at him. "I need you to be a man, for once! This isn't about you, this isn't about Alvin, it's about doing the decent thing for people who need you."

Some of what she was saying finally penetrated Calvin's hazy mind. "Yes," he said. "Tell me what to do."

"Something to take their minds off their anger," she said. "What we need is a heavy storm. Wind and rain. Lightning!"

"I can't do lightning."

"How do you know you can't?"

"Cause I grew up trying." He looked down at his hand. The bare bone of one finger was exposed. "Margaret, what's happening to me!"

"You were too long out of your body," she said. "Alvin's hurrying here to save you."

"He don't want to help me, he wants me dead!"

"Stop thinking about yourself, Calvin!" she said sternly. "I need something that feels like a force of nature."

"I can do fires. I can set the city on fire."

As he spoke, a couple of tiny flames danced around on the floor beside him.

"No!" cried Margaret. "Good heavens, are you insane? The slaves will be blamed for setting the fires, it would make everything even worse! Not fire."

"I don't know how anything works," Calvin said. "Not deep enough to change it. Alvin tried to teach me but all I wanted was the showy stuff." He wept again. Margaret had to seize his wrists to keep him from rubbing the skin off his face.

"Get control of yourself," she said. She turned helplessly to Gullah Joe. "Isn't there something—"

Gullah Joe laughed madly. "I tell you! No good this way! Zombi no good! All he think be, I so dead! He be sad, all sad, him."

"What about the water?" she asked Calvin. "I know you and Alvin played with water, he told me. Making it splash without throwing in a stone—that's a game you played. Remember?"

"Big splash," he said.

"Yes, that's right. Make it splash out there. In the river, really big splashes. Slosh the water up on the shore. Make it flood."

"All we did was little splashes," said Calvin.

"Well this time do a big one!" Margaret shouted, her patience wearing thin. If, in fact, she had any patience left at all.

"I'll try, I'll try, I'll try." He cried again.

"Stop that! Just do it!"

She felt someone kneel down beside her. Fishy? No, Denmark's wife. She had a damp cloth. Gently she pressed it against Calvin's forehead. Then his cheek. She mumbled something unintelligible, but the music of it was calm and comforting. Calvin closed his eyes and began trying to make the water in the river splash.

Margaret also closed her eyes and cast about for heartfires near the river. She skipped from one to another, up and down the shore, on the north side of the peninsula and the south. No one was looking toward the water. They were all watching inland, fearful of the howling from the slaves.

Then one of them noticed that the boats were rocking in the water. Masts tipped, then tipped back again. He looked out at the water. Wave after wave was coming, as if from giant stones falling, or perhaps something pulsing deep under the water. Each wave was higher than the one before. They began breaking onto the docks.

More and more people were seeing the waves now, and those near the water began to run farther inland. The waves were coming up onto the streets, forming rivers that flowed over the cobblestones. Farther inland the water came until it was streaming across the peninsula. Ships battered against the dock and began to break into kindling. People ran screaming through the streets, pounding on doors, begging to be let inside.

And the slaves also pounded on the doors. Where a moment before all they could think of was murder and vengeance, now in their ground-floor quarters a new passion had taken hold: to get to the first floor before this flood drowned them. Wave after wave swept through the slave quarters. The howling and singing stopped, to be replaced by a cacophony of panicked cries.

Many of the Whites, seeing the flood, opened the doors and let their slaves, now chastened and afraid, come up to safety. Others, though, kept the doors locked, and more than one discharged a weapon through the door, warning the slaves to stay back.

There were no more thoughts of killing the White families they worked for. Already the slaves were telling the stories that made sense to them. "God be telling us, Thou shalt not kill, or I send a flood like Noah!" "Lord, I don't want to die!" Terror took the place of rage, damped it down, swept it out, drowned it, for the moment, at least.

"Enough," said Margaret. "You did it, Calvin. Enough."

Calvin sobbed in relief. "That was so hard!" He lay back down, rolled over, curled up and wept. Or rather, tried to curl up. As he dragged his legs across the floor, his right foot was pulled away from his body. Margaret gagged at the sight. But Denmark's woman reached down, picked up the foot, and put it in place at the end of the damaged leg.

"He just about dead," said Denmark.

"No," moaned Margaret. "Oh, Calvin, not now, not when you finally did something good."

"That the best time a-die," said Fishy helpfully. "You get in heaven."

Margaret turned again to Gullah Joe.

"No look me, you!" he said. "I do all you say, look what happen!"

"What if he sent out his doodlebug again? Like before? Even if he dies, can't you hold on to it? Keep it from getting away?"

"What you think I be? I a witchy man! You want God, him!"

"You held him captive before. Do it again! Try it!"

Even as she insisted, she could see the paths of the future change. When she finally saw one in which Calvin was still alive at dawn, she shouted at him, "That's it! Do that!"

"Do what?"

"What you were thinking! Right when I shouted."

Gullah Joe threw up his hands in despair, but he set to work, making Denmark and Fishy help him, moving charms into a new circle, then putting an open box in the midst of it. "Tell him go in box. Put him whole self in box."

"Did you understand him, Calvin?"

Calvin moaned in pain.

"Send out your doodlebug! Let him catch it and save it. It's your only chance, Calvin! Send your doodlebug to Gullah Joe, go into the box he's holding. Do it, Calvin!"

Panting shallowly, Calvin complied as best he could. Gullah Joe kept tossing a fine powder into the circle. It wasn't till the tenth throw that he shouted. "You see that? Part him go in! Look a-that!"

Another cast of the powder, and this time Margaret also saw the spark.

"All bright him! Inside, go all inside!"

"Do it, Calvin. Your whole attention, put it inside that box. Everything that's you, into the box!"

He stopped moaning. He rolled onto his back, his eyes staring straight up.

"He's done all he can do!" cried Margaret. "He's exhausted."

"He dead," said Fishy.

Gullah Joe slammed the lid on the box, turned it upside down, and sat on it.

"You hatching that?" asked Fishy.

"Inside circle, inside my hair." Gullah Joe grinned. "This time he no get out!"

"All right, Alvin," Margaret murmured. "Come quickly."

She leaned back against Denmark's wife, who knelt behind her like a cushion. "I'm so tired," she said.

"We all sleep now," said Denmark.

"Not me," said Gullah Joe.

Margaret closed her eyes and looked out into the city again. The water was calm again and the panic had died down, but the revolt was over for the night. Killing had been driven out of the hearts of the Blacks.

But now the thought of killing was showing up in other hearts. Whites were rushing to the palace, demanding that someone find out who started the plot. It had to be a plot, all the slaves starting up at once. Only the miraculous intervention of the waves had saved them. Do something, they demanded. Catch the ringleaders of the revolt.

And King Arthur listened. He called in his advisers and listened to them. Soon there were questioners in the streets, directing groups of soldiers as they gathered Blacks for questioning.

How long? thought Margaret. How long before Denmark Vesey's name comes up?

Long before dawn.

Margaret rose to her feet. "No time for rest now," she said. "Alvin will come here. Tell him what you've done. Don't harm Calvin's body in any way. Keep it as fresh as you can."

Gullah Joe rolled his eyes. "Where you go?"

"It's time for my audience with the King."

Lady Ashworth spent the entire rebellion throwing up in her bedroom. The flood, too. For her husband had found out about her liaison with that boy—slaves who had once been docile now suddenly seemed to take relish in sowing dissension between her and Lord Ashworth. In vain did she plead that it was only once, in vain did she beg for forgiveness. For an hour she sat in the parlor, trembling and weeping, as her husband brandished a pistol in one hand, a sword in the other, one of which he would set down from time to time in order to take another swig of bourbon.

It was only the howling of the slaves that broke off his drunken, murderous, suicidal ranting. This was one house where none of the Blacks wanted to brave a crazed White man with a gun, but he was all for shooting them anyway if they didn't shut up and stop all that chanting and moaning. As soon as he left her alone, Lady Ashworth fled to her room and locked the door. She threw up so abruptly that she didn't have time to move first—her vomit was a smear down the door and onto the floor beneath it. By the time the flood came she had nothing left to throw up, but she kept retching.

With the Blacks terrified and Lady Ashworth indisposed, the only person able to answer Margaret's insistent ringing at the door was Lord Ashworth himself, who stood there drunken and disheveled, the pistol still in his hand, hanging by the trigger. Margaret immediately reached down and took the gun away from him.

"What are you doing?" he demanded. "That's my gun. Who are you?"

Margaret took in the situation with a few probes into his heartfire. "You poor stupid man," she said. "Your wife wasn't seduced. She was raped."

"Then why didn't she say so?"

"Because she *thought* it was a seduction."

"What do you know about any of this?"

"Take me to your wife at once, sir!"

"Get out of my house!"

"Very well," said Margaret. "You leave me no choice. I will be forced to report to the press that a trusted officer of the King has had a liaison for the past two years with the wife of a certain plantation owner in Savannah. Not to mention the number of times he has accepted the hospitality of slaveowners who make sure he doesn't have to sleep alone. I believe sexual congress between White and Black is still a crime in this city?"

He backed away from her, raising his hand to point the gun at her, until he remembered that she had his pistol. "Who sent you?" he said.

"I sent myself," she said. "I have urgent business with the King. Your wife is in no condition to take me. So you'll have to do it."

"Business with the King! You want him to throw me out of office?"

"I know the ringleader of the slave revolt!"

Lord Ashworth was confused. "Slave revolt? When?"

"Tonight, while you were threatening to kill your wife. She's a shallow woman, Lord Ashworth, and she has a mean streak, but she's more faithful to your marriage than *you* are. You might take that into account before you terrify her again. Now, will you take me to the King or not?"

"Tell me what you know, and I'll tell him."

"An audience with the King!" demanded Margaret. "Now!"

Lord Ashworth finally stumbled into the realization that he had no choice. "I have to change clothes," he said. "I'm drunk."

"Yes, by all means, change." Lord Ashworth staggered from the room.

Margaret strode into the house, calling out as she went. "Doe! Lion! Where are you?"

She didn't find them till she opened the door down to the ground floor. Half soaked in floodwater, the slaves were as frightened and miserable a group as she had ever seen. "Come upstairs now," she said. "Lion, your master needs help dressing himself. He's very drunk, but I have the gun." She showed him the pistol. Then, certain that Lion had no murder in his heart, she handed the gun to him. "I suggest you lose this and then don't find it for a few days." He carried the gun upstairs with him, only dropping it into his pocket at the last minute.

"You sure he don't kill the master?" asked Doe.

"Doe, I know you're a free woman, but can you go to Lady Ashworth? As a friend. No harm will come to you from it. She needs comforting. She needs you to tell her that the man who had the use of her was more than a trickster. He forced her against her will. If she doesn't remember it that way, it just proves how powerful he is."

Doe looked studious. "That a long message, ma'am," she said.

"You remember the sense of it. Find your own words."

King Arthur and his council had been meeting for an hour before Lord Ashworth finally bothered to show up, and it was obvious he had been drinking. It was rather shocking and would have been a scandal on any other night, but all the King could think about was that finally he was here, perhaps he could break the impasse over what to do. Hotheaded John Calhoun was all for hanging one out of every three slaves as an example. "Make them think twice before they plot again!" On the other hand, as several of the older men reminded him, one didn't seize one-third of the city's most valuable property and destroy it, just to make a point.

Lord Ashworth, however, did not seem interested in the argument. "I have someone to see you," he said.

"An audience! At a time like this!"

"She claims to know about the conspiracy."

"We know about it already," said the King. "We have soldiers searching for the hideout right now. If they're wise, they'll drown themselves in the river before they let us take them."

"Your Majesty, I beg you to hear her."

The intensity of his tone, despite his drunkenness, was sobering. "All right, then," said the King. "For my dear friend."

Margaret was ushered in, and she introduced herself. Impatiently, the King got to the point at once. "We know all about the conspiracy. What can you possibly add to what we know?"

"What I know is that it wasn't a conspiracy, it was an accident."

She poured out the story, keeping it as close to the truth as possible without announcing just how powerful Calvin was before, and how helpless he had become. A young White man of her acquaintance noticed a man taking something from each slave that disembarked. It turned out that they were charms that held the slaves' true names, along with their anger and their fear. Tonight there had been an accident that destroyed the name-strings, and the slaves suddenly found themselves filled with the long-hidden rage. "But the flood frightened it out of them, and you'll have no rebellion now."

"Claptrap," said Calhoun.

Margaret looked at him coldly. "The tragedy of *your* life, sir, is that despite all your ambition, you'll never be king."

Calhoun turned red and started to answer, but the King raised a hand to silence him. He was quite a young man, perhaps younger than Margaret and there was an air of quiet assurance about him that she rather liked, especially since he seemed interested in what she had said. "All I want to know," he said, "is the name of the one they call the taker of names."

"But you already know it," she said to him. "Several witnesses have told you about Denmark Vesey."

"Ah, but *we* know about him because of excellent investigative work. How do *you* know?"

"I know that he's innocent of any ill intent," she said.

A man handed the King a paper. "Ah, here it is," the King said. "Your name is Margaret Smith, yes? Married to an accused slave thief. And you're here in Camelot to meddle in our ancient practice of servitude. Well, tonight we've seen where leniency takes us. Do you know how many slaves told us about plans to kill entire White families in their sleep? And now I find that there's a White woman intimately involved with the conspirators."

With sick dread, Margaret saw herself playing the leading role in some nasty futures in the King's heartfire. She hadn't bargained on this. She should have probed into her own future before coming to the King with wild-sounding stories about Blacks giving up their names voluntarily, for safekeeping, and then getting them back suddenly. "You must admit it sounds like a fable," the King explained kindly.

"Your Majesty," said Margaret, "I know that there are those who urge you to punish this revolt with brutality. You may think this is necessary to make your subjects feel secure in their homes, but Your Majesty, extravagant measures like the one Mr. Calhoun proposes will only bring greater danger down upon you."

"It's hard to imagine a more heinous danger than our servants turning their knives on us," said Calhoun.

"What about war? What about bloody, terrible war, that kills or injures or spiritually maims a generation of young men?"

"War?" asked the King. "Punishing revolt will lead to *war?*"

"The rhetoric surrounding the issue of whether the western territories of Appalachee will be slave or free is already out of hand. A wholesale slaughter of innocent Black men and women will outrage and unify the people of the United States and Appalachee, and stiffen their resolve that slavery will have no place among them."

"Enough of this," said the King. "All you have succeeded in proving to me is that you are part of a conspiracy that must include at least one of the servants in the palace. How else could you know what John Calhoun's proposal is? As for the rest, when I need advice from an abolitionist woman on affairs of state, you're the very person I'll call upon."

"Your Majesty," said Calhoun, "it's obvious this woman knows far more about the conspiracy than she's letting on. It would be a mistake to let her leave so easily."

"What I know is that there *is* no conspiracy," said Margaret. "By all means, arrest me, if you're prepared to bear the outcry that would follow."

"If we hang one slave in three, no one will be asking around about *you*," said Calhoun. "Now arrest her!"

This last order was flung at the soldiers standing at the door. At once they strode in and took Margaret by the arms.

"She'll confess soon enough," said Calhoun. "In treason cases, they always do."

"I don't like knowing about things like that," said the King.

"Neither do I," said another man's voice. It took a moment for them to realize that it wasn't one of the King's advisers who spoke.

Instead, it was a tall man dressed like a workingman on holiday—clothes that were meant to be somewhat dressy, but succeeded only in looking vaguely pathetic and ill-fitting. And beside him, a half-Black boy two-thirds grown.

"How did you get in here!" cried several men at once. But the stranger answered not a word. He walked up to Margaret and kissed her gently on the lips. Then he looked steadily into the gaze of one of the soldiers holding her by the arm. Shuddering, he let go of her and backed away. So did the other soldier.

"Well, Margaret," said the man, "it looks like I can't leave you alone for a few minutes."

"Who are you?" asked the King. "Her foreign-policy adviser?"

"I'm her husband, Alvin Smith."

"It was thoughtful of you to show up just as we've arrested your wife. No doubt you're part of the conspiracy as well. As for this Black boy—it's not proper to bring your slave into the presence of the King, especially one too young to have been reliably trained."

"I came here to try to keep you from making the mistake that will eventually take you off your throne," said Margaret. "If you don't heed the warning, then I at least am blameless."

"Let's get her out of here," said Calhoun. "We've got hours of work ahead of us, and it's obvious she needs to be interrogated as a member of the conspiracy. Her husband, too, and this child."

Margaret and Alvin looked at each other and laughed. Arthur, on the other hand, was too busy gazing at the magnificence of the council room to care much about what was going on. He didn't really notice the King until now, when Alvin pointed him out. "There you are, Arthur Stuart. That's the man you were named for. The King of England, in exile in the Crown Colonies. Behold the majesty of the crownèd head."

"Nice to meet you, sir," said Arthur Stuart to the King.

Calhoun's outrage reached a new level. "You dare to mock the King in this fashion? Not to mention naming a Black child after him in the first place."

"Since you've already got me hanged in your mind," said Alvin, "what harm will it do if I compound the crime?"

"Compound nothing, Alvin," Margaret said to him. "He's been warned that if he takes retribution against this revolt that didn't even happen, killing slaves without reference to guilt or innocence, it will lead to war."

"I have no fear of war," said Arthur Stuart. "That's when kings get to show their mettle."

"You're thinking of chess," said Margaret. "In war, everyone has their chance to bleed." She turned to Alvin. "My message was delivered. It's out of my hands. And your brother needs you."

Alvin nodded. He turned to the company surrounding him. "Gentlemen, you may return to your deliberations. I ran down here from New England this afternoon and I have no more time to spend with you. Good evening."

Alvin took Arthur by one hand and Margaret by the other. "Make way please," he said.

The men blocking his path didn't move.

And then, suddenly, they did. Or rather, their feet did, sliding right out from under them. Alvin took another stride toward the door.

The King drew a sword. So did the other men, though they had to get them from the wall where they hung during the meeting. And two guards by the door drew pistols.

"Really, Your Majesty," said Alvin, "the essence of courtesy is that one must allow one's guests to leave."

Before he finished talking, he already reached out to change the iron in the swords and the pistols. To their horror, the armed men found their weapons dissolving and dribbling into pools of cold wet iron on the floor. They dropped their weapons and recoiled.

"What are you, sir!" cried the King.

"Isn't it obvious?" said Calhoun. "It's the devil, the devil's dam, and their bastard son!"

"Hey," protested Arthur Stuart. "I may be a bastard, but I'm not *their* bastard."

"Sorry we have to be on our way so quickly," said Alvin. "Have a nice future, Your Majesty." With that, Alvin reached down, pulled the lockset out of the massive door, and then pushed gently on it, making it fall away from its dissolving hinges and land with a crash on the floor outside the council room. They walked away unmolested.

*   *   *

The stink of Calvin's dead body filled the attic when Margaret led Alvin and Arthur into the place. Alvin went at once to the corpse and knelt by it, weeping. "Calvin, I came as fast as I could."

"You want to cry," said Denmark, "cry for the dead."

"I already explained to him about holding Calvin's heartfire in the box," Margaret said.

"I can't repair the body without the heartfire in it," said Alvin. "And it can't hold the heartfire until it's repaired."

"Do both at once," said Margaret. "You can do it, can't you, Gullah Joe? Feed the heartfire back into the body, bit by bit?"

"You lose you mind?" asked Gullah Joe. "How many miracle you want tonight?"

"I'll just do my best," said Alvin.

He worked on Calvin's body for three hours. No sooner did he start in on one repair than the one he just completed started to decay again. Working steadily and methodically, though, he was able to get the heart and brain back into working order. "Now," he said.

Gullah Joe slid off the box, carried it close to Calvin's body, and opened it.

Alvin and Margaret both saw the heartfire leap into the body. The heart beat convulsively. Once. Twice. Blood moved through the collapsing arteries. Alvin paid no heed to that problem—it was the lungs he had to repair now, quickly, instantly. But with the heartfire inside the body, it became far easier, for now he could make a pattern and the body would imitate it, passing the information along through the living tissues. A half-ruined diaphragm contracted, then expanded the lungs. The blood that pumped feebly through the body now bore steadily increasing amounts of oxygen.

That was only the beginning. Dawn had fully come before Alvin's work was done. Calvin breathed easily and normally. The flesh had healed, leaving no scars. He was as clean as a newborn.

"What I see this night," said Gullah Joe. "What god you be?"

Alvin shook his head. "Is there a god of weariness?"

Someone started pounding on the door downstairs.

"Ignore them," said Margaret. "There are only two of them. They won't break in until there are more soldiers to back them up."

"How long do we have?" asked Alvin.

"Not long," said Margaret. "I suggest we leave now."

"Is there no rest for the devil?" asked Alvin.

"You a devil too?" asked Gullah Joe.

"That was a joke," said Alvin. "Margaret, who *are* these people?"

"Time enough to explain on the road." Margaret turned to the others. "It's not safe for you to stay here, Denmark, Gullah Joe. Come away with us. Alvin can keep you safe until you're in the North, out of this miserable place." She turned to Fishy and Denmark's wife. "You aren't in the same danger, but why should you stay? We'll take you north with us. If you like, you can go on to Vigor Church. Or Hatrack River." Margaret looked at Gullah Joe and smiled. "I'd like to see what all the knackish folk in Hatrack River would make of *you*."

Denmark tugged at Alvin's sleeve. "What you done for your brother. Raise him from the dead. What about my wife?" He brought her forward.

Alvin closed his eyes and studied her for a few moments. "It's an old injury, and it's all connected with the brain. I don't know. Let's get away from here, and when we're safely in the North, I'll do what I can."

They all agreed to come along. What choice did they have? "Can't you take all us?" asked Fishy. "All the slave in this place, take us!"

Margaret put her arm around Fishy. "If it was in our power, we'd take them. But such a large group—who would take so many thousands of free Blacks all at once? We'd bring them north, only to have them turned away. *You* we can bring with us."

Fishy nodded. "I know you mean to do good. It never be enough."

"No," said Margaret. "Never enough. But we do our best, and pray that in the long run, it *will* be enough."

Alvin knelt again by Calvin, shook him gently, woke him. Calvin opened his eyes and saw Alvin. He laughed in delight. "You," he said. "You came and saved me."

❖ 15 ❖

Fathers and Mothers

MIKE FINK AND Jean-Jacques Audubon waited a discreet distance away
as Hezekiah Study led Verily and Purity through the graveyard. The
graves were located in a curious alcove in the wall of the cemetery.
Purity knelt at her parents' graves and wept for them. Verily knelt beside
her, and after a while she reached for Hezekiah and drew him down
with her as well. "You're all I have left of them," she said to Hezekiah.
"Since I have no memories of my own, I have to rely on yours. Come
with us."

"I'll travel with you as far as Philadelphia," said Hezekiah. "Beyond
that I can't promise."

"Once Alvin starts talking about the Crystal City, you'll catch the
vision of it," said Verily. "I promise."

Hezekiah smiled ruefully. "Will there be a need for an old Puritan
minister?"

"No doubt of it," said Verily. "But a scholar like you—I think we'll
have to tear you away from the things you can learn there in order to
get a sermon out of you."

"My heart isn't much in sermonizing anyway," said Hezekiah. "I'm tired of the sound of my own mouth."

"Then don't listen," said Purity. "Why should we miss out on your sermons just because *you* don't want to hear them?"

They lingered near the graves for some time. Only when they were leaving did it occur to Verily how odd it was to have such an alcove enclosing just those two graves. Otherwise the graveyard walls marked out a simple rectangle.

Hezekiah heard the question and nodded. "Well, you see, when they were buried, the witcher insisted the graves had to be outside the churchyard. Can't have witches in hallowed ground. Then the witchers left, and all the neighbors who knew them and loved them, they tore down the wall at that place, and laid out a new course, and now they're inside the wall of the churchyard after all."

They stood on the south bank of the Potomac, waiting for the ferry to return to their shore to carry them across into the United States—specifically New Sweden, which despite its name was now almost as thoroughly English-speaking as Pennsylvania. A long-legged waterbird swept down into the water, elegant in its graceful passage from a creature of air to a creature of water.

"Too bad Audubon ain't here to tell us what bird that is," said Alvin.

Arthur Stuart took Margaret by the hand. "You were there," he said. "You know. What kind of bird was it that carried me?"

Margaret looked at him in puzzlement. "What do you mean?"

"I remember flying," said Arthur. "Hour after hour, all the way north. What kind of bird was that?"

"It wasn't a bird," she said. "It was your mother. She knew some of the witchy lore that Gullah Joe uses. She made wings and she flew, carrying you the whole way."

"But I saw a bird," said Arthur.

"You were a newborn," said Margaret. "How could you possibly remember?"

"Wings, so wide," said Arthur. "It was so beautiful to fly. I still dream about it all the time."

"Your mother wasn't a bird, Arthur Stuart," said Margaret.

"Yes she was," said Arthur. "A bird in the air, and then a woman when she came to earth."

Alvin remembered now how a question had nagged at Arthur the whole time he was with Audubon, a question that he could never quite frame in a way to get the answer he needed. Now Alvin had the answer for him. "She *is* waiting for you, Arthur Stuart," said Alvin. "With wings or without, your mother bird is still alive, waiting for you when the time comes."

Arthur Stuart nodded. "I think you're right," he said. "I feel her sometimes in the sky, so high I can't see her, but she's looking down and she sees me." He looked to Alvin and Margaret for reassurance. "That's not silly, is it?"

"They'd have to have a thousand angels watching her every minute in heaven," said Margaret, "to keep your mama from watching over you."

Arthur Stuart nodded. "When I see her," he said, "that's when I'll find out my true name."

"All names are true on that day," said Alvin. "When we see each other for what we really are."

Margaret said nothing. She took no comfort in thinking of a day of resurrection far in the distant future, for she had never seen that day in any heartfire. All her visions ended, sooner or later, in death. That's what was real to her.

Real and yet not terribly important. She felt her own swelling abdomen, where the baby's tiny heartfire was growing. As long as she had enough time to see this through, to bring this girl into the world and raise her to adulthood, she'd have no complaint when death came for her.

The ferry pulled in and the people from the New Sweden side disembarked noisily. Alvin, Margaret, and Arthur walked back to where Fishy, Gullah Joe, and Denmark and his wife waited for them. Fast as they were traveling, news had already reached them of mass hangings of rebel slaves in Camelot. They feared the worst—John Calhoun's proposal to hang one in every three. But it turned out to be only twenty.

Only twenty.

In addition, a warrant had been issued for a scoundrel named Denmark Vesey, an illegally freed half-Black who had plotted the whole thing, meeting every slave ship that came to port. Well, that would never happen again. Blacktown was cleaned out and the laws concerning the movements of slaves without their masters were going to be tightened considerably. The days of soft treatment were over for the slaves of the Crown Colonies. They'd learn who was boss.

Once the stories crossed the Potomac, however, they changed. The facts were the same, but now the story was told with growing anger. Even Blacks want to be free, that's what the Northerners said. Whatever they might have planned, they didn't kill a single White. And now the Crown Colonies are cracking down even harder on these poor souls. Enough. The line had to be drawn. No slavery in the western territories. And no more rights for Slave Finders in the United States. Repudiate the treaty. If the Congress we've got won't do it, then we'll elect one that will. Never again will a human being on northern territory be the property of another man. People might not know it yet, but this was the rumor of war, and soon enough these seeds would bear fruit. Margaret had spent many months trying to forestall it. Now she knew that war was the only hope of ending slavery. Dreadful as it might be, it was a war that had to be fought. And here in New Sweden, the chatter of war was from the right side. It was her people talking.

Overhearing such conversation at a roadside inn, where the whole party could sit at a table together, Black, White, and all in between, led Denmark to lean back in his chair, fold his hands behind his head, and say, "It be good to be home!"

All along the road, Alvin worked steadily at trying to heal the damage to Denmark's wife. Margaret assured him that all her memories were still in her heartfire, somewhere, hidden from Margaret because they were hidden from the woman herself. It was slow, meticulous work, healing only a few nerves at a time, a few tiny regions of the brain. But they could all see the improvement in her. She limped less and less. Her hands became more deft. Her speech became clearer. She remembered more and more.

There came one morning when she woke up screaming from a terrible dream. Fishy was with her, but Denmark soon came at a run. When he entered the room, his wife looked up at him and said, "I dream you try a-kill me!"

Weeping, Denmark confessed his terrible sin to her, and begged forgiveness. "I not that man no more," he said.

That healing, too, would be long and slow.

The journey that Alvin had made in one night, running with the greensong to carry him along, took them more than a week at their leisurely pace. But it ended at last, on a familiar street in Philadelphia. Arthur Stuart recognized the rooming house and ran on ahead. Soon Mike Fink rushed out into the street to greet them, followed more slowly but no less happily by Verily, Purity, and Hezekiah. And when Alvin came into the house, there was Mistress Louder, covered in flour but not to be restrained from hugging him. She immediately adopted Margaret as her favorite daughter, and fussed over the unborn baby so much that Alvin joked that Mistress Louder thought she was the mother.

Alvin and Margaret were given the best room, the one with a balcony overlooking the garden. They sat there that first evening, taking in the peace of their first night together in so long that Alvin marveled aloud that the child had ever managed to get itself conceived.

"Let's not be apart again like that," said Margaret.

"Well, not to point the finger, but you were traveling as much as me."

"Never again," said Margaret. "You won't be rid of me."

Alvin sighed. "I never want to be rid of you, but I also want the baby to be safe. I'll take you home—Hatrack or Vigor Church, whichever you want—but I've got to go to a place in Tennizy calling itself Crystal City."

"Take me with you."

"And run the risk of you giving birth on the road? No thanks," said Alvin.

Margaret sighed. "All this wandering, all this separation, and what have we accomplished? The war is still coming. And you still don't know how to use that plow of yours, or what the Crystal City really is, or how to build it."

"I know a few things, though," said Alvin. "And maybe the main reason for all this travel wasn't the tasks we had in mind. Maybe it was those folks in the other rooms. Denmark and Gullah Joe and Fishy and Denmark's lady—I think we'll get them all to the Crystal City, in the end. And Purity and Hezekiah—I think they'll come along, too."

"And Calvin," said Margaret. "He's changed."

"Couldn't bring himself to travel with us, though."

"I think he's ashamed of what his carelessness set off back in Camelot," said Margaret. "But he's steadier. His heartfire has a lot of paths that lead somewhere. And . . ."

"And?"

She brought his hand up to her mouth and kissed it. "And maybe I have other reasons to look into the future with more hope."

"I reckon now he owes his life to me, somewhat, he's got to think different."

"Well, don't count on gratitude. It's the most fleeting of all human virtues. The change in him has to run deeper than that. I think it was when he raised that wave to stop the slave revolt from happening. Thousands of lives were saved when he did that."

Alvin chuckled.

"Why are you laughing?"

"Well, I was on the road, but I was looking ahead. I saw him trying to make a splash in the water, like the old game we played. But he was so weak, he wasn't up to it, he couldn't concentrate."

"So you did it," said Margaret.

"It wasn't easy even for me," said Alvin, "and I was healthy and experienced."

"Well, don't tell *him* that he didn't make that flood."

Alvin laughed. "And take away his one memory of doing something heroic? Not likely."

They sat a while longer in silence. Then Margaret patted her belly and sighed.

"What?"

"I was just thinking how much my mother would have loved to be here. She set such store by babies. Lost a couple before I came along and managed to live through infancy."

"But your mother *is* here," said Alvin. He reached over and laid his hand on her chest, over her heart. "Every heartbeat, she put it there, she heard those heartbeats in the womb, month after month. She's in your heartfire now, as you were in hers. That doesn't go away just because of a little thing like death."

She smiled at him. "I imagine you're right, Al. You usually are."

He kissed her. They sat there a little while longer, till the mosquitoes drove them back inside. They fell asleep clinging to each other, and even in their sleep they kept reaching out to touch each other, for fear that one might have slipped away in the night. Miraculously, they were still there in the morning, touching, breathing, hearts beating together; heartfires bright; lives entwined.